GHOST

~ IN THE ~

MIST

GHOST ~ IN THE ~ MIST

Mists of Redemption ~ Book 2

M. L. REID

GHOST
~ IN THE ~
MIST

CHAPTER 1

I hated the smell of hospitals. Hated the sounds—or sometimes, the lack of sounds. Hated the "calming" monochromatic colors they were decorated in. Hated the maze of halls I had to walk through every time I wanted to see Mom. Hated opening the door and seeing the wonder woman from my memory look like a fading doll on a white bed. Hated seeing the breathing mask over her face and a feeding tube snaking out from under the edge of her white quilt.

For financial reasons, she shared the room with three other women, all Dreamers. All had fallen unconscious on the same day six years ago. They never spoke a word to each other, but they'd spent every day together since coming to this hospital. From interacting with their family members over the years, I knew the other women pretty well. Luckily, I was the only visitor right now.

My senses were good enough now that I was aware of doctors and nurses walking up and down the hall outside Mom's room, even through the closed door. I ignored them as I picked up a padded metal chair from the wall and carried it to my mother's bedside, sinking down as I smiled softly. "Good afternoon, Mom." I reached out and gently touched her light brown hair, the same color as mine and Aliya's. There were graying strands at her temples, something she would have been proud of if she were awake.

"I'm not getting older; I'm getting more experienced. It's an honor," she used to say when I'd tease her for aging.

I opened up the bedside drawer and pulled out a red brush. "I'm going to brush your hair now, okay?"

She never answered, but it seemed rude to just start doing things without asking. Maybe it was because there was a small part of me which hoped that Mom could actually hear me, even if she couldn't respond. As I carefully drew the soft bristles through her hair, I started to speak about anything and everything that came to my mind.

"It's been a long time since I last visited, huh? I'm sorry; I've been busy. Things have changed a lot recently. Like, *a lot*." I paused. I bet I couldn't even tell her about the System, even though she wasn't conscious. "I'm not an E anymore."

That single letter *E* had plagued me for the last year. When Mom fell into a coma, I hoped I would become a Hunter. It meant a life of blood and battle, killing monsters in the Gate every day. It also meant I could improve my family's life. Every Hunter was ranked based on their stats, the highest being S, then A, and so on down to E. The stronger the Hunter, the better their perks such as income, housing, treatment and, well, over- all state of life were. Everyone around me fit in that lucky place.

Everyone, except me—an E-ranked Hunter, and the weakest one in the short history of Hunters. So weak, there were humans stronger than me. That one letter plunged me into the depths of hell, and every day was a battle just to survive.

That is, until a couple months ago. Since getting my System, I've been able to get stronger and level up like a video game—something that was supposed to be impossible. A Hunter was stuck with their stats till death, but by collecting EXP from killing monsters, I'd managed to scrap my way up from level one all the way up to level twenty-two.

Even though I was now D ranked, the visible rank which other peo- ple could see was stuck at E. Since a Hunter shouldn't be able to change their stats, it was safer to hide it until I was strong enough to ensure I wasn't killed by someone threatened by my future prospects. Or become an experimental rat for some scientist trying to figure out a method to level up.

As for what my System was, well, it was complicated. Unlike the Guides all Hunters had which simply provided information and a form of com- munication, my System had a consciousness. It enabled me to improve my stats, learn skills and abilities, and even gave me magic.

In return, it wanted me to get revenge for it. Revenge on what, I didn't know yet. I wasn't strong enough to know. And honestly, I didn't care why. As long as I could keep my family safe and fed, I'd pay any price.

"I can't tell you why, and honestly, it's really complicated. But I've been doing some pretty dangerous stuff lately. Nothing too out of control." I paused when I thought of everything that'd happened the last couple days.

"Okay, that's a lie. You would pull my ear off and yell yourself hoarse if you knew what I've done lately." I laughed, despite myself.

God, I would give anything to have her do that right now. I'd go deaf for life if it meant Mom smiled at me again.

"I, ah . . . " My voice cracked, and I had to swallow before I could force another smile. "I just wanted to say I'm sorry." I leaned back and let my hands drop into my lap as I stared up at the fluorescent light. "I'm sorry, Mom. About the Feng Jungle energy crystal." It had been wonderful, watching that asshole Blake's face fall into despair when I broke the crystal in front of him. But now that I was face-to-face with Mom, guilt tore at me.

"I promise, there's a reason why I did it. I know it probably put the hospital in a desperate position, and I don't even know how many innocent people this will affect, but I couldn't let that energy crystal come into Earth. It's not even just because of the task." My heart felt like it was ripping apart just thinking about it. "But it would have been worse if it came into Earth."

When the Gates first appeared twenty years ago and spilled out millions of unbeatable monsters, cities were decimated, countries fell apart, and electricity failed because there was no one left to man the plants. Once Hunters evolved out of the remaining humans and were finally able to kill the monsters, a new power source was found. Every creature had a blue gem in them, just bursting with clean energy, and since every Gate had an unlimited number of monsters in it, there would never be an energy crystal shortage. It was the Hunters' job to go into the Gates every day to bring out one or more of them.

What nobody knew was that there was an interdimensional parasitic planet hanging over Earth. And those seemingly innocent energy crystals were bits of that planet, slowly poisoning Earth until the ginormous monster could strike and eat the planet. Monsters, and even the manifestation of Hunters, were caused by the toxic magic leaking from the energy crystals and Gates they came from. Sounded far-fetched, huh? If only it wasn't true. But it was. And no one believed me.

I sighed and rubbed my face. "Still, it's just one energy crystal," I said, thinking about the mission in Feng Jungle. "A huge one, sure, but how many millions of crystals are brought out of the Gates around the world every day? How many Hunters get turned into monsters and killed by their own people weekly? Is what I'm doing even doing anything? Am I really helping? But I can't just sit back and do nothing. If it were just me, maybe I could close my eyes and pretend, but knowing that you, Aliya, Aunt Mina, and Uncle Carl are in danger, I can't just sit still. Even though I'm pretty sure all my efforts are useless." I took a long breath and held it before letting it out. A bitter smile curled my lips. "I wonder if this is how Kesstel felt? Or did he get blindsided by it, too, and that's why he's so pessimistic?"

A picture of him, so tall and powerful walking toward me through the mist came to my mind. I blinked out of my thoughts and sat up straight. "Ah, I haven't told you about Kesstel, have I?" I forced all the bitter uncertainty away and replaced it with a bright smile. Putting the brush away, I pulled out a special lotion from Mom's side drawer. Her skin was paper pale from lack of sunlight for the last six years and needed to be frequently lotioned. Glancing at the chart over her nightstand, I guessed it was about time to do that.

"Kesstel is . . . well, out of this world." I laughed at my own joke. Literally. He wasn't from Earth but from a planet the parasite had destroyed long ago.

Gently, I rubbed the lotion onto Mom's cheeks, around the clear oxygen mask, and over her nose and mouth. "He's cold and standoffish. Honestly, he scared the hel—*heck* out of me when I first met him, and the next couple times after that. He's not a bad guy, I think. I don't know much about him, but I've seen him enough that I'm getting used to him. I actually even forgot he was an S rank for a while yesterday. Then when he got mad, I was actually shocked—even more so when he made it so I wasn't affected by his aura."

I paused, my hand at her throat. Mom's faint pulse pumped under my fingertips. "I don't know what I should do about him. Should I keep a distance between us or try to be friends with him? It seems like he has all the answers I need; I just don't know how to get them from him." Another bitter smile pulled at my lips. "What right do I have to be friends with an S god?" Then I laughed. "And how many assassins are going to come at me just for trying?"

Seriously, who got assassins sent after them for simply talking to a guy? Me, apparently. And the person commissioning them wasn't his wife, or even his girlfriend. They had no relationship at all. It made the situation all the more unreasonable. And sucky.

I let out a long sigh and started to rub lotion onto her left hand, feeling her bones and veins through her tissue-thin skin. "Ah, Mom. What should I do?" I whispered and lapsed into silence, listening to the ticking clock on the wall.

I noticed a human in the hallway stop at Mom's room. A moment later, there was a light rap on the wooden door.

I looked over my shoulder as Uncle Carl stepped into the doorway. "Hey." I smiled and stood up to give him a tight hug. "I didn't know I was going to see you here."

"Jynn, it's good to see you." Dark bags circled his eyes, yet he smiled and hugged me back. His thin face had aged since I last saw him, and there was more gray in his dark hair. "It's been a while, huh?" He grabbed a chair from the wall and set it next to mine. How many times had we sat like this in this sad hospital room throughout the years? Too many times.

I bobbed my head. "Yeah, you were out the last time I visited."

He paused and nodded. "I find myself coming here a lot."

I glanced at him, surprised. "Why?"

A tired smile pulled at his lips as he gave me a side glance. "Your mom is a good listener, I guess." His face brightened, and he pointed to the fanged snapper bracelet on my wrist. "You're wearing yours too. Aliya never takes it off, I swear. She can't wait to show it to everyone she meets. Sometimes, I see her just sitting there and twisting her wrist to make the scales rattle. She says she likes the sound."

I smiled and touched my own bracelet. "I'm glad she likes it." I wore mine as long as I wasn't in armor. The shop clerk had been right—the bracelet did give a small +2 magic boost, but I couldn't fit it over or under my arm bracers. I'd thought about enlarging it, but I didn't want it to get damaged in a fight. I'd rather not use it in the Gate and keep it longer.

I swallowed hard so my voice didn't crack. "Mom is a good listener. I'm a good listener, too." I looked into his brown eyes. "I mean, we're a family. And you've been an amazing uncle to me and Aliya all our lives. I owe you a lot. I want to do anything I can to help, and if listening is what you need, that's what I'll do."

His smile wobbled, and tears pooled in his eyes. He reached out and hugged my shoulders hard. "I don't deserve you or Mina or Aliya." His voice broke, and he took a couple deep breaths until he calmed down.

"I was just spilling my guts to her, too." I sat back and straightened Mom's blanket. "What were you going to talk to her about?"

He took a big breath. "The usual," he said slowly. "About job hunting and worrying about your aunt's health. About how . . . " He paused. "I wish I could do more. I wish I wasn't such a failure."

My mouth cracked open, but it took me a couple of seconds to speak. "I don't think you're a failure. You're just in a slump, but you can pull yourself out. We're all here for you, believing in you."

I knew depression wasn't like a cold, where you felt bad for a couple days then *poof*, it was gone. It would be great if it were, but it wasn't. I didn't know what to say to help him. This was the man who'd helped raise me. Every time I felt like a failure, he was there to buoy me up. I should be able to do the same for him, but what if I said something which made it worse?

He gave a sad laugh. "Right. A slump." He sighed. "I've always been in a *slump*. I took in two sweet girls and raised them in poverty." He started talking faster, as if spilling out words he'd kept bottled up for too long. "I'm in such a *slump* that I need my little niece to work herself to the bone to put food on *my* table. And don't think I have the same magical illusion as Mina and Aliya. I heard the stories your dad told when we were sharing a beer; the ones he didn't dare tell your mom. I know how it is on the other side of that Wall."

His breathing sped up. "No matter how many applications I send out, I'm getting old, and there are younger, more capable people out there. When I did get that telemarketing job, there was just so much noise. I couldn't think, my brain shut down, and I couldn't breathe. The next thing I knew, I was walking out in the middle of training." He buried his face in his hands. "I failed. I failed to help my family. Again." His voice broke. "I'm worth more dead. At least you'd get the life insurance money."

My eyes widened, and my heart stopped. "Shut up!" I jumped to my feet as my chair skidded across the ground then fell over.

Uncle Carl jumped and looked up with red eyes.

I glared down at him, heaving out fast breaths. "You are not a failure. You never have been. You could have abandoned me and Aliya at an orphanage when Mom fell into a coma, but you didn't. You raised us with all the love and encouragement you could. We might not have had the newest clothes, but we knew what family meant. That's better than what half the people in this city have." I jabbed a finger out the window. "No amount of money is going to replace that. I know. *I know.* I got a lump sum of money instead of a dad. That money never hugged me. That money never told me it was going to be okay. That money didn't stay up with me till one in the morning helping me with homework even though he had work in the morning like you did."

The anger burning in me fizzled out, leaving a deep sadness in my heart. "Why can't you see how much we need you? Especially Aliya and

Aunt Mina. You're the only father figure that Aliya remembers, and Aunt Mina would fall apart without you. Our family is already so broken, we'd fall apart if something else happened." Tears burned my eyes. "I've been trying so hard. I'm literally putting everything I have into keeping you safe. I bleed, I struggle, I run in circles trying to figure out what to do, I end every day so damn tired that I feel like I can't get up in the morning. But I do anyway. Willingly. Not just for Aliya and Aunt Mina—it's for you, too, Uncle Carl."

I took a deep breath, shocked at the words that had come out of my mouth. I'd never wanted to tell him any of this. And I sure as hell shouldn't be talking like this in a hospital room.

I sighed and covered my face. "You don't have to hurry. You can take all the time you need to find the right job for you. I'll take care of everything until you're on your feet again." I lowered my hands and looked at him with pleading eyes. "Just please, don't give up. Don't disregard the love we all have for you. Please."

He bowed his head. Big drops of water plopped down on the knees of his khaki pants.

I stared down at his head. *God, please tell me I didn't say the wrong thing this time.* I just wanted to help; I didn't mean to lose it on him.

There was a soft knock on the door.

I turned my head and saw a doctor standing there in a long white robe. "Is this a bad time?" His soft voice carried through the room.

Shoot, I must have been too loud. I forced a smile. "No. Is there a problem?"

"Ah, yes. There actually is." The doctor stepped into the room and closed the door behind him. He held a manila folder in his hands.

I glanced at Uncle Carl, who was still trying to get his emotions under control. Well, I was the one yelling, so I should take the heat for it. I walked over to the doctor. "Sorry about the noise," I said, sheepishly. If I apologized right off the bat, maybe I'd only be warned and not asked to leave.

The doctor nodded to the side. "Hunters have strong emotions; it's nothing out of the ordinary." He smiled kindly, but his droopy eyes were sad. "It's actually about Annette Devhro I need to talk to you about."

My stomach plunged to the ground. "What's wrong with my mom?" She seemed just fine to me. Nothing had changed in six years.

"Nothing, technically. She's showing all the correct symptoms of a Dreamer, and that's why I need to talk to you." He handed me the folder. "In a little over half a year, it will be her seventh year in the Dreamer state."

He looked me in the eye. "It's usually about that time that a Dreamer's health starts to rapidly decline. We, at Garden City Hospital, don't keep Dreamers here longer than seven years. The equipment they need is a lot more costly, and it only preserves their lives for another year or two at most."

My eyes widened. I did know that Dreamers didn't live more than ten years after they fell asleep, but it was something I'd always pushed to the back of my mind. When Mom passed out six years ago, I told myself there was plenty of time to find a cure. That's why we didn't pull her plug years ago. There was always hope she'd wake up—even though it had never happened before.

I swallowed hard. "Have they come up with an antidote yet?"

The doctor shook his head like it was something he'd done thousands of times. Probably because he had. "I won't lie. The scientists aren't any closer than they were twenty years ago." As if he hadn't just crushed my heart, he continued, "You'll need to start making some decisions. If you're going to move her to another city, you need to make preparations now. All hospitals put a tight cap on how many Dreamers they take, and spots fill quickly. If you aren't going to move her, there are other preparations you need to make."

He didn't say it, but he was talking about funeral arrangements.

My hands fisted as my thoughts raced and jumbled together, trying to find a solution to the problem.

System? I asked in my mind. *Is there a cure for Dreamers?*

[. . . **Not yet.**]

CHAPTER 2

There wasn't a cure for Dreamers . . . yet. I had clung to that hope for years so I wouldn't collapse. I needed that sliver of hope. Life could—and did—beat me all it wanted, but my family had to be okay. I wasn't a chemistry expert, but I knew that antidotes and vaccines were made by joining ingredients together.

A given, yes, but it only worked if they were the right ingredients. After twenty years of experimenting, if they hadn't found the right combination yet, it meant one thing: the right ingredients weren't on Earth, which meant they had to be in Gate Vale.

The fact that the disease didn't exist until after the dimensional Gates appeared solidified that thought all the more in my mind. The sleeping disease must have come from the parasite . . .

Gears started turning in my head.

. . . so something from the parasite must cure it, right? If that were true, it meant there were one or more monsters that Hunters hadn't found or that hadn't been turned into the Research Department who was working on the cure.

So I needed to start collecting monsters, every single kind, until I found the ones that were missing. My System agreed to notify me when I came across a helpful drop item for my personal cause, so all that was left was getting strong enough to take on the Gate and mastering the skills I had.

Gate Vale was divided into sections, like a puzzle tossed together with no rhyme or reason as to what piece went where. Like how Feng Jungle, which was full of beautiful silvery trees and rainbow crystal clusters, was right next to a muggy marshland. Each location had a dividing boundary line—literally just a three-foot-wide stretch of clear dirt—around it. That gap was like a physical barrier, keeping all the weather from one section out of the next.

Gate Vale was set up like a target, with the two-hundred-foot-tall black Gate in the middle. The lower-ranked locations were closer to the Gate, and the higher-ranked ones were on the outside, right next to the mountains rimming the valley. At this point, I wasn't strong enough to enter the high-ranked locations—I'd die in a heartbeat—but someday, hopefully, I'd be able to walk all over Gate Vale.

For now, I could make a checklist of every known monster in the weaker areas and work from there.

I started in Edmond Woods, hunting down every monster on the list and checking their drop items. Since it was an E level forest, it wasn't a problem mining; the hardest part was finding all the rare monsters. Three days later, I moved on to Glenn Holt. I'd sworn I would never step in there again, but I did. Between a grudge and helping my mom, it was obvious which way the scales would tip. Four days later, I scratched off all the monsters on that list and gained another level. I got a lot of loot in that week, but none of it triggered a response from my System that I'd found something helpful.

Next, I went to Fogmire. I'd spent a lot of time there, but I hadn't hunted down every kind of monster in it yet. It was also the best place to practice using Mist because I could manipulate the natural fog already there. It was a bigger region, and certain smaller monsters were harder to find, but a week and another level later, I finally checked off my whole list—and still came up empty-handed for ingredients.

After a day of grinding on unhelpful monsters, I stood in front of a level sixteen treant and took a silent breath. Thick fog filled the creepy forest, but I was completely dry and comfortable in my black leather armor, courtesy of my Mist ability. I held my kindjal in my right hand, a gorgeous weapon with a bright steel handle which fit perfectly in my palm, and a blade that was a swirled mix of clear crystal and steel. It looked like a fancy showpiece, but it was the strongest and sharpest weapon I'd ever encountered. And it was mine.

Late evening light cracked through the misty air and left hazy highlights on the monster tree's gnarly bark. It seemed so harmless. If it weren't for my heightened senses, I might have overlooked the thin lines indicating its closed eyes and mouth.

Pressing my hands together, I cast Mirror. Once I separated them, a second kindjal—an exact mirror image of the one in my right hand—appeared in my left. I spun the swords in my hands and whistled short and shrill.

The tree monster's eyes popped open.

I let out another whistle.

Two of its limbs shot at me. Months ago, the attacks had been so fast, I could barely see it move. Now . . . *Hah.*

I swiped my left kindjal in an arc in front of me, solidifying the mist as I did and creating a half-circle barrier. The treant's studded hands, with tiny little twigs as fingers, smashed into it, stopping a foot from my forehead. Before the monster could react, I jumped high and threw my left blade, which sank into the bark at a sharp angle right between the treant's creepy, slanted eyes. The monster let out a guttural rumble and twisted as the blade wobbled between its eyes.

Still in the air, I kicked off a line of solid mist and shot at the treant before it could retract its limbs, landing on the blade's handle with all my weight. A huge chunk of bark and tree flesh popped off with a crack as I forced the kindjal down toward the monster's mouth. Black, sappy blood dripped from the gouge, and the treant let out another rumbling wail. Twisting, I thrust the kindjal still in my hand right between the monster's eyes, through the divot of exposed wood. An inch before the guard hit the tree, my blade stopped—had its energy crystal blocked it?

The crystal shattered, and the treant instantly disappeared into a million tiny lights which faded away in seconds.

[+95 EXP]

[You have Leveled Up!]

[Gained Skill: High Jump.]

"Yes!" I whispered, throwing my hands into the air. I knew that last treant would do the job and get me to the next level. I was finally a quarter of the way to where Kesstel was.

. . . Okay, I didn't actually know if he was level one hundred or not; I just assumed he was. In my mind, he was the pinnacle of power. He would have to be to survive more than one planet collapsing, right?

But more importantly, I was getting stronger and checking off monsters, steadily narrowing down the possibilities toward helping find a cure for Dreamers.

I couldn't help but feel good about myself, even if leveling up was a small victory in the grander scheme of things. It felt good to be at the top of the food chain. I felt like I was actually doing things instead of running away from everything like I had once upon a time in Feng Jungle.

I smiled and picked up the drop items—a huge chunk of treant bark and a piece of lumber—then opened my menu.

Jynn Devhro

Rank C   **Level** 25

                                            EXP to Next Level 1175

HP 248/537   **Stat Points** 0
MP 115/245

Strength 50 (+20)   **Agility** 48
Magic 44   **Perception** 42
Constitution 44 (+20)   **Intelligence** 42

Skills   **Abilities**
Throw   Mist (Improved) (40 ft)
Critical Hit   Feather Step
Quick Hit   Regen (Limited)
Mirror   Stealth (Limited)
High Jump

I gasped. I was C ranked? I was finally a C! For the first time in my life, I was on par with most of the Hunters in the world. C was the most common designation, but there were obviously different levels within each rank. Levels one to nine were E. Levels ten to twenty-four were D. So how many levels until I was a B? Emma was a C-ranked Hunter, but she was level forty-eight, so she must be on the high side. I think.

Either way, this called for a celebration.

I was practically humming as I exited the Gate. *Where should I go for dinner?* My debt to Henry was officially paid off, and I still had some money left over from my Stone Mace contract, so I could spare to treat myself. My day date with Aliya was the first time I'd eaten at a restaurant in Eden, so it wasn't like I had a regular haunt.

A familiar presence approached from the right, pulling me out of my thoughts. I looked over as Kesstel walked up to me. He was in khaki pants and a button-up plaid shirt with the sleeves rolled up, showing off his strong forearms. Every inch of his tall frame, from his walk to the way he held himself, depicted the royal upbringing he'd been raised with. It paired perfectly with his bred-to-be-gorgeous face and pale blond hair. Although I was getting used to him, he was still intimidating to be by sometimes. Never mind the insanely powerful Hunter aura he had, which he always restricted when he was with me.

I blinked, wondering what he was doing here. Then again, I was starting to get used to him just randomly appearing. "Good evening?" I left the question open, tossing the ball onto his side of the conversation court.

"Evening. It's getting close to closing time." He nodded his head toward the sun, low enough to be barely visible between city buildings. "You shouldn't cut it so close."

I bobbed my head absentmindedly. "I'll remember that next time." As if that wasn't something every single Hunter knew. There were only twelve people in Eden who had a chance at surviving inside the Gate at night, and one of them was standing beside me.

A horrifying thought suddenly struck me. What if the reason why there wasn't a cure for Dreamers was because the needed ingredients were from monsters that only emerged within the Gate at night? God, was I going to have to work up to an S to find out? Would I even have the time before Mom passed away?

Kesstel tapped my forehead gently. "Hey. You're spacing out on me."

I jumped and focused on him. "I-I was just thinking about something."

He tipped his head to the side and started to walk. "Come on."

With a sense of déjà vu, I caught up, and we walked side by side. "Where are we going?"

"To celebrate," he announced.

"What?" He wasn't seriously psychic, was he? I mean, if he were, that was a line that shouldn't be crossed.

His lips pulled up in the corner. "Today was my last day on the job, and now I'm free. That's cause for celebration, right?"

Oh, right. He did say he only had two weeks left. Had it really been that long? I'd been so busy throwing myself into grinding that I'd lost track of time.

I paused when Kesstel turned and started walking toward A District. Even with my splurge money, there wasn't a single restaurant I could afford there, and I shuddered to think about the entry prices of the few clubs there. They were rumored to be the best in the city on food and drinks—and their prices were rumored to reflect it. There was a reason why only A-ranked and higher Hunters went to them.

He noticed my hesitation and looked at me. Then he reached out and lightly took my wrist. If I wanted to pull away, it would be really easy. "Come on. It's getting late."

I bit my lip. "I'm actually not that hungry," I lied. "And I'm not really a party girl, you know? I'm sure there are others—"

"None that I want to spend time with," he cut me off. "This restaurant tastes great, and there's nothing *party* about it. Even if you aren't that hungry, I'm sure you'll find something you like. As a gentleman, I'm paying, and I don't care if you waste my money." He paused and looked right into my eyes. "Eat with me?" He tugged on my wrist just enough to catch my attention.

Oh my god, what right did he have to act like an abandoned puppy? He was on the pinnacle of everything. That should be illegal!

For a second, I wanted to scratch his ridiculously bred-to-be-handsome face for having the gall to guilt-trip me like this. I took a deep breath and looked to the side. "Okay."

I didn't know if he was worried I'd back out or something, but before I knew it, I was seated at a table at an Italian restaurant in A District. The decor was classy and sophisticated, with lots of space between the tables. Kesstel requested a booth in the back corner behind a couple decorative ferns where the lighting was low, and it was next to a tinted window which looked out over the street.

I stared at the menu, trying to figure out what to do. This place served all their dishes family style, so everything was huge and expensive. Jeez, I was just going to go somewhere for cheap fast food to celebrate. Finally, I settled on one of the cheaper things on the expensive menu—Chicken Alfredo. That should be good enough, right?

I glanced at Kesstel. I thought someone like him would be celebrating in a bar with loud music and a flashy entourage, like the glamorous lives I'd seen on the TV. I never would have thought he'd choose a nice Italian place to celebrate.

It was all I could do not to shift on my bench. It wasn't that the navy-blue cushioning or the dark wood backing were uncomfortable to sit on, but I didn't know what to do or say. Sitting together like this, with diners stealthily eyeing us from across the room, was unnerving. It was so different from when we were walking in the forest, where now I was forced to focus on the person seated in front of me—someone whom I had already decided I was going to stay away from.

I blinked and realized I was still in my armor. It was so comfortable that I'd forgotten I was even wearing it. I bit my lips. I had a spare pair of clothes in my Items Bag—just a pair of jeans and a T-shirt, nothing fancy and not appropriate for a place like this, but it was better than dirty armor.

The waiter stopped by our table and smiled at us, his eyes flicking nervously at Kesstel. Even though he was holding back his aura, the D-ranked young man was still obviously affected. "Are you ready? What can I get for you?" The pen in his hand shook with a fine tremble.

I glanced at Kesstel. Was there anyone who treated him like a normal person?

He was looking at me. "Do you know what you want?"

I blinked and looked down at the menu. "Ah, yes. A Chicken Alfredo and a side salad with ranch, please."

The waiter wrote it down. "And what to drink?"

"Just water is fine." I motioned to the full glass in front of me.

The young man turned to Kesstel, and his back became a little straighter. "What can I get for you, sir?"

"A Chicken Parmigiana, a Shrimp Scampi, a Lasagna Classico, some steamed vegetables, a side salad, and a basket of breadsticks," Kesstel said without batting an eye. He closed his menu and handed it to the young man after he was done scribbling. "And water is fine for me, too."

I nearly choked on my breath and tried not to stare at Kesstel. I leaned on the table and lowered my voice. "These dishes are family style."

Kesstel gave me an odd look. "I know."

My brows rose. Did he seriously plan on eating all of it?

CHAPTER 3

After the waiter left, I excused myself. "Um, I'll be back in a minute." He nodded to the side. "Of course."

I nearly jumped out of my seat and hurried to the bathroom. Thankfully, it was all one big room with cream tile and soothing maroon walls. In a snap, my armor was slotted in my Items Bag and my spare clothes were sitting on the marble counter next to the sink. I took a second to wash my hands, arms, and face, then I patted my body down with my towel before I put it back in my bag. Since blundering through Feng Jungle, the extra things I kept in my Items Bag had grown, including a full first aid kit and rope.

I quickly put on my clothes and buckled my hip satchel on. Jeans and a pale green T-shirt were a far cry from fine-dining attire, but these were some of the new clothes in my closet. I quickly smoothed out my ponytail with a brush and nodded at the mirror. At least I looked suitable for a civilized conversation.

Feeling like I was ready for battle, I walked back to the table.

Kesstel gazed out the window with his hands motionless on the table, completely oblivious of all the stares covertly shot his way. The apathetic gleam was back, making his eyes look like blue topaz jewels instead of the eyes of a person. Yet again, I was struck with how separated he was from the world around him.

I hesitated. He wouldn't react violently if I broke his concentration, would he? I had a feeling he wouldn't hurt me, even though I didn't know where that confidence came from, but I doubted the owners would appreciate it if he broke something by mistake. Then again, I guessed that was a risk all store owners faced in Eden.

Before I could decide, Kesstel turned his head toward me, and his face softened into an almost smile.

I slid into my seat. "Sorry that took a while."

He shook his head. "Not at all. You could have taken even more time. I did ambush you, after all, as soon as you came out of the Gate."

I bobbed my head and fidgeted with my glass of water, feeling the cool condensation on the outside of the smooth surface. I couldn't help but want to convert it into mist, but I shouldn't do that in public. I didn't have a problem with it in front of Kesstel, since he already knew, but there were more people other than him inside this public space.

I glanced up at him. "I have to ask, is there really a reason to celebrate not working for Councilman Wilks anymore? The job couldn't have been that bad."

Kesstel flexed his hand, and a domed barrier covering just our table appeared around us, just like the first time we seriously talked. "I find it more comfortable talking without prying ears, don't you? It doesn't restrict movement, just noise."

I nodded, appreciating the silence that settled over us. No more silverware clicking or accidentally overhearing other people talking. And knowing no one would overhear me was reassuring. If I said something stupid, at least Kesstel was the only one who would know.

He nodded. "It's not that it was a bad job; I did learn a lot about the inner workings of the Hunter society and hierarchy. But does anyone really want to be strapped to the same routine over and over again for seven years? Miss Wilks is your typical wealthy young miss. Endless shopping and parties with excessive glamor and loud music. Once a week, I'd escort her into the Gate and kill a monster for her to fulfill her Hunter requirements." He reached out and picked up his glass, twisting it between his hands.

I did the same things every day, but I didn't have the time to think they were boring. "That sounds like a cushy job which anyone else would kill for," I muttered, taking a drink.

His lips thinned into a tight smile. "I would have gladly traded. It was boring, and being shown off like a pet was annoying. In my youth, I spent a lot of time at balls and parties, though none of them were loud and dark like the ones Miss Wilks likes to dance at. But it never bored me because I had a mission—to improve my connections and establish my place in the minds of the gentry around me. A far cry from standing along a wall, turning down dance requests and keeping men from getting too handsy on my ward. Or holding yet another shopping bag and walking up and down the same street again." He motioned to the restaurant. "I'd rather spend the day in Gate Vale, feeling my blood pumping with the kill, and then relaxing in a place like this or at my home."

I had to admit, I was in the same boat as him.

The waiter approached our table with a large black tray full of food platters on his shoulder. He was oblivious to the barrier around us as he opened a stand and set the tray down before he started to arrange the food on our table. The smell of pasta, sauces, cheese, shrimp, and garlic bread filled my nose and sent my stomach into a hungry roll. The young man disappeared for a second and came back with a clear glass pitcher. He refilled our drinks. "Is there anything else I can get for you?"

Kesstel shook his head.

The waiter disappeared like the wind.

I stared at all the food. My stomach was so empty, I knew it was going to start roaring at any second. God, how long had it been since I'd seen this much food on a table in front of me? Every single plate was a culinary masterpiece. I peeked up at Kesstel, my brow wrinkled. He was the one who'd ordered most of the food. Would he get mad if I sampled all the dishes? I was dying to taste everything.

I nearly jumped out of my skin when I found he was watching me with his piercing blue eyes. He was relaxed, and an almost smile was touching his hard mouth, as if he was enjoying watching me agonize. "What are you waiting for? Eat."

He picked up the serving spoon and scooped a large helping of food onto my plate. And it wasn't just from the Chicken Alfredo I'd ordered. He added something from every dish onto my plate until it was piled high with food.

I couldn't help but pause as a small smile curled my lips. He was feeding me again. Seriously, what was his obsession with feeding me? It was so . . . silly.

Well, I guess that solved the food problem. Next came eating gracefully. I couldn't seem to figure out where to put my hands or how to chew without looking like a starving cow. I'd never really thought about eating before. Sure, I knew proper dining etiquette and stuff, but it all seemed subpar now that I was sitting across from this guy. As delicious as the food was, I could barely taste half of it because I was overly conscious.

He didn't seem to have the trouble I did, his movements as smooth as ever. All the while, his attention was on me.

For the life of me, I couldn't figure out why.

I took a bite, savoring the taste of perfectly cooked shrimp, and tried to think of something to say.

"Do you have any family?" he suddenly asked.

I blinked and looked up at him. "Ah, yes. I have a little sister who lives with my aunt and uncle. My mom is a Dreamer, so my aunt has been raising us for the last six years." I paused, the news of my mother's condition still too fresh to want to talk about it more.

He paused. "No father?" He picked up another serving platter and pushed more food onto my plate before he added more to his own.

I took another bite, delighted by the crust on the parmesan chicken. "He was one of the first-generation Hunters. He died in the Gate ten years ago. I was seven and my sister was five at the time. My mom held our family together, but, well, there's no cure against the Dreamer's disease yet." I picked at the food on my plate, feeling a little more relaxed. Even though it still pricked my heart, it was a subject I could talk about to anyone because it was all common knowledge.

"She sounds like a strong woman," he commented, watching me with clear eyes.

I smiled. "She is—was." I couldn't help but start to ramble about my family. I didn't know how long I went on before I realized I'd totally dominated the conversation. I bit my fork and glanced at Kesstel. "Did you have any family?"

What if he'd been married? He had talked about how his parents were engaged as children. Had it been the same with him? He looked like he was in his early twenties, but how long had he actually been alive?

Kesstel's expression softened, the likes of which I'd never seen before. I couldn't breathe and I couldn't tear my eyes away from his face, either, as the food in my mouth turned to dust. Who was he thinking about to make that expression?

His face was gentle, but there was a lingering pain in his voice. "You already know my father was a prominent duke in Kathar. He was stern but fair, and our lands were very successful under his care. My mother was a gentle woman, as beautiful inside as she was out." A smile flashed across his face as the vibrancy in his eyes faded out like he was looking at something far away. "But that didn't mean she was a pushover. She couldn't be, raising three boys. Even my father bowed in submission when she was mad."

It was fun, listening to him talk about his world. It brought up thoughts of kings, knights, and princesses. And it sounded like our mothers had something in common, but I would bet that Kesstel took after his father in temperament. "So you had two brothers? Were they younger or older?" I took another bite, enjoying the sound of his voice.

"Both younger. A couple of hotheads. They had good hearts, but they gave my parents the runaround and created a lot of extra work for me," he grumbled, but there was love in his tone.

I smiled, recalling the love I had for my sister. I felt like that sometimes, too. "What kind of work? What did your family do?"

Nostalgia was heavy in his gaze. "My world was a lot smaller than Earth, as I said previously. The total landmass comprised about the same size of your Americas. Most of it was controlled by one country—my country. Ten generations ago, the emperor had a set of twin boys. They were both outstanding and loved each other, so the oldest became the reigning emperor while the younger became the empire's sword and shield. And thus, the Noblé Duchy was created.

"We assisted in running the empire and smoothing over disturbances before they reached the emperor's table. We also managed about a third of the empire's land, including a few gold and silver mines. Since the beginning, my family's line has always been close to the royals. In fact, every four or so generations, a princess would marry into my family and one of our daughters would marry a lesser prince. Not only did it keep relationships tight, but the Noblé line had a pact of allegiance with the ruling house. My ancestors saved the royal family from extinction several times and built them back up to glory." There was a lot of pride in his voice.

I smiled and scooped more food into my mouth.

"More?" he asked.

I nodded, thinking he was asking about his story. He must have thought I meant food because he put more on my plate. I couldn't help but stare at it, seriously doubting that it could be eaten.

While I was still agonizing over the portion on my plate, Kesstel started to talk again. "While my mother ruled the household, my father and I ran the businesses and intelligence. My brothers were training to be my cousin's, the crown prince, personal aid and bodyguard." He paused. "We were unprepared when the Gates appeared."

"Did your family become Hunters, too?" I went to take another bite but found there was finally nothing on my plate. It wasn't just my plate— the entire table was empty of food. When did that happen? I seriously couldn't believe we'd eaten it all!

The thought had just come to my mind when two servers appeared at our table. One quickly removed all the empty plates while the other set down two huge bowls in the middle of the table. One was a brownie sundae. The other was a fruit tart.

I gaped at them.

A brownie! Oh, my holy awesomeness, it was a brownie! And ice cream and whipped cream and all the heavenly goodness that came with it. I could barely take my eyes off that to gape at the fruit tart in all of its colorful glory. The crust looked perfectly flakey, the peaches and strawberries could have passed for gems. It was a work of art!

But still, that brownie . . .

Kesstel held out a long spoon.

I reached for it, but paused just before my finger touched the metal. Wasn't this just too much?

He leaned forward and pushed the spoon into my hand, then he leaned back and took a scoop of the fruit tart. "Yes, they were all Hunters. My brothers and father were melee. My mother was a very strong mage. In my world, there was a third class, a magical knight type. I belonged in that class."

I didn't think that was possible before the System took over my life. But now I was an odd in-between, too.

"We could never get a handle on the Gates. My uncle, the emperor, was killed when one of the first Gates opened in the palace garden. My cousin, the crown prince, was visiting my castle at the time and became the only surviving royal left. We tried our best, but he was still a teenager, and no one knew what we were doing. Even my father. We never thought we'd face extinction." He took a slow drink. "Lack of advanced technology and communication led to unorganized panic and the government folding until it was each town desperately fighting for their own survival. It only took my world five years to collapse. By then, only my youngest brother was alive." He paused, his brows tightening into a straight line. "But he died in the next world."

"I'm sorry," I said softly. How awful would that be, to watch your family die, then to see your world be erased? All for the sake of a monster planet to feed.

Kesstel opened his mouth, then frowned. A threatening presence entered my area of awareness, and I paused. We looked over at the same time.

Bethany Wilks charged across the room in a purple wraparound dress and diamond-studded stilettos, her blonde curls and breasts just as big and bouncy as the last time I'd seen her. She stopped at our table, inside the bubble that Kesstel had cast.

"There you are, Kesstel. I've been looking everywhere since you disappeared." She playfully glared at Kesstel.

He looked up at her with a blank expression.

Bethany looked at me, her mouth twisting. "What are you doing here?" Behind that beautiful face was a look I knew very well. Disdain. It was clear she'd judged me and found me lacking.

I guess that would merit another round of assassins, huh?

CHAPTER 4

It wasn't too unreasonable that people would think I shouldn't be near Kesstel. I mean, who was he? An S god. Who was I? Even if it wasn't true anymore, my title still indicated I was the weakest Hunter recorded in history. Not to mention the fact I was a poor girl in cheap clothes. What was I doing with a man as amazing as Kesstel?

I put my spoon gently on the table and looked up at the woman who wanted to kill me. "I'm—"

My words were cut off when Kesstel suddenly shoved a mouthful of brownie sundae in my mouth. I choked on creamy decadence as cold vanilla slipped down my throat and chocolate coated my tongue. I gasped and coughed so much that I could smell the sugar in my nose.

Kesstel leaned forward and patted my back. When my coughing slowed down, he leveled Bethany Wilks with a weighted stare. "My partner," he announced. "She's my partner, and we're having dinner."

I gaped at him through watering eyes, still trying to swallow the bite. *I'm his what? Since when?*

Bethany looked just as floored. "What do you mean? *I'm* your partner."

"You were my ward, the daughter of my employer," Kesstel corrected her, his voice just as flat. "But that changed two hours ago. Please excuse yourself from our table, Miss Wilks. There's only seating for two." He picked up a navy-blue linen napkin and handed it to me.

I grabbed it and buried my red face in the thick material. When I could finally breathe and the tears were wiped from my cheeks, I lowered the linen enough to stare at him over the hem. I wasn't necessarily glaring, but I definitely wasn't shining stars out of my eyes at him, either. He seriously had just dug my grave.

So the question now was: would it be death by hitman later, or brownie sundae homicide now?

"Excuse myself? Just leave, that's it?" Bethany's eyes turned red, and huge tears streamed down her pale cheeks. "And after everything we've been through for the last seven years. Does that really mean nothing to you?"

More and more, this was looking like a breakup scene, and I was in the middle of it all. Even with the temptation of the brownie, all I wanted to do was run away.

As if he knew what I was thinking, Kesstel touched the back of my hand with his and nudged the brownie sundae bowl closer to me. At least he didn't try to shove it down my throat again.

"Our time together never meant anything to me to begin with. It was a job. I reminded you of that repeatedly, Miss Wilks. I've already returned everything that you gave me to your father. None of it was used and is in new condition, so you can regift or return it as you like." He shot her a look. "Please leave, Miss Wilks."

I stared down at the brownie, watching fudge slowly drip off it. What should I do? I felt shackled to this moment, the table, even the sundae. The discomfort somehow kept me from fleeing even though I wanted to, *so badly*. If only Bethany and Kesstel would fight it out—a couple swings of the sword always solved the problem. Granted, Bethany would be dead after . . .

Instead, each word they exchanged felt like another shovel of dirt digging me closer and closer to six feet under.

I looked at Kesstel. What was going on in his head right now?

Bethany sobbed wretchedly and spun around with a flourish. She smacked right into a waiter walking past who was balancing a tray full of food.

The waiter gasped and lost his footing as the tray slipped from his hand and fell toward my head.

Kesstel reached out in a blur of movement and grabbed the lowering side of the platter, balancing it and shifting the food back into place. Bethany staggered around the waiter then tripped and fell onto her butt with a yelp. Her pointed heels gouged the waiter's legs, who yelled in shock and pain then fell toward me. I gasped and reached out to steady the young man; at the same time, Kesstel reached out one hand and grabbed the waiter's shoulder so he didn't land on me, but in the process, the platter fell out of the waiter's hand and Kesstel's grip on it twisted.

Five plates of food hit Kesstel's shoulder, covering his back and arm with pasta, breadsticks, creamy garlic sauces, and soda glasses. It all continued to slide over him and landed on the polished floor in a messy slop.

Silence blanketed the entire restaurant.

A couple specks of food hit my cheek, and I winced at how hot it was. Yet he'd been hit by the whole thing. "Kesstel! Are you okay?"

A dense, heavy ripple of power filled the air, radiating from Kesstel. The oppressive power was so much stronger than me, goose bumps covered my body, and I couldn't help but shiver. At least it wasn't as heavy as when he'd taught Blake a lesson. No one collapsed, but a collective breath was heard as the pressure settled over the restaurant. Kesstel lifted his head up, and I shivered again. His eyes . . . they were faintly glowing blue. From the way they glowed to the hard slant of his mouth—he looked like a demon. Gorgeous, but freakishly scary.

His one clean hand brushed the food specks off my cheek. It took everything I had not to flinch, just in case it made him angrier. But the gentle way he touched my cheek instantly soothed my fear. I couldn't help but stare at him, conflicted. He was scary. My body was still reacting to the angry energy he emitted, but my heart and mind calmed.

He focused on my cheek as if making sure I was unmarred. He must have liked what he saw because the angry energy ceased.

The whole restaurant sighed with relief as one. I blinked, realizing that at some point, the barrier around Kesstel and me had disappeared.

What no one could see was that Kesstel was still glaring, but at least his eyes weren't glowing like a demon anymore. He turned his head and focused on Bethany.

Her hands were fisted at her side so tightly that her knuckles were as white as her face. Her brows were pulled low over her wet deep blue eyes. Her expression slipped between humiliation and fear as she used our table to pull herself up off the floor and stand on visibly shaking legs. From the shock on her face, it was clear that Kesstel had never been angry with her before. She turned and ran out of the restaurant like a wraith was chasing her.

The waiter shifted away from the hold that Kesstel had on his shoulder, his mouth opening and closing like a goldfish. His brain was so obviously fried, he was glued speechless to the spot staring at the S god.

Kesstel stood up, his body angling so he didn't drip any food on me. "Are you okay?"

I gaped at him. "I should be asking you that. Isn't the food hot?"

"Compared to the flames inside the Gate?" The corner of his mouth hooked up.

Ah, I guess he did have a point there. I'd seen high-ranked Hunters get blasted with flames from aggressive monsters and walk away without being singed. Compared to Kesstel's crazy-high rank, what would something like this do to him? Still, that didn't make me feel any better.

Not sure what else to do, I raised my wrinkled napkin and started to wipe away the food that slipped down his arm. "Um, thank—"

"Oh my god!" A man in a blue vest with a shiny name badge pinned to his chest came running down the aisle. "I'm so, so sorry, sir!" He held a stack of white towels in his arms. Several servers hurried behind him, holding towels and cleaners, too.

Kesstel tore his eyes off me and looked up, frowning.

The man bent over and draped a towel over Kesstel's shoulder. "I'm so terribly sorry. Something like this . . . in my restaurant . . . " He couldn't seem to string a full sentence together.

The server who had been rooted to the spot finally blinked out of his shock. He dropped to the ground and helped the arriving waiters pick up the mess of food and broken plates.

Kesstel took an offered towel and mopped at his shirt. "Are you okay, Jynn?" he asked again, apparently unwilling to let it go until I answered.

I blinked at him and nodded slowly. Seriously, how could he ask me that question in this situation?

Kesstel turned to the owner. "It's no trouble. None of this was caused by any of your staff." He flicked a glance at the door where Bethany had disappeared through. It looked like he'd found someone to hold accountable.

The owner didn't look pleased. "Even so, please allow me to pay for your meal and get your clothes cleaned."

Kesstel stepped out of the booth. "That isn't necessary. If you'll excuse me." I started to get up, but Kesstel held up his hand in a stop motion. "I'll be back in a moment. If you come out now, you'll get dirty. Just wait until it's cleaned up first." He waited until I slowly nodded before he turned and walked to the back of the restaurant where the bathrooms were.

I bit my lip, watching him go. I'd just changed in the bathrooms a bit ago, so I knew what was going on. With his rank, his Items Bag was probably large enough to fit everything inside a house and then some; he had to have a pair of clothes. And I didn't want him to walk around in soiled, food-stained clothes, either, so I didn't put up a fight. The problem was, now that he was gone, I was the center of attention.

The owner turned his attention to me. I wasn't as scary, so he hit me with all the fawning and apologizing he couldn't squeeze out with Kesstel. If it weren't for the fact that it was rude to leave while Kesstel was gone—and I was hugely indebted to him at this point, what with the meal and saving me from the raining food—I would have run away within the first tortuous minute of Bethany arriving. The owner wouldn't stop shoving gift cards and small gifts in my hands while the servers worked like bees to clean around me.

"No, it's really okay," I muttered for the millionth time as I tried to hand the gift cards back. I wasn't paying for the meal to begin with, so why should I get the gift cards?

I almost broke out in the "Hallelujah Chorus" when Kesstel returned. His hair was wet and slicked back from his face, a few stray strands dangling over his forehead. His slacks and button-up shirt had been traded out for jeans and a T-shirt, but he didn't look any less appealing. I wasn't the only one who noticed, by the way numerous women stared at him.

For the first time, I didn't want to run from him. In fact, I couldn't wait to scramble out of the booth, no matter what its cleaned state was. I dodged around the workers and hurried over to Kesstel.

He took one look at my tense expression and asked, "Shall we go?"

"Yes." I nodded. Anything to get out of here.

The owner still tried to comp the meal, but Kesstel insisted on paying. He even paid for the food that was spilled on him, much to the owner's chagrin. It wasn't until we were walking down the sidewalk away from the restaurant that Kesstel pointed to my hands.

"What are these?"

I blinked down and gasped. I'd been in such a hurry to leave, I didn't notice I was still holding them. "Oh no! They're gift cards. The owner kept giving them to me, even though I told him not to." I glanced behind me, torn. I really didn't want to go back. Never mind my nerves—I was sure the owner would have a heart attack if he saw us return. I pushed the cards into Kesstel's hands. "They're for you." He was the one who'd paid, anyway.

His brows lifted. "But they were given to you." He tried to give them back.

I shook my head and stepped away. "I don't want them. I won't use them, anyway, so you should keep them." If it wasn't for Kesstel, I doubted I would have been let into that restaurant to begin with. This restaurant cared more about the ranks of diners than the pastry shop I'd visited with Aliya.

He frowned at me. After a second, he motioned to my pants. "You got dirty after all."

I blinked in surprise at the small tomato spots on my right thigh. When did that happen? When the food fell or when I got up? It didn't really matter; the spots were barely bigger than a quarter. It didn't even come close to some of the stuff that had covered me from my visits to the Gate. "Ah, it's okay."

He shook his head. "No. Let's go get you a new outfit that isn't dirty."

My eyes widened and I put my hands up in a stop position. "No, seriously. It's okay. It'll clean out without a stain. There's no reason for you to buy me clothes."

He leaned to the side and planted a hand on his hip. "I was the one who took you there, and it was my acquaintance who caused the spill. Do you expect me to let you walk about with messy clothes?"

He was admittedly fun to talk to. Even when he was scary, I was starting to understand he wasn't a danger to me. But I had a feeling that this evening had gotten me even deeper in the quagmire of Bethany Wilks's anger.

I took another step back, putting considerable distance between us. "I'm grateful for the meal. It was delicious, thank you. But I need to get back home already." I smiled at him as convincingly as I could.

He frowned and stepped closer. "Let me take you home, then."

And let him see where I lived? The E Hostel was a far cry from a castle.

I shook my head. "No, really. I'll be fine. Thank you, again, for everything. And I'm sorry that you got messy because of me." I took a couple steps back. "See you around." I waved and took off running before he could stop me.

I felt so ungrateful, I almost felt sick. But I didn't have the right to stand by him. I didn't know what he wanted, but whatever it was, I couldn't give it to him. I was too weak, too poor, too much of a *nothing*. Maybe in sixty or seventy more levels, I'd finally be worthy to stand within ten feet of him.

CHAPTER 5

When I opened my eyes the next day, I was immediately notified of my new tasks.

[Daily Task: Destroy five Energy Crystals.]

[Daily Task: Cultivate for forty-five minutes.]

[Task: Collect three Cyan-Agarics.]

I stared at the last one, trying to make heads or tails of it. What was a cyan-agaric? I rolled off my bed and took a second to stretch while I opened my *Monster Manual* and flipped through it. By the time I was done stretching, I concluded that, whatever it was, it wasn't in the *Monster Manual*. Frowning, I piled up my laundry and headed down to the first floor. It was early enough in the morning that I should be able to get a washer and dryer. In theory.

As early as it was, Henry was already in the kitchen, wearing a blue apron and humming an off-tune Chinese folk song under his breath. The air was thick with bacon, eggs, and spiced oatmeal. He looked up.

"Morning, Jynn girl. Come, eat." He pointed at the plate with his metal spatula.

I bobbed my head and smiled. "Morning. I'll be there in a minute."

There was only one other person in the room, a man in a hoodie and sweatpants at the far dining table. He leaned over his food, obviously more asleep than he was awake. I walked past the dining room tables and into the long living room area. It was big enough to fit a couple lengthy L-shaped couches surrounding a mounted TV. I'd walked through this room countless times, but I think I'd sat on the community couches only four times since I came to the hostel. Like most tenants here, I preferred to hang out in my room instead.

On the right wall was a door which led to the laundry room. Ten washing and mounted drying machines lined the walls of the narrow white room, five on each side, with a long wooden slat bench in the middle. There was a basket of rumpled clothes still on it, a flaming pink bra very visible on top. Three of the machines had laundry in them, left over from the night before from the looks of it, with empty or half empty baskets on their lids. Other than that, I had my pick.

Habit directed me to the right wall, and I started to stuff my things into the machine. Henry's bedroom was on the other side of the left wall. I knew he was used to it, but I always felt that the laundry machines were unreasonably loud, and I hoped dryers running at night didn't disturb him.

When I picked up the jeans I wore yesterday, I took a second to spray some stain-fighter solution on the sauce spots. Then I pushed my hands into my jean pockets for a last-minute check and felt five thin plastic cards in there. I yelped in surprise and nearly jumped out of my skin. The pants slipped from my fingers and plopped onto the worn cream-and-white linoleum. Five shiny restaurant gift cards slid from the pocket and scattered across the floor. No way. How? When? I'd clearly put those in Kesstel's hands. What were they doing in my pocket?

"Jynn?" Henry's voice came through the open doorway. "Everything okay?"

I jumped again, suddenly feeling like a thief. I just couldn't handle this. I was seriously going to die from a heart attack. Grabbing the cards, I stuffed them into my Items Bag. I mean, what would anyone think if they saw an E rank with hundreds of dollars' worth of gift cards for a swanky restaurant?

"Ah, yeah," I shouted over my shoulder at the door. "I just—" *died* "—slipped."

The more pressing matter was, how was I going to give these back to Kesstel? I didn't have any way to contact him. The only times we had talked was when he took the initiative to seek me out. I mean, what did an S do all day? They were in charge of sweeping out all the overbearing monsters in the Gate before the other Hunters went in, but what about after that? I guess until yesterday, Kesstel would have spent his days being Bethany Wilks's bodyguard. But what did he do now?

It's not like I had all day to look for him. I had laundry, my daily tasks, and nondaily tasks.

I also needed to go to Maveric Armory to sell all the loot still in my Items Bag from yesterday. Because of grinding and looking for ingredients for the Dreamer cure, I'd forgotten I hadn't sold my drop items until the armory was already closed. A morning trip there would take up time to get to the Gate and potentially lose needed kills, but I'd hate to leave drop items behind because I couldn't fit them in my Items Bag.

Besides, I didn't even know what a cyan-agaric was yet.

I finished putting my laundry in the machine, added soap, and turned it on. While that washed, I headed out to breakfast.

Henry handed me a loaded plate, and I sat down on the corner of the table closest to him. I ate a couple bites before I looked at him. "Can I use your computer? I need to look something up."

Using a pair of tongs, he began flipping over sizzling bacon while he dodged the splattering grease. "What are you looking for?"

I swallowed a big bite of bacon, trying not to feel guilty. He'd never let me help him with his chores. They were his job security, he always said. As long as they needed to be done, he had a living. As soon as his jobs were taken away and he became obsolete, he was done for.

"Do you know what a cyan-agaric is? All I know is that it's somewhere in Gate Vale." I didn't really expect Henry to know. It had been nearly ten years since he last stepped inside the Gate, but there was always a possibility.

He placed a steel mesh covering over the pan to keep the grease from popping out and shook his head with a sigh. "Ah, Jynn girl, I've never heard of that. Is it a monster?"

I chewed slowly, thinking, then swallowed. "I don't know. It might be, but it's not in the *Monster Manual*. But it could be a plant, I guess?" I doubted the System would send me out there to collect a bunch of dirt . . . maybe.

"If you don't even know that, how do you know what its name is?" Henry asked incredulously.

I paused. What should I say? I really hated lying to Henry.

The Hunter on the other side of the dining room gave a loud snore. His chin slipped off his palm, and he face-planted into the table, rattling his mostly empty plate. He jumped awake, snorting and gasping in shock.

I bit my fork to keep from laughing out loud.

Henry guffawed. "Hey, Mateo, go back to bed or stay awake and get moving. Either way, don't break my table with your head."

The man's face burned red. He inhaled the rest of his food as fast as possible and hurried from the room.

Henry watched him go, hands on his hips and shaking his head. When Mateo was gone, Henry turned back to the stove, apparently forgetting all about his question.

I laughed under my breath and finished my meal. Walking the plate over to the sink, I washed it off before Henry could notice, and since he was still playing with the eggs, I took the time to clean Mateo's plate and put it on the drying rack next to mine.

Henry took the eggs off the burner and looked at me before glancing at the plates on the rack and scowling. Sniffing, he lifted his nose in the air in mock anger. "Well, since you're done, I'll go unlock the office for you." He turned and walked down the hall.

I followed him to the office and waited as he touched the fingerprint sensor with his thumb. Once the lock clicked, Henry swung the door open for me. "When you're done, just shut the door," he instructed, hurrying back to finish making breakfast for twenty-two more people. From the sounds of the ceiling starting to creak overhead, the morning rush was going to start soon.

I walked around the L-shaped honey oak desk and sat down before I turned on the computer. While it booted up, my attention was drawn to a picture on the far corner of the desk.

Age had worn the quality of the photo paper, but it couldn't diminish the joy of the faces in the frame. A much younger Henry sat holding hands with a round-faced, smiling woman. Behind Henry was a black-haired young man arm-in-arm with a pretty young woman and holding a plump baby in a frilly pink dress. Behind Henry's wife was another young man, his arm resting on his mother's shoulder and grinning so wide that his eyes narrowed just like Henry's.

My gaze traced the frame, noting the faded spots the size of fingers on the tarnished wood frame. Even after more than fifteen years, how often did Henry stop and hold this picture?

The computer played a tune, drawing my attention as the login screen appeared. I signed in as a guest and opened the internet. From there, I typed in the name and hit enter.

The first result popped up a drawing beside a small body of text.

I stared at the picture, memorizing the slender off-white stem under the blue perfectly curved umbrella-shaped top dotted with three bright white circles.

"It's a . . . mushroom?" I muttered under my breath, surprised. How hard could this task be?

I scanned the text.

The cyan-agaric is found in the Josu Rainforest. It is estimated that only one emerges a day, if at all, and the location is never the same. The cyan-agaric is extremely toxic if consumed, and there is no known antidote. Never attempt to handle without the proper equipment.

It's confirmed—the System was obsessed with sending me after stupidly dangerous stuff.

Maveric looked up when I walked into his shop, a surprised smile spreading over his kind face. "Well, good morning, Miss Jynn. I think this is the first time I've ever said that to you." He finished fastening a piece of paper to a corkboard on the wall behind the display counter then walked along till he was in front of me. "I was a little surprised when you didn't come in last night."

It's true. I'd seen Maveric nearly every night since I'd started leveling up to sell my drop items. It had gotten to the point where we didn't even haggle that much anymore. He knew he'd get a good-quality item, and I knew I'd get a fair—and more often than not, generous—price.

I smiled at him. "Good morning. Things were a little hectic last night, so I'm here now."

He looked over my armor and sighed with appreciation. His gaze could have been considered completely inappropriate, but I knew him well enough not to be offended. "Are you ever going to tell me who makes your armor? I'd love to pick his or her brain."

I shook my head. "Nope. And I still don't know what kind of material it is, either."

He gave another exaggerated forlorn sigh, then brightened up and rubbed his hands together.

"Alright. What do you have for me this time?"

I emptied all the drop items out of my Items Bag. Thirty minutes later, I accepted the last transfer payment and watched as Maveric put the large piece of treant lumber into his Items Bag. My eyes drifted over the corkboard yet again. I couldn't fully see what was written on the paper, but there were two words that had caught my attention as we talked money: *Josu Rainforest.*

Now that business was complete, I couldn't help but wander over to get a better look.

Wanted: Two aero-teuthida from Josu Rainforest.

Reward: $500

Poster: Maveric

I pointed to the paper. "What's this?"

Maveric walked over and rubbed his hand through the back of his short, pale brown hair. "Ah, a client wanted something specific for his armor, and I need two aero-teuthida for it. I'm too busy to go into the Gate anymore, so I thought I'd post a reward for someone to get it for me. It should cover the cost of getting it and pay for the price of the aero-teuthida, granted that they don't ruin it while bringing it back. They need to be handled very carefully because they fall apart easily, even inside an Items Bag."

It took me all of a second to make a decision. "I'll take the bill."

He blinked at me. "What?"

I bobbed my head to the side. "I'm going there, anyway. I'll take the bill."

Maveric frowned. "Is that where your team is going today? The Josu Rainforest?"

The fact that I was an E couldn't be more obvious to anyone who looked at the title bar over my head. But now that I was bringing in harder monsters, I'd had to come up with a reason why. As far as Maveric knew, a little after I met him, I joined a team of Hunters. It wasn't all that uncommon for Es to join stronger teams and do all the grunt work for a living.

I nodded. "There are a couple things they want to find there. What's one more item on the list?"

He still frowned at me. "The Josu Rainforest is no casual matter, Miss Jynn. Especially for an E, even with a party. It might be a C-ranked location, but there's a reason why most of the Hunters who enter it are higher ranked. It's nearly impossible to stay on the ground. The velociorhea there hunt in packs, and they are very fast. And you can't evade them on foot—tree roots pose a huge problem. They latch onto living things and don't let go until they've sucked all the moisture out of the body."

CHAPTER 6

I paused, absorbing Maveric's words of warning. But he also gave important information on how I could handle the Josu Rainforest. I didn't know what a velociorhea was yet, but at least I knew where to look. If it was common knowledge, it definitely was in the *Monster Manual.* "Thanks for the information."

He looked at me hard. "I take it you still want the post?"

I nodded.

Since I was going to be there anyway, I might as well do this and get some extra cash. I still had a long way to go before I could afford a house for when Aliya came to live in Eden.

Ah, I guess that should be *if* she came? I knew it was still up in the air, but in my mind, it was a done deal. If I were ranked as a C, I would be in a guild and have a salary on top of the loot income, as well as better designated housing. Granted, I could have had that right now if I had accepted President Price's offer, but I wasn't stupid enough to make a deal with the devil when I knew I was going to be the one losing in the end.

Haha, scratch that. I'd already made a deal with the devil without thinking about the consequences when I was dying under the red orc's blade. I'd lucked out, since the System ended up being a nicer master—it obviously didn't want to kill me . . . maybe?—but I knew right off the bat that Price wouldn't be as lenient.

Maveric sighed loudly, bringing my attention back to him. "Well, if you want it." He pulled the paper off the pin and wrote my name on it. "You shouldn't let your team pull you into too many dangerous situations, you know." He opened a metal filing cabinet behind the counter so well designed and flush with the wall that I didn't even know it was a cabinet until then. He leafed through the files inside then added the bill to a large group of papers. "I'll need the aero-teuthida by the end of the week." He lifted his hand, and a blue screen appeared, much like the one we used when I sold my loot. Only this one was a contract of services. It clearly laid out that I would exchange two aero-teuthida by the end of the week for the agreed-upon amount, and that he wasn't going to give my post away to anyone else until the time was up.

I reached out and accepted the contract.

A teal-colored System notice popped open. [**Additional Task has been added.**]

I nodded with satisfaction. "Alright. I'll see you later." I paused mid-turn. "Oh, I know this isn't your area of expertise, but I don't suppose you have any teleportation tokens to the Josu Rainforest, do you?" He gave me a blank stare. I shrugged. "It would save me time at the Transportation Office if I just bought it off you."

He gave a disgusted grunt and ran a hand through his already messily spiked brown hair. "Ah, this team of yours! Not only do they make a young girl do all the grunt work, but they won't even help you out by picking up a transportation token while they're at the office?" He turned and started to rummage through one metal filing cabinet after another.

Man, was that whole wall a massive storage unit? I thought it was just a gray wall.

"Here they are." Maveric straightened, holding a blue cloth bag. "It's been about eight years since I had to trek through the Gate myself for supplies. Now I just sit here, and Hunters come to me, you know? I didn't think I still had these." He opened the bag and dumped nine circular copper tokens out onto the glass counter. "Nowadays they use energy crystals because the magic on them lasts longer than a week, but these should still work." He pushed them around until he found one with a raindrop etched on it and picked it up. "You got lucky. I don't know what the price is now, but I bought it for a hundred dollars. I'll sell it to you for that much." He created another blue screen and offered it to me.

I'd deal with a copper piece over an energy crystal any day. "You are surprisingly kind to Es," I commented as I accepted his offer. Even if I wasn't an E in strength, it still was what everyone thought I was. "It's different."

He handed me the token. "Well, there are quite a few of my clients who are Es. Even if the loot they bring in is from lower monsters, they aren't that much different from the higher-ranked Hunters. Everyone is just trying to live and make a living." He scooped the tokens back into the bag. "Not to mention, my older brother is an E, and he has a kid not much younger than you. So, you know, I get it." He smiled sadly. "He slaved his guts out to support me and his son until I could get my business up and running."

It sounded like a familiar story. You know, just like my own life. But after all this time, the only person I'd ever talked shop with was Maveric. "You two don't work together?" Blood was thicker than water.

He gave a hapless smile. "We do. I wanted him to help with the business stuff in Eden, but he kept saying he didn't want to drag me down. And he hates numbers. He'd rather be in the Gate, collecting materials for me. He's dealt with a few shitty teams over the years, so I know how unfair it is for Es." Maveric pulled out a couple long metal containers and explained how to put the aero-teuthida in them so I didn't damage the carcasses, then he handed them over. "Take care of yourself out there."

I smiled at him. "Will do. See you later."

Inside the Gate, I walked southeast of the entrance to a small trail that led between a thicket of thin trees. There were a few A-ranked Hunters along the short path, one already looking bored out of his mind while the other two paced up and down the path vigilantly. They each had a Hunter's Association symbol on their chest, a deep red *H* atop a navy-blue sword and axe all stitched with precision over a pale-yellow circular flame. It made sense that the Association guarded this area, since they were the ones who manned it.

The path opened up to a small natural clearing in the trees where twenty transportation circles, arranged in two rows, hovered off the dirt ground. A good ten feet separated each glowing purple circle. An A- or B-ranked mage stood by each, guiding the lines of Hunters and making sure everything went smoothly. All but two magic circles had lines of Hunters in front of them. Before I could wonder why the two lonely ones were left with a single mage standing guard, one of them flashed bright, and a second later, an armored woman appeared and took a couple quick steps before she regained her balance. She turned and watched as another Hunter appeared after her.

Oh, those two were returning circles. According to the Guide, unlike the magic circle I'd used when I was working with Emma, these specific transport circles weren't tied to a specific location. The Hunter who entered went to wherever their token designated them to go. It would make sense that some would be for going and others for returning. It wouldn't surprise me if most of them were used for going in the morning but were changed to returning in the evening when Hunters were done with the day.

Given the cost of a transport token, it wasn't surprising to see that nearly all the Hunters lining up were either C or higher. Well, it wasn't just the cost. It was also the fact that the farther you were from the Gate, the stronger the monsters became. The ten or so lower-ranked Hunters in the clearing were standing next to strong Hunters. Most of the weaker ones looked nervous and a little afraid, while a few were confident that their party would protect them.

Quite a few eyes glanced my way when I joined the shortest line. I was obviously alone and an E. A couple in the line next to me snorted and leaned into each other, sharing amused glances and making it apparent that they thought I was insane. I sighed, ignored all the looks, and retrieved a printed map of Josu Rainforest from my Items Bag.

The Guide in my System had a map of Gate Vale, something all Hunters had access to. Only, it was just a general overview. If a Hunter wanted a more detailed map of a certain location—like the one Mason had of Feng Jungle—they had to buy one. Or in my case, print it off the internet.

It was a little more archaic and earned me even more looks of ridicule.

A mage in line ahead of me turned around and shifted the tall metal staff in his hand. "Are you lost?"

I glanced up at him in surprise. "No."

He glanced between the paper and my title bar. His brows rose so high on his forehead they disappeared under his baggy, brown fringe. "Oh." He turned around, shot a couple looks at me over his shoulder, then dismissed me entirely.

The couple melee Hunters next to him nudged his shoulder and snickered.

I went back to my paper.

I had no idea where the cyan-agaric would appear. All I knew was that it was seven inches tall and only one grew a day somewhere in the rainforest—if one grew at all that day. On the ground . . . where I shouldn't be because of the predatory velociorhea that traveled in packs, and the human-sucking roots. So the plan was to scout the entire rainforest from the treetops, every day, until I found three of the blue mushrooms. At least the aero-teuthida that Maveric wanted lived in the treetops. That was a bonus, I guess.

My line was quickly dwindling. Since there was a little bit more time, I opened my *Monster Manual* and looked up the velociorhea. It was a C-ranked monster that stood around five feet tall and looked like a mix between a dinosaur and a bald, rainbow-headed ostrich. It didn't have a beak, just a long snout full of pointed teeth below bright yellow eyes. While its head and long neck were bare, its oval body was covered in fine gray-brown feathers. It couldn't fly, and there were very sharp claws at the end of its wings. Two strong, bald gray legs supported the body and ended in vicious-looking talons bigger than my fingers. These velociorhea were fast, agile, and lived in packs of three to four.

To my left, one of the return circles lit up, and a Hunter in cobalt-gray armor and black under armor appeared. He stepped to the side and watched another Hunter come out in the exact same armor.

The group ahead of me got to the front of the line and started to disappear into the transportation circle.

Finally, it was my turn. I closed my Guide just as another Hunter appeared out of the magic circle next to me.

Bethany Wilks took a couple quick steps attempting to regain her balance. Her tight, rich-blue mage robe shifted over her body, revealing her curves. She huffed a breath, a pout on her red lips as she smoothed her clothes down and walked forward, her eyes narrowed pensively. For once, there was nothing coquettish about her. More men in identical armor came out of the magic circle behind her, but she didn't spare any of them a glance as she walked right past me.

Just as I turned my head to look at her go by, she glanced at me. Our gazes collided.

Ah, shit.

Her eyes flared in anger. "You!"

"Miss? It's your turn." The mage at the front of the line prompted me forward.

Between staying with a woman who looked full of hellfire and following the mellow voice of the Association mage, I knew exactly where I was going. I turned my back on Bethany Wilks and quickly stepped forward.

"Please show me your token," the middle-aged man directed.

The token appeared in my hand, and I showed it to him.

"Ah, the Josu Rainforest." The mage nodded his head.

As soon as he said the name, I wanted to shake him. *You didn't have to say it out loud! That crazy chick is right behind me! She's trying to kill me, and now you told her exactly where I'm going!*

He motioned with his hand toward the circle. "Be careful."

My head was high, and my back was straight like I wasn't on edge, but I ducked around him before he was even fully out of my way.

"Hey, wait!" Bethany Wilks screeched behind me.

Without looking back, I stepped into the magic circle and let it take me away.

CHAPTER 7

I landed on the small clear borderline that divided the Josu Rainforest and the Pointe Tundra, casting Stealth as soon as my feet hit the ground. My body disappeared as momentum from traveling sent me a couple steps forward, right into the rainforest.

The light overhead dimmed to the glow of dawn. Glancing up, I saw, high above my head, how the umbrella of leaves on the top of every tall pale tree tangled together without letting a single beam of light through. The air was hot and heavy with humidity, and it took me a second to adapt to the muggy atmosphere, and another second to accept the slight smell of decay in the air. It wasn't rotting flesh—I knew that smell well enough—but of organic things decomposing. Like how Henry's little flower garden in the hostel smelled in the spring after he mixed in the fertilizer.

A light drizzle sprinkled down around me, but I couldn't see where the rain was coming from. I turned in a half circle. At the edge of the rainforest, where its border collided with a different region, the sky was as blue as ever over a sprawling tundra. No rain over there. But it definitely was lightly raining over here. Droplets clung to the branches overhead and to the random bursts of bright-green fern-like plants which grew right out of the wonky-shaped tree trunks.

In fact, there were more plants growing out the sides of trees than on the moist ground. From where I stood, the rainforest floor was a blanket of moss which covered rocks and grew up the sides of trees. There was no way to tell which way was north in this forest because the moss grew all over the trunks.

The only other things I could find on the ground were mushrooms. I examined them more closely. *Hm.* They were small and white. Not what I was looking for, but it was a step in the right direction.

I finished my quick survey of the area and jumped up to a tree branch which connected to others like a jungle gym obstacle course. My new skill, High Jump, took me right up to the first level of branches. I landed lightly and couldn't help the wide grin that spread over my face. Oh my god, that was so fun just being able to jump like that. It was like flying!

I couldn't resist looking around for somewhere else to leap to. It was the first time I'd been able to use this skill. Practicing it a little by jumping around like a caffeinated bunny wouldn't hurt anything, right?

Before I could make that fantasy a reality, three Hunters came out of the transportation circle one at a time. Still invisible, I looked down at the C-ranked men.

The one with a bushy red beard and tank armor looked around the rainforest. "Which way do you think she went? A little E insect can't get that far, right?"

I frowned. *Damn, that was fast.* Clearly, my playtime was over—before it even began.

Another Hunter in light armor with a large, beaked nose looked around the forest and shifted his shield around nervously. "I don't see anyone. But we need to get off the ground."

The third man, a mage in green robes and holding a gnarly wooden staff, motioned to the right. "There are some low branches there. We could use that to climb up."

"Ugh," Red Beard moaned. "I don't do well with heights."

Beak Nose thumped him over the head with his shield. "Dumbass! That money is wasted on you." The sound of metal on metal echoed off the trees.

My brows rose, a little surprised that he would make such a stupid move. At the moment, I couldn't feel any monsters, but that didn't mean much, since he'd just announced their location so clearly.

"*Sh!*" the mage hissed. "We gotta go, now." He glanced around and scowled. On the ground next to his brown boot, an inch thick tree root slowly slithered closer to him. He stabbed it with his staff, and the root recoiled as if in pain. He didn't bother looking back as he ran to the closest low-hanging branch.

Luckily, it was in the opposite direction from me. Content, I turned and got ready to leave. Between Stealth and Feather Step, I should be able to get away from them easily enough, especially if one of them didn't do well with heights. From Red Beard's clunky armor, he probably wasn't going to be moving that fast, anyway.

A jolt went through my body as I became aware of several monsters coming in our direction—fast.

Red Beard held out his arm and let the mage jump to his forearm then spring off, landing on a low-hanging branch. The mage grabbed at the tree and hoisted himself up. Looking down at his companions, his staff appeared back in his hand, and he lifted it slightly in the air to cast a spell.

Suddenly, Beak Nose stiffened. He gasped, obviously feeling the monsters closing in, and let out a yelp as he ran toward Red Beard. He didn't even ask or pause before he climbed on top of the large man and jumped up onto the branch next to the mage.

Red Beard was thrown off balance from his teammate's frantic moves and he stumbled to the side, his head bowed so that his helmet covered his face. When he tipped his head back up, his face alternated between pale white and as red as the hair on his face. "Hurry, lift me up!"

The mage frowned in concentration, and the tip of his staff started to glow green.

A green film covered Red Beard, and he rose into the air. "Hurry!" he pressed.

Three soundless blurs darted around the wet trees. In the dim light, I caught sight of the rainbow-colored heads of the velociorhea. Like lightning, they bolted toward the floating Hunter.

Red Beard looked over his shoulder. His eyes widened, and his face settled to a frightened pale white. He gripped his bastard sword and swung it at the first velociorhea that jumped at him. His blade struck the monster right on its gray feathered chest and flung it to the side.

From his perch in the tree, Beak Nose pulled out a dagger and threw it at the next monster. It dodged to the side, and the dagger sank into the ground.

"Hurry!" Red Beard screamed.

The mage jerked his staff up, sweating like he was reeling in a ton of bricks. "Shut it . . . This isn't . . . my natural element!" He groaned under the pressure but kept at it.

The Hunter jerked higher in the air, halfway up to the branch. Beak Nose dropped to his stomach and reached out for Red Beard's gloved hand.

The largest velociorhea jumped onto Red Beard, its giant talons digging between the stomach sections of the Hunter's armor. The monster ignored the Hunter's agony and stretched its neck up toward Beak Nose's hand, who screamed and jerked back just in time as the monster's mouth *clomped* shut. He scrambled to his feet, but in the process, he knocked into the sweating mage.

The mage swore, and the green glow disappeared from his staff.

The screaming Hunter and monster dropped to the ground with a thud that echoed around us. I was stiff with horror and could only watch as the downed man swung his sword frantically, screaming. His first swing missed the quick monster, and before he could swing again, the third velociorhea closed in and stood on his arm, pinning it to the ground.

"Fire!" Red Beard howled. "Fire!"

A fireball shot from the mage's staff and soared toward the monsters.

They jumped safely to the side. The third velociorhea looked up at the mage and let out a screech which sounded like a combination of a dog's growl and a crow's caw.

The only injured monster recovered and rejoined the attack even though black blood leaked from the gash on its chest. It lunged at the downed Hunter and grabbed his helmet with its talons. Red Beard screamed as the claws left red trails from chin to forehead, his cries deepening once the monster started jerking at his helmet. The buckle broke under his chin, and the helmet ripped right off his head. Red Beard's bellows were silenced when the largest velociorhea dove at him and snapped his neck in its mouth. There was an audible crunch that twisted my gut.

I pressed my fingers to my mouth. *Dear god.*

The two remaining Hunters stood on their branch and stared down with pale, shocked faces as the velociorhea pack started to tear apart their companion's corpse with feral savagery. There was no reason to fight against them now, and the realization seemed to render them dumb.

I glanced away. Red Beard was being eaten in front of me, and it had all happened so fast. The velociorheas were clearly well-coordinated monsters. And they weren't the only ones in the rainforest. Concealed within the dim light between the trees, there were many more.

I hadn't taken Maveric's advice for granted, but the seriousness of his warnings didn't hit me until now. I took one more look at the blood-smeared monsters pushing at each other to get another bite before I jumped to the next tree. I had to put some ground between them and me with the last remaining minute of my Stealth.

As empty as the ground was, sixty feet up, the canopy was full of things. The air was a little fresher, and it was a bit brighter, the faint sunlight taking on a green shade as it glowed through the thick layer of leaves. Sturdy branches spread out of endless bridges which twisted and turned around each other. The dense connectivity made traveling easy; when one branch turned or became too thin to walk on anymore, another was just a step away.

Small ferns and bushy plants with twisted white flowers spotted the branches. Well, they were white until accidentally touched; then they turned red, full of blood. I learned that the hard way. As annoying as it was, they didn't have energy crystals in them, and I didn't take the energy to destroy every one that I saw.

Slowly moving through the rainforest, I shifted every which way to peer at the ground below. All I could see was green moss and white mushrooms. One of those stupid white flowers came into my periphery, and I twisted on the branch so I could step over it. Just as I raised my left foot into the air, a sharp sting zinged up my right leg.

I gasped, shocked. *When did a monster get close to me?* Pausing, I looked down.

A vine as thick as my finger had wrapped around my ankle. Its tip had bored a hole through my boot and was latched onto my leg like a leech. The green of the vine was starting to turn red.

Gritting my teeth, I lashed out with my kindjal and severed the vine. The part attached to me fell off, my own blood oozing from its severed end. It landed limply on the branch then rolled right off, dropping twenty meters to the ground. That must be where the decaying smell came from—the dead things from up here. Since it wasn't fleshy, it wouldn't have a meaty decaying smell.

The rest of the vine shrank back like a cut rubber band and slid to the underside of the branch. Leaning around, I saw a bulbous plant attached to the bottom of where I was standing, its body almost looking like a swollen green pepper with purple veins webbing across it. Three vines swayed around as if the air wasn't stagnant. The fourth vine, still dripping blood, was curled up like a wounded animal against the body. A red title bar appeared: [**Assassin Vine Lv20**].

The three fine vines shot toward my face. Jerking back, I swung my kindjal, and another vine was cut in half, the green tip falling down with the light rain to the dim land below. As the other two pulled back, I cast Mist.

The foggy particles spread through the humid air like an infection, pushing away the musky smell and replacing it with a fresh scent. It covered the whole branch, especially under it like I wanted, and I jumped down and landed on solid mist with the assassin vine at eye level.

As I thrust at the bloody plant with my blade, it stretched out its remaining uncut vines toward my chest in a suicide attack. The first vine struck just as my weapon hit the bulbous center of the monster plant and I jerked my kindjal to the side, slicing it in half. Clear liquid with a faint red tint that stank like bad onion gushed from the split center. The body gaped open to reveal a pale blue glow on the base of the plant where it attached to the branch. While the vines writhed through the air like insane worms, I sliced at the plant once more and cut its energy crystal in half. The assassin vine exploded into little fading lights.

[**+95 EXP**]

I caught the drop orb before it fell to the ground. A vial of assassin vine juice, probably the stuff that fell from the bulbous center, was added to my Items Bag. My nose wrinkled, thinking about its smell. The faint red in the liquid must have been my blood. Did that mean that some of me was in that vial? If so, it would feel a little wrong to sell it to Maveric.

A jolt of awareness went down my spine. Four monsters were moving toward my location very quickly. Jumping back onto the branch, I crouched low as I looked down through the mist. Out of the dim light, four velociorheas appeared through the trees. Even though they didn't have any distinguishing features, the red letters over their heads—which displayed a range of level thirty-five to forty-five—indicated they were different from the ones I'd seen earlier. Which meant these monsters were probably hungry.

The largest one with the highest level, which I was starting to understand meant the leader, stepped up to where the severed vines had landed. It sidestepped around and sniffed at the ground intently, then it lifted its head, nostrils flaring on its toothy snout as it drew in large breaths, and looked through the tree branches and mist right at me.

CHAPTER 8

I crept a couple feet farther down the branch and watched the velociorhea below me, waiting to see what it would do. Its nose didn't follow my exact movements, but after a minute, its nostrils flared again, and it tilted its head. Beady yellow eyes followed the branch I crouched on, but it seemed to have lost my exact location.

The other three slightly smaller monsters sniffed at the ground then lifted their bald, rainbow-colored heads to look in my general direction. They obviously couldn't see me through the thick mist that clung to the branch hiding me, but they could smell me through the drizzling rain. The question now was, were they like bloodhounds that kept after a scent come hell or high water? Or would they give up after a while since their target was sixty feet above their heads?

Trying to find a tiny blue mushroom on the ground was hard enough from this height, even with my improved sight. When I did find one, going down and getting it with those hungry monsters hanging around would be more than a little tricky.

I sat down and retrieved a pencil and the Josu Rainforest printed map from my Items Bag. The paper wilted a little because of the mist, but I laid it on my leg and hunched over it to protect it from the light rain as I marked where I was, indicating I'd already searched this area. I also added a few details and landmarks to the map so I could distinguish one tree-filled section from another. It wouldn't do any good for me to go in circles, and this was the best way I could think of to mark off territory. If this didn't work, then maybe I'd look into dropping a hundred bucks to buy a map of the rainforest for my Guide, but for now, that thought made my stomach hurt. The cost of traveling to this location was hard enough to swallow. My transportation token was only valid for a week, so if I didn't finish this task by week's end, I'd have to buy another one.

I glanced down at the velociorhea still sniffing so intently on my direction, it was like they expected me to spring into their mouths. Creepy, but I could live with it for now. What else was I going to do? As long as they stayed down there and I stayed up here, they could stare all they wanted.

As I put the map away and stood, a glint of silver in my periphery caught my attention, and I turned quickly. About forty feet away, a squid flew through the air, drifting around trees like a silvery ghost. Its pointed, cylindrical body was roughly a foot long, and eight arms added another foot. The arms wiggled, flexing and straightening, propelling the monster through the moist air as if it was swimming underwater. Two long tentacles ending in suction cups trailed behind almost lazily.

I couldn't resist perking up. That was an aero-teuthida, one of the two I needed for Maveric.

One of the long tentacles twitched. Like a bullet, the squid monster shot at the tree to its left, and its arms opened up wide like a squiggly maw, revealing a sharp white beak as big as my fist. It chomped down on the body of an assassin vine, engulfing the whole thing in one bite. The green vines tangled with the silver arms for a couple seconds before they went limp. The aero-teuthida pushed off the side of the tree, ripping the assassin vine right off, then the floating squid started pumping through the air casually, as if its body wasn't bloated from digesting another monster, and several inches of the green vines weren't still hanging out its beak.

Sneak attacks. Was this whole rainforest full of sneak attacks? And wiggly vine-like things? Ah well, if the aero-teuthida was going to show itself to me so fast, I'd take advantage of the chance to catch it.

My lips curled up, and I activated Feather Step. I leaped from my branch, the toes of my boots barely touching damp bark before I was shooting to the next tree. At this speed, the rain was hard on my face and body, but my defense was high enough to take away the sting. It was almost a little odd to get wet now, after spending so much time in mist and staying dry. The mist I had cast earlier stayed around my body, swirling like a hurricane as it kept up with me, spilling over the branches and encasing trees. I kept it smaller, only about ten feet in diameter for now. If I needed to, I could open it up to its whole forty feet without paying the extra MP, but for now, this was good enough.

The other thing that kept up with me were the velociorheas. They ran below me, darting around trees and changing directions, keeping up with their target as I closed in on mine.

Twenty feet from the aero-teuthida, I Mirrored my kindjal and got ready to throw one at the monster. If I could pin it to a tree, that would make it a lot easier to kill. But I had to be careful—Maveric needed the carcass to be as intact as possible. If I mangled the body too much, I'd need to get another one, which also meant I couldn't destroy the energy crystal.

A bright flash of light arched through the sky, and a bolt of lightning cut through the aero-teuthida, leaving a gash big enough that the semidecomposed assassin vine fell right out of its stomach.

I skidded to a stop, my boots slipping on wet bark till my toes hung over the branch's edge, just one leap away from my thoroughly damaged target. The blackened monster flailed in the air, body punctured and flattening like a slowly deflating balloon.

To add insult to injury, a black arrow thudded into the dying squid.

It dropped to the ground.

Mouth parted, I watched it fall in the middle of the velociorheas. They apparently weren't picky because I hadn't even heard the thud of its fall before the dino-birds started tearing apart the fried squid. I sighed and looked in the direction the arrow came from.

I'd gotten so used to feeling monsters around me in these woods, I'd just let the presence of Hunters blend with them when I went after the aero-teuthida. Not smart, but I was counting on my mist to keep me concealed. I mean, who in their right mind would attack a swirling cloud when they couldn't see what was at its center? Now, if they knew there was a person inside, that would be another matter, but I wasn't going to let that happen. Mist was, after all, a limited ability. Limited to one person: me. I wasn't strong enough to let the world know about me yet.

A group of Hunters stood on branches roughly fifty feet away. There were six of them, all C ranked, and all of them had a different color dyed in their hair.

A female mage with yellow streaks in her long brown locks smiled at a man with bright green hair. "I told you I could get it first. Who's the quickest shot now?" She brushed at her red sleeves with an exaggerated movement.

The green-haired man shifted his compound bow from one hand to the other. "What? It's not like you actually have to notch a lightning bolt." He scowled.

Yellow tilted her head back and smirked with pride. "Right, i.e. I'm faster."

My lips pursed together in accepted defeat. Yeah, I'd just totally lost two hundred and fifty bucks to a couple of show-offs. Ah, the irony.

The oldest member in the group, a man who looked about thirty with blue hair peeking out of his helmet, rolled his eyes. "Why don't you two compete to see who's going to get the energy crystal now?" He looked pointedly down at the monsters eating their kill.

Green and Yellow immediately shut up. They looked into each other's eyes, then slowly turned their heads to the side, as if pretending they weren't there at all.

Blue looked at them. "Well?"

A girl in dark pink robes and pale pink locks blended into her blonde hair piped up. "We should get out of here soon. I'm almost out of MP."

I turned, ready to leave them to their bickering. I was still 0/2 on flying squids, *and* I still had a mushroom to find.

"We can't leave yet," Green objected. "We haven't found that damn blue mushroom."

For the second time in five minutes, I skidded to a stop. My mouth gaped open as I turned back toward the colorful group. *Now, wait just a damn minute!* The words nearly exploded out of my mouth, but I was able to choke them back just in time. First, they took my kill, and now they were looking for a blue mushroom too?

Pink glared up at him. "Then stop getting stabbed by plants. Half of my MP has gone to patching you up alone!"

"Sorry, sorry!" He gave her a helpless smile. "What did that quack want with a blue mushroom again, anyway?" Green glanced at Yellow as if she might know.

She shrugged.

"Hey." A quiet-looking man with orange hair and wearing tank armor motioned in my direction. "Does anyone else think that cloud is weird?"

"That's what I was just thinking," the remaining Hunter with purple woven through her black hair commented. "I saw it moving earlier before you guys attacked. But it hasn't moved since. I don't think it's a real cloud."

"Huh." Green notched an arrow and aimed it right at my chest.

I instantly dropped like a stone, flattening myself on solid mist behind the branch. An arrow rocketed through the middle of the mist, missing me by half a second. Carefully, I peeked over the branch in their general direction.

Is he shitting me? Who just shoots randomly like that? How many arrows does he lose a year?

Green gave Yellow a cocky smile. "How was that for a quick shot?"

"You missed," she said in a deadpan voice.

Blue thumped Green on top of his helmet. "Knock it off." Then he peered closely in my direction. "But there is something in there." His eyes narrowed, trying to see through my billowing barrier.

" . . . Do you think it's a ghost?" Pink spoke quietly, looking nervous.

Purple shot her a glance. "Monsters, magic, and morons are real. Ghosts are not."

Orange chuckled under his breath.

I'm done. So done with them.

They didn't come across as bad people, but I needed to get going, and fast. Especially if I was going to have competition riding my coat-tails. There wasn't a time limit on how fast I got the cyan-agaric—I think it's because the System knew that one might not appear every day—but the sooner I found everything, the sooner I could go back to harvesting every monster in a zone and finding ingredients for the Dreamer cure.

I wish I could say I was ready to do that here, but lying to myself would get me dead fast. I wasn't ready to take on the velociorheas. Not yet.

Maybe the reason why the System wanted me to get the cyan-agaric had to do with the antidote, maybe not. I wouldn't know until I found them. But right now, I thought the best thing for me and Mom would be to get this task over with quickly so I could go back to the level D locations and grind to get stronger and get lots of drop items.

A sting shot up my leg. I gasped and glared down at the now red flower drifting away from the hole in my boot.

Luckily, my gasp was masked when Green yelped. "Damn flowers!"

I couldn't help but smirk at the shared misery. Letting out a silent sigh, I leaned my forehead on my arms, looking down. How many people would be freaked out right now, lying on air sixty feet above the ground? I'd gotten so used to heights that I was quite comfortable . . . as long as I wasn't bitten by another flower.

The largest velociorhea snapped at another one, chasing it away, then the monster leaned down and picked up the devoured aero-teuthida's glowing energy crystal with its mouth. With a crunch that echoed all the way up here, the crystal broke into pieces and disappeared down the monster's gullet before it looked up and licked its lips, as if waiting for another meal to drop.

"Well," Orange's flat voice drifted through the air, "at least we don't have to get the energy crystal now."

CHAPTER 9

My brows rose. I knew monsters ate each other—it was common knowledge that they ate anything weaker than them, human and monster alike—but it'd never dawned on me that the stronger monsters might eat the crystals.

Huh. Wonder what happened to the digesting energy crystals inside them?

The largest velociorhea shuddered, its long black feathers ruffling over its oval body. With one last large shake of its colorful head, it relaxed and looked back up into the treetops, its yellow gaze flicking from me to the rainbow brigade of Hunters fifty feet away as the red title bar above its head changed. The level increased from forty-five to forty-six.

I let out a silent breath. So eating energy crystals made monsters stronger. That made sense, since they improved the levels of the Hunters who absorbed them as well.

"What do you think?" Yellow asked. "Do you think we should go check out the ghost?"

I frowned and shifted to a crouch, casting Stealth and getting ready to finally slip away, but I paused once again.

Two Hunter auras neared from the treetops. The two surviving Hunters—Beak Nose and the mage—were fighting with each other.

"You shit. You're just half assing around, saying she went this way when you don't actually know!" The mage threw his hands in the air. "It's one measly E. What's taking you so long?"

"Shut it!" Beak Nose snarled. "I know exactly where I'm going. I'm not the one who's half assing! You are! It's your fault Bern died!"

Bern? Ah. Red Beard.

"Says the man who used him like a ladder just to save his own skin." The mage grabbed Beak Nose's collar and thrust his wooden staff into the man's face. The edge of his staff started to glow. "I'll show you half assed. It's not my fault Bern died, but I could be yours."

I hoped they'd kill each other. Unfortunately, Beak Nose took a deep breath and lifted his hands in surrender. "Hey, why don't we calm down a bit? Let's just work together, get this mark done, and get outta this bleeding place."

The light faded from the tip of the mage's staff. He released the man's collar and stepped back. "Fine." Then he gasped and looked down. "Damn flowers!" He kicked out and sent a flutter of red pedals into the air.

Could my venture into Josu Rainforest get any better? Enemies behind and on my right, and monsters down below. So onward it was. I wanted to backtrack so I could keep scouring the ground from where I'd first spotted the aero-teuthida, but that wasn't an option now.

. . . Or was it?

I lunged forward and Feather Stepped back from where I came, the mist following me. I expanded the radius of the white particles, spreading them out the full forty feet. Mist cascaded over tree branches like waterfalls and pooled in the air around me as the pale light from above gleamed green on the top of my cloud, giving it an eerie look.

"Gah!" Pink screamed from behind. "It's moving! It really is a ghost!"

The mist swelled right over Beak Nose and the mage, swallowing them in the thick whiteness as I jumped off my branch and ran on the fog right beneath them. I could hear them swearing, and a blast of fire lit up the inside of my mist, but they couldn't attack what they couldn't see. Moments later, the mist cloud passed by, and they looked around in shock.

I hopped back on a branch and let go of Mist. Still in Stealth mode, I ran back to my starting location from before I'd seen the aero-teuthida earlier. The rainbow brigade had become a blockade, so I turned west to go in search of my mushroom.

Two hours later, I flopped down on a branch after clearing it of every flower, vine, and anything else that wasn't bark. Even then, I had half a mind to strip that off, too, just so I knew I could rest without being stabbed or bitten. I was obviously still alive, but my whole body hurt, from my chin to my toes. My armor was still intact, but my body was riddled with tiny punctures that were still bleeding because I hadn't had time to rest and Regen.

My HP took a ding with every vegetation nibble, and I'd lost about a third of my HP. But my exhaustion was more of a mental thing. It was like sitting on a doctor's exam table, knowing you were just about to get a painful shot, but not knowing *when*. Then after that shot, another one would come. Then another. On and on, for hours.

Even the bird monsters that looked like small vultures had tongues that shot out and wrapped around their prey like vines. And these tongues ended in pincers which sank easily into flesh. If I was any less nimble, I'd be dead five times over by now.

But even though I was tired, I'd already more than filled my energy crystal quota for the day, and I was getting close to leveling up, so that was a pro, I guess.

The con was, I still hadn't seen a single speck of bright blue . . . besides the blue on the velociorheas' crests.

I scowled at the group of monster stalkers below. When I'd run away from the two Hunter groups, I'd lost that foursome of velociorheas. An hour ago, though, a new group—this one with a level thirty-two, thirty-seven, and forty-four—had noticed me and hadn't left since.

Too tired to care about their obsessed staring, I took my lunch out of my Items Bag and ate it while I pored over my map and monster list. There were currently ten different kinds of monsters that appeared in the Josu Rainforest, and I'd killed four of them. One of them—I glanced down at the dino-birds—was beyond my skill level to kill. Maybe I could handle the weakest one in that group, but not with the other two so near. The other five monster types I hadn't found yet, including another aero-teuthida.

In the three hours I'd been in this rainforest, I'd covered about a quarter of it. That gave me eight hours to scour the rest of the region.

I sighed and put away the wrapper before taking a healthy drink of water. Feeling refreshed, I turned over and laid on the thick branch, looking up at the dripping canopy. Did it ever stop raining?

I felt movement to my left and instinctively flipped to my feet, kindjal out. An assassin vine which hadn't been near my leg a minute ago paused, trying to act like a lifeless plant. With a scowl, I lashed out to cut it. Clear liquid gushed forth, and the vine shrank back to the other side of the tree.

I ran after it, ready to find the main body. I thought I'd gotten everything on this tree. If I wanted to actually rest, I needed to get rid of this monster, too. Not to mention, it might give me enough EXP to level up.

Slipping around the tree trunk, I paused, looking for the assassin vine's body. Its vines weren't that long, so it had to be somewhere close.

Shivers of awareness spread across my body, and I jerked to the side. I wasn't fast enough.

Vines slapped around my legs and arms, the thick tentacles strangling my limbs so tight that I could feel bruises forming under my armor. I twisted and thrashed, trying to loosen the hold. Then my senses screamed in alarm, and I jerked to the side as a cold, smooth vine touched the back of my neck. Desperation fueled a burst of speed and strength, and my hand jerked up as the vine slid higher.

When it encountered my hand, it slid over it on its way to wrapping around my throat, pinning my fist against my neck. This angle pulled at the muscles in my shoulder and upper arm, but it was a hell of a lot better than being strangled. The vine tightened painfully, but it couldn't close my airway.

Panic set alarms off in my head as the plant monster lifted me right off the branch. I jerked and wiggled, but the vines didn't let go as I was pulled to the right and lifted higher into the air.

What had me? This wasn't an assassin vine. They didn't grow big or strong enough to do this.

Okay, okay, calm down, girl, and think. I took a breath and forced my mind to stop screaming, then I thought about the list of monsters in this area.

Just then, I caught sight of a skyward-facing, bell-shaped plant resting on a huge branch overhead with vines coming out of the base—the same vines holding me prisoner. Unlike the small assassin vines, this plant monster was over seven feet tall and about three feet wide. The outside of it was green, nearly the same color as the glowing canopy tree line. If it wasn't for the fact that the darker green vines around me were attached to its base, I didn't think I would have noticed it at all.

As soon as I saw it, I knew exactly what it was. It was a level thirty-one hell's pitfall, one of the more dangerous monster plants in the rainforest because of the acidic, paralyzing juice inside its giant bell-like flower. I said flower, but it was all one petal. There were no cracks or seams, just a mouth ready for something to drop in.

The vines suspended me over the opening, and I looked down into the greenish khaki-colored inside of the bell. A clear juice filled over half the flower.

It wasn't just fear which made my limbs tingle; the vines were so tight that no blood was circulating, and my legs and arms were going numb.

The vines lowered me into the giant pitcher-shaped flower, and I was immediately surrounded by a thick, decaying smell. Unlike the rest of the rainforest, this was a putrid meat stench, enough to unsettle my stomach even more than it already was. Just before the soles of my boots touched the liquid, the vines let me go.

For a second, I was free . . . then gravity grabbed me and pulled me down into the open mouth of the hell's pitfall.

Reaching out, I grabbed the edges of the monster with my numb hands, but there was a clear mucus coating the surface, and no matter how hard I gripped and tried to pull myself up, my fingers kept sliding in. I curved my body up and pulled my still tingling feet out of the thick liquid, trying to prop my boots up against either side of the flower, but it was only three feet wide. Not only could I not get into a good position in the space, but the walls were covered in the same super lubricant that was on top of the monster.

"Ah!" I couldn't help the scream as I felt myself continue to slide inside. I didn't even dare move my hand from its precarious grip to summon my kindjal.

My fingertips finally slipped right off the edge, and I dropped down into the expansive flower, frigid-cold liquid covering my body up to my chest. The bottom of the plant wasn't flat but curved and bumpy. I stumbled on the unevenness and bumped onto the side of the monster, which nearly caused me to slip all the way into the thick liquid.

I instantly became aware of every single hole and cut on my armor, yelling as the acidic liquid seeped right in, stinging and burning my body in mind-numbing pain. It was torture, as if my skin was being dissolved right off my body.

In the corner of my eye, I could see my HP steadily dropping at an alarming rate. I could see that the flower's energy crystal was somewhere below my feet, but to get there, I'd have to dive through all the acid and hope that my kindjal was long enough to pierce the crystal. The problem was, I didn't know how thick the main body of the monster was, and I didn't dare put my face in the liquid. It was so fast acting, I didn't want to go blind before I could do anything. I needed to get out of here first, then I could do something about the monster.

Over my head, vines crisscrossed the opening of the flower, caging me in.

Panting in pain, I summoned my kindjal to my still tingling, numb fingers and lifted it awkwardly in the tight space. Through one of the holes on my arm bracer, I could see the skin under was pickled and red. Cracks were forming and slowly seeping blood. Just as I lifted the sword, the strength started to drain out of my body. The kindjal that had always felt like a feather in my palm suddenly felt like a hundred-pound weight.

I sagged against the side of the flower and gasped, nearly slipping into the liquid again. The paralyzing effect was that fast?

No! No, I am not going to die in a damn plant. I gritted my teeth and forced my arm to lift. My hand shook as I sliced the blade into the side of the flower.

CHAPTER 10

The tip of my kindjal punctured the wall of the hell's pitfall by about an inch. The monster shuddered and writhed, agitating the liquid around me and making it splatter on my shoulders and chin. My numb feet slipped on the uneven bottom again, and my unfeeling fingers nearly slipped off the handle, but I gripped it with both hands and leaned into it, using my weight to push the blade through the thick wall.

My weak knees buckled, but I hung on. The kindjal sliced downward, leaving a two-foot-long gash. Liquid gushed through the open cut, and the surface level decreased. The lucky result wasn't good enough, however; I was still stuck in this monster that wanted to digest me alive.

I jerked my weapon out and aimed for the plant wall again, ready to make a crosscut. Since I couldn't escape out of the top, I would just have to cut my way out through the side of this huge flower monster.

At the mouth of the flower, more vines appeared, sliding between the gaps of the ones caging me in. They slapped at me, leaving sharp, painful welts, but every time they tried to wind around me, they recoiled. It took a second to realize they were getting burned by the same juices burning me. Crazy! This monster's "arms" weren't immune to its own digestive juices? The instant realization helped me. I could live with its slaps and hits, even if each one made my weak body stagger, as long as the vines didn't tie me up again.

I gripped my kindjal with both hands and stabbed the wall again. The monster thrashed more than ever, and one of the vines slapped at my face, but I reached up and grabbed it with damp gloved hands. The vine jerked back before my numb fingers closed around it and then disappeared over the edge of the flower. My smile was more like a grimace as I leaned on my blade and forced it down at an angle, creating an *X* on the wall.

The volume of the liquid lowered another inch around me. Holes had started to erode in my armor, revealing ruined skin, and my hip satchel was looking just as worn, but I hoped that its function wasn't damaged—there was a lot of stuff in there that I needed or wanted to sell.

I couldn't feel my legs anymore, just pain. My whole body felt sluggish and heavy, even though my mind raced a million miles per hour.

I jerked my kindjal out of the hell's pitfall's wall, then jabbed it into the middle of the *X*. The wall gave way, and my body fell forward as my hands rushed right through the plant. Cracks snaked across the flower wall, wedging the *X* wider, and even more liquid spilled out.

The plant shook and thrashed, and my legs gave out. I slouched forward, my arms guiding my dead weight against the flower's wound, forcing the opening to widen.

Almost there.

The weapon fell from my numb fingers, but I wasn't too worried about it. It would come back. Shifting, I leaned my head into the hole my arms created. The tearing crosscut wasn't big enough to fit through yet, so I tried to lift a leg to press against the side of the flower, but I couldn't raise it high enough.

Reaching back, I lifted my right leg with my hand and propped my foot against the slippery wall. My eroding boot kept sliding off the side, but I held it in place with a trembling grip.

In the corner of my vision, my HP flashed red, signaling it was less than twenty-five percent.

A System window popped open. [**HP is low. Please seek medical assistance.**]

Very unhelpful.

"Working on it," I muttered. Then I kicked with all the strength I had left in my body.

My head and one shoulder finally popped through the hole, and I jerked the rest of my arm through to try to push against the outside wall of the bell flower. My movements were awkward and clumsy because I could barely feel my arms now.

The vines came back, slapping at me and attempting to wrap around my slippery limbs, but they kept jerking away because of the acidic liquid that clung to my body. Still, every time they grabbed me, I used them to help pull myself another inch through the hole.

A vine wound around my wrist. Twisting my hand, I gripped it, and with another desperate burst of strength, I held on as it tried to pull away. With a squelching pop, my other shoulder popped out of the hole.

And then I was airborne.

The vine I'd gripped ripped from my hand, and wind rushed past my face, whipping my hair about. Through watering eyes, I could see branches zooming past me, and the ground getting closer.

Below, the three velociorheas that had been stalking me for the last hour looked up and opened their mouths wide.

My heart stuttered in fear, and panic sparked through my mind. Instinctively, mist exploded out of me and solidified beneath me. I slammed into the solid surface hard enough to knock out what little air remained in my weak lungs, and bright lights swarmed my dim vision. My nose felt wet and warm; hopefully, it wasn't broken, but if it were, it wouldn't be the end of the world. Even though I felt dizzy and numb, I squinted my eyes open . . .

The foaming mouth of a velociorhea widened before my face.

I yelled and tried to jerk back, but my body was slow to listen.

The monster's mouth clamped shut with a snap less than a foot from my aching nose. Its size diminished, its body falling away, and I understood what was happening. Fifteen feet below my mist, a velociorhea stood still while the other two took turns jumping on its back and using it like a springboard to get closer to me. They jumped one after another, reaching as high as they could with their mouths, only to come up short over and over again.

Even though they couldn't get to me, it was still terrifying seeing them come so close. When they were a safe sixty feet below, it was almost comical how they followed me around. Now . . .

I gasped out a couple breaths, trying to calm my freaked nerves and force the muggy air into my stiff lungs. No matter how much I tried, I couldn't get a full breath, as if there was a tight band constricting my chest.

All the while, the velociorheas continued to jump at me, their mouths shutting with a steady *clump, clump, clump* sound. Though I was safe, my nerves frayed.

I wedged my hands under me and started to push up with the speed of a turtle. I hadn't found a cyan-agaric or an aero-teuthida, but I couldn't go on. If I got cut open, lost a finger, or reduced my HP to one, my Regen would fix it. But poisons weren't a part of that deal. I needed to get to a healer before the hell's pitfall poison paralyzed my lungs more.

My head lolled to the right. My eyelids were heavy, every fiber of my body screaming to simply stop moving.

A flash of color caught my attention, and my eyes widened. In a nook eroded away at the base of a tree was a small, bright cyan-blue circle. It was so dark inside the hole, and it was formed at such an odd angle, that I wouldn't have seen the circle if I wasn't right here.

"No . . . way," I whispered. I'd been looking everywhere for that thing, and now here it was, the cyan-agaric, just twenty feet away, and I couldn't get it. There was no way. Not in this condition, with less than twenty percent HP left, semiparalyzed, and with a group of velociorheas playing piñata below.

A deep sigh moved through me—one of resignation. I couldn't get to it now, but I could come back. I knew my location because of my map. I could make a mental note, come back tomorrow, and hope it was still there. Unfortunately, knowing my luck, I wasn't too optimistic. Still, hope was better than nothing.

I pushed to standing and stumbled to the side. Since I controlled the mist with my mind instead of my body, I didn't have a risk of stepping off the edge and dropping to the open mouths below. The solid mist stayed right under my unsteady feet as I staggered through the rainforest toward the transportation circle.

If I had the strength to Feather Step, I could have made it back in less than thirty minutes; now that I wasn't going through the rainforest one layer at a time, I could have just cut a straight line to the exit. As it was, I had to stop every twenty minutes or so just so I could have a breather or pick myself up after my legs gave way. I lost track of the time; all I knew was that it took me a long time to go only a little ways. I was going slow enough that the velociorheas stalking me still had time to leapfrog off each other, never once falling behind. The sounds of their mouths snapping shut were more frequent than my heavy footsteps.

The drizzle kept falling. It did a good job of washing away the blood that stuck to my body, but it stung when the cold liquid hit my raw skin. The acidic plant juices seemed to resist the rain, clinging stubbornly to my body and continuing to slowly eat away at my skin and armor. Though I wasn't at risk of indecent exposure, the holes in my black leather and gray under armor were growing.

When I finally caught sight of the pale purple circle through the trees, I nearly collapsed with relief. I was almost there.

The last I'd checked, it was already past three. I'd gotten in my daily energy crystal amounts, but I hadn't cultivated yet. With all the liquid in the air, this might be a good place for that. The problem was, there wasn't a single safe place to sit down here.

Since I'd already given up on getting an aero-teuthida and a cyan-agaric for the day, my daily list shortened to just getting healed and getting back to Fogmire to cultivate.

I staggered to the magic circle, watching as it slowly got closer and closer. When I was ten feet away, I suddenly realized I had a problem. Or rather, three problems, all hungrily waiting below my feet. How was I going to get inside the circle at ground level with those monsters there? Just how smart were these things? Would a distraction work on them?

I opened up my Items Bag and looked at the drop items in there. Pulling out the fleshiest thing I had—a piece of breast meat from a big, monstrous bird—I lifted my left hand and wiped the blood still flowing from my nose onto my fingers before smearing it on the meat. Then I gripped it with my right hand, barely able to feel the thing at all, and lifted my shaking arm, throwing the meat as far as I could. It was more like trying to drill it into the ground twenty feet away as opposed to actually throwing it like I meant to.

The velociorheas immediately turned and ran after the meat, snapping at each other for dominance.

I turned and jumped. As soon as my body was in the air, I lost all control of it. Like a limp doll falling through the air, I tipped head down, arms dangling and facing the rainforest as I fell. I could only watch helplessly as the largest velociorhea turned and sprinted for me, yellow eyes fixed on my throat and toothy mouth open. The question was, which would happen first? Would I land on my head, or would the monster snap my neck?

Five feet away, a bright yellow barrier flared up and out into a circle around me. The monster smacked right into the barrier and was blown back thirty feet. It screeched as it landed on the ground and skidded across the moist dirt right into a tree, leaving a trail of ruined feathers behind. It took a second for my dizzy mind to realize there was a protective wall around the magic circle. From the looks of it, it had been cast by someone A rank or higher. At least I wasn't going to be mauled to death.

My hand touched the ground just inside the glowing transportation circle. Instantly, the purple magic flared, and the gravity pulling me down disappeared. A nauseous wave of disorientation washed over my body as I was shot the opposite direction up into the sky.

I made it. I actually made it to the magic circle. As relieved as I was, the speed I was flying at was too much for my air-deprived mind. I blinked furiously, trying to keep my eyes open and force away the black that was creeping around my vision, but each time I blinked, my eyes would stay closed longer than the last time.

Stay awake! I ordered myself. *Breathe slowly and don't faint!*

The other side of the transportation arch came into view. All I could see was the ground getting closer, with dozens of colorful people flitting around it. I braced myself as much as I could, but I didn't have control of my body. My feet hit the ground, followed closely by my body, and I rolled across the ground, seeing only a mix of brown, green, and black. The System was flashing some red message in my face, but I couldn't focus enough to read it.

I stopped rolling face up, my whole body screaming in pain, but I couldn't make a sound.

Noise erupted around me as people yelled and words jumbled together.

"Oh my god! She's still alive!"

"Where's the rest of her team?"

"Careful, don't touch her! That's hell's pitfall juice!"

"Healer! Is there a healer here?"

"Quick! Get the—!"

Everything disappeared into inky black silence.

CHAPTER 11

—

When I opened my eyes, it took me a second to recognize the familiar white room. Through the white curtains hanging over the window, a sliver of late evening sun slashed through and left a splash of yellow orange on the white wall across from me. I was lying on a hospital bed, bleach-white blanket pulled up to my chin, and the metal side rails up. At least this time I wasn't hooked up to a bunch of machines.

Several months ago, I woke up in a room identical to this, and my life changed forever. I didn't feel as traumatized as the last time I was in an Eden hospital room, but I was disappointed in myself for being in this bed. Disappointed that I let myself get that close to danger.

I sat up and looked at my hands and arms, grateful that they were back to normal, as if I'd never touched the hell's pitfall acid to begin with. Next, I touched my face. It felt right; nothing out of the ordinary. My clothes had been changed into a hospital gown, and my damaged armor was folded neatly on a chair against the wall. It pained my heart to see my awesome armor in that condition, but not as much as the sight of my beat-up hip satchel. The armor would heal itself at midnight, but it was another matter for my Items Bag. I'd just barely bought it, using money that me and my family has scraped together. Once I sold the items in it, I could buy a new one, but it wouldn't be the one my sister helped pay for. No matter what, the new one wouldn't mean as much.

With a miserable sigh, I dropped my face in my hands.

Someone stopped right outside my door, drawing my attention. That person knocked on the door, then it opened.

Healer Jonovan stepped into the room, leaving the door open, a gentle smile gracing his handsome face as he walked to my bedside. His long brown hair was tied over his right shoulder as usual, and he wore black slacks and a white shirt under a deep blue mage robe.

"Good evening, Miss Jynn. I'm glad to see you're not dead." He sat on the chair next to my bed and reached for my hand.

I held it out, palm up. "Hello, Mister Jonovan. Was I that close to dying?"

I glanced at the clock on the wall. It was six thirty; I only had an hour and a half left to finish my last task of cultivating. The task didn't specify where, so maybe doing it here on the hospital bed would check it off? But I didn't have to think hard to know it wouldn't do me any good. If push came to shove, I would, but I'd rather do it in the Gate so it was actually beneficial.

Jonovan touched my wrist with his fingers and used his powers to check on the condition of my body. "Yes and no. You looked worse than what you actually were, but another hour covered in hell's pitfall poison would have stopped your lungs." He must have liked what he found because he sat back on the chair and crossed his arms over his chest, obviously getting comfortable for a chat.

I watched him, trying to not feel uneasy under his stare. It had been months since I'd seen him. First, because with my Regen, I didn't need a healer for the most part—a ninety-minute nap fixed any injuries I got. And second, because I didn't know to what extent he could sense the change in me, and it's not like I could actually tell him about the System.

"It's been a long time since I last saw you, Miss Jynn," he commented. "Usually, when I stop seeing people, it's because they're dead. I have a bad habit of reading the weekly list of deceased Hunters—there are a few I've treated enough that I like to keep track of, you included. I was glad your name was never listed there, but it doesn't explain why you stopped coming for free healing. I take it you joined up with a group with a competent healer?"

I bobbed my head, going along with the lie I'd been telling Maveric for months. "Ah, yeah."

"Hm." Jonovan considered. "Where are they? Everyone who came out of the Josu Rainforest was questioned, but we couldn't find anyone missing an E Hunter in their group. Are you the only survivor in your team?"

My lips pressed together, and I gripped the blanket pooled around my waist. How big was I going to let this lie get? If I said my team was dead, there would be a slew of paperwork that would need to be done. I would have to report the incident, and the Hunter's Association would investigate the "dead people" so they could compensate the families. With how strict the Association was registering Hunters, I couldn't just make up names and throw that out.

I bit my lips and tried to think of how I should answer without actually giving the real answer.

When I didn't talk, Jonovan stepped in. "There isn't a team, is there? You went to the Josu Rainforest, a C-rank location, all by yourself. Didn't you?"

"Ah . . . " I swallowed and tried to think through my panic to answer.

"That's a yes or a no question." Jonovan hummed like he was trying to help, his gentle smile strained.

" . . . Yes." I stopped trying to avoid his eyes and met his gaze.

He stared at me for a moment, the smile sliding off as he studied me. "Well, I'm glad I don't have to report any deaths. It's my least favorite thing about this job. Now, do you care to tell me why you were in an area that's above your rank?"

"No," I said without breaking eye contact.

He looked at me for a couple seconds then shifted forward to rest his elbows on his knees. "You've changed, Jynn. Since I was the one who first looked at your stats, I feel confident in saying that, outside of yourself, I'm the most aware of what your stats are. And I still remember them. It's hard to forget how sick I felt dashing a young girl's dreams like I did."

I looked down at the blanket and twisted my fingers in the material, frowning. I'd never forget that moment, either. It'd changed my life forever.

He kept talking, his soothing voice drilling into my ears. "I can't legally check your stats right now; not without your permission. And when healers use their magic, we don't see the exact number of a Hunter's HP, just a bar that goes from red to yellow to green as it gets filled up. Some Hunters are more susceptible than others to treatment, which is why any other healer wouldn't think twice about healing you. They'd think that it took so long because you weren't compatible with them." He paused. "But I've healed you hundreds of times. I know what it should be like. And I know that when I healed you a couple hours ago, it was different. Your HP is different. Your body is different. Stronger. And . . . something else." He shook his head as if confused. "What happened to you?"

I pressed my lips together tightly. I couldn't answer him, even if I tried.

He leaned his head to the side. "Does it have to do with you passing out in the Gate a couple months ago?"

My eyes narrowed. He hit that on the head, but I wasn't going to let him know.

"Did you Reawaken?" Jonovan continued to press.

My mouth opened, then I paused and shut it again. Finally, I said softly, "Not exactly. But I can't tell you about it. It doesn't matter how much you ask; I can't tell you."

He stared at me long enough to make me fidget. Then he sighed. "I thought you trusted me more than that."

The smile that danced on my lips was shallow. "It's not a matter of trust. I'm sorry."

He leaned back against the chair. "Well, you have a clean bill of health. Healthier than the last time I saw you, in fact. You can go at any time." He stood up.

"Healer Jonovan?" I looked up at him. "Can I ask you a question?"

He paused. "Yes."

I licked my lips and tried to organize my thoughts. "How close are they to making a cure for Dreamers? Do you know?"

His eyes narrowed for a second, then he slowly sat back down. "Is there someone you know who's a Dreamer? A family member or friend?"

I nodded. "My mother."

He frowned. "Does this have to do with why you were in Josu Rainforest?"

I smoothed the blanket out over my legs. "No," I replied honestly. In fact, I'd been honest this whole time. I think that's why Jonovan wasn't mad. He wasn't yelling—he's just not like that—but I could tell by his rigid posture he wasn't happy. "But is there anyone I can talk to about the cure? I want to know what I can help with."

Jonovan's mouth twitched, and he folded his arms across his chest again. "I would actually be the best contact for you about the cure. I am a healer yes, but the other part of my job is assisting in creating the cure."

My breath stopped for a second. "Really? Since when?"

"For the last ten months or so. More and more people are being afflicted with the disease, so they started bringing in the top healers to come up with a solution."

My brows furrowed as I thought. "But healing doesn't actually help with Dreamers. I mean, healing magic doesn't work on humans at all. It can't even regress the damage that happens to bodies from being in a coma."

Jonovan nodded in agreement. "Correct. They're hoping that someone can create a new spell or combine the right components to create a vaccine for it. Nothing has worked."

This was exactly what I wanted to know. Maybe with this knowledge, I could use my System to create a cure. "How close are they to making a cure or vaccine?"

"As for a vaccine, it's just a pipe dream. They don't even know why certain people fall unconscious and others don't; there seems to be no rhyme or reason to it. Until they do, the research has nowhere to go." His words weren't new. It was something everyone knew. "As for the cure, I have a colleague who swears he's close to completing a prototype, but he's missing something. Ironically, he thinks that the something he needs is the reason why people are afflicted with the disease to begin with."

I nodded slowly. "Can I talk with him?"

"No," Jonovan denied me without mercy. "You might somehow be stronger, but you are not strong enough to do anything about this subject. I don't want to see you running recklessly into danger for something which might or might not help. You'd be risking your life for no reason."

I frowned at him. "I think it's worth it."

He stood up and walked toward the door. "I have nothing else to add to this conversation."

"Jonovan," I called after him.

He stopped at the entrance and frowned at me. "Yes, Miss Jynn?"

I smiled at him. He was this mad, yet he still turned around for me. "Thank you. Really. Thank you for helping me, healing me, and caring for what happens to me. I really do appreciate it."

He paused then nodded.

"And . . . " My voice died as I thought about what had come to my mind. Would he actually accept it? "If I told you there was . . . something or someone behind the Gates . . . like a whole other planet, would you believe me?" I watched his expression closely, ready to take in any reaction he had.

As it was, I didn't have to watch that closely. Jonovan looked like he'd been struck by lightning. His eyes widened, and he laid a fist on the door. "What did you say?" Before I could answer, he thumped his hand on the wood. "Dammit, Jynn, don't you dare listen to that cult!"

My mouth dropped open. A . . . cult? There was a cult about the parasite?

Jonovan went on, looking like he was the one who'd lost his marbles. "Is that what this is about? You got brainwashed by that crazy cult and now you're running around in dangerous places for them? What the hell are they thinking, sending a young girl like you into a place like the Josu

Rainforest?" He stalked toward me and stood over me, glaring down. "Where are they meeting? By god, I'll get their asses arrested for conspiracy and inciting panic so fast, they won't be able to brainwash anyone else."

I gaped at him. "Wait, Jonovan! There's no cult. Or at least, I didn't know there was. Is there one? But seriously, calm down! I was just asking a question . . . about a theory I heard once. That's all." I didn't know if I wanted to laugh or cry at his explosive reaction.

I was just telling the truth. I thought that out of anyone in Eden, he'd be the most likely to believe me. I didn't expect him to react like this.

Jonovan pinched his brow and let out a long breath. "Sorry, Miss Jynn. It's just . . . that damn cult is horrible. Like a pack of rabid rats that keep slipping through officials' fingers. They secretly lure people to their meetings and fill their heads with nonsense while releasing into the air a vaporized drug produced by components found in the Gate. It causes a high and adds to the hysteria. It's addicting and sometimes deadly for humans. Hunters handle the effects better, but not by much."

He scowled and dropped his hand. "Apparently there was a meeting just last night. By the time the police got there, the cult had cleared out, leaving several dead bodies in their wake. It's been a mess how they mix dangerous Gate plants or monster parts to create drugs and give out doses to the human population. We have the Wall and stick to regulations for a reason, you know."

"I . . . didn't even know that was happening," I admitted with a sinking feeling.

It was going to be a million times harder to convince anyone of the danger Earth was in if there was a cult running around, killing people like that. Was that why no one would believe me?

Jonovan nodded in relief, the anger draining from his body. "I'm glad. I don't want you anywhere near them. They're dangerous, and their favorite people to entice are humans and E-ranked Hunters."

"How long has this cult been around?" I asked.

He shook his head. "Not long. I don't even know exactly, since the authorities only started putting their activities together recently." He looked into my eyes. "Promise that you won't ever talk to them. Please?"

He was so serious, I could only nod in agreement.

But honestly, I was dying to know more about them.

CHAPTER 12

I couldn't wait to leave the hospital. Okay, it was more like I ran out of there like my butt was on fire, but there wasn't a lot of time before 8:00 p.m. hit and the Gate closed.

Since my armor wasn't in any shape to fight in, I wore the spare jeans and a T-shirt that I had in my Items Bag. Yes, I called myself crazy for doing it, but I didn't have anything else to wear. Her Resistance was the only armor I owned.

Technically, I could just step right inside the Gate, sit down, and cultivate there, but that meant I'd be visible to any Hunter who entered or exited. With so many people after my head right now, that didn't seem like a good idea. If I hurried, there was enough time to sprint to Fogmire, cultivate, and sprint back.

"Lesson learned. *Again*," I mumbled to myself as I walked into Gate Square. "Cultivate first, then go on dangerous missions." It was a stupid move, and not the first time I'd made that mistake. You'd think I'd have learned it by heart by now.

It was late enough in the day that there were only a handful of people going into the large square. Everyone else was exiting the Gate and leaving to go home or joining the line forming at the hospital, all in various battle-worn stages. Lights were starting to turn on in the surrounding red brick buildings, getting ready for nightfall. Construction workers who were reassembling the buildings from the worldwide Gate Surge were already gone. From the looks of it, they were just about to start on the finishing touches.

A familiar presence approached me, and I looked over to see Kesstel in casual wear, walking up to me. He looked at me as if he didn't know what expression he should show—concern or a smile.

"All better?"

I paused. "What do you mean?"

He nodded over my shoulder toward the hospital. "You were in there for a couple hours. What happened?" He glanced at my damaged hip satchel, and his lips thinned.

My head tilted to the side, completely not knowing what to feel. Exasperation? Still, a small part of me appreciated his concern. "You always know where I am. Did you know there's a word for that? *Stalker*, I think is the term." Really, with him, he just kinda showed up whenever he wanted, like a cat. A very dangerous cat.

He winced and ran a hand through his hair. "I know. I don't purposefully do it, but I do notice when you're in my vicinity. And I've never noticed you in the hospital before, especially for such a long time."

I started to walk toward the Gate, and he fell into step with me. "How widespread is your area of awareness?"

He frowned and didn't answer.

I looked up, waiting for a response.

His head tilted to the side. "If I focused my mind on searching, and if I was standing at the Gate in the middle of the city, I could find you anywhere in Eden. If you were in Garden City and I was at the Gate, that would be beyond my reach."

My eyes widened. "That's . . . really far." Miles. That was like over five miles.

He nodded. "I know. Unless you're close, I only check your general direction in the evenings to make sure you made it out of the Gate." He looked up at the giant black arch looming over us. "Which still makes me think like I'm out of my mind."

I stopped walking and turned to face him. Hunters were walking out of the Gate less than thirty feet away, but I couldn't hold back my questions. "What do you want from me?" I shook my head, frowning and confused. "You told Bethany Wilks that I was your partner. It's a joke, right? Even if we did partner up, I'm so much weaker than you, no one—not even me—would take it seriously."

An invisible barrier surrounded us, blocking out the noise. He really didn't like people overhearing him, did he? "But you won't always be. Although I don't know how, you are stronger every time I see you. You could be the same as me someday." He paused, frowning. "I want . . . to be friends." His mouth wrinkled, and he looked away.

Wait, were the tips of his ears pink?

My eyes widened. "What?"

He glanced at me out of the corner of his eyes without turning his face. Then he tipped his head back and looked back up at the Gate. "I forgot . . . how nice it was to *feel* something. It's been so long. I forgot how wonderful it felt to talk freely. About my past, about the present. And to think that the future might not be so lonely. It's nice to care about the well-being of a person again."

His hands fisted at his side. "I've gotten good at displaying the right emotion at the right time, but it's all been superficial. No matter where I go, there's always a . . . barrier around me. Separating me from the current intelligent species. It's like standing in the middle of a play, watching face-less dolls move about. Or maybe I was the empty doll, just biding my time until I moved to the next world. The next stage," he whispered. He pressed his right hand over the lower left side of his chest. He looked at me, his brows wrinkled in confusion. "I don't know why it's you. The irony almost kills me. But I enjoy being with you; I enjoy smiling again. I enjoy feeling *emotions*. And I want to do that more. That only happens around you."

I stared at him, so frazzled I felt like my head was going to explode. Honestly, I didn't think being friends was a good idea. It was like a noose around my neck, tightening the more I was around him. But I did like hanging out with him. I felt . . . safe with him. Even when he was angry. It was stupid, but I felt that as long as he was there, I wasn't going to get hurt; there wasn't a single person in the whole world I could say that about. Not even at Aunt Mina's home in Garden City, where I could have fun but had to guard my words to protect my family.

That fact alone made me want to run away. I didn't want to lean on anyone. I didn't want to need someone there as a crutch. I couldn't bare my soul to someone and let them have that control over me.

But I also couldn't kick Kesstel away. Not when he was so honest and open about a simple wish for a friend. Because I knew what it was like to look around and know you were completely alone in another world.

I bit my lips and looked up at him. "I . . . don't partner up," I said softly. I'd never level up if he was around, since apparently, I didn't get EXP for monsters that other people helped me kill. "But I don't mind hanging out and stuff." I smiled softly.

He nodded. "I can do that." Then he paused and smiled. "Can I get your number so I can just text you instead of hunting you down every time?"

The smile slipped from my face. "Ah, I don't have a phone."

"Hm. We should go buy one for you," he muttered.

I shook my head. "No, I have more important things to do first. I'll get one when I have the money for it. For now, I really do have to go." This conversation was eating up valuable time.

I took a couple steps toward the Gate, and the sound barrier popped.

Kesstel frowned. "Where are you going?"

I motioned to the huge black arch ahead of me. "I have something I have to do in there. Right now."

He fell into step beside me. "What? It's getting too late for you to be in the Gate. And you're not even in armor."

I checked the clock on my System. I had enough time—barely. I glanced at him then passed through the Gate. "I know."

Kesstel stayed at my side; he even kept up with me as I activated Feather Step and sprinted as fast as I could.

"Where are we going?" Kesstel's running form was almost leisurely, as if he wasn't even putting effort into it. Then again, with his stats, he didn't need to.

I glanced at him, trying to decide if I should chase him away or not. But he already knew about me being a Warrior of Mist. I didn't know what all I couldn't show him, but it shouldn't be a problem if he saw me cultivate, right? Then again, if weaker monsters ran away from him, I wouldn't have to worry about attacks breaking up my time and spending longer than I wanted to inside. "Fogmire. I have something to do there."

The golden plains between the Gate and Fogmire flashed by us. The metallic stalks of six-foot-tall grass whispered as they swayed and brushed around us. Hunters followed the path that cut through the plain, all walking toward the Gate to go home. Every person we passed wore armor of some sort or another. I bet Kesstel and I were the only ones in the whole Vale who were in street clothes.

Some Hunters jumped out of the way as we ran by. Others scowled and glared as if daring us to make them move. Before I could jump over one such guy, Kesstel's hand flicked out, and a bright blue flash of light like a whip smacked the man to the side, flinging him over ten feet into the golden grass. Kesstel did it so smoothly, he and I didn't even have to break a step. He only had to do that one more time for others to realize it was better to just get out of the way.

Kesstel glanced at me. "You know, I could carry you and we'd be there a lot faster."

"I bet." And I'd die before I asked him to carry me. "But there's nothing wrong with a little exercise."

He bobbed his head. "Are you going to tell me what you have to do that's so important before we get there?"

I shook my head. "Nope. Honestly, I'm not even sure that I *can* tell you."

"What's that supposed to mean?" His brows pulled together.

My lips twisted. "It's just . . . complicated."

We sprinted around a corner, and Fogmire came into view at the end of the path. Its gloomy, misty treed border loomed over the brightly flashing fields in sharp contrast.

There wasn't a need to go far into the forest, so I leaped onto a tree just a couple feet in where the mist really started to pool and sat down on a thick branch. Kesstel landed lightly on the branch next to me and watched with interest as I crossed my legs and put my hands together in the correct position.

"Is there a particular reason why you came out here to do yoga?" He didn't even bother lowering his voice.

Right next to us, a treant peeked its eyes open and looked at Kesstel. It immediately shut them and pretended to be a dead tree.

My mouth twitched, looking between the monster and the man. "Cultivating. It's called cultivating. It's a lot different from yoga." It wasn't until the words were out that I realized what I'd said. I got my Mist power by cultivating, so I always thought it was in the "you can't tell anyone about this" category. Could I tell Kesstel about it, since he already knew what I was? "It's going to take forty-five minutes, and I can't talk. If you want to go back, you can."

He hopped onto a tree a couple feet away and sat down, leaning back onto the trunk. "I'll be fine." He rested his hands behind his head with one leg dangling down as if he didn't care he was lying on a treant. He probably didn't.

The monster didn't budge a millimeter.

Should I laugh, sigh, or cry? *Someday,* I told myself. *Someday, I'll be that strong.* And to get there, I needed to cultivate.

Since I'd first figured out how, I'd never put a lot of thought into it. But now that I had an audience, my body felt so rigid, and my hands were awkward.

Stop it, I ordered myself, closing my eyes. I reached out my awareness and instantly felt Kesstel's presence. Frowning, I disregarded him. As soon as I did, I felt the familiar and soothing mist swirling and pooling in the air. Mentally, I grabbed onto the particles and drew them to me. All thoughts outside of cultivating disappeared, and my mind cleared as habit took over.

In no time at all, my System dinged, letting me know that my task was done.

I slowly opened my eyes. Kesstel was sitting right next to me, watching me closely.

With a jump, I nearly fell out of the tree. I'd known he was around me, but last I looked, he was on a different tree. When did he move right beside me? I righted myself and sat normally on the branch, letting my feet hang down.

When I originally planned to come, it was for a quick in-and-out. With Kesstel here, the sense of urgency lowered, and I felt like I could actually take my time. It was turning into a bad habit—a really bad habit. But I was curious about what he was curious about.

"So that was cultivating. I've never heard of or seen it before." Slowly, Kesstel reached out and touched my stomach with the barest touch of his fingertips—the mist I drew in pooled there. "It's almost like an energy crystal, but not," he observed. "Just raw power collecting without an item to anchor it in place." His features were solemn.

I nodded, wondering how much he understood. "Cultivating is basically absorbing the compatible elements around me to strengthen myself. It's a Warrior of Mist thing. It's very helpful." I lifted my hand and summoned a thick cloud of mist around my fingers.

Interest gleamed in his eyes, and he reached out to touch the fog. It swirled and curled around his fingers. The gleam in his eyes turned to a sharp glint, but I didn't feel threatened. Pulling back, he shook the waterdrops that had collected on his fingers, then looked around the forest where the white particles were so thick, the naked eye couldn't see more than five feet away. "I imagine this place is perfect for you, then."

A thought came to me. "Ah, but I don't want you to cultivate." He glanced at me with surprise. "I'm not saying that because I don't want you to get stronger. It's just, the other Hunter I saw cultivate turned into a monster. He used an energy crystal. I told you about this a bit ago, remember? But even so . . . " My voice died out, pathetically.

The corner of Kesstel's mouth hooked up. "It wouldn't do me any good, anyway. There isn't an element compatible to me here." His sword appeared in his hand, so beautiful and noble looking. A second later, a pale blue glow surrounded the pattern-welded blade. "My magic is more of a force type, where I can add nonelemental magic damage to my attacks. It's pliable, but really only meant for offense."

I could feel the power radiating from the light, not daring to touch it like he did my mist.

"How did you learn to cultivate?" he asked.

My lips twisted together. Should I try? He knew so much about everything else; if he also knew about the System, maybe we could work together to find a cure for the Dreamers and figure out a way to save Earth. I paused.

"I ha—" My voice cut out.

[Warning! Sharing information about the System with outsiders is restricted. Please cease your actions.]

"You what?" Kesstel encouraged.

I sighed and rubbed my forehead with exasperation. "Nothing. It's nothing." I jumped lightly to the ground and nodded toward the Gate. "Let's go."

CHAPTER 13

—

We ran back toward the Gate, me Feather Stepping and Kesstel keeping pace right beside me. Halfway through the tall golden grass field, a loud siren went off from the direction of the entrance. It echoed through the air, a warning to everyone still in Gate Vale.

The sound made the hair on my arms stand up. I'd never heard the five-minute warning before, since I always made sure I was out beforehand. Just hearing it was enough to know that something bad could happen if we didn't make it out on time.

I glanced at Kesstel. Nighttime was when the S-ranked monsters came out. Could he handle something like that?

He noticed my stare. "Do you want me to carry you?" The corner of his mouth hooked up.

Was he teasing me?

"Hey, I'm a big girl. I can buckle my own boots and everything." I shook my head; it almost made me dizzy because of the speed we were going. "I was wondering how you would hold up staying here at night."

"Hm." He didn't answer for a couple seconds. "I'd be fine." His voice was quiet. If it wasn't for my Hunter stats, I wouldn't have heard him.

The long golden grass ended, and we came into the large clearing around the Gate. Ahead, Hunters ran across the field like they were being chased by hellbats. It didn't matter what their level was, the clock was ticking.

Another siren wailed—one last short warning.

Simultaneously, the ever-blue, clear sky overhead turned blood red.

I yelped and ducked in surprise. The only time that ever happened was when a Portal Burst occurred. My heart seized up tight in my chest from

PTSD, and my lips parted as I glanced around, trying to find where the new portal would open up. Small lights appeared in the red sky, like stars but not quite. They were bigger than the ones I saw on Earth, not a lot but noticeable at first glance. And they weren't just one color, but a rainbow that shifted and swirled.

Kesstel followed my gaze to the stars above. "Those are remnants of worlds the parasite has eaten. If one portal attached to Earth fails, one of those will take its place—assuming that the remnant world hasn't lost all power and dissolved up there first. Or if the parasite creates another Gate, pieces of the remnant worlds are patched together to make the Vale inside the Gate."

I gasped and looked at him. "Are you serious? It's eaten that many planets?" The lights above were not numberless, but they were numerous.

Kesstel's head tipped in my direction as he glanced at me out of the corner of his eye. The red light gleamed off his white-blond hair, turning it nearly the same color. In the dim light, a pale light seemed to glow from his blue eyes. Not nearly as obvious as in the restaurant the other day, and there was no angry emotion attached to the light, but it was enough that I knew it wasn't a trick of the light.

His lips thinned, then he tipped his head back up to look at the stars. All the emotion slid off his face, replaced with a razor-sharp glint in his eyes. "Who knows how long that parasitic planet has existed? Do you think such a sophisticated trap could be developed in a short time?"

It really was a good trap. So good that humans had no clue they were helping themselves fall into destruction. And anyone who talked bad about it was silenced—or thrown in together with a crazy cult.

A ripple shook the ground, the Gate at the epicenter of the jarring pulse. The few Hunters trying to exit fell to the ground before they scrambled to their feet and threw themselves through the black arch.

I jumped over the ripple; only, the ground continued moving, and I staggered when I landed. It was like trying to walk on an inflatable instead of solid earth. Kesstel reached out and grabbed my elbow to help steady me.

In the valley around us, six black arches grew out of the ground—Portal Bursts—like mini Gates. There didn't seem to be any rhyme or reason to where they showed up, whether it was in the middle of a forest, a desert, or over an icy tundra. As soon as they appeared, monsters started to spill from their black depths. At the same time, from the dark pits of the portals in the mountains around Gate Vale, thousands of monsters added to them.

From my position just inside the clearing around the Gate, it was difficult to see every portal's activity in the regions around me, but I knew it was happening. I could feel it, just like I could feel the goose bumps that spread over my whole body. A heavy, dense pressure settled over the valley, as if the sky was pressing down. The air seemed too thin, and I couldn't get enough in my lungs. My knees weakened. If it wasn't for Kesstel's grip on my arm, I would have fallen to the shaking ground.

He frowned and transferred his hold from my elbow to the shoulder, holding me to his side as we sprinted the last bit to the Gate.

Overhead, a dozen black holes opened in the red sky. From the Portal Bursts depths, huge flying monsters appeared, one of them right above us. Well over a hundred yards long, it looked like an Eastern dragon, only with eight legs. It twisted its green body and roared, the triangular silver spikes on its back like knives cutting through the air.

My knees gave out entirely, and I stumbled to a stop, staring up at it. I should keep going. Somewhere in the back of my mind, I knew that. But in the presence of an S-ranked monster, my body froze up, and my mind went numb.

Oh god, it was huge. Even though it was high in the air, the power radiating from it sapped all the strength from my body and left me like a rag doll flopping to the ground.

Kesstel used his hold on my shoulder to pull me up and continued heading toward the Gate.

That wasn't the only S-ranked monster that came out of the Bursts. Each portal released one—some big, some smaller—into the Vale, along with other lower-ranked monsters.

Human screams came from behind me. I turned my head just in time to see four Hunters running out of Glenn Holt as fast as they could. But it wasn't fast enough. Monsters rained down on them from above, and the Hunters were taken down as fast as you could count *one, two, three, four.* What was left were dozens of monsters fighting each other for rights to eat the kills.

The dragon above let out another roar, this time closer.

My head tipped back, and I looked up numbly to see the S-ranked creature dive at us like a green comet.

Kesstel's sword appeared in his right hand. He swung his blade, slashing at the air, and in its wake, a bright blue magical arc exploded, creating a crescent-shaped wave which shot toward the dragon so fast that I could barely keep track of it. The magic grew stronger and bigger as it soared until it was half the size of the monster. It lit up the dimness, casting a blue highlight on the red tint smothering Gate Vale.

The dragon tried to dive to the side, but it wasn't fast enough. The attack hit the monster, gouging out long holes and splattering black blood into the air. As horrible as that hit was, the monster didn't die. It just arched its back and sailed up higher.

Then Kesstel pulled me through the Gate.

The usual disorienting tingle swept through my body as we passed into Earth. It helped jump-start my mind, but my body was still a mess, shaking and limp. I couldn't even stand up straight. Even though the horrible pressure was gone, my feet couldn't seem to walk in a straight line.

Kesstel semicarried me away from the black arch and stopped at the edge of Gate Square. He shifted, trying to look at my bowed face. "Are you okay, Jynn?"

G-get it together, I ordered myself, but I couldn't seem to stop the violent shivering which rattled my bones. "Yeah," I whispered. I cleared my throat and forced out a stronger, "Yes. I'm okay."

I pressed my trembling hand to his chest and pushed away from his grip. As soon as his hand fell away from my shoulder, my fingers instinctively clutched at his shirt. But I didn't let myself hold on to him. Instead, I forced my hand to let go as I straightened my back.

A Hunter's Association employee approached us, looking at Kesstel. "You were the last one out of the Gate. Did you see anyone else in there?" His voice was bland, like it was a question he'd asked a million times and never expected a different answer.

Kesstel flicked a glance at him and shook his head. "None who lived."

The employee gave a curt nod and walked away.

It was just a small distraction, but it was enough for me to catch my breath and finally get some fresh air into my lungs. I took another shuddering breath but couldn't quite bring myself to look at Kesstel.

It was humiliating how he'd had to drag me around in there. I'd been nothing but a useless bag of flesh. Sure, now that we were friends, some people would say I should make use of him. He was so strong, it would be easy to stand behind him and let him shield me from danger while I hopped about, doing my tasks. But I didn't want to stay weak. I didn't want to stand *behind* him. I wanted to stand *beside* him, as equals, so if he got hurt, I could be there to save him.

Right now, staring down at my trembling fingers, that seemed like such an unobtainable dream.

Kesstel's hand appeared before my face, a snacks bag resting in his palm.

I blinked at the cookies and couldn't resist the slight smile which curled my lips. I looked up at him, noticing how his eyes were no longer glowing, and took the treat.

"I told you before, you don't have to feed me all the time. It's not helping your cold, dukely, sophisticated look." I broke the bag open and popped a small cookie in my mouth. The bite-size treat had a satisfying crunch, while the fudgy chocolate strips melted and coated my tongue nicely.

It was so silly, but it helped break the negative thoughts crashing through my mind.

Kesstel took out a bag of trail mix and started eating it. Every time an M&M fell into his palm, he'd drop it into my bag of cookies. "I know."

I smiled before I glanced back at the Gate. Not a single Hunter had come out of it since we had. Given what was going on in there, no one would. Not until tomorrow morning, when the Ss and the higher As went in.

The cookie turned to dust in my mouth, and I forced it down my throat. "Are you going to have to fight all those monsters tomorrow, Kesstel?"

He tilted his head back. The apathetic gaze returned to his eyes as he frowned. "No, not all of them. Most of them will be gone by morning, eaten by other monsters. I'll just have to deal with the biggest threats remaining before the other Hunters enter by 8:00 a.m."

Now that the Gate was closed for the night, there were only a handful of people in the square with us. Most of them were Hunter's Association workers with badges on their chests, talking and motioning to the Gate. They were probably talking callously about who had died tonight.

I looked around and saw a couple benches not far away. One was under a lamppost, while another sat just outside the circle of light. Turning, I walked over to the one in the dark and sat down. As soon as I did, my feet started to pulse painfully, letting me know this spare pair of gym shoes was too worn for the running I'd done today. I wiggled my toes, feeling a slight breeze where a hole was wearing at the tip.

Kesstel sat down beside me.

I added an M&M to a cookie and ate it. "Did you know that monsters eat each other's energy crystals?"

He tipped his head back and poured the rest of his trail mix into his mouth. He nodded while he chewed and swallowed. "Yes. Like I said, the energy crystals can change as much as the parasite needs. When a monster eats another monster, the energy inside the weaker crystal is added to the stronger one. And the surviving monster gets stronger."

I nodded. "I noticed." I ate the last cookie. "So the monsters you handle in the morning will be stronger than the ones in there right now." Habit had me smoothing the plastic bag flat. As soon as it was satisfactorily pressed, I started to fold it smaller and smaller.

Kesstel watched me. "Yes. But there will be less to handle at once, so it doesn't matter either way."

When I couldn't fold it anymore, I twisted the wrapper in my fingers, smoothing over the edges. "Would you really be fine, staying in there all night?" That didn't seem possible, but at the same time, I'd just witnessed him taking on an S-ranked dragon. And winning.

He smirked and reached out, taking the garbage from me to put it away in his Items Bag. "Of course I would be."

I rolled my eyes. "Of course you would be." Then I sighed and looked up at the Gate. "How much would I have to pay you to keep me alive in the Gate all night?"

CHAPTER 14

Kesstel stilled, his blue eyes brightening with surprise. Then his face darkened like the night falling around us. "There's not enough money in this world or any other which would tempt me enough to take you into the Gate at night."

I was just as surprised by his words. "Is it really such a big deal? You really couldn't do it?"

He shook his head. "It's not a matter of not being able to do it—I absolutely *refuse* to do it." I'd gotten so used to how his tone softened around me, it was a shock to hear the hard edge in his voice directed at me. "There is no reason for you to be in there at night. You just saw what it's like. I personally saw how you were affected—you couldn't even stand up without help. If you try to stay overnight, I will personally go in and haul you out."

So I was just going to have to get strong enough to stay in there overnight by myself. After all, there wasn't anyone else I believed in enough to ask for help.

Okay, I didn't know any other Ss, and I doubted an A could do it.

"Why the hell would you want to spend a whole night in there, anyway?"

I swallowed and picked my words carefully. "It's been twenty years since the Dreamer's disease appeared, and the doctors still haven't come up with a cure. I think the missing component might be in one of the monsters that only come out at night. It's the only place which hasn't been thoroughly searched yet. I have . . . something which can help me figure out what that missing component is." I looked up into his face. "That's why I want to go into the Gate at night. I want to help find a cure for Dreamers—help find a cure for my mom."

His lips pressed into a hard line, not sympathetic at all. "There is no cure for Dreamers. There never will be. Not as long as the parasite is attached to Earth, and it won't let go until this world collapses. Then the last thing you'll need to worry about is the Dreamers."

A jolt of shock and fear stung my heart. It wasn't the first time I'd heard there was no cure and to not expect a miracle, but hearing Kesstel say it was completely different. I mean, he was whom I considered the expert on anything related to the parasite. My throat was so tight that I had to swallow a couple times before I could force out any words. "Why? What does that parasite have to do with Dreamers?"

Although there was no way to prove it, most people believed the disease was tied to the Gates. Hearing Kesstel say it cemented the fact in my mind.

He leaned against the back of the bench, staring off into the distance across Gate Square. With his stats, I was sure he could still see perfectly fine. "It's like a weeding-out system from the parasite. The parasite is flooding this world with its magic. Those who are compatible with it turn into Hunters. The ones who aren't susceptible stay human. The people whose bodies reject the magic fall into a coma—or as humans call it, become Dreamers." He frowned and glanced at me out of the corner of his eyes. "When this world collapses, the only ones who might survive it are the compatible ones. Anyone else will dissolve and be eaten with the planet when the parasite absorbs it and adds the remains to the collection of stars you saw in the Gate's red sky."

My breathing stopped, and all I could do was stare at him. Every word was like a hammer striking deeper and deeper into my chest.

There was no mercy in his face as he laid out the facts at my feet. "Like I said, there is no cure for Dreamers. There never will be; not unless the parasite lets go of Earth. And that won't happen." He paused. "If you can accept that now, it will save a lot of heartache later."

I looked down at my lap and finally noticed that my fingers were clenched together. They were so tight, my hands were shaking. Silence settled over us, as heavy as the weight in my heart.

My family was everything. The whole reason I was still breathing right now—the reason why I'd accepted the System to begin with—was because of my family. Now Kesstel was telling me they were all going to die, just like that? That I'd have to watch Mom slowly wither first, then be helpless as the rest of my family vanished in front of my eyes?

. . . No. No, I wasn't going to let that happen.

"I . . . " my voice cracked the silence. "I don't believe that there's no cure." I knew Kesstel was frowning at me, but I continued to stare at my clenched hands. "There *is* a cure. I know there is. And I'm going to find it." I had to believe that. If I didn't, I'd collapse.

He sighed. "You're setting yourself up for disappointment and pain." There wasn't any glee in his tone at all, just a resolute honesty in the face of my stubborn wishful thinking.

"Maybe," I said. "But I believe I can find a cure." I looked up at him, full of determination—a determination which might very well walk me right into a bad situation. "And I'm not going to let the parasite destroy Earth."

Pity bled into his expression. "Now you're just thinking the impossible."

"Why can't I?" I challenged. "There has to be something, somewhere, which can make the parasite let go."

Even I knew I was talking big now. It was a literal planet, and I was just an eighteen-year-old girl. But I wasn't going to lie down and die. I'd never been able to before, not when my family was on the line. *I'm not about to start now.*

Kesstel shook his head. "After so much work, do you really think the parasite is going to just let go when its prey is so close to falling? Honestly, Earth just needs another couple major events, and it will collapse."

Another couple major events? Like a couple more big energy crystals or Gate Surges? I guess I really needed to prevent those as much as I could. Unfortunately, I had no ability to affect the other Gates around the world. What if all the other big crystals appeared in, say, Germany or Japan? I wouldn't even know about it.

There had to be another way. Instead of waiting for the parasite to act, was there a way to attack it? I frowned, thinking. "Kesstel, is there any way to get to the parasite planet?" What if we just nuked it? That always worked in the movies. Ah, wait. Nukes didn't work on monsters; would they really work on the parasite? I doubted it.

Now that the conversation had slipped away from me going into the Gate at night, the tension was slowly easing out of his body, and his features were softening. "It's on the other side of a portal. The Gates are like veins, connecting the parasite to Earth, remember?" he said, referring to one of the first times we'd talked and he'd drawn a picture in the dirt. "And the portals ring the Gate Vales like a pearl necklace. The Gate itself isn't the vein or path to the parasite—one of the portals is. Only, finding the exact portal is harder than you'd think. I've never been able to find the right one." He leaned forward and rested his elbow on his knees. "I think it might be one of the stars in the red night sky. The only way to make those worlds come down is by collapsing the portals around the Vale." His eyes narrowed. "Then one of those will take the place of the collapsed portal."

My eyes widened. "The last time a portal collapsed, there was a world-wide Gate Surge." There were hundreds, if not thousands, of world-fragment stars in the Gate Vale sky. If the only way to get them down to check if they were the right one was to collapse a portal, and each time it caused a worldwide Gate Surge . . . Humanity wouldn't last until the right portal was found.

Kesstel sighed. "Yes. That's why I don't do it very often."

So he'd caused that last Gate Surge. Hundreds of thousands of people had died from it. In fact, there were still some areas that weren't completely under control yet. "How often have you done it?"

"One happened when I came out of the portal to Earth." Kesstel shrugged. "The only other time I caused a Gate Surge on Earth was a couple months ago. Although, I caused quite a few of them in the last world I was in. That's how I figured out how the portals worked." He tapped his fingers together. "I wanted to find the parasite as fast as possible."

That's right, he'd mentioned that before. "What will you do when you find it?"

His eyes narrowed, and a mean smile curled his lip. "It gave me this power. I thought I'd give it back. And take it down with me." Wisps of power started dancing on the bricks around our feet.

I sat up straight and stared at him with wide eyes. "What? You . . . you're talking about killing yourself?"

He shrugged. "My world and everything I love is gone. What else do I have to live for? The only reason I've made it this far is because I refuse to die if the parasite doesn't die with me."

My hand fisted at my side. Before I even realized what I was doing, I swung out and bashed him up the side of his head . . . and instantly regretted it. It was like punching iron. My hand pulsed painfully and instantly swelled.

I yelped and hugged my hand to my chest, blowing on it while glaring at him.

The blow that was turning my hand purple barely made his head dip forward. He blinked and gave me a *what-are-you-doing?* look.

I scowled at him. Who on Earth had a skull that thick? And I meant that in a couple different ways. Since I didn't have any other advantages over him, I stood up until I was towering over him. "You can't just ask to be my friend then say you have nothing to live for," I snarled at him. "Does my friendship really mean nothing to you?"

There was no way I thought lightly of him losing his family and home. I would be devastated if that happened to me; I understood the thought of just wanting to fade away if they weren't there for me. But after all the effort he'd put into making me lower my guard around him, when he talked like that, all I could think was *what about me?* It felt selfish, but I couldn't deny the anger that rose when he implied he was just going to throw me away.

He paused, obviously shocked. "Ah."

I opened my mouth to let out a torrent of emotion, but he beat me to the punch.

"I'm sorry."

I paused.

Hang on, that wasn't fair! I hadn't even let out all my steam yet. Why was he jumping to the end and apologizing already? Where was the noble, unbending duke who made everyone quake in their boots? I'd thought I would be the loser here, but now I was left in a no-man's-land without winning or losing.

A small, apologetic smile curled his mouth. "I am sorry. I didn't mean to disregard your feelings. I'm so used to being alone, I guess I haven't changed my mentality yet."

I drew in a deep breath and slowly let the pressure in my chest out with the air. With another huff, I dropped on the bench beside him. The feeling was coming back to my hand in the form of pins and needles. I scowled as I shook it, willing it to go back to normal. "Damn, what is your skull made out of, anyway?"

He smirked. "My mother swore it was granite."

"Sure, sure. Throw in a joke to distract me." I moaned and leaned against the bench.

Looking at the Gate was too depressing right now, so I tipped my head back and looked at the real stars in the sky. The light pollution from the city washed out most of their brilliance, but there were still enough to appreciate. I couldn't help but wonder about how long it took for the light from one galaxy to reach Earth. How many of those stars had already been winked out but we just couldn't tell yet? If so, how was the parasite able to move around so fast?

"Hey, Kesstel?" I whispered.

"Hm?" He tipped his head back, staring up at the stars too.

"I think you and I want the same thing." I paused, collecting my thoughts. "You want to find the right portal to avenge your world, right?" I didn't have to look at him to know I was right. I still had issues with the idea of him going all kamikaze, but I didn't want to bring that up again right now. "And I want to find the right one to find a way to make the parasite let go of Earth. So we both need to find the right portal. Why don't we team up and look for it together?"

He was quiet for long enough that I finally tilted my head and looked at him.

"I wouldn't mind working together. The problem is you aren't strong enough yet," he answered. "Not mentioning any monster we might meet, if I go all out, the simple backlash of my attacks would injure you, and the portals aren't a place to fight half-heartedly."

As depressing as it was, that was a simple fact. "But I won't always be weak. You said so yourself."

"That's true," he agreed. "Inside each portal is a Boss—a monster much stronger than all the others, like a king. They're all S ranked. The existence of the portal is tied to the Boss. Unless it loses enough energy and collapses by itself, the easiest way to destroy a portal is to kill the Boss."

A king. Instantly, my mind conjured up the image of the red orc sitting on a huge golden throne wearing a black robe and with red orc females kneeling at his feet. The image of his chilly red eyes as he stared down in glee while I was sliced to death sent a shiver through my body.

My hands clenched tight. *No*, I ordered myself. *Don't think about it.*

"I'm not going to give up on Earth; it's my home. And I'm not going to give up on my family; they're the reason why I fight. They used to be the only reason." A small smile touched my mouth. "But lately, I've been adding more. It's . . . different. New. But I'm starting to think it's not a bad thing. I'm going to get stronger and find the portal to the parasite, and while I do so, I'm going to keep looking for the cure for Dreamers. I know what you said, but I still believe there's a cure out there."

Kesstel laced his hands behind his head, still staring at the stars. "If it makes you feel better, go ahead. Concentrate on getting stronger, and I'll examine the portals around the Vale again. Maybe I missed something. If I find anything, I'll let you know."

I tilted my head and grinned at him. "Deal."

CHAPTER 15

It was odd going back into the Gate. After the red nightmare from last night, the bright blue sky and perfect weather were a little jarring. The Vale's segments were spread out before me, green where it needed to be, golden or off-white where it wasn't. So peaceful, like last night's Portal Bursts and giant eight-armed dragon had never happened. I was so used to seeing Gate Vale in the daytime, I'd had no clue what it was like after nightfall. And I couldn't even think about what Gate Vale must be like when Kesstel and the rest of the high-leveled Hunters entered several hours before the rest of us.

I made sure to run to Fogmire and cultivate first. I even took the time to track down some creatures and destroyed my daily quota of crystals there. Since I was in a hurry, I wasn't picky and just went after the closest monster. The Josu Rainforest was so complicated, I just wanted to make sure I got all my daily tasks done first before I went back.

Once I got the confirmation from the System, I walked to the Association's transportation area. As soon as I was in line, someone called out to me.

"Jynn!"

I turned at the sound of Emma's voice to see her walking with the rest of her group out of the path which led to the transport area. She looked as spritely as ever, a happy hop in her step and her brown ponytail swishing behind her. Emma walked up to me and caught me in a hug. "It's been so long!" She leaned back and smiled.

I smiled, too. "It has been. Good morning," I said, nodding at her group.

They greeted me back as they got in line behind me. Their body language was relaxed and friendly, but obviously not as excited to see me as

Emma was. There was a new person in the group, a young man in light armor. He must be the one filling the hole Reina left. I couldn't help but glance at Billy. He didn't look agitated.

Emma glanced over my shoulder at the pale purple circles. "Are you with another party today? Where are you headed?"

She wasn't going to invite me to go with her group, was she? At least she gave me a way out. I quickly glanced around to make sure I couldn't see anyone I didn't want to overhear me. Such as a rich, spoiled brat and her hitmen guards, or the two assassins she'd sent after me. Since it was safe, I answered Emma. "I'm going to Josu Rainforest today."

The whole team looked at me in surprise.

Billy let out a low whistle. "Do all Es like to go to dangerous places like you? Even with a team, that's a rough region."

It took everything I had not to roll my eyes at him. "It pays the bills." *And for new equipment,* I thought as I brushed my hand lightly over the new hip satchel buckled around my waist. At least I'd gotten a five percent discount since I was trading in one that was only a month old. Unfortunately, that benefit was a one-time deal. The next time, I'd have to pay full price.

"Wow." Emma's brows scrunched up together in worry. "You're really going there? What if you meet the Josu Ghost?"

I moved up with the line then turned back to her. "Josu Ghost? What's that?" Now that I was interested in killing one of each monster, I'd looked up every monster in the area. As far as I knew, there wasn't a ghost in the rainforest. Ghost-type monsters like that were usually found in the bog on the other side of the Vale—outside of the petra-squirrels in Fogmire. Or was there a new monster I hadn't heard about yet?

Emma bobbed her head. "Yes. The forums have been going crazy all morning about a new monster someone reported in the Josu Rainforest. It's a cloud that moves around under the canopy erratically and can shrink and grow without warning. It doesn't seem to have a solid body, and they don't know what to classify it as."

The muscles on my face completely froze in a shallow smile. Well, except for the ones that were twitching like mad with shock. Okay . . . I really didn't think I'd get labeled as a ghost. I mean, a cloud under the canopy that can grow and shrink? That could only be me. Although it wasn't really a cloud, but that wasn't important.

What it meant was that I had to be careful using my mist in Josu Rainforest until people forgot about it. There were a lot of Hunters out there who changed up the monotony of going in the Gate daily by hunting rare and new monsters.

The impulse to crouch down, bury my face in my hands, and laugh my guts out was so strong, I almost dropped right there. Since I didn't want to come across as a crazy person to one of my few friends, I resisted the action.

Sure, what were a couple hundred more Hunters aiming at me? Bring it on.

I smiled and tipped my head back while I let out a huge sigh.

"You're acting weird," Billy pointed out.

"Yep," I muttered, then focused on Emma and Mason. "Where are you going?"

"We're going back to the Feng Jungle," Emma said.

"We thought it was a good place to work out any kinks with our teamwork," Mason spoke up. "It's not too hard but challenging enough that we can see what needs to be worked on." Then he motioned to the new young man with brown hair and a pleasant face hanging out in the back of the group. "This is Russel, by the way. Russel, this is Jynn."

Russel looked at me, his gaze flicking to where my title bar would be over my head. Even though he looked puzzled about why he was being introduced to someone like me, he still waved.

I nodded back, not offended at all. There weren't many teams who would talk to a lone E like this. The line moved up, leaving only a couple more people in front of me.

"Jynn." Mason caught my attention. He held out his hand, and a white envelope appeared on his palm. "President Price wanted me to pass this on to you. He's hoping you'll take the time to come talk with him."

Now the new guy, Russel, looked downright confused. The rest of the team shifted, looking a little tense.

Emma frowned. "President Price has been paying a lot of attention to us lately and asking about you. I haven't told him much." She gave a bitter smile. "I . . . don't know much about you." She peeked at me. "I'd like to learn more, but at the same time, maybe that's a good thing right now. At least until you, um, decide."

"I already gave my answer." I really didn't want to take the letter, but I also didn't want the failure of delivering it to fall on Mason's head. Who knew how petty President Price might be?

I took the letter and pinched the smooth paper, almost bending it in half. Before I could damage it any more, I put it away in my Items Bag.

Throwing a letter away from their president right under their nose would be too rude to Emma and her party.

It was funny. Price had offered me a deal because he thought I was friends with Kesstel. I turned it down then because at the time, I wasn't—and I didn't want to be within a hundred feet of Blake. Now that I was friends with Kesstel, I still didn't have any inclination to join. Mostly because I still didn't want to be within a hundred feet of Blake. It was a little distressing, knowing Price hadn't backed off yet. How many more things were going to get piled on my plate before it tipped over?

I came to the front of the line, and Emma gave me another quick hug before I stepped into the transportation circle.

As soon as my feet touched the ground, I took a couple running steps and jumped up into the trees. I didn't want to give the velociorheas a chance to find me so early in the game. Yesterday hadn't gone so well, but it was different now. Unlike yesterday, I knew where to look for one of my targets—as long as the rainbow team hadn't found the cyan-agaric while I was out of commission, anyway.

I Feather Stepped at a sprint and shot through the rainforest treetops, my toes barely touching the wet branches as I went fast enough not to be assaulted by obnoxious flowers. Vines twisted around the branches and reached for me, but I always slipped out of their grasp. And that was the goal: go fast enough that I could get the cyan-agaric before I was injured or attracted the attention of the velociorheas. From what I could tell, they were drawn by the smell of blood, so if I wasn't bleeding, they'd be more likely to overlook me.

The Josu Rainforest was just like yesterday: muggy air, a constant drizzle, and full of slithering vines and interlocking branches. What was different was the number of Hunters in the area. More than once I was forced to jump to the neighboring branch to go around a group of Hunters walking single file along the treetops. I didn't have to wonder for long why there were so many people. A single line from a conversation I overheard as I ran by answered the question.

"So, where's the Josu Ghost again?"

Crud. Hunters really were out here hunting for the Josu Ghost. So any time I used Mist as a cover, I'd be targeted by nearly every Hunter who had a visual of me.

I huffed a breath in annoyance and kept running.

But it wasn't just Hunters I found more of, but velociorheas. Any time there was a group of injured Hunters, there was a group of expecting monsters below begging for a free meal. Luckily, they were more interested in the other Hunters than in me.

I finally came to a resting spot and took out my paper map from yesterday. The paper was crinkly and weatherworn, but the ink was still legible. Looking at the notes I made, I glanced around. That was the branch I'd tried to rest on yesterday, although it was covered in biting flowers and assassin vines again. That meant that up and to the right should be the hell's pitfall.

I shifted before looking up around the thick tree trunk. Sure enough, there was the seven-foot-tall monster plant with a cross-shaped tear on the side of the pitcher flower. Vines dangled down from the base, several of them severed at different lengths. Frankly, I was impressed it hadn't been eaten by other monsters overnight.

But it was a good thing, too. It meant I had a chance to even the score today. But first, I had to get my mushroom.

Based on my fuzzy memory, my eyes followed the line of where I would have fallen out of the hell's pitfall plant. My gaze stopped roughly twenty feet from the ground, where I'd landed on solid mist and broken my nose. When lying there, I had looked to the side and seen the cyanagaric in the nook of a tree. I think it was the tree I was currently standing on. Only, the mushroom was on the ground.

My stomach twisted painfully as my mind unhelpfully replayed the scene of the guy getting eaten by velociorheas. I closed my eyes and put all my attention into feeling for anything moving around me. There was a group of six Hunters to my left, but I couldn't tell if they were being trailed below.

Ah, and an assassin vine on my right. Just as a tendril shot at my ankle, I stepped to the side and slashed down. The tip of the vine fell to the rainforest floor, and the rest of the plant retracted.

At the same time, I heard a familiar shout.

"Damn flowers!"

I glanced over to see the rainbow brigade from yesterday walking along the branches toward me. Green scowled and shook his leg, obviously still smarting from a sting.

"It could be worse; they could be poisonous," Yellow said, her lips curled up in silent glee. She brushed her wet yellow-and-brown hair out of her face.

"But why do they only go after me?" Green whined. A black arrow appeared in his hand, and he started to swing it, aiming at all the small plants at his feet. "The rest of you aren't getting bitten."

"IQ?" Purple piped up.

Blue, in the front of the line, sighed. "It's just that we aren't making that big of a deal about it. Don't be a baby. Just keep your eyes peeled." He motioned with his sword ahead of him.

That was when they noticed me.

"Ah," I muttered. Were they still looking for the mushroom? That was the only thing which made sense to me. So the one from yesterday was most likely still there . . . only now my competitors were going to watch me get it.

Oh, what the hell? I wasn't going to walk away just because of them. It just meant I needed to grab it without them knowing.

I glanced around the ground one more time before stepping off the branch. Through the wind in my ears, I heard the pink healer gasp.

"Suicide?!"

I kicked off the side of the tree trunk next to me, trying to use that as a shield between me and the party. Once I was comfortable, I created a small, one-foot block of mist halfway between me and the ground. Because of High Jump, I knew I could land safely from a fall of thirty feet, but I had no guarantees on sixty feet—better safe than sorry.

I tapped on the block to control my fall, then dropped the rest of the way.

Landing on the ground, my stomach churned painfully the second my boots touched down, and an instant alarm went off in my head, screaming that I needed to get off the ground. *Now.*

I couldn't. Not yet.

I stilled my body and raging heart, trying to sense my surroundings. I couldn't sense anything moving around me. Slowly, I turned around and faced the tree behind me, looking toward a small hole that had eroded away between the thick roots where wet wood met wet dirt. Even from this angle, I couldn't see inside. As silently as possible, I walked up to it and knelt down.

A slight blue glow emitted from inside the dark hole. No, it wasn't the cyan that was glowing but the three white, perfectly circular scales on the blue cap. In the dark hole, the glow reflected off the cap and cast a faint blue onto the white moss pooling around the cyan-agaric's creamy stem. For a five-inch-tall mushroom, it gave off quite the pretty picture. The drawn images I saw online definitely didn't do it justice.

I glanced around my surroundings one more time before I reached into the hole, taking a cloth handkerchief out of my Items Bag. According to all the information I'd read, I couldn't touch the cyan-agaric because it was extremely toxic. But I had to touch it if I wanted to put it in my Items Bag because I didn't own it yet. Once it was in, I could take it in and out without handling it. I had a feeling I wouldn't get the chance to do that, though. Since the System wanted me to collect it, I bet it would disappear as soon as I got it. Just like the Essence of Nothing and the pearl duku—another poisonous plant the System had me get.

The question now was if I would get poisoned before I could slot the cyan-agaric. I really didn't want to go through that again after yesterday. I just hoped that the hanky would shield me enough.

Covering the mushroom with the material, I carefully touched it with the back of my knuckle where my leather gloves covered. With a single thought, the handkerchief and mushroom disappeared altogether into my Items Bag.

[**Task: Collect three Cyan-Agarics. (1/3)**]

I breathed out a long sigh of relief, the tension leaking from my body.

From inside the hole, something wrapped around my hand so tightly that my fingers instantly went numb.

CHAPTER 16

I gasped and shoved my left hand against the tree to pull my hand out of the hole. Without the light from the cyan-agaric, I couldn't see what was holding me, but from the thick, rope-like binding, experience would say it was a vine. Or a root.

Out of the corner of my eye, a dull brown snake-like creature wiggled and slithered across the mossy ground. A root, probably one from the tree right in front of me, drew closer, aiming at my feet. Several more rose from the moss and into the air like wooden spikes. Then they bent and grew toward me.

Shit! I jerked at the one keeping my hand captive, and a stinging pain jolted from my wrist up through my arm as something wedged beneath my arm bracer and pierced my flesh. A second later, the smell of blood—my blood—wafted in the air.

I silently gasped and pulled back with more intensity, but I'd been forced into an awkward angle to gain what little leverage I could as the additional roots continued to stretch toward me.

A twinge of alarm went down my spine as I felt three monsters moving toward me on the ground, *very* quickly.

Damn, they found me.

I summoned my kindjal and thrust it into the hole. It was at an odd angle, and I couldn't see what I was aiming for, but if I ground it against my wrist, it should cut the root. Anyone else would have cut their own hand off trying this, but since my blade was connected to me, I wasn't at risk of being maimed.

Another root wrapped around my leg, sliding all the way up to my thigh and binding me into a crouched position. Its tip nuzzled around my thigh, searching for a place to puncture.

Damn, damn, damn. I gritted my teeth and put more strength into pressing my kindjal to my wrist. Suddenly, the root snapped in half, and I nearly fell over. A severed piece of root slipped off my aching wrist and leaked blood all over the moss at my feet.

Behind me, I could feel the velociorheas getting closer. *Thirty feet.*

I sliced the root wrapped around my thigh, only to have two more latch on as a new attack, something fast from above, shot toward me. My eyes widened. I'd never get out of this.

A black arrow stabbed into the base of one of the roots binding me, nearly cutting the plant in half. A second arrow followed in a flash and finished the root. In that same moment, I stabbed down at the one holding me, and as soon as it was cut, I grabbed the arrows and High Jumped with everything I had. I shot into the air just as three velociorheas flashed around a tree, barely more than a blur of colorful heads. They lunged into the air, snapping at my feet, but couldn't get to me.

I continued to soar upward, then felt the weightlessness of reaching the peak of my jump. I stabbed my kindjal into the tree trunk and anchored my feet against the wet bark. Too high for the velociorheas and too low for biting vines and flowers—I hoped—I took a second to finally breathe and lower my pounding pulse. The monsters growled and screeched at the base of the tree, leaving deep cuts in the wood as they vented their frustration. The roots that had plagued me retracted back into the moss under the velociorheas' feet. Monsters ate monsters all the time, but apparently, the roots didn't care much for the blood of giant chickens.

I tipped my head back and looked above me.

The rainbow brigade stood on the branch above, all with different expressions ranging from impressed to surprised. Green, that loud-mouthed man, still had a black arrow notched loosely in his compound bow, as if ready to let another one loose in a second.

"Hm," Orange muttered. "An E with High Jump. Who would have thought?"

I gulped in another breath. Since they already knew, I guess I didn't have to hide it from them. Flipping up onto my kindjal, I used it as a springboard to jump the rest of the way into the treetops—and was instantly bit by a now-red flower. *Gah.* Looking down to find the flower, I had a moment of lethargic dizziness. *Just how much blood did that root suck up in the seconds it had me?* I stepped back to brace myself and kept my head up like I didn't feel like falling over. Granted, the velociorheas still making a racket below would be overjoyed if I did.

I took a steady breath before focusing on the group of Hunters walking across the branches toward me. They hadn't seen me take the cyan-agaric; there was no way they'd have been able to from the angle they were above me. And since one of them had just helped me escape, they shouldn't be a threat. In theory. It would be better to act casual and friendly just in case.

I bobbed my head at them and gave a small smile. "Thank you for helping me." I looked at all of them but let my eyes rest on Green the longest, since he was the one who actually helped. I held the arrows out to him.

Green's face turned beet red under his kiwi-colored hair. The bow and arrow vanished from his hand before he took the ones from me. He lifted his chin with pride. "Don't mention it." Despite his words, his expression screamed, *praise me more!*

Blue, the obvious leader, gave me a complicated look. He folded his arms across his chest, tall and imposing in his full armor. "Where's your party? What were you doing down there?"

Pink leaned around his broad back and blinked at me with huge deep blue eyes. "Hasn't anyone told you it's dangerous down there? Why wasn't your party protecting you?"

I was dying to run away, all the better to keep my mushroom hoarding a secret from them, but they obviously wanted answers. It was unusual, really. The fact that they'd helped me to begin with was odd, but now they were talking to me, a lone, weak E.

But since they wanted answers, I'd give it to them.

"I dropped something earlier," I lied right to their faces. I did feel bad about it, but what was I going to do? Tell them we were competing for the same thing and that I got it first? "My party wanted me to get it. I should catch up with them now. Thanks for your help."

"Hey," Blue called out before I could turn away. "We're looking for something. A blue mushroom with three white circles on top. Have you seen one?"

So that's why they helped me. They wanted information. I paused like I was thinking, then I slowly shook my head. "I can't help you. Sorry." That at least was the truth. I couldn't help them. And if I saw another one, I'd keep that one for myself, too. Maybe after I completed my task, I'd tell them where to look. But for now, they were on their own.

The leader nodded. "Well then, you should get back to your team fast. Es shouldn't even be allowed in here."

Green hissed and winced. "Damn flowers." He jerked his right foot to the side.

Yellow, right behind him, snickered. Purple rolled her eyes and leaned on a hip.

I nodded slowly. "Right. Well, good luck finding your blue mush-room." *Because I'm going to find them all first.*

Pink, Green, and Yellow waved goodbye to me before they left. Blue, Purple, and Orange simply turned and walked away.

I took a second and checked under the branch for any assassin vines. There weren't any, and since all the little flowers around me had already turned red and wouldn't bite me for the time being, I sat down on the branch and took out some food and water.

Only one cyan-agaric appeared in the Josu Rainforest at a time. Once that one was picked, another one wouldn't show up until the next morn-ing, so searching for another cyan-agaric was pointless right now. What I needed to do now was start looking for another aero-teuthida.

And I would, right after I took a break for some needed calories and revenge.

Twenty minutes later, I stood up, ready to go. Walking across the branches until I was under the hell's pitfall that had nearly killed me yes-terday, I saw that below the hole I dug on its side, trails of black, blistered plant flesh streaked where the digestive acids still leaked out. Even the branch under the base of the seven-foot-tall flower had been burned and withered away. Six vines hung down from the base, still charred or cut from my encounter.

Was it a bad thing that I felt a strong sense of satisfaction when I saw how damaged it still was? That damn freak plant was going to get me to the next level.

My lips curled, and I focused on the base—the receptacle—truly see-ing it for the first time. It was three feet wide, the same as the bell-shaped flower, and about two feet thick. I couldn't see any roots. For all I knew, the hell's pitfall could be anchored to the thick branch with magic.

I frowned, trying to come up with an attack strategy. Even though it was injured, it was still five levels higher than me, and the last time I tan-gled with it, I nearly died.

From what I could tell, the energy crystal was in the middle of the receptacle, nearly at the top. Stabbing up through the branch for it wouldn't work; my sword wasn't long enough. Stabbing from the top meant that I'd have to go through at least three feet of paralyzing liquid to get to it, and I wanted to avoid touching that stuff as much as possible. So, a side attack and dealing with the vines was the way to go. Which meant I needed a lot of speed to deal with the vines. I couldn't sense any Hunters around me, but I didn't know how long that would last.

Let's do this. Now.

I cast Mist and pooled a thin cloud around my left hand. From there, I Mirrored my kindjal and activated Feather Step before I High Jumped till I was level with the hell's pitfall. The mist pooled under my feet and solidified, giving me a surface to fight on ten feet away from the monster flower—close enough to deal with the vines, but far enough away that I could move freely.

It sensed me. Three vines shot toward me, and even though I was still smarting from the last plant that grabbed me, I slashed at the vines, slicing and cutting as I twisted and turned out of their reach. They were nimbler than I was—after all, they didn't have the restriction of a skeleton—but now that they didn't have the element of surprise, I was able to keep up. Every time another foot of vine was lobbed off and fell to the open mouths of the velociorheas below, my lips curled up a little more.

The other three vines joined the attack. They were from the other side of the monster plant's receptacle, so they didn't have as much reach, but they still attacked me with gusto, whipping, slapping, and trying to wrap around anything they could latch onto. It really put my agility to the test. Try as I might, I still couldn't block everything. My body was littered with welts that twinged whenever I moved, but I was able to avoid all the stabbing attacks.

A vine wrapped around my upper left arm and jerked me to the side, trying to flap me in the air like laundry on a line, while the rest of the vines shot forward to wrap around or puncture me. I gritted my teeth and opened my left hand in front of me, converting the slow rain to mist and creating a solid barrier between me and the monster. It was bigger than I wanted to make, but hopefully, a Hunter wouldn't notice it. Being mistaken for the Josu Ghost wasn't going to help right now.

The vines hit the barrier and slowed down, but since the hell's pitfall was stronger than me, they were still inching their way through the barrier. Once they got to the other side, the barrier would shatter, and they would have full movement again. I took the time to swing the kindjal in my right hand at the vine around my arm. A large section fell to the ground below.

I jumped up, stepping on the barrier that held all the vines temporarily motionless, and lunged at the hell's pitfall receptacle. As soon as the monster felt me coming, it began withdrawing its vines from the barrier. But not fast enough.

I stabbed my kindjal into the monster's base, aiming right at the energy crystal. A vine twisted around my waist, punishingly tight, trying to squeeze out all my air. Gritting my teeth, I pushed harder with my sword, sinking it in farther. I felt a slight resistance before the energy crystal shattered.

[+153 EXP]

[**You have Leveled Up!**]

Jynn Devhro

Rank	C	**Level**	26
		EXP to Next Level	1145
HP	373/583	**Stat Points**	0
MP	105/265		
Strength	51 (+20)	**Agility**	50
Magic	45	**Perception**	44
Constitution	46 (+20)	**Intelligence**	43

Skills	**Abilities**
Throw	Mist (Improved) (40 ft)
Critical Hit	Feather Step
Quick Hit	Regen (Limited)
Mirror	Stealth (Limited)
High Jump	

CHAPTER 17

That night, I left the Josu Rainforest feeling conflicted. I'd found a cyan-agaric, which was good. But I didn't find an aero-teuthida, which was the task that actually had a time limit. I knew they were hard to find, but I didn't think it would be *this* hard. Two days, and I still hadn't caught a single one.

At least the Josu Rainforest was a good place to level up—for a bloody price. Just shy of achieving another level, I had to give up and leave. My HP was a breath away from red, my body hurt, and I felt more like a lump of Swiss cheese than a person as I slowly walked across the clear, grassy field surrounding the Gate. Timewise, I still had a couple more hours to look for one of those flying squids, but physically and emotionally, I was done.

Just before I stepped through the Gate, a deep voice called out. "Miss Devhro."

I frowned, trying to place the voice. I think I knew it? I turned toward the sound and blinked at the group of Hunters walking toward me.

At the lead, walking just a half step ahead of Blake, was President Price. He flashed a smile which slightly softened his square, somewhat handsome face. Too bad my thoughts weren't anywhere near friendly right now.

"Fancy meeting you here." Price waltzed right over, completely oblivious to the look Blake was giving me over his shoulder.

I'd say if looks could kill, I'd be dead . . . but the cold gleam in Blake's eyes went a little further than that. He obviously didn't just want me dead—he wanted me to disappear as if I'd never existed to begin with. What, he just couldn't accept that his guild leader was catering to a little E insect?

I forced a stiff smile while mentally screaming a round of crude cuss words. "President Price, good evening."

Price gazed down at me. In full black armor, he gave off the impression that he was larger than life. But wait, was it just me, or were his lips starting to twitch from smiling? It looked painful. "It's ironic that we ran into each other today, when I was just talking to Mason and Emma this morning." From his tone, it sounded like he was talking about hanging out with his best friends. The complete opposite of the awkward stances Emma and her team gave off this morning when talking about interacting with Price.

I nodded slowly. "They are fun to talk to." Why did this guy have to find me now? All I wanted to do was snuggle in my bed and sleep.

He paused tactfully; such an odd thing for such an imposing man. "I don't suppose you've talked to them recently? I gave them a letter to pass on to you. Did you get it?" His mouth twitched again, and a cool glint flashed across his eyes.

I nodded again, this time with more surety. "Yes, I ran into them earlier, and they gave me your letter." What would have happened if they hadn't given it to me? Nothing good, that was for sure. "But I've been busy." I motioned to the Vale behind me. "I haven't read it yet." Maybe it was ballsy to tell that to his face, but if it gave me a chance to leave, I'd take it.

He stiffened as his lips thinned to a straight line. How many people had told him to his face that his words weren't important enough to read right away and lived? Very few, I bet.

"Ah, well." He forced the smile back on, this time, his right eye twitching like a tick. "Well, where are my manners? You look exhausted; let me help you with that."

Blake quickly schooled his expression, so when Price turned toward the party of Hunters, the president missed his killer look. God, what a fun game. Standing just behind Blake was the ever-present Mark, Penny, and Daniella—the first two sneaking glances at Blake.

Price motioned to a healer in the back of the group. "Quickly come heal this young woman." He smirked, likely thinking he was being gracious. "One of the many perks about being in the Stone Mace guild. Free healing from the best healers in Eden."

Right, as if the second-best healer in America wasn't available in the Eden hospital for free, too. At least Jonovan didn't glare at me like I was worthless, I thought, watching the healer come to me. Still, I was too tired to care, so I let the woman touch me with her glowing fingers. I wasn't that versed in healing, but I could tell her ability was subpar to Jonovan's. Maybe I was spoiled or biased, but right now, I just wanted to leave.

When she stepped back, I pressed out a better smile than before. "Thank you."

She jerked her head in a nod and slipped to the back of the group again, apparently not wanting anything to do with me.

Price smiled at me. "Miss Devhro, I just wanted to extend you another offer to join the Stone Mace guild."

The smile almost slipped off my lips again, but I kept it in place since I didn't want to be rude. The guild president might be catering to me right now because of Kesstel, but in reality, Price could crush me like a bug if I insulted him too much, and it wasn't like Kesstel was here right now anyway if Price lost control.

"Thank you for the consideration, but no." Once again, I didn't leave any room for compromise in my tone.

If his smile was twitching before, now it was full-on spasming. His Hunter power flickered out, flattening the grass around him in a ten-foot radius. I staggered back, my head pulsing painfully and feeling like an ant pressed under a giant's thumb, but I refused to let my legs buckle. I would not bow down to him; no way in hell.

It took a couple seconds for Price to control himself. As his features smoothed, he retracted his aura. "Well, I hope the next time we chat, you'll have a more favorable answer." With that, he looked at the group behind him and jerked his chin toward the Gate. He didn't wait for them to respond before he walked away and disappeared through the black arch.

Now it wasn't just Blake who scowled at me with disgust. Nearly the entire team of Hunters clearly thought I was scum who deserved to die for turning down their leader. The only one who stared at me with curiosity instead of contempt was Penny, who obviously thought I was off my rocker but in a comedic way. The only saving grace I had was the fact that President Price was personally pursuing me to join their guild—even if I pissed him off. But as long as he was interested in me, Blake's team wouldn't attack me. Instead, they walked past like I was trash on the side of the road.

I watched them disappear. Man, if I were a petty person, I wouldn't join for that alone.

Ah, okay, I might be turning into a petty person. Still, Price's people weren't selling his guild very well. Not if they treated everyone who wanted to join like that.

The last two people to walk through the Gate were Mark and Penny. Both of them glanced back at me with confused expressions before they disappeared.

I huffed out a breath and finally relaxed. God, I hoped that was the end of it.

I took a quick stop at Maveric's shop to sell my drop items on my way home. Luckily, he didn't pressure me about the aero-teuthida even though I hadn't turned in one yet. I still had another three days till the deadline, so another two days before I'd start panicking.

My mood had finally lifted by the time I got back to the hostel. Henry handed me a plate of ham, mashed potatoes, and gravy, then motioned me over to the table. I sat down and started to eat while he washed the dishes.

The downstairs common room as a whole was rather empty. Aside from me and Henry, there was a woman reading on one of the couches in the living room, and two men sitting on the other end of my long table, talking quietly with each other. Granted, that didn't mean a lot, since I could hear every word they said.

" . . . God, it felt great. Like flying," the man farthest from me said. He brushed a hand through his dark hair and sighed. There was a skull eating a flower on his red shirt and a chain hanging on his jeans. I usually recognized everyone, although I didn't know most people's names in the hostel. He was one of the exceptions. Mateo, the guy who'd face-planted into the table a couple days ago during breakfast.

Mateo's friend hummed under his breath. With his back to me, all I could see was his pale brown hair and blue T-shirt. "I don't know. It's just . . . weird, you know? I mean, do you really believe all that shit?" He tapped his fork against his empty plate, beating out a nervous rhythm.

Mateo laughed. "Nah, that shit's whack. That nut job can talk all he wants. I just go to feel good; it helps to unwind after a hard week in the Gate." He grabbed his cup and gulped down the rest of the liquid, then set it down with a clunk.

"Seriously, man, I don't think you should go anymore," the friend muttered. "People are calling it a cult. I hear the Hunter's Association is trying to catch them. What happens if you're there when they show up? You'll get sent to the Holding Place. No high is worth wasting away in there until you die."

One word grabbed my attention like a noose. *Cult.* This guy, Mateo, knew about the cult, and he'd even been there before. I glanced up at

Henry, but he must have been too into washing the dishes or he couldn't hear them from where he was. That was probably for the better.

I stood up and walked over to the men. They looked up when I stopped right behind them.

Mateo donned a guarded expression. "What do you want?"

"I want to know more about what you're talking about," I said softly.

Jonovan was very clear on his opinion about the whole thing and had warned me away. But I wanted to know more about them. I wanted to know what they were saying. If it was crazy, druggy babbling, or if there was some truth to it. If it was true—and I could get the drug away from them—maybe I'd have enough backing to make the Council believe me when I met with them in three and a half months. With multiple testimonies and hopefully solid evidence about the crystal caterpillars and human-changing white tunnels, maybe I could get enough help to hold off the parasitic planet until more people other than just me could come up with a plan to save Earth.

The friend laughed nervously. "Ahaha, I don't know what you're talking about?"

I nearly rolled my eyes at him. Honestly, with Hunter hearing, it was hard to not overhear things. If they really wanted to keep it a secret, they should have talked about it in their room. Then again, most E ranks' hearing was about on par with most humans', so I guess it wasn't too much of a stretch for them to talk down here.

"The cult," I stressed in a whisper. "I want to know more about it. Where are they meeting and when?"

Mateo looked at me like I was crazy. "Nah, wait. You seriously don't believe in that shit, do you?"

My lips twitched. Didn't his friend just ask him nearly the exact same question a second ago? "I don't know. It seems really far-fetched, but I want to know more about it." I needed to know if there was more to this cult or not. If it was real or just a bunch of junkies getting high.

Mateo's friend let out a long breath and stood up, his chair skidding across the wooden floor as he rose. "I'm out." He took his plate over to Henry in the kitchen and disappeared through the doorway to the stairs.

Mateo watched him go before glancing back at me. "Hey, I don't know you. But I know you aren't strong. A place like that isn't for someone like you. Some weird shit goes on in there. Too weird for a cute little girl." He glanced at my figure, adding emphasis to his words.

I frowned and tilted my chin up. If he was trying to freak me out, it wasn't working. "I heard it was mostly full of humans and Es. If they can go, why can't I?" Especially since I wasn't an E anymore. And if that's the only people who attended, I doubted any of them could hurt me.

He scowled and shoved off the table to his feet. Now that he was up, he towered over me, a full head-and-a-half taller. "I aint telling you shit. Everyone knows that Henry's taken a shining to you, and he's a good guy for an old man." He picked up his plate, put it on the counter, and left.

I watched him go, frowning. *Huh*, that wasn't how I thought this would end. I thought I'd get a one-way ticket to the cult. I mean, in movies and stuff, they were climbing over themselves to get people to join, right? Especially if their numbers kept dying off, even if it was their own fault.

Well, now what do I do?

CHAPTER 18

The next day, I couldn't stop thinking about Mateo as I cultivated in Fogmire then walked toward the Association's transportation area. Just inside the clearing around the Gate, I saw a familiar bleached-blond man.

Kesstel was dressed in a blue tunic, black pants and boots, and a bright steel breastplate today. He looked toward me from across the short grass, his face completely disinterested in whatever the woman in front of him was saying.

That woman was Bethany Wilks, decked out in a maroon mage's robe with magic stones dangling from her neck, wrists, and ears. Her wavy blonde hair was in a thick braid which hung over her right shoulder nearly to her slender waist. When Kesstel looked away from her, her mouth clamped shut, and an angry flush colored her cheeks. "Kesstel!" she yelled, trying to get his attention.

He glanced at her before walking away, her mouth dropping open when he left her so easily to come to me. He stopped in front of me, his back to her. It was only then that his face softened from a blank slate to a sorta smile. "Good morning."

Mentally, I slapped my palm on my forehead and laughed. This man, he had no idea what he put me through just to be his friend. Probably because he couldn't see how Bethany looked right now, her face flushed with anger and wild magic swirling around her feet. Okay, knowing him, Kesstel would know about the magic. The sad thing was he obviously didn't care. Probably because he didn't know what her temper meant to my safety.

And it wasn't just Bethany Wilks I had to worry about. There was also President Price, who apparently wasn't finished with me yet; what pressure would he apply to get me to join his guild?

All this because Kesstel wanted someone to talk to. And I found I liked talking to him.

Helplessly, I smiled at him. "Good morning. How long have you been in the Gate now?" What time did he have to get up to take out all the dangerous stuff before the rest of the Hunters got here?

Kesstel shrugged. "A couple hours. I normally get here around six. Some of the Portal Bursts are still open at that time, and I can look inside. I just ate breakfast, so now I'm going to check another couple things out before I'm done."

I couldn't help frowning at the nonchalant way he talked about his usual morning. So dangerous. The only time I'd ever gone into a portal, I died. "Do you get hurt when you go in?"

He smirked and waved a hand in dismissal. "Occasionally."

"Right, because you're Superman," I muttered. Should I even bother worrying about him? I huffed a breath and tapped on his simple breastplate. "Just don't do anything dangerous, okay?"

Now the smile touching his lips was genuine. "Okay."

I nearly snorted. Did I have any room to ask that of him? I mean, everything I did was dangerous. In fact, I was on my way to an area that was putting me to the test more than any other place I'd ever been to. "Where are you headed?"

The smirk was back. "To a portal." He lifted a hand and pointed to the east side of the Vale. "Don't worry; I won't collapse it."

So much for not doing anything dangerous. God, we were a pair, weren't we? This time, I couldn't stop my hand as it pressed against my forehead. Should I laugh or cry? I was so torn, all I could do was give a wobbly smile. "Okay."

"What about you? Are you going back to the Josu Rainforest? You are being careful there, aren't you? You've grabbed quite a few Hunters' attention lately."

I blinked at him. How did he know that's where I'd been the last couple days? And what did he mean by that?

From over his shoulder, I saw Bethany Wilks march toward us, her face set to kill as she leveled her eyes on me. As she arrived at Kesstel's side, that glare shifted to a hurt, coquettish expression. "Kesstel, you didn't let me finish talking to you." She reached out to take a hold of his arm.

He smoothly stepped out of her reach and came to my side. Or should I say, a half step behind me. If it wouldn't hurt me more, I would have elbowed him. Okay, I didn't have the guts to do that just yet, but the thought definitely crossed my mind.

"Miss Wilks, I've explained and explained again." Kesstel's tone was like a subzero freezer. "Please stop drawing this out. Not everything fits perfectly into your rose-tinted world. Every interaction we had together was because of a contract, nothing more, nothing less."

"But—"

"Goodbye, Miss Wilks." Kesstel put his hand on my shoulder and directed me toward the teleportation area. His hand was gentle on my back, but he forced me to keep up with his long-legged stride.

I couldn't resist glancing over my shoulder at the woman Kesstel had left in his dust. I thought she'd be burning with anger, fire flickering around her, ready to burn me to a cinder. But she stood there, watching us walk away. Her shoulders drooped, and her hands were fisted in the folds of her robe. She didn't take a single step forward or even try to talk as we turned the bend in the tunnel leading to the transportation circles.

I glanced up at Kesstel. "That was a little mean, you know." Hang on, this was the woman who was trying to kill me. Why should I care?

He huffed with frustration. "You have no idea how persistent that woman is. She's never been told *no* before, so she doesn't know when to stop. I've tried to be nice, but she just won't get the message."

I didn't want to talk about her anymore. Seriously, I'd had enough of that woman. "How did you know I've been in the Josu Rainforest? Are you stalking me again?" I tilted my head to the side, giving him a stink eye.

He finally relaxed enough to slow down to a normal pace for me. "No, not even close. I was trained to collect data from the time I was ten. It's a habit that dies hard. With your unique abilities, as soon as I heard about a moving cloud under the rainforest canopy, I knew exactly what it was." He tapped his hand on my back, as if to prove I was corporeal. "Definitely not a ghost." He dropped his hand and strolled along beside me.

"How long do you think it'll take for the hype to die down?" I fought the best when surrounded by Mist, but with so many people hunting the Josu Ghost, I didn't dare expand it any farther than necessary. In a location that was as dangerous and over my level as the rainforest, it would be a lot easier if I could use my mist.

Kesstel shrugged. "Until someone catches that ghost, I guess."

"You're not helping," I muttered.

"Do you want me to?" He glanced at me out of the corner of his eye.

I had a feeling that if I asked, he'd drop what he was doing and help. But I wasn't going to leech off of him. I shook my head. "I'm fine. It's not the worst thing that's ever happened to me." Not even close.

To my surprise, Kesstel waited with me the whole time I was in line. He, as usual, drew a lot of stares, but since he didn't care, I tried not to as well. Even more surprising was the fact that Bethany Wilks didn't come after us. After a short wait, I waved goodbye to Kesstel and shot up through the transportation circle.

I landed at the edge of Josu Rainforest and used the momentum to jump right up into the trees. Since I'd picked the cyan-agaric yesterday, a new one would be growing somewhere in the rainforest today. Unfortunately, they never grew in the same place twice, which meant I was back to square one. Really, the mushroom could be ten feet from where I stood right now for all I knew.

I needed two more, but my goal today was to catch an aero-teuthida—two would be preferred. I'd only seen one so far in my scour of the west half of the rainforest. I knew they were hard to find, but this was a little ridiculous. Then again, there wasn't much I could do if another Hunter killed all of them before I even got to them. Maybe I'd have better luck on the east side of the rainforest.

With that in mind, I sprinted east along the road-like branches. Like yesterday, there were a lot of Hunters prowling around the treetops, killing whatever moved and making it difficult to run in a straight line. The sounds of the activities—the yells of attacks, yelps of flower sneak bites, and sounds of trees being rendered into pieces and crashing to the ground—filled the musky, stale air. The velociorheas below were hyped up, ready to eat whatever fell, be it human or monster. Some of the Hunters dropped to the ground to kill several velociorheas, but as soon as they landed, dozens more of the monsters appeared as if out of thin air and joined the fight. As soon as one monster died, three more would arrive, and it wasn't long before the overzealous Hunters were forced back up into the trees.

I'd been hoping to have an easy time—well, as easy as it could be in this place—leveling up today, since I was so close to the next level. But right then, I worried I wouldn't even get a kill at all.

Luckily, the amount of Hunters seemed to thin a bit by the time I made it to the east side of the rainforest. I stopped on a branch, breathing a little hard while I looked through the drizzle that wet my body. I wiped my face with my hand, even though I knew it was going to get wet again immediately. Jeez, all this moisture was going to make me mold, I swear.

A shiver of awareness went down my back, and I leaned to the side just as a bat-like monster flew right past. Its body missed me, but the hooked thumb at the end of its three-foot wingspan clipped my shoulder. I wobbled on the slick branch before I caught my balance, pain throbbing from my shoulder down my left arm where the monster's talon had pierced through my armor. Scowling, I Mirrored my kindjal and brandished them at the creature.

It looked like a bat for the most part. It had black bat-like wings, and a black bat face and ears. But its dark green body was more like a wasp's, with a small thorax and a bulbous abdomen. The wings stretched all the way from the monster's neck to halfway down the abdomen, leaving room for stubby feet. Oh, and yes, there was a giant stinger on its butt.

The level thirty zotz shrieked at me and swooped around to attack once more. I swung at it with my left hand, trying to force it off its trajectory again, and moved to stab it with my right, but the monster curled its body and wings around my left sword, willingly taking damage as it thrust its seven-inch stinger into my torso. My right kindjal was just in time to strike against the steel-hard stinger, forcing it to the side. My brows pinched together, and I groaned as the stinger pierced me. It hurt like hell, but the wound wasn't fatal.

The zotz opened its mouth wide, revealing long canines, and arched around my kindjal to bite at my wrist.

I canceled Mirror. The kindjal disappeared from my left hand, and the bat monster shrieked when it suddenly didn't have anything to hold on to and fell backward. The zotz let go of my hand and pulled its stinger out of my side, arching its wings wide to fly.

My right hand slashed up, cutting into the thin skin. The bat jerked away, preventing me from cutting the appendage all the way off.

It flapped awkwardly in the air, its left damaged wing flailing like a tattered sheet, the skin closest to its body flowing freely in the air. But it didn't fly away. I Mirrored my kindjal again and brandished the blades at it, my lips curling in a sneer. The zotz opened its mouth and let out another shriek, but this was different from before. A high-pitched ring echoed through my ears and rattled my mind, making me see double. I groaned in pain and narrowed my eyes, trying to join my vision back together. The bat monster dived at me, aiming at my head this time.

I gritted my teeth and cast Mist, converting all the drizzling rain around me into thick vapor. The zotz paused, obviously thrown off by the sudden distortion around it. I, however, relaxed. My vision was still affected by the shriek attack, but inside the mist I didn't *see* with my eyes. A black-and-white 3D picture of my surroundings within twenty feet of me formed in my head, making me aware of every nook and cranny of every tree and shrub.

As well as of a wiggling squid hiding in a tree hollow fifteen feet away.

I focused on the bat monster and jumped into the air, both blades ready. The zotz thrust its stinger out, aiming at my chest yet again, but I stabbed my left blade down into its abdomen, just above the stinger, and forced it away from my body. The bat opened its mouth again, and I stabbed my right blade through its open mouth. With a crack, my weapon broke through the monster's skull.

The carcass went limp, dragging me down toward the ground. Solid mist appeared under my feet, and I jerked my blades out of its body before I quickly thrust down where the energy crystal was inside the monster's thorax. The zotz exploded into little lights, brightening up my mist cloud from the inside and leaving two drop items.

[**+95 EXP**]

[**You have Leveled Up!**]

Several voices rang through the air, leaving me no time to celebrate getting to level twenty-seven.

"Look! The Josu Ghost!"

"Get it!"

"No, it's mine!"

A group of mid- to high-leveled Hunters entered my mist from the north, south, and east. They hurried along the tree branches to reach the middle as fast as they could, even though they didn't know what was at the center of this mist.

Me.

I hissed in my mind as I focused to the east of me, where the aero-teuthida remained hidden in the tree.

Dammit!

CHAPTER 19

I knew casting Mist would likely bring me trouble—with so many Hunters interested in snagging a unique kill, being found was bound to happen. I just didn't think it would happen so fast. Unfortunately, I didn't have a way to explain why a melee E Hunter had magic, but even if I shouted through the mist letting them know about me, it was a real possibility I'd be dead before they understood they were killing one of their own. And an even bigger possibility that they wouldn't care anyway.

I could run away, but after looking for so long, I didn't want to let the aero-teuthida get away. Unfortunately, there were ten Hunters inside my mist, three of which were between me and my target.

A mage on a branch fifteen feet away thrust her hand toward me, and I moved at the same time that foot-long icicles formed and shot at me as fast as arrows. Two of them missed me entirely, but the third one brushed my cheek, leaving behind an icy hot pain. A second later, I felt a cool drip of blood sliding down to my chin. The icicles kept going behind me until they smashed into trees, leaving huge holes as they exploded on contact.

I gritted my teeth and cast Stealth before jumping off my ledge. Hopefully, it would be enough to hide me from them. Just as my toe left the solid mist, a fire blast from the north and south landed where I'd been. I dropped ten feet but kept the center of my mist at its original starting point. If I moved it with me, the Hunters would follow, and I wanted them as far away as possible from the aero-teuthida. I'd already lost one to a random show of, well, pride. I didn't need to lose another one for another stupid reason. Two feet above the bottom of my cloud, my foot landed on solid mist, and I sprinted toward my target hiding at the edge of my fog. There wasn't even a ripple in the vapor around me as I moved.

"I didn't hit it, did I?" a woman yelled.

"Wait, where did it go?" a man gasped.

"Is it gone? Why is the cloud still here?" a different man asked.

The Hunters shifted around, trying to see around me as I slipped right under them.

One of the melee Hunters turned in my direction. "I think I can feel something," he muttered. Luckily, he was part of the north group and too far away from me to do any damage.

"Where?" a female mage asked. "God, this fog is so thick! It's distorting my perception."

"That way." He lifted his hand and pointed.

Since I had eyes in the back of my head right now, I knew exactly where he was pointing, and I was already out of the way by the time a fireball lit up the mist. Slipping around the tree, I put the thick trunk between me and the other Hunters. Technically, I could easily cancel Mist right now, since Stealth was doing a good enough job of concealing me, but it would reveal my monster—my kill.

I wasn't sharing.

Looking up through the tree, a couple feet above me was a bushy fan of fat, green leaves. Just under the bush, where I wouldn't have even seen it if I wasn't searching from this angle, was a hole only three or four inches wide. The monster was in there.

I gripped my kindjal and got ready to stab into the hole. If I was fast enough, I should be able to critically injure it before it flew away.

"So frustrating!" a man roared. "I know it's here somewhere! Damn ghost! Damn cloud!" He swung his sword and struck the tree I was hiding behind.

The tree groaned as a violent shudder rained leaves down from above. A crack appeared in the trunk below me, and the whole tree tilted a couple inches in my direction. Startled, I pushed my hands out against the trunk. I didn't know if I was trying to right the tree or keep it from falling. I couldn't do either, anyway. Although the Hunters weren't standing on this particular tree, wasn't he worried that it would fall and hit the branches they were standing on? If they fell, who knew who would survive?

The vibrations shook the cluster of leaves over my head. Suddenly, the aero-teuthida burst out of its hiding hole and shot through the fog like a silver torpedo, right out of my cloud.

Ah, damn! I lunged after it, pulling my mist with me.

"What? After it!"

I could hear the yells of the Hunters I was leaving behind, but there were more important things to worry about. Like the absurd speed of the flying squid as it darted around the trees. Seriously, between me and the monster, I knew which was more like a ghost. If it wasn't for the mist I kept ten feet ahead of me that the aero-teuthida kept slipping in and out of, I would have lost it long ago.

The Hunters were still loudly running after me, shooting magic into the cloud. I guess the one good thing about the aero-teuthida zigzagging around the trees was that the Hunters kept running into dead ends. The bad thing was it only hung them up for a second before they jumped to another branch and kept coming for me. And it wasn't just a dozen Hunters chasing me anymore—the group had doubled in size at an alarming rate.

The silvery squid slipped around a tree, trying to throw me off again.

I formed a triangular block at an angle just past the tree and landed on it, using it to shoot off and change my trajectory. All the while, I kept my eyes on the prize. Mirroring my kindjal, I got ready to throw it. If I used Critical Hit, it would make things a lot easier because I was guaranteed to hit the monster. Unfortunately, it would target the energy crystal and make the whole creature disappear. Then I'd be back to square one. I was going to have to hit it with my own skill, no cheating allowed.

Taking aim, I threw my kindjal just as the monster darted in front of a wide, wet tree. The short sword cut through the light rain and hit the flying squid, piercing through one of its arms and nailing the monster to the trunk.

Elation bubbled in my chest. A perfect hi—

My eyes widened. Two icicles cut through the mist, too fast for me to dodge. The first skimmed my left side, slicing right through my armor and leaving a frigid, burning gash. The second embedded in my left shoulder, just under the clavicle, its sharp point tearing through my skin and muscle. A second later, the ice, so cold that it burned, spread over my skin, forming an inch-wide ring around the wound. It stopped the bleeding, but jolt after jolt of agony shot through my body, racing from my shoulder down to my toes.

A scream ripped from my throat, and the momentum of my jump faded, causing me to drop. My mind was seminumb with pain, but I was conscious enough to create a solid platform to land on. Crouched on my hands and knees, my left arm jostled and sent another intense, agonizing pulse tormenting my body. I screamed again and knelt there, gasping in pain.

"Stop shooting at me, you sons of bitches!" My voice was distorted with pain. "I'm not a monster!"

Silence greeted my words as twenty-five Hunters stopped running, about half of them just inside my cloud. The ones in my mist that I could actually "see" looked at each other.

"Did you hear that?" the mage who shot me asked, her eyes wide. "Could the Josu Ghost be a person?"

"It's a trick!" the melee Hunter next to her insisted, his beard wafting with each heavy breath he took. "The monster is trying to trick us!"

Other Hunters joined in the argument, throwing options around.

While they were stalled, I shifted back onto my knees, biting back a painful groan. My right hand shook as I reached up and gripped the icicle in my shoulder. About two inches were inside my body, leaving six inches sticking out.

With a quick jerk, I snapped it in half. It wasn't a clean snap at my skin, so there was about an inch still sticking out which hurt when it rubbed against my armor, but the ice had stopped the bleeding, so it was okay to leave it in until I got healed.

As soon as the ice was broken, the pulsing pain it kept emitting disappeared and gave me a second to breathe. I was still in intense pain, but at least I felt like I could handle it.

"But monsters don't have a language!" another Hunter spoke up, looking just as concerned as the mage.

"If it wasn't a monster, why would it hide?" the first melee Hunter demanded.

I gritted my teeth and threw the broken piece of ice at him. "Because I want some peace and quiet!" I gasped out, almost regretting my actions—the movement of throwing hurt, but *god* if I didn't want to peg him between the eyes with that ice.

He jerked to the side barely fast enough, so I missed his face. The ice dinged off the side of his helmet and fell to the ground. "It's attacking me!" he gasped, brandishing his sword.

Instantly, the other Hunters, especially the ones in the back, went into attack mode.

I jumped forward toward my aero-teuthida hanging on the tree. Just as I flattened myself against the trunk, two fire blasts, an arch of lightning, and another round of icicles filled the space I used to be on. The magic hit each other and exploded, illuminating the mist with brilliant colors.

Fury boiled in my mind and overflowed in an eruption of spite. "Damn you! Leave me alone!" I snarled and thrust my hand out toward the Hunters. *You want a ghost? Well, eat it!*

Three solid mist walls appeared in front of the line of Hunters lined along the tree branches, one on each group. With the movement of my hand, they shot toward them. I didn't even know I could do that, but I wasn't thinking rationally right now.

They couldn't see nor feel the presence of the walls and were caught completely off guard. Since I was a lower level than them, they should have been able to break through my barriers, but because I had the element of surprise, several Hunters were pushed off the branches before the walls disintegrated in a puff of smoke. Teammates reached out and grabbed at their falling companions, and all but one was caught—the loudmouthed, unlucky melee Hunter who'd pissed me off so badly dropped to the ground like a pile of steel.

With just a moment of hesitation, three other Hunters jumped after him. I guess he wasn't too unlucky if his team was willing to take on velociorheas for him. There weren't any under us right now, but I could feel them coming.

I didn't have any time to revel in my new ability because all thoughts were cut off when four sharp hooks stabbed into my right arm. I hissed and focused on the manus at the end of the aero-teuthida's tentacle, the four barbs along the flattened area digging into my skin. With a jerk, the silvery squid convulsed against the blade keeping it pinned. Just as I stabbed my second kindjal toward the monster, it ripped away from the tree, leaving its damaged leg still nailed to the bark. My attack sank uselessly into the trunk as my target slipped through the air and out of my mist, leaving me with four throbbing gashes on my arm as it pulled away.

Oh, no, you don't! Like a madwoman, I lunged after the aero-teuthida and gave chase, dragging my mist with me to hide my monster from unwanted eyes. The chaotic group of Hunters faded in the distance behind me. Some were still trying to pull their companions up, while others were trying to get around them to chase after me. On the ground, I could hear the sounds of fighting and velociorhea screeches. But they could all kiss my ass for all I cared.

What mattered was catching that flying squid.

As I ran, I couldn't help but notice there was something wrong with the cuts on my arm. The blood wasn't coagulating. The bright red liquid just kept leaking through the holes in my armor and leaving a trail of drops behind me—a trail which was quickly gathering a growing group of velociorheas. These things just didn't stop, did they?

It hurt to move my left shoulder, and my right hand was slick with blood, but I kept chasing. The aero-teuthida darted around a tree, trying to wiggle away again, but I thrust my right hand up, and a solid barrier shot out and smashed the squid against the wet bark. It was momentarily stunned before it started to wiggle and push through the barrier toward freedom.

But that moment was all I needed.

Landing in front of it, I raised my foot. My boot crushed the flailing arms and tentacles, holding the monster in place while I stabbed into its large, circular eye just like how Maveric instructed me to. My blade sliced through like the monster was made out of warm butter until the tip hit the trunk. I had to be careful of the angle it went in. The energy crystal was between the eyes—I didn't want to hit it and make the monster disappear.

The aero-teuthida struggled for a couple seconds before it finally died.

[+85 EXP]

[Task: Collect two Aero-Teuthida. (1/2)]

Breathing heavy and hurting all over, I took a second to simply lean on the tree. Even though it wasn't from the ocean, the monster still gave off a strong fishy smell, and combined with the rusty smell of my blood, the already muggy air smelled nauseating.

I glanced at my still freshly bleeding arm and sighed. Once I was ready to move again, I took out the special container Maveric gave me and carefully put the monster's carcass in it. I knew the System wanted me to destroy the energy crystal without it even asking, but I didn't. It would be counterproductive.

Now that I knew about the crystals, it felt wrong to purposefully bring one out of the Gate. But I hadn't been thinking of that when I took Maveric's post. I'd only been thinking about money.

I condensed the mist to a thin strip under me and sat down with my back against the tree. My Stealth was about to run out, but it was worth it to pay the MP again. I glanced at the giant bird monsters under me and the Hunters above me who were trying to figure out where the Josu Ghost went.

Next time, I needed to think a little harder before I sold myself into a difficult situation.

My lips pulled up in a sneer as I tipped my head back and let the cool rain fall on my face. *Psh, yeah, right.* I couldn't resist jumping headfirst right into these stupid situations, huh?

CHAPTER 20

Josu Rainforest really was testing me, be it health, mental and physical endurance, or my abilities. The current issue, yet again, involved my limited Regen. When I got scratched by the aero-teuthida, I noticed almost right away that it didn't scab over, but it wasn't until I caught the monster and rested that I realized there was a problem. A quick check at my status while adjusting my new stat points confirmed what I was worried about.

The aero-teuthida had inflicted me with Bleed, which meant that my wounds wouldn't coagulate. Since it was a status ailment, my limited Regen wouldn't fix it. Ironically, the only reason why I hadn't bled dry was because of Regen. It healed just a pinch faster than Bleed drained my HP. Because of Bleed, I didn't dare take the ice out of my shoulder, either. Right now, it was stopping the blood from gushing. If the ice was gone, who knew how long it would take for me to pass out from blood loss? As painful as it was to move with a chunk of ice wedged between my shoulder bones and muscles, it proved that I was alive. That had to be good enough for now.

But I couldn't be more excited to touch the ground on the other side of the transportation circle clearing. In the late afternoon, there was hardly anyone around the purple circles besides the staff. Most people had already gone where they wanted to go, and it was a little early for most Hunters to call it quits for the day. The few Hunters I saw as I walked back to the Gate were in the same condition I was—too battered to go on.

While I walked across the clearing to the Gate, a bright flash of light caught my attention. I paused midstep and gaped.

Bethany Wilks was sitting on the grass surrounding the Gate. Dressed in her full glory, she sat with her arms folded on her bent knees and her chin tucked into the rich material of her mage robe's sleeves. Her blonde hair shimmered in the sun as her bangs fell into her face, concealing her features.

My mouth wrinkled. If I stayed on course, I was going to walk right by her. I could swing to the right and loop around, but that felt a little cowardly.

Taking a breath, I lifted my chin. Then I marched on.

Five feet away, Bethany raised her head a little.

I swallowed hard to keep from jumping. My hand stiffened, ready to summon my kindjal at any moment. She wouldn't attack me here, would she?

She tilted her head and glared at me from beneath her bangs. Her eyes were red-rimmed and puffy. "Don't get ahead of yourself," she said, her voice nasal and hoarse as if she was trying not to cry. The fact that her makeup wasn't smeared at all was a testament to how high-end it was.

I stopped and looked at her. Like, really looked at her. Looked at the wet material on her sleeves where her face had rested. Looked at the way her fingers were trembling as she gripped her elbows tight enough to make her knuckles blanch. Looked at how flat the grass was around her, like she'd been there for a long time. From what Kesstel had said, there were typically nine bodyguards who accompanied her. So where were they? Why was she sitting here alone?

For the first time, she didn't come across as a stuck-up princess. She looked . . . pathetic. Almost defeated. I admit I didn't like her; maybe even hated her. After all, she had tried to kill me. I thought I'd feel wonderful seeing her beaten down like this. If this was Blake, for sure I'd be laughing and dancing on cloud nine. But for some reason, I didn't feel that way when I saw Bethany here. I just . . . didn't feel anything.

She jerked her chin in the air. "Soon enough, Kesstel is going to come back to me. I mean, I'm prettier than you, richer than you, and more connected." It was like those facts were a badge of honor for her. A crutch she clung to to feel better.

My mouth twisted as I paused, trying to decide what to do. I should just walk away. The less drama I got tangled up in, the better my life would be. And Bethany was nothing but drama. Still, I found myself saying, "You're right."

Her eyes widened in surprise, and she looked me full in the face. "What?"

"You're right." I watched her closely, ready to move at a moment's notice in case she tried anything. Then again, with how battered I was, there wasn't much I could do if she did attack. The thing I was banking on was that she wouldn't hurt me in the open like this. "You are prettier, richer, and more connected than me. In fact, I couldn't be more opposite than you if I tried. I don't even know why Kesstel picked me to be friends with."

Her hands loosened on her sleeves. "Friends?" The harsh lines on her face softened, leaving a lost look.

I nodded. "Yes. He and I are friends. Odd friends, if you ask me. I don't think we have anything in common." I paused. "But I've found that he's nice to talk to."

"And . . . he talks to you? A lot?" Bethany asked softly.

I nodded.

Her eyes narrowed, and she tilted her head arrogantly. "Why would he talk to you and not me? What could you offer him that I can't?"

I could only shake my head. "I can't answer that because I don't know. I literally have nothing I could offer him. But he doesn't want anything from me. Just my friendship and some of my time. So just leave me alone, okay?" A jolt of pain went from my shoulder to the tip of my toes. I drew in a shallow breath to keep from hissing in pain. "I've got to go now. Bye."

She didn't respond, but I could feel her eyes on me until I disappeared through the Gate.

Jonovan wasn't at the hospital when I stopped by to get healed, but right now, that was a plus. I really did think of him like a friend, but I didn't want to get guilt-tripped right now. Especially since I was doing two things that would piss him off: going to Josu Rainforest without a team, and trying to hunt down the cult he hated so much.

Feeling a hundred percent, I headed for Maveric's shop.

I opened the door and walked in. He glanced up and waved a hand in greeting before he turned back to the pair of Hunters at his counter.

Drifting to the side of the store, I kept my distance. I couldn't do anything about overhearing their conversation as the pair sold their loot to Maveric, but I could at least give them some space while they bartered for a better deal. Unfortunately for them, their quality of skinning wasn't good enough to raise the price. In the end, they left huffing but unable to really complain.

I watched them leave, grateful for my System. It made that whole process so easy for me. Too easy, but given all the dangerous crap it made me do, I personally thought I deserved it.

"Evening, Miss Jynn," Maveric greeted me and put his hands on the counter, an excited grin on his face. "What do you have today?"

I unloaded my drop items in front of him.

He nodded slowly, his eyes already assessing them. "Good haul."

"And this." I waved my hand and set the container with the aero-teuthida on the glass top. The carcass floated in the frosted red glass tube like an alien. "It's just one for now. I'll bring you the other one by the end of the week. They aren't the easiest thing to find, are they?"

Maveric picked up the container and turned it around in his hand, examining the body. "Perfect. Just like I expected from you." He set it down and tapped on the lid. "Give my compliments to your team. With this, I can at least get started with my client's armor."

I nodded. *Yep, because "they" worked so hard.* "Oh, they wanted to know if the aero-teuthida's energy crystal was included in the price you were paying, or if it was ours to keep?" I paused tactfully. "We never really talked about it before I took the post."

Maveric paused. "Oh, we didn't. I just need the body, not the energy crystal. I thought you'd take it out." He picked up the container again and looked into it closely. "But you haven't," he muttered under his breath.

I shook my head. "We didn't want to accidentally ruin the body." Honestly, I had a hundred percent confidence there'd be nothing left of the carcass if I tried to take the energy crystal out myself.

Maveric tapped on the container and looked at my loot on the counter, thinking. "Let's exchange all this stuff first, then I'll take out the energy crystal for you."

I smiled and nodded. Perfect. One more step to payday, plus I got to rid the world of one more parasitic crystal.

Then I paused and thought, *System, if I destroy the energy crystal after he gives it to me, is it still going to make the monster's body vanish?* I'd hate for it to disappear on him after all the work I went through to get it here.

I didn't have to wait too long before the System responded with a teal screen. [**No. But it is recommended that you don't take up too many of these tasks. Introducing monster byproducts to Earth is also detrimental to the planet's environment.**]

Unlike the Hunters before me, Maveric and I negotiated the prices of my loot smoothly. Thirty minutes later, he took the aero-teuthida container into the back, and I wandered over to marvel at the beautiful quality of the armor displayed in the corner of the shop. The first time I came in here, the displayed armor had a fish-scale pattern weld over it. This new armor had faintly red-tinted steel blended with the silvery metal, creating an overall flame-like pattern. Red magic stones adorned the armor in just the right places, and two phoenix feathers arched out of the top of the helmet. God, Maveric's ability left nothing wanting.

He came back into the room. "Pretty, isn't it? I'm proud of how it turned out." He held out the energy crystal.

I returned to him. "It is beautiful." And pretty expensive. "The person who buys this is lucky." A handkerchief appeared over my hand as I reached out and took the energy crystal from him. I carefully wrapped up the glowing blue orb so it didn't touch my skin before I tucked it into the pouch of my hip satchel.

Maveric watched me, obviously puzzled, but he didn't comment. "Yeah. The project that the aero-teuthidas are going toward is armor which helps the wearer weigh less without compromising their attack. Frankly, my client wants to be lighter than air, but no one can walk on air." He paused. "Oh, except for that one Hunter a month or so ago that people saw running on air over Prine Lake. But no one knows anything about her. Or have seen her since." He shrugged. "Either way, that's the reason why I'm making this armor. My client thought it would be fun to run around on air. It's impossible, but I'm getting paid to help anyway. And so are you."

I paused and slowly nodded. First, I was a ghost, now I was an inspiration for specialized armor? This was getting too weird.

Maveric's words were on my mind as I returned to the hostel. After greeting Henry, I went up to my room. I needed to find a safe place to destroy the energy crystal. Sure, I could whip out my kindjal anywhere, but I didn't want to deal with the drama of someone seeing me destroy one. It felt like that damn thing was burning a hole in my hip satchel. Even though I couldn't see or feel it, I knew it was there, like a disgusting stain that I wanted to wash clean as soon as possible.

Halfway down the girls' hallway, I paused and focused on my door at the end of the corridor. There was a small, square letter wedged between my handle and the doorframe. That was weird. Aside from Henry, I didn't have any friends in the hostel, and everyone's mail was delivered to Henry, who personally handed it out to the Hunters. So who would leave a letter on my door? Very few people were allowed down this hall. To give it a number, just thirteen people—twelve women and Henry.

I plucked out the letter. My brows wrinkled as I turned the envelope around, but there wasn't anything written on the outside. My System didn't send out an alarm that it was dangerous, so I carried it into my room before I closed and locked the door. Making quick work of destroying the energy crystal, I finally turned my attention to the letter.

With a quick slice, I cut it open and pulled a piece of white paper out. The message typed on it was simple:

Do you want to know the truth? Saturday, 11:00 p.m.

Under the message was an address. I stared at the words, trying to make sense of them. My brows rose high on my forehead once it clicked.

Ah. It looked like I didn't have to search for the cult anymore. They'd found me.

CHAPTER 21

I now had an address and date for when the—I rolled my eyes—*End of the World* cult was going to meet, but I still didn't know who left me the note.

I asked Henry to see the security footage of the hall so I could see who it was. He was worried but accepted that it was nonthreatening—I was just curious.

Unfortunately, the footage didn't reveal anything. Roughly thirty minutes before I walked up the stairs, a figure in a hoodie and sweatpants climbed the stairs and hurried down the narrow hallway. Her hood was pulled low, obscuring her face as she stuffed the envelope quickly between my handle and door. Then she practically ran back down the hall, head bowed, and disappeared down the stairs.

I watched her rush down two flights of stairs and right out the front door, all without encountering anyone.

I was left stumped. Besides noting a possible curve at the hips, there was nothing distinguishing about this person at all. Her body, covered in baggy clothes, appeared of average height. There wasn't even a hint of hair falling out of her dark hood. She'd even worn gloves while handling the letter.

Huffing out a breath, I leaned back in the chair in front of the computer. "Well, she has to at least live here," I muttered to myself. "Only people who live here can go up the stairs. That narrows it down to a dozen people."

Henry, standing behind me and staring at the screen with a confused look, gave a questioning hum. "Not necessarily, Jynn girl."

I craned my head to look back at him. "Huh?"

He folded his arms over his round belly and tapped his fingers on his arm. "Friends of the occupants are allowed upstairs, too. There's a two-hour window from the time a woman has been invited upstairs—or they've physically left upstairs—to when the barrier prevents them from reentering that level. At that time, the only restriction is that men can't go on the women's floor, and women can't go on the men's floor."

I blinked at him. I totally forgot that! I'd never invited anyone to my room, so there was never a need for me to remember that rule. "So you're saying that as long as a girl invites another girl upstairs, they have two hours to access?"

He nodded.

My mouth wrinkled as I turned back to the computer and rewound the security footage, searching for the last person to enter or leave the hallway. The last person to leave was Leticia, lazily strolling out of her room dressed like a cheap socialite. She left at 12:13 p.m. The letter was left on my door at 3:23 p.m.

"So it was obviously someone who was invited to go upstairs by some-one else." In other words, it could be anyone.

Henry hummed again. "I could ask all the girls whom they invited upstairs. We could narrow it down that way." He squinted at me. "This is all very mysterious. Why exactly are you wanting to know again? Are you sure it's nothing dangerous?"

I shook my head and closed out of the security program. I stood up and smiled at Henry. "No, it's nothing bad. At least I don't think so. I was invited to a party, but the note didn't say who it was from."

He hummed a third time; this time, his nasally tone was thick with dis-approval. "Don't go. If you don't know who gave it to you, it's dangerous." He waved his arms. "There are too many dangerous things out there for a young woman. Monsters aren't only inside the Gate, you know."

My smile turned genuine. "I know. Thanks for caring, Henry. It means a lot." I paused as another thought came to me. "Oh, has Mateo come back yet? I wanna ask him something."

Henry frowned for a minute before he nodded. "Is Mateo involved in this party, too? He's a good enough guy, but you need to keep your dis-tance. He likes to hang with the wrong crowd too often."

Funny, they'd both said each other was a good guy, followed immedi-ately with a *but*. I shook my head. "It has nothing to do with the party." Okay, it had everything to do with the party. But Henry didn't need to worry about that.

Henry scrutinized me for another minute before he went upstairs to find Mateo. I waited at the bottom of the stairs and leaned against the wall. Finally, Henry came back down and said that Mateo would be down in a minute. A minute turned into twenty. By the time he came down, the hostel was starting to fill up with Hunters coming back for the day, and Henry was in the kitchen, busy as a bee.

Mateo dropped off the last step heavily and looked at me with an almost scowl. "What?"

I nodded out the front door. "I wanna ask you something. Let's go into the gym and talk, okay?"

His almost scowl shifted to a full-on scowl. "I don't wanna. I have nothing to say to you."

I met his gaze, not intimidated in the slightest. "I'll just ask you some pretty private questions right here in the middle of everyone, then." I glanced down the hallway where chatter echoed from the living room, battling Henry's off-tune humming. As if to nail it in harder, the front door opened, and two women walked in. They glanced between Mateo and me with interest.

Mateo huffed in annoyance and swung around. "Ah, hell. Let's go. But I think you're an idiot to wanna get tangled in this shit."

And you're already tangled up to your eyeballs. So what does that make you? Man, I'd switch you any day. I'll take on the crazed cultists, and you deal with the planet-eating monster. I followed him out, my inner monologue running wild as we went.

We walked around the side of the hostel, past a small ten-by-ten patch of dirt surrounded by concrete that Henry had turned into a vegetable garden, and to the dilapidated gym building in the back. The metal door squeaked as it opened, the sound echoing in the dark room on the other side.

Mateo stepped inside and folded his arms, glancing around with dislike. "Turn on the lights already."

I blinked at him. He didn't even know where they were? Was I the only one who used this building? *Ah, never mind.* I probably was. Every time the System added a new fighting move to my Guide, this was where I practiced until the move became second nature and I used it in battle. And those were the only times I ever saw this place lit up.

I took five steps along the right wall and flicked the switch with a practiced hand.

Fluorescent lights high overhead lit up with a slight buzz, and the ones over the weight set and other exercise equipment on the left side of the building flickered three or four times before they finally stayed on. The faded blue flooring was just as depressing as usual, and the off-white walls were chipping and peeling, especially in the places where I hit when I fumbled a move while practicing.

"Okay, we're here. What do you want?" Mateo snapped.

I couldn't help but give him an odd look. Seriously, what was his deal? "Why are you so defensive with me? I'm not going to hurt you, you know."

He snorted and rolled his eyes. "As if you could." He tipped his head back and glared down his nose at me. "I just don't want you to go reporting me. If word got around that I was involved in the cult at all, I could get locked up forever. And so will you, idiot."

I nearly slapped him upside the head and yelled, *Then why were you talking about it to your friend in the common room, where anyone could overhear you?* Instead, I counted to five to cool my irritation. "I just want to know if there's anyone else in the hostel who's involved in the cult."

He gaped at me. "Huh?"

My day had been way too long to handle this guy. Resisting the urge to massage my aching temples, I carefully explained, "This afternoon, someone left an invitation at my door to the next meeting, this Saturday. I don't have to explain how hard it is to access the women's hall. I just want to know who left the note."

Mateo flinched away from me. "Someone else was listening? Oh god!" He looked around as if expecting to see a crowd of people peering at him from the corners of the gym.

I nodded to the side. "If it's that important, don't talk about it in the middle of a common place." It was a lesson I knew well. "Anyway, is there anyone else?"

He shook his head frantically. "No. It's just me. I think. Everyone wears masks, so it's hard to tell, you know? Besides, I don't go to talk to people . . . " he trailed off.

So he really had no idea? I wondered how much he actually paid attention to the people around him when he was there. From the sounds of it, he was really only there to "feel good" from the drugs the cultists used.

"I'm outta here." Mateo swung around.

[**DOWN!**] A red System message flashed in front of my face.

I dropped to the ground and swept Mateo's feet out from under him at the same time the window behind me shattered. Mateo screamed as he fell, blood exploding out of a bullet hole in the fleshy part of his shoulder.

He howled as he landed on the ground, hugging his wound and rolling around frantically.

I twisted and tried to look out the broken window, but it was dark outside. With the light pollution from fluorescent lights overhead, there was no way I could see who'd attacked. That was assuming the attacker wasn't using a concealing spell or device.

A bright light flashed on the other side of the window. From this angle, it could only be from on top of a building. I didn't have time to think too hard about it because all my senses went off in alarm. Grabbing the screaming Mateo on the floor, I scrambled to the side as a fireball shot through the broken window and landed where we had been. As soon as it hit the ground, it exploded like a bomb.

I gasped and threw my hands up, casting Mist and solidifying it at the same time. A millisecond later, the explosion hit the barrier around Mateo and me. We were blown to the other side of the gym, where I hit the wall and was knocked dizzy, only to have a second dizzying impact when Mateo's big body slammed into mine. I gasped for air as he flopped to the ground and lay motionless on the damaged flooring. At least he was still breathing. Cracks webbed across my barrier, but it still stayed intact around us.

The explosion set off a fire, instantly igniting everything around us. The walls, the ceiling, even the pads on the exercise equipment were on fire. Smoke quickly took over the stale, sweaty odor of the gym and pooled around ceiling beams. Head still swimming, I glanced through the fire to the only door in the entire building. We'd never make it across the fire. The hotter the room got, the more my mist evaporated. Even now, my barrier was on the verge of collapsing. The only reason why it hadn't yet was because I was steadily draining the reserve mist I kept inside me to replace the evaporated portions. But it wouldn't last forever.

Black smoke permeated the air around us, swirling within the white barrier and further weakening it. I blinked as my eyes started to sting. At my feet, Mateo coughed but remained unconscious. Sweat leaked down his forehead and darkened his shirt. As an E, he was more affected by the fire than I was.

I scowled and looked up. If I couldn't get to the door, I had to take a window out. I didn't know how carrying Mateo would affect my High Jump. In theory, I should be strong enough to carry him the twenty feet up to the window directly over my head. I could just leave him here, but since I was the one who invited him into the gym, I felt responsible for getting him back out.

Not to mention, I was pretty sure I was the reason why the gym was on fire at all. Just because I hadn't seen Bethany's hitmen in a couple days didn't mean they weren't still there. I thought talking to Bethany would solve her problem with me, but apparently, I was wrong.

My kindjal appeared in my hand. As soon as the smooth handle touched my skin, I flung it up at the window. It smashed into the glass and shattered it, raining down shards that bounced off my dome-like barrier and pooled in a circle around us. A second later, my kindjal appeared back in my Items Bag.

I gritted my teeth and grabbed Mateo. Awkwardly, I hauled his heavy body over my shoulder. I'd never thought I was that short. I mean, I was five and a half feet tall. That was average, according to the internet. But with Mateo's body draped over me like this, his head hanging past my hip on one side and his knees touching mine on the other, I felt small. And awkward.

The cracks in my barrier spread with a sudden *clack*, and more black smoke contaminated my mist.

I took a deep breath and looked up to focus on the window overhead. I bent my legs slightly and bunched my muscles, putting all my strength into the action. Pushing off the ground, I jumped with everything I had.

A second fire blast hit the outside of the door and exploded like a grenade.

In midair, I watched the metal wall before me tremble.

Then warp.

Metal wrenched against metal in an earsplitting squeal as the ceiling suddenly collapsed into itself, pulling the whole building down with it.

CHAPTER 22

I huddled under the wreckage, my barrier like a small cocoon just big enough for me and Mateo. As someone who hated touching people, it was like torture. He was sweaty and badly needed a piece of gum. Distorted ceiling beams, bits of wall, and half a light fixture pressed down on my barrier. Through the rubble, I could see the flicker of a fire, but for the most part, it was put out when the gym collapsed.

I didn't dare push out of the rubble just yet. I could hear yells as people drew closer to my location, but I didn't know if the hitmen were gone.

"Oh my god, I think there's someone in there!" a woman's voice exclaimed.

"Get them out!" Henry yelled, his voice cracking with panic. "Water mages, get on that fire. Where's Nora? You need to heal them until the ambulance gets here."

The rubble shifted on my left, and a piece of burnt Sheetrock—lifted by several men—let in a blast of fresh air. One of the guys was Mateo's friend. He gasped. "Mateo! What the hell is going on? Hey, hang on—you're that girl!"

Between my barrier and them holding the Sheetrock up, there was just enough room to crawl out of the wreckage. I wiggled forward, grabbing Mateo's arm to drag him with me. As soon as I was close enough, many hands pulled us from the hole. Once we were clear, the men holding the Sheetrock let go, and I released my barrier. The whole pile collapsed with a crash, and a spark of electricity arched ten feet in the air.

I dropped to the ground, gasping for fresh air.

God, I thought Mateo's smell was going to kill me. If he couldn't afford deodorant, I would gladly buy him some.

"Jynn girl!" Henry howled, his gaze frantic. "Are you hurt? Where are you hurt?" He patted my shoulders, stomach, and legs, looking for injuries—he was short enough that I didn't have to stand up for him to check me. When I didn't show any signs of intense pain, he sighed and grabbed my arm. "How? Wh-what happened?" He looked at the wreckage.

The gym was a total loss. There wasn't a single wall, part of the ceiling, or piece of equipment that wasn't on fire or twisted like a pretzel. Even the metal door was bent in half inside the dilapidated frame. Two mages stood next to the fire, hands outstretched and shooting water on the flames; as Es, the water they could summon was the equivalent of a garden hose. In the distance, I could hear sirens wailing, their sounds echoing off the buildings around us and getting closer.

I tipped my head back and looked in the direction the attacks had come from, but the roof was empty. I didn't really expect them to hang around. Hopefully, they thought I was dead and would leave it at that.

I glanced at Henry. "I-I don't know," I said, finally answering his question and pretending to be confused.

Nora, the healer, dropped next to Mateo's side. She reached out and gasped, widening the lapels of his blood-covered shirt. "Oh my god! He's been shot!"

Everyone within hearing distance froze and looked our way. Guns weren't necessarily banned in Eden. They just, for the most part, were pretty ineffective weapons on this side of the Wall. They didn't work in the Gate at all, no matter what material they were made from. And anything ranked upper B or higher, be it Hunter or monster, was fast enough to dodge the bullet. Even most upper-C Hunters could move fast enough to prevent a fatal wound.

For that reason alone, any gun shot in Eden was a big deal, because it just didn't happen often.

Mateo's friend knelt by him. "Is he dead?"

The healer shook her head. "No, not yet." She reached out and started healing him. I wasn't an expert on magic, but I could tell how weak hers was. Maybe I'd just been spending too much time with powerful people.

Henry shook my arm, pulling my attention back. "Jynn! What happened?"

I looked up at him with big eyes and decided to play dumb. "I don't know. We were talking, and suddenly, Mateo screamed and fell down. The next thing I know, the whole building blew up." I loosened the control I had on my muscles and let the aftereffects of an adrenaline rush take over, making my arms and legs shake.

"Who did it?" Henry looked sympathetic but didn't let up like I'd hoped.

I shook my head. "I don't know."

At least that much was true. I knew what they looked like, as long as Beak Nose and Mage Buddy hadn't died in Josu Rainforest. But I didn't know their names, and I had no way to prove who'd sent them after me.

The siren grew closer, its blaring howl making me flinch and cover my ears. On the other side of the hostel, a bright light pulsed as a fire engine drove between the hostel and the neighboring building. There was barely enough room for it to maneuver, and it was in a hurry. Henry's garden didn't stand a chance against the large tires.

The fire engine was followed by an ambulance and a police car. Another police car tried to join, but there simply wasn't enough room. Between the three automobiles and all the Hunters, the basketball court–size space between the hostel and the rubble was completely filled. The second police car stopped in the lane, right on top of Henry's thrashed garden.

Henry groaned and covered his face.

"Your garden!" I gasped.

Henry dropped his hands with a sigh. "Yes, but it's not as important as someone's life."

I glanced at him. It was that mentality which made me glad that Henry didn't go in the Gate anymore. The younger generation would eat him in there.

Firemen burst out of the truck, mages wearing black-and-red heat resistant robes and headgear. They pooled their powers together, creating a giant water ball in the air the size of the rubble which they carefully lowered over the burning steel and debris. A loud sizzle permeated the air and was cut short as the liquid settled down. A minute later, the mages raised their arms, and it levitated back up, leaving a completely dry and cool pile of wreckage behind. Another wave of their arms, and the water disappeared. Just like that, the fire was out.

At the same time, the A-ranked healers rushed out of the ambulance. They wore white robes with a thick dark blue stripe all the way down the left side of the robe, just like the black-and-red firemen robes, with a Hunter's Association logo on the left breast. Two of them went to Mateo, shooing the E healer to the side. One reached out and cast a green glow over him while the other cast a gold healing magic. His injuries healed at a visible rate, but he didn't wake up. It probably had something to do with the green magic on him. Once he was fine, the two healers stepped back, and another mage stepped up and cast a levitation spell. Mateo lifted into the air and flew over to the back of the ambulance.

Two other healers came to my side. They looked at me as critically as I looked at them. "How are you feeling?" the man on the right asked, reaching out. He carefully touched my shoulder and cast Heal. Immediately, I felt the uplifting warmth of the spell.

"I'm fine, I think. My body aches and my lungs hurt from the smoke, but I don't think there's anything really wrong." My natural body constitution was enough to prevent me getting too injured, even without my armor. Or maybe I was just too used to such extreme injuries that this didn't seem like a big deal. If I had taken a direct hit by either the gun or the exploding fire magic, it would be a different matter entirely though.

The man hummed and released me after I was a hundred percent healed. Then he opened his Guide and started asking me questions like my name and other identifying details. He recorded my responses on his Guide, his fingers flying over the blue screen, before he paused and read something. He glanced at me.

I stared at him. It was times like this I wished I could read other people's Guide screens. What did he see? Did it have to do with me?

Henry stood at my side the whole time. "What's wrong?" he prompted.

The healer looked Henry up and down. "Are you related to Miss Devhro?"

Henry stilled and shook his head. Without another word, he turned and walked away. I watched him go without needing to ask why. If there was something personal to discuss, the healer wouldn't be able to say it around Henry. Then again, with other high-leveled Hunters around, there was no privacy. "Is there something wrong?" I asked the healer.

He glanced at me and shook his head slowly. "No. You are a rank E Hunter, aren't you, Miss Devhro?"

"Yes," I said without guilt. I was. Maybe E wasn't my literal rank, but that's what it was on record.

He tapped a little longer on his screen. "Well, Miss Devhro, you were lucky. There are no lasting effects of your run-in with a collapsing building. But if you feel any discomfort or sharp pains, it would be best if you check into the hospital to see if there's any embedded shrapnel that I didn't notice."

Just then, a pair of police officers approached me. They wore green police uniforms, nearly identical to the navy ones in Garden City. The difference was, the green material was magically enhanced, so it wasn't just normal cloth. It was much easier to make armor, since the cost of making fabric which acted like plate mail was ridiculously expensive and difficult, but the Hunter's Association thought it was better to match their sister city's public authority to create unity. Even though the two cities were kept as separated as possible.

The younger of the policemen, who had a badge which read Officer Nix, spoke up. "You are not in trouble, Miss Devhro. But you're going to have to come with us and recount what happened." There was nothing kind about his expression at all. It was obviously just a job he was going through the motions with.

Inside the Gate, it was a free-for-all. It was expected that people, especially weak people, would die. And sometimes, those deaths were caused by Hunters. As long as there was no evidence, it didn't happen. They were just one more missing Hunter on the growing list.

However, the rules were different in Eden. There were laws and codes, ones which were expected to be followed. The mentality from the Gate often spilled over into Eden, but if something was done, it had to be done quietly. Blowing up a building—a Hunter's Association–owned building—didn't count as *quiet*.

Add a gun wound on that, and it was guaranteed to be investigated.

I stood up and brushed the soot and grime off my clothes the best I could. "Can I change first?" I asked Officer Nix. Between what happened in Josu Rainforest earlier today and now, I felt downright gross.

He shook his head. "It won't take long." He motioned to the police car parked in Henry's garden. It seemed almost sacrilegious to sit in the car that was desecrating Henry's precious garden.

The firemen were already back in their fire engine, and the healers were loading up. The policeman and woman who had been in the other car were talking to the hostel inhabitants and taking statements. Henry had the policeman nearly by the ear, demanding to talk to the Hunter's Association president about the collapsed building as the poor Hunter reassured him over and over again that Incident Management was on their way over right then.

There really was nothing left for me to do, so I followed the officers to the car and sat in the back. At least they didn't make me sit on the side with a cage around it. I was a good girl growing up; my family had enough going on, and I didn't want to pile more on top of it. Needless to say, this was my first time in a police car. Even though I wasn't in trouble, I felt like it.

The ride was relatively short, but in the suffocating silence, it felt like it took forever. The older officer drove to the Hunter's Association building then parked around the back side. The police station, a box of a building that was missing all the grandioseness of the Association's building, was tucked up against the back. The car was parked, and Officer Nix opened my door.

He gave me a thin smile. "This way." He motioned to the front door.

I followed the older officer as Officer Nix followed me, his eyes boring holes in my back.

CHAPTER 23

Officer Nix scrutinized me from the other side of the table. His Guide screen was out, ready to type. This wasn't an interrogation inside a cramped room under the pressure of A-ranked Hunters. We were actually in a pleasantly bright room with a painting of Gate Vale on the wall and matching mahogany table and chairs to sit at. If there was one thing upsetting in the whole room, it was the security camera blatantly hanging in the corner.

So not only was my every action under the sharp eyes of the men across the table, but someone else whom I couldn't even see was probably watching on the other side of the camera.

The older officer seated next to Nix—named Officer Garth—tapped on his own Guide screen. "Can you tell us what happened this evening, Miss Devhro? Why were you in the gym with Mr. Iglesias? What did you talk about? What happened when the building collapsed?"

I paused, thinking. What was Mateo going to say when they asked him what we were talking about? Technically, he was the one who would get in trouble if he was tied to the cult. I still had clean hands—for now.

"Mateo and I were invited to the same party this weekend," I said, being as vague about the details as I could, tying a lie with the truth. "Going alone made me nervous, so I was trying to find someone to hang out with while I was there. Mateo and I don't know each other that well, so I wanted to know if there was another girl going. You know, power-in-numbers kind of thing." After being a good girl my whole life, I didn't know if it was a good thing or not that I was getting better at lying with a straight face and calm voice.

The men typed on their screens while I talked. When they were done, Officer Nix looked at me. "What happened after you were done talking?"

I shook my head. "We weren't done talking yet. Out of nowhere, Mateo just got shot. He screamed and fell down. Then a fireball landed in the gym and blew up. Everything was on fire, and Mateo was unconscious. Then another fireball hit the outside of the gym, and the building collapsed on us." I hugged myself like I was freaked out. "It was so scary. I don't know how we weren't crushed. It was a miracle." Yeah, a miracle of my own creation because of leveling up from all the dumb things I'd lived through over the past few months.

"Do you have any idea why this happened? Anything funny going on around you or Mr. Iglesias that you've noticed lately?" Officer Nix asked after he was done typing on his screen.

I frowned and looked at the painting of the Gate. "I don't know about Mateo. Like I said, I really don't know him. We've talked only a couple times, both very recent." I took a breath and jumped off the deep end. "But I think someone is trying to kill *me*."

Both of the officers paused and looked at me. "Has something like this happened before?" Officer Garth asked.

I frowned, trying to figure out how much to tell them. Technically, right now would be the perfect time to lay it on the table. "Not in Eden. But several weeks ago, a man attacked me in the Gate. He died because he wasn't careful in the Feng Jungle. And I know there are two men stalking me right now."

Officer Garth's dark eyes narrowed. "Have you reported this?"

I shook my head.

"Why not?" Officer Nix demanded. "We can't do anything if we don't know anything."

I looked at them, thinking about what I wanted to reveal. What I could even reveal. This was the main problem why I hadn't reported it yet: there were a couple people I knew who wanted me dead, number one being Bethany Wilks. If there was another person—*cough, cough*, Blake—well, he'd already tried to kill me with his own hands once. Unfortunately, both were high profile people, and I couldn't prove they were behind the attempts on my life. Without proper evidence, any accusations I presented would be swept under the table. After all, both people had the money and backing to make any report disappear, especially Bethany Wilks, the daughter of a Hunter Councilman.

"Honestly, I can't prove for sure who's after me or why. I only know because of things I overheard the attackers say while I was hiding, which implied they were going to kill me."

"So you've seen them? What do they look like?"

I took a breath, thinking back to the first day I entered the Josu Rainforest. Luckily, it was still fresh in my mind. Something about seeing a man getting eaten alive in front of you was hard to forget. Slowly, I described Beak Nose and Mage Buddy the best I could.

After I was done, the officers looked at each with a knowing glance.

My eyes narrowed, catching their looks. "Do you know who they are? Are they hitmen for hire?"

Officer Nix sighed. "Can you think of any reason they'd want to kill you?" he asked instead of answering my question.

"No." I shook my head. "I don't know why anyone would kill me. I haven't done anything wrong." Really, I hadn't. I'd never stolen anything from them; I never even said anything bad. My only offense was that I existed. Me, a measly E. God, it was frustrating being labeled like that for something I couldn't control.

But at least I finally reported the issue. After the gym blew up, the police couldn't ignore the problem now that it was brought into Eden.

The next morning, I found out that I exploded the Hunter forum chat again—twice.

Hunters kept talking about how someone got shot in E District, which led to the Hunter's Association conducting a search on every gun owner in Eden—and even some surprise searches on some suspected unregistered gun owners. A couple of people were arrested, but that was all forum posters knew about the subject. The Association was very effective at plugging up any leaking information.

But even the Association couldn't hide the fact that the building where the man got shot exploded. I mean, the building was *gone*. By the time I woke up, every beam, piece of wall, broken shard of glass, and heat-warped exercise equipment was gone. They even peeled up the ruined blue flooring. Other than the blackened concrete in the shape of the missing gym, it was like the building had never been there.

When I came down the stairs, the Hunters in the common room were talking about it so loudly, throwing out speculations about what happened and why, that I simply walked right out the front door. There was no way I was going to get interrogated by them. I simply bought breakfast and a lunch for later at a shop, and ate the breakfast sandwich on the tram to the Gate.

The second way I made a splash in the Hunter pool was because of my behavior in the Josu Rainforest yesterday. Outside of the Gate, it was all about the gunshot and the exploding building. In Gate Vale, nearly every conversation I overheard was about how the Josu Ghost was apparently a Hunter. Probably the same woman who people saw months ago fleeing from a plesiosaurus by running on air. Back then, she appeared out of nowhere and disappeared just as fast. Now she was back again. People were dying to know about her unique magic style and how they could get her to join their teams.

When I landed in Josu Rainforest, a dozen or more teams were waiting around the transportation circle. Some were in the trees; some were on the ground taking up so much space that someone apparently had to put up another protective barrier to keep the ground monsters at bay.

Outside the faintly glowing large barrier, packs of velociorheas stalked the circle, staring hungrily at the Hunters inside. Whenever a pack got too close to another one, they would shriek and snarl at each other. Thick tree roots clumped around the bottom of the barrier, twisting and wiggling around each other, and slithering up the barrier like snakes, searching for a weak spot to get in.

As soon as I landed on the ground, every eye focused on me. A second later, every eye looked away as a collective disappointed sigh whooshed through the musky air. My lips twitched in humor. Oh, if only they knew. But I wasn't going to announce to the world who I was. Before I got these powers, all I wanted was a quiet life. Now that I had them, I still wanted that normal life. Just like I wanted a normal planet to live that life on.

I took a couple running steps and leapt into the trees. From there, I sprinted away from the crowd as fast as I could. When I was sure no one was looking, I activated Stealth and jumped off the branch. Thirty feet from the ground, I activated Mist and spread my cloud out the full forty feet.

After yesterday, I had some serious doubts about using Mist in the rainforest again with all the people headhunting me, but the vision it gave was such a bonus, it was worth the risk. Especially now that people were convinced that I wasn't a monster.

My mist spilled across the ground and lower trees, filling in every nook and crevice. As it did, a thorough 3D image of my surroundings appeared in my head. I could see every patch of moss, every decaying leaf on the ground, inside every hidden cavity in every tree.

God, why was I doing it the hard way for so long? Like this, I could search so much faster. If sprinting, I could cover the bottom half of the forest in the afternoon, looking for the cyan-agaric. Then I could search the treetops for the aero-teuthida in the evening. I could kill two birds with one stone.

"Ma'am! Wait, ma'am!" a woman yelled above me.

It took me a second to realize she was talking to me. I paused and looked up to see the rainbow brigade standing on a branch above me. The pink-colored healer waved at me, a big smile on her face.

As soon as I stopped, I noticed a large group rushing in my direction. Most of whatever was coming was in the treetops, but there were a couple dozen on land, obviously velociorheas. A moment later, a mob of Hunters pushed and shoved each other as they ran on the wet branches.

"I wanted," Pink yelled down toward me, "to ask you if you would join our team? We think you're really cool." She obviously couldn't tell where I was because she was looking at a spot five feet from me.

I blinked at her. *If I did, what color would I have to be?*

"Hey, back off! We're going to recruit her!" a tall Hunter yelled as she skidded to a stop on the branch right next to the rainbow brigade. Her boots slid across the wet bark, carrying her nearly right into Green, who was at the end of the line.

He stepped back to give her more room. When he did, his brawny elbow bumped into Purple right behind him. She gasped and stumbled back in surprise, waving her arms while she wobbled for balance. Green spun around and grabbed Purple to hold her steady, but not before Purple's hand smacked Pink across the head.

Pink yelped and jerked in an exaggerated movement. The soles of her boots slipped right off the wet bark, and she shrieked as she fell backward. Orange, right next to her, dropped to his knees and reached for her, but his fingers closed on air, missing her pink robe by inches. Pink's blood-curdling scream ripped through the air as she plummeted.

On the ground, the velociorheas looked up expectantly.

CHAPTER 24

Pink screamed as she plunged into the thick mist, falling to the ground.

I gasped and ran toward her, and she dropped right in my outstretched arms, nearly breaking my waist in half and ripping my arms from their sockets. How the hell did movie actors make it look so easy? Why couldn't real magic be like movie magic sometimes? Even though my face contorted in a grimace, I didn't drop her. With a big breath, I stood up straight.

Pink's eyes were closed, and though she was safe, she continued screaming like she was dying. As soon as I grabbed her, she thrashed violently, put more effort into her scream, and her face began turning purple. Did she think I was a velociorhea?

My sensitive ears rang painfully. "Please, stop screaming."

She jerked and froze. Her eyes popped open, and she gasped like a fish, staring at the mist around her and then toward me. "Wha—wha—huh?" She reached out and touched my arms, shoulder, neck, and face. "What?"

Oh, right, I still had Stealth activated. She couldn't visibly see me even though she could feel me. From her perspective, she was being held by an invisible person.

Man, I just took the Josu Ghost a step further, didn't I?

"Ah, could you not touch my face?" I asked, tilting it away when she fingered my nose. "It's a little awkward."

She gasped and tucked her hands into her chest. "Oh yes! I'm so sorry, ma'am. That was so rude of me." She blinked at me with big blue eyes.

She's fantastic at selling cute, isn't she? And I was such a sucker Big Sis type that I fell for every Little Sister person I saw. Pink might have a baby face, but I bet a hundred bucks that she was at least five years older than me. The items she wore—a red magic stone necklace and matching brace-let—plus the fine material of her pink robe were high quality. I didn't get the impression that her team was rich, so she must have saved up to get these items.

Below us, I could hear the velociorheas' mouths snap—*clop, clop, clop*—as they jumped below. Did they ever tire of jumping?

Up on the branch, Pink's teammates were freaking out, yelling her name and walking around, trying to see through the mist. Other Hunters were quietly attentive, listening for what was going to happen on the ground.

Pink looked at her frantic teammates overhead. "I'm okay!" she yelled up at them.

Their leader, Blue, paced up and down the branch. "Where are you? I can't see you!"

"I'm fine! The Josu Ghost caught me, so I'm okay!"

While she was talking to them, my attention was drawn to the base of a tree which my mist had just rolled into after moving to catch Pink. Inside the crevice was a very familiar-looking mushroom. I couldn't verify that it was what I was looking for since I couldn't see the color, but I had a feeling it was a cyan-agaric.

The question was how to get it with all the Hunters above and the monsters below?

Pink looked back at me, catching my attention. "Thank you. Like, really, thank you so much." Then she paused. "But I have to admit, it's really weird talking to an invisible person." What a tactful way to say, *let me see your face.*

I rolled my eyes. "If I wanted people to know what I looked like, I wouldn't be hiding in a cloud." Okay, that was mostly true. It also helped with searching for what I needed. "I like my privacy, and that's not going to change. Thank you for saying that I'm cool and wanting me to join your team, but I don't partner up." Even though I had good impressions of this colorful team, I still wasn't going to give them my back. There was only one person whom I felt confident enough to do that with, and I simply wasn't at his level yet.

"Oh." Pink sighed in disappointment.

My mouth twitched, and I resisted the urge to ask what color I would be if I did join. I wasn't part of their team, but that didn't mean I couldn't use them. "I'm going to put you down now." With my improved Strength, she wasn't heavy, but she also wasn't on my very short list of people I let touch me.

Clop, clop, clop still echoed from below.

She squealed and flung her arms around my neck. "Don't put me down! I don't want to die!" Her arms were so tight, her grip kinked my neck at an uncomfortable angle. If she was trying to convince me not to drop her, she was going about it the wrong way. But the pure panic in her voice was very obvious.

"I'm not going to drop you. You won't fall; I promise." Maybe it was a good thing she couldn't see through the mist at the monsters that circled and jumped at us from below.

She loosened her arms and looked over her shoulder. "What are you standing on?"

"Magic." That was the only answer I was going to give her. The platform I was standing on extended out, and I set her feet down on it.

She gasped and tapped her booted toes against the solid mist for a second before she stood up, but that didn't stop her from keeping a death grip on my arm. At least I had breathing room, so I let it slide.

But as long as I had her here, I might as well take advantage of her. "Hey." I pulled her attention to me. "I don't do stuff for free. I saved you, so you owe me. And I want payback now."

Pink's eyes widened. Her thin dark brows scrunched up, and she looked like she had been betrayed. "Okay? What do you want? If it's anything too expensive, I'll have to talk to my team first."

I snorted. "It's not going to cost you a cent." *But it will make you run around this rainforest for at least another day.* "I need to get something off the ground, so I want your team to distract the velociorheas until I get it."

Pink gaped at me. "You want . . . what?"

Her team was all C ranked, with the leader Blue the only one in the high-C range. I honestly didn't think they had much of a chance against four velociorheas. "I can promise that none of you will get hurt. You'll stand in the air like this and distract them while I jump down and get what I need."

She bit her lip, thinking.

"It's not like I'm asking for money, just a bit of your time. A small price for saving your life, I'd say," I pressed. "Do I really have to mention the outrageous prices anyone else would demand?" Yes, blackmailing was a thing among Hunters. A Hunter scraping by every day just to make a meager living in a bloody world would never pass up the opportunity to take advantage of a weaker Hunter.

Pink bit her lip, looking conflicted. "I don't know that I can make a decision like that for my team." She looked up, even though I knew she couldn't see through the mist.

"Call your leader down here and let's talk." Of course, that meant I would have one more life I could use as ransom to get what I wanted. God, I was good at this evil person, blackmailing persona. Maybe I'd found my true calling.

I almost laughed out loud.

Pink took a deep breath before she called out, "Tarek? Can you come down here?"

The leader, Blue, paused. "What?"

I looked up at him. "Jump down here. Don't worry, I won't let you hit the ground. Expect a thirty-foot drop. You won't be able to see what you land on, but it's solid."

Some of the other Hunters, especially the one who'd caused Pink to fall, got excited and looked down into my mist. It was obvious from their expressions they were all thinking about jumping down. They shifted and whispered to each other, some even pointing in my direction.

I frowned. "That guarantee only applies to him," I called up to the rest of the Hunters. "I will not catch anyone else who falls. Period. Just leave me alone. I'm not going to join any teams or guilds." Just like when I'd dealt with President Price, my tone was strong and unyielding. With the natural tenacity of Hunters, if I sounded anything less than commanding, they'd never leave me alone. After all, a weak-willed Hunter wouldn't live long enough to make it to this rainforest.

"Now, Mr. Leader," I called up to Blue. "Jump on down here."

His thin lips pressed in a frown. Then he jumped. The mist puffed and pooled around him as he dropped through, but with Pink as a marker, he landed on the platform cleaner than I expected.

"Tarek!" Pink cried out as soon as he was beside her, pooled tears in her eyes. She reached for him with her left hand, but it came up a couple inches short because she didn't seem to be able to let go of me yet.

I held her arm and stepped forward, bringing her with me.

Blue reached out and grabbed Pink's hand. She jumped onto him and wrapped her arms around his neck, sniffling.

He patted her back and let her cling. "Are you hurt?"

She shook her head. "No, I was just so scared. Give me a minute." It couldn't have been comfortable pressing her face into his metal chest plate, but she didn't seem to mind.

Blue continued to pat her back as he looked up and around. "Is anyone else here?"

I crossed my arms and leaned on a hip. "I'm here."

He turned in my direction and frowned. "I can't see you."

"I like my privacy. Something that people just don't seem to understand." I glanced at the group of Hunters who remained above and didn't act like they'd clear out any time soon. "Anyway, the reason why I called you down was to complete a transaction. Pin—*she*," the words slurred in my mouth as I changed it midsyllable, "said that she didn't have the authority to pay me back for saving her life. That's why I called you down."

Blue scowled. "Are there no good people in the world nowadays?"

"Not in Eden. Only an idiot would do something for free." If I was going to pour black paint on my head, I might as well play the part to the fullest. Hell, even though Green had helped save me the other day, it was still to get information from me. He was still paid for his help in the end.

"I want your team's cooperation," I explained simply. "I need to get something off the ground. All the ruckus above drew the velociorheas here, and now I'm in a bind. I want your team to distract the monsters while I hop down and get it."

He frowned before he slowly bit out the words, "We don't have the strength to take them on." No Hunter wanted to admit they weren't strong enough. It was one of the most shameful admissions in Eden.

Pink pursed her lips to the side, scowling at her feet.

I nodded, then remembered they couldn't see it. "I know. And I don't expect you to take them on. In fact, I can guarantee that none of you will get hurt."

He tilted his head to the side. "How can you guarantee that?"

I swept my hand in front of me. The mist below our feet thinned out until there was just enough left to hold the solid platform under our feet. At the same time, a velociorhea springboarded off another's back and jumped up toward us.

Pink screamed as its open mouth shot closer to her feet. She jumped right onto Blue and clung to his shoulder, tucking her feet into her chest. Blue swore, wrapped an arm around her waist to anchor her to him, and materialized his longsword.

The monster's mouth snapped shut ten inches from where Pink's toes had been before falling back to the ground. Blue didn't even have time to strike before gravity took the monster away. He simply stared down at the group of velociorheas as they jumped over and over toward us, only to come up short every time.

"See?" I said. "Invisible barrier. All I want you to do is stand here and distract them for a while."

He slowly turned his dumbfounded face toward me. Then he looked shocked all over again. "You're invisible!"

I facepalmed and sighed hard. *I swear, I just went over that. Am I going to have to start all over again?*

CHAPTER 25

I know that we kill and dissect monsters for a living," Yellow muttered under her breath. "But this is one of the freakier, grosser things I've done in a while." She shifted a piece of raw steak in her hand and wiggled it in front of her. Rainwater collected on the meat and formed a fat red drop of liquid which dripped off a corner. It dropped to the ground below.

The four velociorheas on the ground went crazy, snapping at the air and climbing over each other to get higher. Try as they might, they couldn't reach the toes of the rainbow brigade, who all held pieces of steak I kept in my Items Bag.

After the first day when I found out an easy way to make the monsters leave long enough to get to the magic circle, I'd stocked up on raw meat. Gross, but effective. And yet another random thing added to my growing list stashed in my hip satchel.

I'd spread my mist out so that the east end covered where the mushroom was, and the west end, forty feet away from me, had Pink and her people distracting the monsters. The mist was thick above them, blocking the view from any persistent spectators, and thin below my helpers so the monsters had a perfect view of their temptation. Hopefully, forty feet and the smell of raw steak were enough to keep the monsters away from me.

Green wriggled his piece of meat, a delighted smile playing over his wide lips. "I think this is awesome. Does anyone have any string? Why don't we try fishing?"

Purple snorted and rolled her eyes.

Blue just sighed.

Orange hummed thoughtfully, then opened his hand. A thin leather cord appeared on his gauntlet. "I don't think this is long enough."

Yellow gasped. "Don't encourage him!"

Green's face lit up like a neon bulb. "Perfect!"

Pink, who adamantly refused to hold a bleeding piece of flesh, laughed behind her hand.

"Guys," Blue moaned.

I couldn't help but roll my eyes and grin at their antics. If nothing else, they were good for a laugh. And they were good at driving the monsters below them crazy. Still invisible, I went to the east end of the mist and looked around carefully. I couldn't feel any monsters around. Taking a hankie out of my Items Bag, I dropped to the ground right in front of the tree, landing noiselessly on soft moss that covered the ground and grew up the tree's trunk.

According to the picture of my surroundings that the mist put in my head, there was a mushroom which looked just like a cyan-agaric. I didn't wait to look inside. I simply covered my hand with the white handkerchief and reached in. As soon as I touched the mushroom, I transferred it into my Items Bag and jumped away from the tree. The retrieval took seconds, but as I pulled away, I felt a root wrap around my fingers.

[Task: Collect three Cyan-Agaric. (2/3)]

I didn't take the time to celebrate—the roots were already starting to pierce through the ground and reach toward me. Instead, I jumped up into my mist. Once I was safe, I let out the breath I was holding. This was the easiest time I had ever retrieved anything the System wanted me to get. Too bad my helpers didn't know I was actually screwing them over behind their backs.

I turned and glanced at them . . . and felt my jaw drop. Technically, the solid mist just stopped their bodies from falling; they could trip and fall flat on their faces, and it wouldn't budge. I really didn't think I needed to consider their items or weapons. If they lost anything . . . well, sucks for them. I mean, what responsible Hunter would lose their junk?

I just didn't think these guys would find the loophole and do . . . this.

Orange had a piece of meat tied up in a leather strip and was dangling it down below his feet. The velociorheas were going crazier than ever, screeching and clawing at the air. When one jumped, Orange would pull the meat up, just out of reach of its jaws. A wide grin covered his face as the rest of the team watched in stupefied awe and distress.

"Come on, baby," Green muttered as he drew a black arrow in his bow. "Wiggle it around," he ordered Orange, taking aim in the direction of the dangling meat.

Orange shook the meat, and a watery red drip fell off. One of the velociorheas jumped off the back of another and lunged at the meat.

Green released his arrow. It shot right through the solid mist and sank right down the monster's open mouth. "Got it!" He whooped and high-fived Orange.

The bird monster screamed and dropped to the ground, flapping its wings while trying to pull the arrow out of its mouth, but it didn't have the dexterity to. The rest of its pack paused and let out loud hissing growls at the colorful group of Hunters. There was nothing but murder in their eyes now. They didn't seem to care about the meat anymore; their focus was one hundred percent on the rainbow brigade.

Green and Orange couldn't care less; they were too busy celebrating while the rest of their team just sighed.

Honestly, it was a happy miracle they'd waited to shoot it until after I was done; since they couldn't see me, they didn't know when I would be finished, and I didn't want to have to deal with riled up velociorheas.

I walked over to them. "You should have gone for the kill shot," I said.

Pink shrieked and grabbed onto Blue's arm. The steak in his hand bumped into her arm. She cringed but didn't let go.

The rest of the team looked in my direction.

"I take it you're done?" Yellow asked, trying to figure out where I was.

I stopped ten feet from them. "Yes. Thank you for the help. It went ten times faster than I thought." I looked down at the velociorhea still trying to get the arrow out of its mouth. "And I got to see something I never thought I'd see. Good job."

Green beamed.

"Can I put this down, then?" Purple asked. "Because I think I'm a vegetarian today."

I didn't blame her. "Yeah. Just toss them. I'll get more later."

Immediately, Purple and Yellow flung the meat away. Blue simply dropped his where he stood, while Green and Orange picked a monster to throw it to like they were feeding ducks. Green actually had the gall to throw it at the injured monster, and was disappointed when it was too distracted dealing with the arrow in its mouth, and another monster ate the meat. A pack of wet wipes appeared in Purple's hand. She pulled one out and started to thoroughly clean her hand, filling the air with the sharp scent of sanitizer. She pulled more wipes out and handed them around to the rest of the team.

Green rubbed it over his hands, grinning. "I totally just found my new favorite sport. Monster fishing."

Yellow huffed. "Dumba—"

The sky dimmed and tinted red. In the already darkened rainforest, it looked just like the Gate Vale during the night. The dim, red light only lasted for a couple seconds before it was gone and the usual daylight was back.

Everyone froze, looking around. We all knew what that meant. A Portal Burst. But where? The trees were so thick, it was impossible to see through them. The Portal Burst could be on the other side of Gate Vale, or it could be fifty feet away, and I'd never know the difference.

"Get back to the transportation circle," Blue whispered. "Go!"

"How?" Pink asked.

The team paused and looked in my direction. Right now, they were stuck on my platform in the middle of the air.

The rest of the Hunters above were already fleeing. They filled the branch-like paths, bumping and pushing at each other. There might be high-leveled Hunters in the fleeing group, but Portal Bursts were dangerous for everyone below an S.

I grabbed Pink. She shrieked as I swung her onto my back, and she clutched onto me like a koala. "This way!" I hissed at them. "Be sure to stay within twenty feet of me." I didn't wait before I ran in the direction of the magic circle.

The team couldn't see me, and honestly, I didn't want to show who I was if I didn't absolutely have to, but they could see Pink; she should be enough of a marker that they didn't get lost. I ran at about eighty percent speed just to make sure they all kept up. It wasn't a problem for most of the team, and I was personally carrying the Healer Pink, but Orange wasn't a sprinter. Green and Blue had a hold of him, though, heavy armor and all, and were dragging him faster so he could keep up.

Even though we started running after the mass of Hunters in the trees, we quickly overtook them. We weren't restricted in the direction we could run based on what way the branches grew, nor did we have to tussle with the Hunter next to us for our spot on said branch.

But what was interesting was the fact that no one was getting attacked by monsters. All the plants like assassin vines and hell's pitfalls, which loved to poke and wrap around Hunters, were curled in on themselves, as if they were trying to diminish their presence on the trees. I only subconsciously noticed it and didn't think any further about it until I saw more than a dozen velociorheas sprinting like arrows right at us. Then right under us. They didn't even pause to look in our direction. A couple seconds later, more velociorheas ran by. Then more.

"Are they . . . " Pink started from my shoulder. "Are they running away?"

Running away from the direction we were headed to.

Suddenly, I was hit by a heavy pressure. It washed over me and settled in my chest, making it hard to breathe. I gasped and stumbled, and Pink shifted on my back and almost slipped off. She shrieked in my ear so loud that I winced and almost dropped her legs just so I could cover my ears. She responded by clutching my throat so tight that my air was cut off.

I had to let go of one of her thighs so I could reach up and loosen her arms enough to breathe. "Don't do that," I panted.

The rest of the team didn't fare much better. Yellow collapsed onto her stomach, and Purple dropped down on her side and grabbed her in a panic, as if she thought Yellow would fall. The men stumbled to a stop, just barely not stepping on the downed women. They hunched over and clutched their chests.

Just as fast as the pressure came, it let up, leaving an unnatural silence in its wake.

I set Pink on her feet and stood up, staring in the direction of the transportation circle. The same direction the pressure came from.

Damn, I had a bad feeling about this.

Pink stumbled over to Purple and gripped her arm. "What should we do?" Even though she whispered her question, in the weirdly still air, it was like she shouted with all her guts. She glanced at the monsters below, which continued to flee in the opposite direction.

"The transportation circle is over there," Blue said, his voice just as hushed. "It's the only way out of the rainforest."

From that pressure we just felt, there was a large chance that the Portal Burst was in the same direction as the transportation circle. Which meant there was a large possibility that there was a high-level monster ahead. We could go the other way like the rest of the monsters, but we were miles from other transportation circles located around Gate Vale, and I wouldn't be able to use them anyway because I didn't have a token for them. The only way I could get back to the Gate was by going forward.

I took a breath and glanced at my stats. My health was full, though I was a little winded from running for so long with baggage. I'd been maintaining Stealth for so long that I was down to two-thirds of my MP. "I'm going ahead," I spoke. "You can come with me, or I can take you back up to the trees with the rest of the Hunters."

The Hunters who had been left in our dust had caught up, but they faced the same dilemma as us: go forward and face whatever was ahead, backtrack through a dangerous rainforest in search of another transportation circle, or wait and hope a high-level monster didn't catch them like sitting ducks.

Blue frowned and looked at his team. "We don't have tokens for any other transportation circles around us," he said softly. "Do you want to stay here or go with the Josu Ghost?"

I frowned at them over my shoulder, even though they couldn't see my expression. "I'm not going to babysit you guys. I'm not all-powerful."

Yellow rested on her knees. She pressed her lips in a smile and gave a sharp nod. "That goes without saying."

"We're grateful you took us this far," Blue added.

I *tsked* and looked to the side. Good people. They were always the first to die. I knew that all too well.

"Well." Green stood straight and flashed a confident grin around his team. "Let's go! We got this!" Fearless energy oozed from his pores, infecting the air. His optimism was perfect for his team. The fear that had settled over them disappeared, replaced with energetic determination.

Yellow grinned big and jumped to her feet. "Don't cry if I deal more damage than you," she razzed Green as she waved her hands in the air, lightning crackling between her fingers.

"No way!" Green took out his bow and notched an arrow.

"If you shoot at me again, I'll get pissed," I warned him.

The whole team jumped and looked in my general direction.

Green gasped loudly. "When did I shoot . . . " he trailed off as if he finally remembered the cloud he'd shot a couple days ago. "Oh damn! That was you? My bad! I had no idea."

Blue winced. "Ah, our apologies."

I huffed a breath. "It's an occupational hazard, I guess." I mean, he really didn't know there was a person in the cloud. "And I think we're all squared away right now, anyway. Just don't shoot any more moving clouds, okay?"

Green bobbed his head.

I glanced over my shoulder. A few of the Hunters in the tree had turned back, heading anywhere but south where the circle was, but most of the

Hunters were cautiously moving forward, leaving behind a small few who apparently decided to stay.

I preferred to work alone, but against a big Boss, there was safety in numbers. As long as I didn't get hit with friendly fire, since I didn't plan on ending Stealth. I was at my best when I was invisible in my mist; there was no way I was going into a big fight with a disadvantage.

I glanced down at the ground. "I think it's safe to get down now. I haven't seen a velociorhea in a while, and I have a feeling the tree roots are hiding like the rest of the plant monsters." I looked at the cowering assassin vine forty feet above us. "I can't keep you in the air during the fight. Too much could happen. Instead of dropping you in the middle of battle, I'd rather put you down now."

The rainbow brigade indicated that they understood, and I made stairs down to the ground for them.

I gingerly stood on the moss and damp dirt, looking around vigilantly for any roots which wanted to prove me wrong. The ground was just as eerily still as the air. Even the constant dripping rain seemed quiet.

Just then, whooping sounds echoed in the trees around us, the high and low pitches ringing off each other in hair-raising resonance. I felt a presence move our way—no, *presences*. At least a hundred monsters were running in our direction, spilling over the tree branches, and swarming across the ground.

CHAPTER 26

Hunters dropped off the branches above, since there wasn't a lot of room for them to fight in. The teams spread out but still kept a sort of formation with each other. Hunters were, by nature, constantly battling against each other for the limited resources available to them, but against this many monsters, it wasn't about resources.

It was a battle of Hunters versus monsters. In instances like this, instinct pulled everyone together with one goal: to win.

Stronger teams stepped forward while weaker teams took the back row, as similar as they could to a Gate Surge formation. There wasn't a designated leader, but we all knew enough to know what to do.

Unfortunately, we were outnumbered.

The whooping sounds grew louder as the monsters got closer.

A couple mages—Yellow included—threw their hands in the air and sent out emergency flares to call for backup. The colorful magic shot up, winding through the branches. Just before it touched the thick layer of leaves which covered the rainforest and dimmed the light, the magic hit an invisible barrier and exploded prematurely.

My lips parted in shock. How was there a barrier there? That shouldn't be.

The mages gasped. Several of them stubbornly sent more emergency flares up, but none of them got through.

"What?" Yellow gasped, looking at her hand like it didn't belong to her. "Where did that barrier come from?"

"If flares can't get through," Purple asked quietly, "do you think the transportation portal still works?"

A chill settled down my back. If that was the case, there was no backup coming even if we could get an emergency flare out.

I Mirrored my kindjal. "The barrier is probably connected to the Portal Burst."

Kesstel said that each world fragment had a Boss. The barrier was probably connected to the Boss of the world fragment on the other side of the Portal Burst. If the barrier was ongoing, that most likely meant the portal had opened but hadn't shut yet.

Just like with the red orcs that kidnapped me months ago.

My fingers tightened around the handles of my swords. "The barrier will disappear when the portal closes." *Or the Boss inside is dead. The S-ranked Boss.*

I took a breath. For some reason, I wasn't as scared as I thought I'd be. Maybe it was because I was stronger. Or maybe because I truly understood what was going on. Either way, there was no way out but going forward.

I walked to the side, away from the rainbow brigade, and commanded my mist to draw back and hover only ten feet around me. I didn't want to disadvantage anyone else. Turning my head, I spoke over my shoulder. "You should stay out of my mist now. It's about to get really thick."

True to my word, the water vapor increased as I pulled in the rain that was ever falling around me. It was so thick, a normal person wouldn't be able to see their hands in front of their face.

Perfect.

"Good luck," I told them.

Monsters swarmed around the thick trees in front of us, finally giving an image that went with the horrible whooping echoing in the air. C-ranked goblins—ugly with large, pointed noses and narrowed yellow eyes—clambered over each other as they darted at the Hunters. Tattered clothes revealed more of their dull gray skin than it covered, but they each carried a weapon, be it a knife or a short sickle.

Let's do this.

I lunged forward toward the east side of the swarm and attacked. Something about my mist disoriented the goblins; I don't think it was just because of the thickness, but as soon as the vapor touched them, they all seemed to jar backward and pause before resuming being their creepy, violent selves. I took advantage of that as much as I could, mowing down goblin after goblin.

I didn't have a team to back me up, but the monsters didn't voluntarily go in my mist, either. It helped to prevent me from getting swarmed, and I was able to deal with the waist-high creatures one or two at a time before going to the next. But that didn't mean that I got away scot-free. Each battle took a toll on my HP, and my MP consistently decreased.

The goblins seemed endless. As soon as one disappeared under my blade or died in front of another Hunter, another goblin took its place.

[You have Leveled Up!]

The goblin stuck on my blade vanished before it could finish its squeal of pain. Breathing heavily, I reached out and grabbed its drop item. Around me, other Hunters were finishing their kills, adding the carcasses to piles that littered the black blood-soaked ground. Right now, there was a little lull in the fighting, but instinctively, I knew this wasn't the end. Every monster we had faced was ranked C. The Boss still hadn't appeared yet.

When the last creature died, nobody celebrated. There was simply a sigh of relief as teams started tending to their people. Injured Hunters sat or lay on the ground, being treated by the healers in their groups. The Hunters who didn't make it to a healer in time were taken away from the piles of goblins, their bodies laid in a row so their companions could bid them goodbye.

As exhausted as I was, I didn't sit down—it was just too gross. Instead, I opened my System menu and assigned the bonus stat points I got. Afterward, I stared at my depleted HP and MP numbers and glanced southward toward the location of the transportation circle. The heavy presence that shook everyone earlier was still there; I simply didn't have enough time to wait for Regen to work—I needed a healer now.

My fist thumped on my thigh as I thought and looked toward the rainbow brigade not far from me. They had survived, but all of them showed wear and tear. Yellow was currently plopped on the ground, breathing hard, while Green squatted next to her, talking low. Purple and Orange, apparently already healed, were as disheveled looking as the rest. No matter who it was, there were scratches and cuts on their armor, robes, or under armor. Purple's ponytail had fallen out, her black and deep purple hair spilling down her back.

Pink's hand hovered over Blue's chest, her golden magic healing him. Once it stopped glowing, she stood back with a cute smile.

I looked around to make sure no one was paying attention to me, canceled Stealth, then crept out of my mist and away from the crowd. I commanded the fog to stay put to give the illusion I was still in it as I walked over to the rainbow brigade.

They looked over and focused on me.

Green was the first to react. "Hey, you're that girl from a couple days ago."

I gave them a small smile. "I got separated from my team again. They turned back"—I motioned to the branches overhead—"but I didn't have another transportation token, so . . . " Before they could think too much about my lie, I got to the main point. "I'd like to exchange information for being healed." I glanced specifically at Blue and Pink.

If this was a normal day, I could simply ask to be healed. But we were facing another battle, with no way of knowing when it would end. As a teammate, Pink was obligated to ensure her team was healed. In fact, there had been cases, although rare, of healers being left behind and discarded in the Gate because they didn't have enough MP to fulfill their roles. I understood this team enough to know that Pink wouldn't be abandoned, but it was still poor form for me to ask for something without an exchange. I mean, the MP she'd use to heal me could mean life or death for her teammates.

Blue frowned at me. "How do you know we want your information?"

I hooked my fingers on the belt around my hips. "You're looking for a cyan-agaric, aren't you?" I ignored the sudden sharpness in the team's expressions and kept talking. "Since you're still here, I assume you haven't found one yet. The one for today is already long gone." I mean, it'd already disappeared from inside my Items Bag, and I had no idea where the System put things after removing them or how to get it back. "I'll exchange information on how to find one for getting healed." I paused. "Or will that not be helpful to you?"

Yellow hissed low. "You aren't trying to steal our post, are you? We already signed the contract with Dr. E. Don't even think about it."

I shook my head. "Believe me, the reason why I know about them has nothing to do with a post." I shifted my weight to my right hip. "Do we have a deal or not?" Out of the Hunters here, this was the group most likely to heal me. And the only ones I had something to offer. If they didn't take it, I'd be in trouble.

"Hey." A Hunter in expensive, full armor approached us from the right. "We're going to make a break for the transportation circle. Who knows how long it will take for the next wave of monsters to attack. We all agree that we should make a move before another wave comes. Or the velociorheas return."

The thought of the bird monsters coming back left a chill in the air. The goblins we'd killed were C ranked, technically the same rank as the velociorheas. The difference was, there was no teamwork or strategy in the goblins' attacks, so they were easier to kill. However, with the velociorheas, what made them so hard to deal with and almost elevated them up higher than their ranks was their flawless teamwork and strategy.

The Hunter focused on Blue. "If you're going to join us, we're heading out now." He jerked his thumb over his shoulder to the Hunters starting to get up. With that, he walked away.

I turned to the rainbow brigade. "So?"

Blue nodded and motioned to Pink. "There's safety in numbers. For everyone." He looked at me specifically. "We gotta go."

Pink walked over to me and touched my shoulder. I didn't know a lot about magic—honestly, until a couple months ago, it was all a bunch of hocus pocus—but I was becoming sensitive enough to tell that Pink's magic, while very effective, was just as soft and fluttery as she came across as.

Cute.

"Thank you," I said to her, then focused on Blue. "The cyan-agarics grow in the trees."

He nodded his head. "We know that."

The corner of my mouth hooked up. "But I don't think you understand; they grow in the *base* of trees." I could tell by the way they stiffened that this was news to them. I looked around until I saw what I wanted and pointed to a tree ten feet away. "You see there? That crevice in the trunk? They grow in places like that. At the bottom of trees, in a dark hole. You also have to be careful of roots. They suck blood and are very fast. I've nearly been caught by them every time." I had a feeling that the reason they weren't bothering us right now was because of the Portal Burst. I glanced at Green. "If it wasn't for your help the other day, that might have been the end of me."

We were still competitors when it came to finding the mushrooms, but I couldn't bring myself to hate them. I also had confidence that I would get another one before they did, since I had skills and abilities they didn't have.

My information startled and worried them.

Blue took a deep breath and nodded slowly. "I understand. Thank you for the information."

My HP bar hit full, and Pink stepped back. "All better."

I smiled at her. "Thank you."

She frowned and tilted her head to the side. Her finger tapped on her lower lip like she was thinking. "Your voice sounds really familiar."

I bet it did. But they didn't need to know why. I waved at them. "Thanks again, and good luck."

With that, I turned and followed the Hunters who were starting to creep through the rainforest. Once I was far enough away, I released my mist and ignored the shock of the people around me when they found it was empty inside.

CHAPTER 27

W e're almost there," a Hunter whispered to her weakened team-mate. "We should be able to see the transportation circle any time now."

I glanced at her and the shivering woman at her side. It was true; we were almost at the location of the transportation circle. It was also true that the closer we got, the heavier the pressure in the air became. Right now, it felt like I was walking through waist-deep water. The already thick air was hard to draw into my lungs, and my knees were getting more and more shaky. Not good for a fight.

From the looks of it, I wasn't the only one affected.

I gripped my kindjal and focused forward, keeping my back straight and head high. A pale purple glow emitted from between thick tree trunks and hovered above the mossy ground. Such a bright color seemed out of place in this damp and gloomy place—felt so wrong mingling with the smell of decomposition and blood. And yet, relief pumped through my veins. If the magic was still there, it meant the transportation circle was still working.

Low, excitable chatter spread between teams as they saw the purple magic circle. A female Hunter in the treetops broke out into a run, full-on sprinting across the branches to the exit. It was like a dam burst as the Hunters in the trees and on the ground reacted, and suddenly, there was a race to get there first and get out of the Josu Rainforest.

"Wait!" I gasped. "You don't know what's ahead!" How could they be so stupid?

I wasn't the only one trying to hold people back. Team leaders and other Hunters tried to catch their companions, but hysteria and fear drove the crowd forward. Who wouldn't want to get out of here as soon as possible?

With nothing else to do, I caught up with the rest of the Hunters, the six members of the rainbow brigade not far behind me.

Hunters on the ground reached the clearing around the transportation circle first, but as soon as they entered, they skidded to a stop and brandished their weapons toward the east. The few Hunters in the trees above didn't pause at all. The first one, a woman in light armor, jumped off the branch, flying thirty feet through the air and arching down to the purple circle. Another woman and a man were quick on her heels.

A swarm of goblins came from the east, whooping and growling. They spilled over the ground, their short, ugly bodies filling up every inch of space in the clearing.

The woman landed in the transportation circle, the magic flashing bright purple, and she shot through the air. Less than a second later, her blurred figure smashed against the barrier covering the rainforest. The barrier rippled, a pale opalescent wave expanding from the point of impact before it smoothed out to an invisible shell again.

The Hunter was thrown from the transportation arch. I didn't know if she was knocked unconscious or if she died from the collision, but she didn't scream as she landed in the middle of the goblins. Either way, from the way they pounced on her with their knives, she wouldn't survive the next couple seconds.

The woman and man who had followed tried to backtrack, but they were already in the air, landing in the small area behind the protective barrier the Hunter's Association had put around the circle. Only, they were stuck. They couldn't use the transportation circle, and there were over a hundred goblins between them and the rest of the Hunters. But that was their problem.

I had my own worries.

On the east side of the clearing was a black arch about fifteen feet tall. Goblins spilled out of the portal, one after another, each one looking as bloodthirsty as the last.

I turned and launched an attack on the goblins that came my way. I didn't have my mist or Stealth to help me this time, but I didn't want to rely too heavily on them, anyway. Instead, I twisted and slashed with my kindjals, hacking the little monsters to pieces. The smell of blood filled the air as bodies covered the ground.

Another level later, I was breathing hard as I maneuvered to the back of the battle. Unlike the first wave of monsters, there was no end to these goblins. Every time one died, another one was there to take its place. It was an endless barrage with endless energy. As for myself, I was getting tired, and my HP was getting low again.

I hurried to a healer in the back. "Please heal me?" I panted.

He scowled at me. "I only have enough to help my people. Go find your healer." He waved me away with the back of his hand and turned to a man who stumbled toward him covered in blood.

What healer? As frustrated as I was, I couldn't force him to heal me. My hands fisted as I looked over the heads to the battle at the black arch. Was there going to be an end to this? We couldn't do anything about the barrier, but there wasn't enough strength to take on the Boss inside the portal.

I could run and hide like some of the other Hunters who'd fled the battle, true. But I refused to be labeled a coward.

A small hand rested on my back.

I stiffened and looked over my shoulder.

Pink smiled softly at me as her hand started to glow, her sweet magic soothing away the aches and pain in my body as my HP filled back up.

Purple glanced at the healer and frowned at me but didn't comment as she hacked another goblin in half with her saber.

I smiled at Pink. "I don't know how I'm going to pay you this time."

She smiled. "I think you might have already paid me back."

Did that mean she'd finally put my voice together with the woman who'd saved her from the velociorheas? But I doubted they paid attention to me as early as when I started paying attention to them.

I opened my mouth to comment but paused as goose bumps spread over my body. I lunged at Pink and dragged her to the ground, then threw myself over her.

She yelped and wiggled. "What are you doing? What's happening?"

"Get down!" I yelled to her shocked team members.

The portal on the other side of the clearing pulsed, growing nearly twice its size. The pressure of it rippled out, flattening anything taller than three feet. Hunters yelled and screamed as they were grounded. Even the goblins that were jumping up to attack dropped with hard thuds. Any magic that was activated fizzled out under the power surge.

The goblins that weren't affected went crazy on the Hunters who were suddenly brought down to their level. The Hunters fought back hard, struggling to their feet under the relentless stabs of the monster's daggers.

I jumped to my feet and swung out, slicing at a goblin as it stabbed toward the downed Green. The goblin squealed as I took off its arm, and a second later, the high-pitched sound was cut off when Green thrust an arrow into the monster's trachea, no bow needed.

"Get up!" Another warning shiver went down my spine. "No! Get down!" I yelled, pushing Pink back down. "Sorry," I muttered.

Her response was muffled by a second power surge from the portal. This time, anything taller than two feet was taken down. Hunters were knocked back yet again, and even most of the goblins were flattened. Those who were already on the ground but higher than the two feet mark were dragged back across the moist ground several feet.

I lifted my head and focused on the black portal. Barely visible through the opaque darkness was a pale color, so muted that I couldn't even clearly make out what it should be. Then the color became more defined—a dull, pale green shade—as a shape took form in the depths of the portal. My eyes widened. Something mostly humanoid was walking out.

No, two somethings.

A second later, two six-foot-tall monsters stepped out of the portal, a layered red loincloth hanging on their bodies. They were just as ugly as the goblins all around me. The biggest difference, besides the height and lean muscles on their arms and legs, was that instead of a flattened, pig-like face, their faces had more of a boar-like snout, complete with tusks. One held a saber in its hand, and the other held a wicked-looking boar spear. Over their heads was a red title bar: [**Goblin Lord Lv75**].

My stomach sank. It wasn't an S-ranked monster—not the portal Boss at all—so even if we killed them, the barrier would remain, and we wouldn't be able to get away. The other problem was, they were also stronger than every Hunter here. If we teamed up and worked together on the goblin lords, it wouldn't be such an issue, but there were still dozens and dozens of goblins around us. And our numbers were getting smaller.

I scowled and *tsked* my tongue. My attacks would probably feel like mosquito bites to the goblin lords, but I might be able to help with backup. I wasn't going to run; I couldn't escape as long as the barrier was up. Sooner or later, I was going to die, whether it be from goblins or when night came.

The goblin lords lifted their snouts in the air and let out bellowing howls. The goblins responded with eerie whoops and howls as they jumped to their feet and started to attack the Hunters again, who reacted with their own moves, and another battle broke out.

Some of the stronger Hunters lunged forward at the goblin lords, working together to take them down. The large monsters looked stupid, but they were fast. Faster than most of the Hunters trying to kill them.

I cast Stealth and Mist at the same time. Pink yelped as the rest of her team gasped when I suddenly disappeared. I Feather Stepped to the goblin lords, not ashamed at all that I was stepping on Hunters to do it. My touch was so light that most of them didn't even really notice what I did. What they *did* notice was the light cloud that whooshed over their heads, and how as soon as I got close, the goblins reacted with fear, squealing and flinching away. So if anything, any inconvenience I gave the Hunter by stepping on them was made up with an easy kill when the monsters dropped their defenses.

As I neared the fight with the goblin lords, I lightened my Mist until the water particles were simply light wisps which rippled and flowed together. Easy to see through, but still there. I landed behind a mage dressed in navy blue robes with a gold-and-white magic stone chain around her waist.

My mist settled over the battle, causing the smaller goblins to flee the area. The goblin lords gave startled, animalistic noises and snorted, obviously bothered by the mist, but the Hunters didn't change a thing. Since most of them came into this rainforest to find the Josu Ghost and recruit her, they knew what my mist was—knew I was there to back them up.

The mage in front of me launched a thick icicle at the spear-holding goblin lord. At the same time, I created a solid mist barrier around its legs. It jerked in agitation and instantly broke my block, but was too distracted to fully dodge the ice. The attack sank right into the monster's left side.

Alright, that worked. From there, I kept watch. Every time the goblin lords moved, whether it was to attack or defend, I would try to lock a block of solid mist around their limbs. They were so much higher level than me that it only deterred them for a second before they broke the barrier. If it was me directly fighting them, that time wouldn't make a difference because I wasn't able to move as fast as them. But for the high-leveled Hunters dodging their attacks or trying to attack themselves, that second was the difference between a hit or a miss. Slowly, instead of the goblin lords having the upper hand, the battle was brought to a deadlock, neither side winning over the other.

At first, all the barriers I made weren't a big deal. But after a while, the mental strain started to get to me. A dull ache formed in my head and grew sharper as the minutes passed. My MP was also starting to drop into the red from holding Stealth, constantly replacing the mist that evaporated in the fight around me, and constantly making the solid mist blocks around the monsters.

A familiar shiver went down my back, and I gasped. "Get down!" I yelled as loud as I could.

Half a dozen Hunters dropped, while the other half ignored me.

Another power surge pulsed from the portal. The goblin lords were completely unaffected, but everyone else who was standing was knocked back. The closer the Hunter was to the portal, the farther they were thrown. I gritted my teeth through my pounding headache and formed solid barriers to catch some of the Hunters in the air. I couldn't say that any of them had graceful landings, since they couldn't even see what they were landing on, but it kept them from falling into the swarm of goblins the rest of the Hunters were trying to kill off.

A third goblin lord, this one holding a giant axe, walked out of the portal. It howled into the air, the sound ear-piercing.

I moaned and covered my ears, trying to block the noise from entering my already throbbing head. Panting, I looked up at the trio of goblin lords . . . and felt the hair rise on the back of my neck.

The axe-wielding goblin lord was staring straight at me. Even though Stealth was still activated, there was no question it was looking at my face. It hoisted its axe high and charged.

CRACK!

CHAPTER 28

—

CRACK!

The goblin lord stumbled to a stop ten feet from me, as if the cracking sound had physically affected it. It lowered the giant war axe and turned its body to look for the source of the sound.

I couldn't resist looking, too.

I gasped, the small sound lost when the rest of the Hunters cheered.

Kesstel stood in full shining armor, a fracture webbing out in the barrier between him and the Josu Rainforest. It was the first time I'd seen him in full armor, and the first time I got to see the crest depicted on his left breast with tiny royal-blue magic stones. It showed a howling wolf and a rose behind an extravagant-looking *N* looped with a crown. Looking at the old-fashioned design, I couldn't help but wonder if it was his family's actual crest.

A frown marred his apathetic face as he looked at me through the barrier.

A self-mocking smile pulled at my mouth when our eyes met. *Yet another being my Stealth doesn't affect.*

The goblin lord roared and hoisted its axe in the air, aiming at me.

Kesstel thrust his palm out and hit the barrier again. The crack in front of him splintered out at a rapid speed until suddenly, the entire wall shattered and exploded into white glitter which faded away within seconds.

The goblin lords howled and collapsed to the ground as if in pain.

Kesstel walked into the rainforest, not bothered at all by the drizzle that fell on his armor and dripped off the tip of his two-toned bastard sword, as his aura spread out, thick as wool. The goblin lords growled, their black eyes narrowed on Kesstel, but not one of them moved off the ground. The goblins curled into balls, whimpering and clutching their heads.

The Hunters weren't nearly as affected as the monsters, although some of their knees gave out, making their companions hold them up. Other Hunters took advantage of Kesstel's entrance and started killing the monsters around them. The goblins didn't even fight back.

I gasped, Kesstel's pressure not helping my headache at all, but still, I struggled to my feet. Somewhat dizzy, I walked over to Kesstel, who came toward me looking like the duke he was. It had been so long since I'd seen him like this, stone-faced and apathetic, that it was a little weird. And funny. What wasn't funny was how he so casually killed the goblin lords with a dismissive flick of his wrist. His stride didn't even pause as he beheaded them.

Kesstel reached out for me, and the kindjal disappeared from my right hand as I reached back. As soon as he touched me, the pressure from his aura vanished; I sighed as the lightheadedness eased up enough to see straight. My knees threatened to give out, so I braced my arm on his bent one while he cupped my elbow.

"Are you okay?" He looked at me.

I nodded. "Mentally strained, but I'll be okay after some rest."

A Hunter still up in the air on one of my mist blocks looked at his teammate. "Who is he talking to?" he whispered, but the area was so quiet, it was impossible not to hear.

The other man shrugged.

I couldn't help but give a tired smile. "You might be labeled as crazy, talking to an invisible person."

Kesstel shrugged. "Like I've ever cared what anyone thought." He looked over to the Hunters, chin high and in obvious command. "Evacuate through the transportation circle. Now. The Hunter's Association is waiting on the other side. Assist the injured; leave the dead."

Right, the magic circle was working again now that the barrier was broken.

Hunters rushed forward, some trying to push through the crowd, but the stronger Hunters and group leaders wrestled everyone into order. Others didn't bother lining up at all, too busy taking revenge on the goblins incapacitated on the ground. Since it wasn't needed anymore, I dissolved my mist, and the Hunters still in the air dropped to the ground with a clatter.

"Why aren't they fighting back?" I asked Kesstel quietly.

"They can't," he said simply. There had to be more to it, but he either didn't want to tell me or wasn't going to talk about it with other people here. He glanced at the cowering goblins, disdain wrinkling his face. A blue glow flashed in his eyes before it was gone.

The goblins huddled into even tighter balls.

I stared up at Kesstel. There was something odd about that light. Sometimes, when a strong mage did a powerful spell, their eyes would glow. Kesstel had strong magic, and it wasn't my first time seeing his eyes light up, but there was something . . . sinister about that flash of light. It was an emotion I'd never seen on his face before.

"Your eyes," I whispered. "Why—"

"Wait!" a familiar voice—Pink's voice—rang out. "What about the Josu Ghost?"

I turned my head and found that Pink was staring right at me. Even though not all the goblins were dead, the people in charge were urging their people to line up to leave, so there weren't many Hunters left.

Purple's hand was on her shoulder. "Hey, we gotta go."

Pink glanced at Purple then shook her head. "But . . . " She looked in my direction. "Aren't you going to leave?" she called, focusing on where Kesstel's hand cupped my elbow. She couldn't see me, but she could see where Kesstel held me. "You are there, aren't you, Josu Ghost?"

The rest of her team turned in our direction, Green and Yellow looking flat-out flabbergasted.

Kesstel shot me a look. His face was still expressionless, but there was a glint of teasing mockery in his blue eyes. *Lord Jerkface.*

I pursed my lips, suddenly hating my title.

I guess it was better than others I could pick up.

"I'm okay," I called back to Pink. "I'm going to stay here. Take care." I could leave, but since Kesstel was here, what did it matter? *Nothing can hurt me*, I thought, glancing at the flattened monsters.

Green gasped. "She really is over there."

Yellow turned to Pink. "How did you know?"

Pink bit her lip and smoothed her battle-crazy hair behind her ear. "Who else do you know who can turn invisible?"

Blue hurried his people ahead. "It's almost our turn. Let's go." When Pink looked up at him, he put a hand on her shoulder and guided her over. "She's with an S. What harm is going to come to her?" This time, Pink didn't resist.

Several minutes later, all the Hunters were gone.

I canceled my Stealth and bent over, tired. "Should I leave, too?" I asked. Now that everyone was gone, it wouldn't be that out of place if a little E came out of the transportation circle.

I couldn't help but look around. This was the first time I'd touched the Josu Rainforest's ground and been safe. It was weird seeing everything from this vantage point. My eyes landed on the fiftyish goblins still cowering on the ground amidst their own dead.

"Why are they like that?" I glanced at Kesstel. "It's because of you. But I've never seen a monster act like that around a Hunter, no matter what the strength difference was." Even an E monster would try to kill an S Hunter, although they normally would try to run first. But to just flop down and die? This was a first.

Kesstel pursed his lips, more and more emotion spreading over his face. "It's because I told them not to move. So they can't move." He left it at that and turned toward the portal. "If you would stay, I would appreciate it." He motioned to the black arch. "I want to see what's on the other side, but I can't say that I want someone to stumble onto me going in and out."

What a roundabout way to ask me to use my mist.

I nodded. "Sure thing." Then I frowned at the portal. I thought, after my trauma, I'd be more scared of the sight. But when the goblins were attacking, I was too busy fighting to think about my past. And with Kesstel here, being scared was one of the last things I felt around him. "What do you think is on the other side? Do you think it's a way to the parasite planet?"

Kesstel shrugged. "I hope so. But I doubt it. Either way, I'm going to kill the Boss inside so the portal collapses."

My heart jumped to my throat. "Isn't that dangerous? What if you get lost in there? Or end up somewhere else?"

"That's possible." He didn't give any more explanations as he looked out the tree line and across the neighboring area to the mountains which surrounded Gate Vale. From this distance, the permanent portals attached to the valley weren't visible, but that didn't change the fact that they were there.

I thumped my fist nervously on my thigh. "What if the Boss kills you?"

Kesstel smirked. "It can try. It's not even strong enough to exit its own portal; I'd like to see what it can do to me." He looked down at me. "Any more questions?"

Wow, confident, wasn't he? Then again, I guess he had reason to be.

I shook my head.

Kesstel nodded. With a flick of his wrist, a barrier appeared around the whole battlefield and portal. Then he turned to the goblins still quivering on the ground and lifted his sword.

"Wait!" I gasped, reaching out to stop him.

He paused and looked at me.

I knew what he was doing. He was going to get rid of the monsters so I was safe. It was a nice thought, but . . . I turned toward the goblins. All I could see were EXP points just lying there for the taking.

I looked up at Kesstel. "Can I kill them? It'll take me a while."

He frowned. "There's a lot of them."

"I'll be fast." I hoped that Kesstel keeping them pinned didn't count as helping and I would lose out on the EXP. If that was the case, me killing them by myself was pointless.

I cast Mist, which drained my MP down to less than ten percent, and filled up Kesstel's barrier with fog. Under the protection of my mist, I walked over to the closest goblin. It felt a little wrong to just stand over it and stab, I'd admit. I'd never been able to kill a monster this easily before. But the goblin didn't move as I thrust my kindjal into its stomach where the energy crystal was, and it disappeared.

[+105 EXP]

A soft smile touched my lips, and I moved on to the next body. Gaining easy EXP caused any tiredness to instantly vanish, and the thought of even more EXP drove me forward. Without the monsters fighting back, even though they were level thirty to thirty-five, most of them were one-hit kills.

[You have Leveled Up!]
[You have Leveled Up!]
[You have Leveled Up!]

I couldn't help but grin when the last goblin vanished. I stood up, put away my kindjal, and clapped the nonexistent dust off my hands.

"Satisfied?" Kesstel asked from his location by the Portal Burst. He stared at me, obviously able to see through the water vapor.

I grinned and nearly skipped back to him. Three levels for less than an hour's work, what a haul.

Next to Kesstel was a carcass of a goblin lord. I paused by it and retrieved my kindjal. "Did you want this one?" I motioned to it with my blade.

Kesstel waved a hand in dismissal. "No."

I nodded, found the spot where the energy crystal faintly glowed in its chest, and stabbed down. It took three more tries to get through the monster's tough body to the crystal, but I finally hit it, and the carcass vanished. I didn't get any EXP or drop items for it, but I didn't want the goblin lord's energy crystal to get into Earth. I paused and looked over the battlefield. There were hundreds of monster carcasses—hundreds of dangerous crystals.

"So, that's how you get stronger?" Kesstel asked, drawing my attention. A towel appeared in his hand, and he held it out to me. "By killing monsters?"

I took the towel and found it damp. Content, I started to clean off my face and hands. "How can you tell?"

"I could feel it every time you got stronger." His gaze fell to the short sword in my hand. "Energy from the crystals was pulled into your sword, and a portion of it was transferred to you." Kesstel tapped his chin, thinking. "But the energy that made you stronger wasn't like the tainted energy inside the crystals. It was . . . pure."

My eyes widened, and I looked down at the kindjal. The dim light from the sun coming from the forest edge to my right caused the crystal-and-steel blade to gleam. That's what it was doing? It was transferring the energy to me and enabling me to get stronger?

I bit my lip and fidgeted with the towel. "It's a little more complicated than that. But . . . I can't tell you about it. I'm sorry." I took a breath and peeked up at him. "What about when I vanish a carcass?" I asked, motioning to where the goblin lords used to be. "What happens to the energy then?"

"The tainted energy simply goes into the sword. Nothing else," Kesstel explained.

It was frustrating how I had to settle for third-party explanations about what was truly going on with my own body. But the System didn't seem to be answering anything lately. I wished there was someone I could talk to.

I couldn't help but glance at the portal.

He followed my gaze. "There should be another two hours before any more Hunters come here, since I told them I wanted time. The barrier will cover the whole battlefield. I'd appreciate it if you kept your mist going until then. If you want to rest, go ahead. If you want to take care of the carcasses, be my guest." He took the dirty towel back and put it away in his Items Bag.

I couldn't take my eyes off the portal. I became a Warrior of Mist by going into a portal months ago . . . "What if there are more people like me in another portal? Warriors of Mist, I mean."

Kesstel was quiet for a second. "There aren't." There was a solid assurance in his soft voice.

I blinked and looked up in surprise. "Why not?"

His mouth opened, and he paused before saying, "Because I personally made sure they were all extinct." He stared into my shocked face. He reached out and gently slid his fingers through the hair falling from my ponytail. "I never thought that so many years later, another one would appear before me. And I'd let her live."

Without waiting for me to respond, he walked into the portal without a backward glance.

Jynn Devhro

Rank C   **Level** 32

EXP to Next Level 2194

HP 926/926   **Stat Points** 0

MP 70/413

Strength 63 (+20)   **Agility** 56

Magic 53   **Perception** 56

Constitution 56 (+20)   **Intelligence** 49

Skills	**Abilities**
Throw	Mist (Improved) (40 ft)
Critical Hit	Feather Step
Quick Hit	Regen (Limited)
Mirror	Stealth (Limited)
High Jump	

W hat's that supposed to mean?" I yelled, glaring at the portal that Kesstel had disappeared through. "You can't just say something like that and leave! You—you . . . *jerkface!*" My voice echoed around the empty rainforest, making it even clearer that I was alone with a bunch of corpses and surrounded by millions of trees.

When I first became a Warrior of Mist, the System told me I was the only one left. I believed it, since the System hadn't ever led me astray before. But somewhere inside, I always hoped there was another one like me. Maybe someone, somewhere, just randomly turned into one like I did.

That tiny, neglected hope had been thoroughly smashed by Kesstel's words. I mean, both he and the System couldn't be wrong, right? Especially if Kesstel was the one who'd . . . personally killed them all.

I dropped my face into my hands and moaned. Why would he kill them all? As uncaring as Kesstel was, he wasn't the kind to move against a group of people without cause. He was too apathetic for that.

My lips curled up in a bitter smile as I lowered my hands. "Well, that explains why I kept feeling like he was going to kill me the first couple times we met. I'm glad we got over that hurdle."

Unfortunately, it didn't give me peace of mind now. The only person who could explain anything was on the other side of the portal entrance right now. As frustrated as I was, I wasn't dumb enough to go charging inside just to chew out a man who was fighting a Boss.

But I could take my frustration out another way.

Turning around, I faced the monster corpses that covered the damp ground. Black blood soaked into the soil and turned the moss on the ground as dark as the dirt. The smell of death mixed with the natural scent of decay the Josu Rainforest had and elevated the repugnant stench to a new level. At least the light rain dulled the smell so it wasn't overpowering.

I walked forward and started to stab monster carcasses, making them disappear. I didn't get any EXP or drop items from them, but according to Kesstel, when I destroyed an energy crystal, the energy was drawn into my blade. Maybe if I destroyed enough of them my kindjal would upgrade again.

That, and I didn't want the velociorheas to eat the crystals and get stronger. They were hard enough to kill as it was. At least I didn't have to deal with them right now. I didn't know if it was the portal or Kesstel's barrier around me, but I couldn't see, feel, or hear any living monsters at all.

Slowly, I made my way through the field, clearing away the bodies. It wouldn't surprise me if the Hunter's Association sent people to clean this up. Maybe even divide up the loot between the Hunters who were involved in the fight, but I didn't plan on giving them the chance. I had two hours; hopefully, that was enough time to destroy all the crystals.

Unfortunately, it wasn't just dead monsters in this pile of bodies. I found several dozen Hunter corpses hiding among the carcasses. I wasn't a ceremonious person, nor was I religious. But I wasn't inhuman enough to leave them twisted together with goblin guts. Each Hunter was a mess of stab wounds and blood, but I still pulled them to the side and lined them up in rows like in the first battle. There wasn't much else I could do. They were already dead, so it was just a matter of time before someone came to collect the bodies—if their family members were lucky. Most Hunters who died in the Gate didn't even have the privilege of retrieval and a proper burial.

An hour and half later, I was huffing and puffing as I added another corpse to the growing line, sighing as I stood up. With the back of my hand, I rubbed my bangs out of my face and looked at my progress. About ninety percent of the battlefield was cleaned up. I didn't know how much energy I'd collected for my kindjal, since there was no way to calculate it, but it was a lot.

My gaze swept over the clearing and zeroed in on the portal's black arch. I would have thought that Kesstel would be back by now. Maybe it was a good thing he was gone so long. Most of my anger had been released on the goblin bodies. I was still frustrated and confused, but at least I was calm enough to have a rational conversation.

My lips pursed to the side, and I walked back to continue cleaning.

A tingle went down my spine, just like during the battle. Instantly, I dropped to the ground. A second later, a large, powerful pulse blew out of the portal.

I gasped and covered my head. The power swept right over my hands, so close that all the hairs stood up on my arms, but luckily, I was low enough to avoid getting hurt.

The trees groaned as the power hit them. Some, even though they were bigger around than I was tall, were knocked to the side, their tangled branches the only thing keeping them standing. Other smaller trees were ripped right out of the ground, crashing down and raining pieces of wood with them.

After the pulse was gone, I looked up toward the portal. What was happening in there? What about Kesstel?

My eyes widened—not because I felt another pulse coming but because the portal was starting to warp. The smooth curve of the black arch wrinkled and bent. As if it were alive and fighting against an internal parasite, the portal twisted and stretched until it could barely be called an arch anymore.

"What?" I gasped, jumping to my feet.

Kesstel was still in there!

I ran toward the portal. Honestly, I didn't know what I was going to do. I mean, there wasn't anything I *could* do. But I wanted to help him. I needed to help Kesstel. Somehow.

Ten feet from the collapsing arch, another pulse burst out of it, knocking me off my feet. I tumbled head over heels before I stopped painfully on the ground. Gasping, I pushed up and looked toward the portal.

It was gone.

Like, *gone* gone. If it wasn't for the blast mark on the ground from the last explosion, it would be like the portal never existed.

At the same time, I felt the barrier that Kesstel had set up vanish like a popped bubble.

"Kesstel?" I gasped, struggling to my feet. "Kesstel!" I looked around, using both my eyes and the enhanced vision that the mist provided. I could see every nook and cranny of the rainforest around me.

But I couldn't see Kesstel.

"Oh my god," I whispered, grabbing my head with my hands.

The portal vanished . . . with Kesstel in it. He'd said it was a possibility, but he was so casual about it, I didn't think it was actually going to happen. Where was he? Where did it go? When a portal collapsed, was it because the world vanished? So did that mean that Kesstel was stuck in space, floating like a comet somewhere between the devoured worlds?

I ran to the edge of the rainforest and stopped at the border between Josu Rainforest and the neighboring location. I pulled the mist back inside my body so there wasn't anything blocking me as I stood there with wide eyes, staring up into Gate Vale's blue, blue sky. Was he up there? And I just couldn't see him because he was too far away?

How did I help him get back? Would he ever come back?

When I first met him, he scared the hell out of me. I couldn't wait to get away from him. But now, the thought of never seeing him again twisted my gut into a painful knot. It was so hard for me to meet someone I trusted. Suddenly losing him seemed surreal.

"No," I whispered to myself. "He's not gone." *He'll come back.* He'd always had the cat-like habit of disappearing and reappearing whenever he wanted. If I waited long enough, he'd come back. Even if it was all lies, it was the only way to comfort myself.

I turned around and stared across the short space to where the portal had been.

It wasn't until then that I realized a portal had collapsed. The last time that happened, there was a worldwide Gate Surge. I could still remember how every monster in the Vale had gone berserk, howling like demons and rushing the Gate.

I held my breath and listened. It was dead quiet around me. There was no howling, no sounds of monsters running. I couldn't even feel anything moving around me. Did that mean there wasn't going to be a Gate Surge? Was it because this was a Portal Burst and not a portal attached to the rim of Gate Vale? That was the only logical reason I could think of. Either way, it was a relief there wouldn't be a Surge. Not only did I doubt that I could make it to the Gate, but according to Kesstel, Earth wouldn't be able to handle another one.

My eyes were yet again drawn to where the Portal Burst used to be. Where I thought Kesstel would come out of.

Frowning, I sat down on the ground. This empty space between the rainforest and the neighboring region was a safe zone. Monsters didn't, or maybe couldn't, leave their zones during the day. Even if one came which I couldn't handle, I was close enough to the transportation circle that I could get away easily.

As it was, I was determined to wait. Until Kesstel came back or I had to leave, whichever came first.

Ten minutes later, the magic circle flashed pale purple.

I jumped to my feet in anticipation.

An S-ranked man in full pattern-weld armor stepped out of the circle, his deep red cape swishing as he walked.

Slowly, I sank back down, cross-legged. I didn't have to see his face to know he wasn't Kesstel—Kesstel didn't wear a cape, and his favored color was royal blue.

The man stepped forward, giving room for the handful of other people who came out of the transportation circle after him. They surveyed their surroundings.

"Where is the Noble?" An A-ranked woman in full armor hummed under her breath. "And where are all the carcasses?" She motioned to their left. "According to the testimonies, there should be hundreds of goblins."

An A-ranked man in leather armor walked farther into the rainforest. "Maybe they ran farther into the forest. Oh, look." He pointed to the row of dead Hunters. "Who put them out like that?" With a few quick steps, he stood next to the closest body. "Nothing's chewed on them. That's different."

Just when I was starting to wonder if they'd ever notice me, the S-ranked Hunter turned and looked at me. I actually recognized him and the red pattern embedded on his chest. S-ranked Hunter Blood Sword. Ironically, the very same Hunter I fell at the feet of when I fled out of the Gate during the last Gate Surge.

"You, girl, what are you doing? And how long have you been there?" Just like the last time I met him, there was nothing discriminating about his mannerisms. But there was also a strong command that I answer his questions.

The rest of the Hunters turned around, revealing Association crests on their gear.

I stared at them from my location a short distance away. "I'm waiting," I answered honestly. "I got left behind." It was true, even if I chose to stay myself.

Blood Sword walked over to me, his armor faintly clanking with each of his heavy steps. "Then you must have seen the Noble. He's an S-ranked Hunter who was sent here to take care of the Portal Burst. Where is he?"

The Noble could only be one person—Kesstel Noblé. I frowned and shook my head. "I don't know. He came and went so fast, I couldn't keep up." I wasn't going to tell them where he actually went, so I came up with something vague enough to satisfy them without straying too far from the truth.

Blood Sword gave a curt nod and turned away.

The woman in full armor came closer to me. "What about the goblins? And the bodies." She motioned over her shoulder.

"The Noble took care of the goblins before he left. Most of them were so destroyed, there wasn't anything left of them." Well, since he wasn't here, I could easily push that on him. I doubted he'd care. "I set the Hunter bodies like that. I thought their teammates might prefer it that way." *Look at me, acting all valiant.* But it didn't make me feel a lick better.

"Let's check the forest," Blood Sword ordered. Then he turned to the man in leather armor. "Give the girl a transportation token so she can leave. Then take care of the bodies."

The man wrinkled his pointed nose, but still walked over to me. He stood over me and held out a hand. A transportation token appeared in his calloused palm.

I blinked at the crystal before I took a hanky out of my Items Bag to cover my fingers and picked it up. Carefully, I stored it in the pocket of my hip satchel. "Thank you."

The man, like everyone else who saw me do the same thing, gave me a look that said I was really weird. He jerked his head in a nod and backed toward the battlefield while the rest of the Hunters ran into the rainforest. They didn't bother climbing the trees to run along the branches. They were three As and an S—what was going to hurt them?

I didn't move from my spot.

I just sat there, watching the man in leather as he put the dead bodies into the transportation circle one at a time before he started to deal with the leftover goblin carcasses at a shocking speed. He kept throwing me glances, obviously thinking I was insane for not leaving.

It didn't matter to me. I just sat there. Waiting.

Kesstel never appeared.

CHAPTER 30

I wasn't tired as I walked back to the Gate. I'd spent enough time waiting in the Josu Rainforest that Regen had completely healed my HP and MP, but my feet still dragged. I couldn't resist glancing at the mountains that surrounded Gate Vale every few steps, hoping Kesstel would pop out of a hidden cave any second. Stupid, really. Even if he did do that, it was so far away that I'd never be able to see him. But I couldn't stop looking.

I stopped halfway through the clearing that circled the Gate and scrubbed my face with my hands. What was I doing, getting so worked up over him? There were so many other things I needed to concentrate on. Leveling up, finding a cure for my mom, finding a way to save Earth from the parasite—something which felt more and more impossible. I didn't even know where to start.

No, Kesstel told me there had to be a portal leading to the parasitic planet. But I wasn't at a high enough level to survive going through one yet. *Come on, Jynn,* I thought. *Concentrate on getting stronger so you can go through the portals. Kesstel is so strong, nothing is going to hurt him.*

A threatening presence closed in on me.

Immediately, I dropped my hands and shifted into a battle position, kindjal warm in my palm. I was close to the Gate, but I wasn't in Eden, so there was always a chance for a monster encounter. Instinctively, I turned toward the presence. And paused.

It wasn't a monster—well, a monster from the Gate.

Blake charged up to me, his handsome face contorted in anger. He was in full armor still, with black blood splashed across his red-tinted steel. He didn't hold a weapon, but he still looked like he was going to lose it at any given moment. Mark and one other Hunter walked behind him, the former scowling at me like I was an irritant. The other guy, whom I didn't even recognize, gave me a look I knew too well; one which said I was too insignificant to bother with, so why care?

I carefully watched Blake's body language just in case he went on the offensive. Preferably, I'd just walk away, but it didn't take a genius to realize I wasn't going to be able to. I gripped my short sword and pulled a trick I'd learned from Kesstel: making my face as blank as possible.

Blake stopped too close and loomed over me as he stared down his nose, brown eyes on fire.

Seriously, what did I do?

"You're supposed to be dead," he hissed in a low growl.

It was late in the day, so there weren't many Hunters around us. Even if there were, I doubted too many would have heard his words.

As for me, I heard them loud and clear. The words punched right into my already reeling mind. I knew he wanted me to die. Hell, he'd personally tried to kill me the first day we met. Was that what he was talking about? Don't tell me it took him this long to put it together.

I returned his hard stare. "Sorry to disappoint you. Oh, actually, I'm not."

His eyes widened in fury, and his hand lunged toward my throat.

The moment he twitched, I was already moving, skipping a couple steps back out of his reach.

What happens in the Gate, stays in the Gate. But that rule only applied if there were no witnesses. Blake's lackeys would obviously back him up, but that didn't apply to the few dozen or so Hunters who were crossing the clearing toward the Gate. They weren't close enough to hear our conversation, but they had eyes.

As soon as I was out of his reach, Blake paused. His hands stayed in the air, fingers like claws that were dying to rip my throat out. "Don't think you're anything special just because you have a powerful backing. Insects like you belong under a boot. Always have, always will. Once the Noble is done whoring you, he'll leave, and you'll have nothing to stand on. Nothing to back up that arrogant attitude."

God, how I wanted to kill him. My mouth hooked up in a sneer. "Between the two of us, I know who likes to parade around like a needy little bitch. How much longer is President Price going to put up with you? How many more millions do you need to lose for him before he kicks *you* aside?"

If he was going to call me a whore, I was going to pass it right back. Of course, I'd seen him interacting with Daniella, but damn, I wasn't going to back down after that comment. I knew I wasn't strong enough to take on a B Hunter—especially one with two A-ranked Hunters behind him—but I was feeling reckless and stupid right now. It almost felt good, venting my worries about Kesstel on this asshole.

It really bothered me when he implied that my only worth was related to Kesstel. Especially the kind of *worth* Blake implied. Did he know how many people wanted to recruit me just this morning? Granted, they would all run as soon as they saw my displayed rank, but my skills still drew them to me.

What did Blake have going for him? He was a B, sure. I couldn't judge his ability because I hadn't ever seen him swing his sword. All of his gear was given to him by President Price, that was no question. So in what way was Blake better than I was? Because he had a posse following his every move? To hell with that.

The faces of the two men behind Blake flushed red with anger.

Blake's face went straight to purple, and his Hunter aura exploded like a bomb around him. An expensive longsword with a black hilt appeared in his hand, and he reached for me. "This time, I'm going to make sure you stay dead," he snarled.

I felt Blake's aura, but it was nothing compared to Kesstel's or even the Josu Portal Burst, so I lifted my kindjal, ready to block. Maybe I could lead him into Eden and out him as the one who kept trying to kill me. Hell, he obviously was going to try right now, witnesses or not.

"Hey!" a female voice yelled out.

Blake froze and looked toward the voice before jumping like he'd been hit by a live wire. His sword vanished, and he shifted into a suave posture like he'd never turned into a raging bull at all.

I blinked, just as shocked at his reaction as I was that someone had actually stepped up for me. When I glanced over my shoulder, I was blown away with another bolt of lightning.

Bethany Wilks stood not far behind wearing a deep purple robe, her arms crossed under her near-bursting chest. She was flanked by two guards wearing black armor, but I knew there were at least seven more close by that I couldn't even see. She frowned at Blake, her head tilted back and to the side. "It's my turn to talk to her. Go away."

Blake hissed in a quick breath, drawing my attention to him. Several emotions twisted his face—shock, anger, denial—before it settled on a reluctant smile. Seriously, it was like someone had carved his face out of wood. "O-Of course, Miss Wilks. Excuse me." He bobbed his head like his neck was a rusted joint in something like a farewell nod/body spasm and turned around. With a violent swing of his hand, he motioned for his posse to follow him.

I watched him stomp away. *Did that really just happen? Is she helping me? Or just wants to take a shot herself?*

Confused, I turned to Bethany. "Are you really helping me?" I asked. "I didn't think you would."

She pursed her lips together and reached up to toy with the sparkling gems decorating the thick blonde braid that hung over her shoulder. "Yeah, well, Kesstel would be upset if something happened to you, right?" She frowned at me. "You really need to find a better team who will actually back you up if you're going to piss off the wrong people."

My head tilted to the side. "I don't have a team."

"Wait," she objected. "What about Kesstel? I thought you two were a team."

I looked at her like she was crazy. "Of course not. There's such a difference in our abilities, if we partnered up, he'd either accidentally kill me with his aura or spend the whole time babysitting me, bored out of his mind." I shook my head. "I'm not like you. You have a whole team of bodyguards watching you all the time." I motioned around since I couldn't pick them out. I bet she'd never been alone in her life. Everything she had was handed to her on a golden platter. Protection, money, food.

Her eyes narrowed. "Yes, they're there. But it's just pieces of paper. Without those contracts with Daddy, do you think they really would stay with me?" she whispered. Her mouth wrinkled in a frown, and her brows furrowed over her sad blue eyes.

I flicked a glance at the men behind her then stared at Bethany, trying to decide what I was supposed to feel. What point was she trying to make?

Bethany bit her lips together in her mouth before she smoothed out her expression. Flinging her hair over her shoulder, she lifted her head, exuding confidence like she was a queen. "Anyway. What did you do to piss off Blake like that?"

I snorted and crossed my arms. "I exist. Do I need another reason?" Before she could agree with me, I moved on. "He's a nasty guy. I didn't think he'd listen to you. He was almost *meek*." Although he almost died just acting like that.

Bethany's mouth curled victoriously as her blue eyes narrowed almost maliciously. "Of course Blake's going to act good around me. His cousin's trying to bang me."

I blinked at her, completely shocked. " . . . What?"

She waved a hand dismissively. "Well, technically, he wants to get married. It's part of his 'make his guild stronger' plan. That man-whore has never been short on women. He's such a stiff, but some women love the submissive play, I guess. *Ugh.* God knows he's not going to let any of his side squeezes go, even after he gives a girl a rock." She scrunched up her nose. "He's actually hoping he can get benefits from me without having to go through the trouble of playing marriage. Scum. He's *so* not hot enough for that."

I simply stared at her, trying to wrap my mind around what she was saying. I couldn't help rubbing my aching forehead. Was everything she said a puzzle? "Hang on. Who is Blake's cousin?"

"Huh?" Bethany gave me a dumbfounded look. "You don't know? Blake Hans is the younger cousin of Wardyn Price, the president of the Stone Mace guild."

CHAPTER 31

———

"W hat?" I gaped at her.

Bethany put her hands on her hips and tilted her head to the side, frowning. "Hang on, you mean you picked a fight with him, and you didn't even know who he was?"

I sighed, long and hard. "He started it."

Wow, I didn't know if this made my comments to him comical or disgusting. But I still didn't regret it.

"Yeah, he would. And he'd get away with it. There aren't many people who are stronger than Wardyn Price. I mean, what he lacks in strength, he makes up for with money and connections. Still not on my level, but he's ambitious." Bethany flapped her hand in the air. "Since you're naive to the situation, here's a quick history lesson for you, so pay attention. The founder of the Stone Mace guild—*something, something* Price—accidentally caused the death of his sister and her husband when the Gates first opened. So he raised his nephew like a son and spoiled the kid rotten. The founder's son—Wardyn Price—became the president after the founder died in the Gate. And the nephew—Blake Hans—continues to be spoiled because it's a habit now. Do you get it?"

. . . Well, that explained a lot. I need to read the tabloids more. And history books. Then again, at this point, I don't think I could be saved anymore. Haa . . .

"And President Price wants to marry you?" I asked, directing the conversation elsewhere.

"Of course. Who doesn't?" Bethany responded like it was a given. "I'm connected and rich. Not to mention gorgeous." She leaned on a hip and struck a pose worthy of any model.

I couldn't help but think of Kesstel and his bred-to-be-gorgeous looks. "Let me guess; you were born with it?"

"Of course not." Bethany rolled her eyes like I was dumb. "I bought it. Well, not all of it." She proudly motioned to her hourglass curves. "Most of it is natural, with just the right amount of tweaks."

My mouth twitched. *Don't laugh,* I thought desperately. *Don't laugh.* She was being a hundred percent serious, and I had a feeling that if I let out the mad laughter screaming in my mind, I'd be in trouble real quick.

I swallowed really, *really* hard. "I see." I couldn't have been prouder of myself at that moment. There was only a slight hiccup in my voice; the rest was pretty natural. *Go me.*

Bethany just shrugged. She looked over my own long, skinny frame with a critical eye. "You know, you're kinda cute and slender, but with the right touches, you'd look great," she muttered like she was talking to herself. "That would be a super easy fix."

As if I had money for that. Besides, high physical activity with a huge chest just . . . seemed like a nightmare. I shuddered. "Ah, hang on. This conversation has gone way off track." I held up my hand. "Um, is there something you wanted to say to me?"

Bethany hummed and looked away. "No, not really. I just wanted to . . . talk. That's all." She glanced at me. "That's what friends do, right?"

My jaw hit the ground. "Wait. Wait!" I took a breath, trying to wrap my mind around what she'd just said. "How can you go from trying to kill someone to friends in one go?"

Her eyes widened. "Wanting to kill someone?" She actually had the gall to sound confused.

"*Yes,*" I insisted. "Does the name *Trace* ring a bell? Melee Hunter, likes knives a little too much? Creepy?"

She stared at me with a blank expression for a good thirty seconds. Then something clicked in her eyes. "Hang on, you mean Trace Martin? Late twenties, plain looking, brown hair, and creepy beyond belief?"

"Yeah." I nodded.

"Ew!" She shuddered heavily and wrapped her arms around herself. "Ah, I've had a restraining order against him for eleven months now. He took *fan* to a hardcore freaky-stalker-fanatic place. Like, he was arrested trying to steal my panties."

I gaped at her. Suddenly, it all clicked in my mind. I gasped and slapped my hand over my forehead. *I'm such an idiot.* His creepy talk and her perfectly timed hostile attitude totally led me to believe he was sent by her.

But Trace never actually said he was working for Bethany. That was something I totally jumped to on my own.

"Ah, wait!" Bethany gasped. "Are you saying he tried to kill you? What happened?"

I dropped my hand. If I didn't know what to think of Bethany before, I didn't have a clue now. "He died in Feng Jungle."

Bethany sighed and patted her chest. "Oh, good. He was a creeper who needed to die." Then she scowled at me. "But I don't appreciate you thinking I wanted to kill you."

So Bethany didn't send Trace, but I knew for a fact there were more hitmen trying to kill me. They'd even collapsed a building on me.

I peeked up at Bethany. "Have you ever tried to kill me?"

She snorted. "Excuse me? Do you know who I am? I am Bethany Wilks." She drew herself up in a gorgeous, well-practiced pose. "I am the face of the Hunters outside of Eden. There are billboards with me on them every mile in Garden City, and thousands more across the country. I have an image to maintain. Rich, powerful, gorgeous, and perfect. *Killer* isn't in that description." *Man*, she walked along that fine line of bragging, stating facts, and complaining very well.

I'd personally seen many of her billboards with my own eyes when I went to visit my family. Each one made being a Hunter seem so appealing, like, *become a Hunter and your life will be perfect like hers*. It helped keep up the illusion humans had. It probably helped keep the mass hysteria down, because they didn't know what a threat the Gate really was to a normal human's existence.

Bethany waved vaguely toward the Gate. "My whole job is to make sure humans on the other side of the Wall keep thinking life is great. You and I both know that isn't how it really is, but the rest of society doesn't need to know. They love their fairy tale, and the Hunter's Council is happy to help them. It helps with distributing taxes, military, and other political mumbo-jumbo that I know way too much about. Which is why I have to keep my hands clean. I can act however I want—it helps with the spoiled princess theme—but my hands have to stay clean. I mean, what would the people think if the face of the Hunters was cold-blooded enough to blatantly kill someone? Even if it's normal in the Gate, the world outside would be in an uproar."

I sighed and thumped my fist on my thigh. "You're right. Sorry," I muttered, still trying to get my thoughts in order. "I think I jumped to conclusions a little too fast."

She was quiet for a minute before snorting in a very unladylike way. "Well, I can't really blame you. I don't make a habit of being nice to people I don't like."

That's because you're strong enough to get away with it, I thought.

So, if she wasn't the one who sent the hitmen after me, that left only one person I could think of. And honestly, it made sense. *I mean, Blake's only been actively trying to kill me since day one.* I just didn't know why he was using hitmen now. Was it because he didn't want Price to find out he was trying to kill the guild's most desired Hunter recruit? Or because he didn't want to take the time to do it himself? Or both?

Either way, it felt a little better to know I had a clear direction.

But only a little bit.

Ahh, this day has been way too long. If I'd known I was going to be harassed about being recruited, caught in a Portal Burst, watch Kesstel disappear maybe forever, and have my opinion of Bethany get flipped on its head, I might have just stayed at home today.

No, I could handle most of what happened today. If I was being honest, it was Kesstel's disappearance that had me twisted in so many emotional knots, I didn't know what to feel.

I need a nap.

Nah, it was late enough in the day that I could call it and just go to bed. Maybe tomorrow I wouldn't feel like I was a step away from collapsing from the mental strain.

"So who is trying to kill you?" Bethany asked casually, as if it was a perfectly natural thing for her to say. She tapped her purple fingernail on her chin. "Let me guess, Blake? He was so charming to you earlier."

I sighed. "I don't know anymore." And I didn't trust her enough to tell her, anyway. Hell, I hadn't even told Kesstel about it. Why would I tell her?

"Hmm, well, when you do, let me know. Suppressing people is one of my specialties," Bethany said with obvious glee.

Yet again, she managed to blow my mind. And the most amazing thing was, even though she knew what I used to think of her, she still obviously looked like she wasn't going to go away. What did I do now to warrant this reaction? Was she really going to latch on to me like a friend? That was just too bizarre. Then again, I'd rather be friends with her than have her trying to kill me.

I didn't even know how to answer that statement, so I changed the subject. "I'm going to head out now. It's been a long day."

Bethany turned and walked with me. Her bodyguards fell into step twenty feet behind us. "I completely understand. God, did you know there was a Portal Burst today? Well, of course you did," she rushed on before I could get a word in. "You must have seen the red sky, right? Isn't that just the freakiest thing? Do you know where it was? The Josu Rainforest. They said that the whole area got sealed off somehow and no one could get in or out of it. Luckily, there was an S Hunter close by who saved the day."

Right before passing through the Gate, Bethany suddenly stopped walking. It was so unexpected, I couldn't help but look around for a threat. Instead, a bodyguard rushed right past me in the blink of an eye and disappeared through the Gate. As soon as he vanished in the opaque blackness, Bethany stepped forward.

Bemused, I followed.

The bodyguard was waiting for her on the other side of the Gate, vigilantly surveying the grounds. Several more bodies slipped through behind me, all dressed in the same matching armor, before they disappeared from sight. I didn't know if they were using powerful magic stones or if their Stealth was that high, but it was unnerving seeing someone disappear like that and not being able to sense them. It just set every Hunter instinct I owned screaming with danger.

Bethany turned to me, completely unconcerned by the men. "Hey, what's your number?" She pulled out a gem-studded cell phone and swiped it open.

Wow, she really was serious about this friend thing. "I don't have one."

She looked at me over her phone. "What? Who doesn't have a phone in this day and age?"

I shrugged. "Me. I've never needed one."

"Hmm," she gave a low hum. Her phone disappeared with a casual wave of her hand. "Well, we can fix that. Meet me here at ten tomorrow morning. No, that's super early. Eleven . . . thirty. Meet me at eleven thirty and—"

"Hang on." I held up my hands before she could go any further. "I'm actually booked tomorrow. Like, all day."

Tomorrow was Saturday, the day the aero-teuthida was due. At least I'd finally found the trick to finding them. And hopefully, people would be scared away from the Josu Rainforest for the day so I could get some work done.

To be honest, even if I didn't have to find another floating squid, I still would go back to that rainforest. It might be the best place to wait for Kesstel, since that's where he'd disappeared.

Tomorrow was also the day the cult was meeting.

CHAPTER 32

Maveric looked up when I entered his shop. "Hey, there's a friendly face."

"Morning." I walked up to the counter.

Maveric met me on the other side. "Just barely." He pointedly looked at the glass-and-steel clock hanging on the white wall beside the counter. The long hand was just centimeters shy of noon.

"Perfect timing then." I tapped on the glass counter between us. A silver canister holding a dead aero-teuthida appeared on it. "And that makes two," I said with satisfaction.

The events of yesterday had scared everyone away from the Josu Rainforest—that, and I think Hunters had given up trying to recruit me. Thank god. It made looking for the second flying squid a million times easier. I could use Mist to help search and didn't have to hide from people—like Beak Nose and Mage Buddy, whom I hadn't seen in a while, anyway. Still, it made it a heck of a lot easier when I wasn't being hunted down for various reasons.

"Yes." Maveric picked up the canister and looked closely through the small window on the side, inspecting the carcass. "You didn't take out the crystal again," he commented, glancing at me.

I spread my hands hopelessly and shrugged. "It's not my forte. I didn't want to ruin it."

He nodded. "Right. Give me a minute." He took the canister into the back, and five minutes later, he returned with an energy crystal, setting it on the counter. "Alright. The deal was two aero-teuthida for five hundred, right?" He flicked his hand in the air, and a blue Guide transaction screen popped up in front of him.

"Yep." I covered the energy crystal with a hanky and slipped it into my hip satchel.

He watched me handle the crystal and lifted an eyebrow. "You don't have to treat them so carefully, you know. They can't be broken or even scratched without special tools."

I smiled at him. "I know." *Like the sword in my Items Bag.*

He shook his head and tapped on his blue screen. A moment later, my System popped up and showed me the details of the contract. I looked it over, grateful that it was straightforward. I just wanted to give him the monsters and get the money. Luckily, the contract was as clear-cut as that. I used my finger to sign the line at the bottom of the screen.

"Did you hear what happened at the Portal Burst?" Maveric asked, making small talk. "Given where it was, I was worried you'd gotten caught in it. I'm glad to see you safe and sound. Especially since an S god disappeared during it."

I paused, my finger still on the screen. Honestly, I could have gotten back to Maveric an hour earlier, but I'd spent some time looking for Kesstel.

I didn't find him.

"Oh, yeah?" I said lightly, like my chest didn't feel heavy. The contract disappeared, and I got a notice that five hundred dollars were added to my account.

"Yeah. Can you believe it? The S Hunters are the big guns, you know. Not a single one has died since the Gates opened. That's why they sent one, the Noble, in to handle the Portal Burst, and he just disappeared. I hear the Association's been looking everywhere for him. But no one knows anything about him. Hell, I don't even know what he looks like, and I maintain his armor." Maveric sighed. "That was my best work. And it's gone."

I looked up at him. "You made his armor? I've seen—ah, pictures of it. It looked amazing. You did a great job on his crest."

Maveric snorted. "Yeah, well, that was a nightmare job. Blood Sword, you know him? He was easy. He just wanted a red sword; didn't really care what it looked like. Easy. The Noble was very picky about how his crest should look. I think I redid it about five times before he let me off the hook. It's not easy changing the design on crystal-infused metal, let me tell you." Despite his words, he couldn't look prouder.

I smiled softly. "Really?"

I bet Kesstel's family crest was important to him. His world was gone, but that didn't mean his memories were. I couldn't even imagine what I'd do if I was in his shoes. Would I be able to go on, knowing I was the only one left? It was an easy answer—no. That's why it was so important to get strong enough to protect Earth.

I tapped my finger on the glass and cut off the thought before I let it run away from me. "Oh, I have some other things to sell, too," I commented.

Maveric's eyes lit up. "Alright. Let's see what you've got."

A half an hour later, I left Maveric's shop and got some lunch. After my stomach was full, I headed back to Gate Vale. There were still seven hours before I had to get ready for tonight. Plenty of time to get EXP and look for Kesstel.

My shoes were noiseless on the pavement as I walked through E District to where the note told me to meet. The nighttime darkness seeped into the concrete and asphalt. So close to the outer wall of Eden, the streets were unkempt, and most of the lampposts were missing bulbs. Even the moon was dark, hiding its newness in the black void above.

I'd say it was quiet, but that would be a lie. The streets appeared deserted, but that was just because the Hunters were hiding in the alleys and doorways. Feeling disgusting eyes on me, I turned my head. With my stats, the night wasn't as dark as it should be. The Es around me might have trouble seeing, but it was like walking through a dimly lit room for me. Dark, but I could still see the blurry-eyed man peeking out at me from a doorway, staring at my body. I scowled and released my Hunter aura— another trick I'd learned from Kesstel. It wouldn't have done a thing for most of the people I was frequently around, but it sure made this drunken E and the other rats hiding scurry away.

I let out a silent sigh. I hated this part of Eden. Seriously, there was nothing good here. It was where all the horrible Hunters who didn't war- rant getting thrown into the Holding Place—*yet*—collected. The Associa- tion knew they were here and came to "clean up" this section every once in a while, from what I'd heard, but it hadn't happened since I came to Eden.

And it wasn't just the street noise that I could hear. On the other side of this particular section of the twenty-foot red brick Wall was the wild outside. Eden was shaped like a circle, off-centered inside the oval-shaped Garden City. Eden was set up like a pie, each of the districts in alphabeti- cal order, but there was a reason why E District was put where it was. If the monsters in the barren land on the other side of the city broke through, the lowly Es should serve as a big enough stumbling block so that the rest of the city could mobilize and defeat the monsters. It was best to sacrifice the weak so the strong could handle the problem. As for the dead Es . . . well, it was less money the government had to waste on room and board.

And everyone in this part of the city knew it.

Still, it was eerie hearing the crying and screeches of monsters on the other side of the Wall while being surrounded by Eden's buildings. Was this how people felt when the Gates first opened? Hiding in their homes while listening to demons from another world hungrily prowl just feet away? My own parents, aunt, and uncle had lived through just that in their high school years.

I stopped outside of a building. There was nothing interesting about it at all; it was just a short brick building with a door. But this was where the note said to go. My bare fingers rubbed together, suddenly missing the feel of my kindjal as I glanced at the surrounding street signs to double-check. This should be it. Then again, this was a cult hiding from the Hunter's Association. What was I expecting? A giant sign that flashed "Cult is meeting right here!"? Yeah, no.

I walked up to the door and knocked on it.

A moment later, a peephole just like in the movies slid open. A man—I assumed from the narrow eyes and bushy brows—assessed me with a glare. "You don't look the type. Scram!" he yelled.

Well, that was inviting. No wonder there were such small numbers in the cult, what with intoxicating their people to death and the unfriendly greetings; I was surprised it was still running.

I held up the note that had been left at my door. "Someone told me to come here." Then I paused. Ah, that didn't sound very encouraging. What would someone say if they wanted to get in? "Um, I wanted to know more about . . . *it*," I finally finished, feeling a little lame. Since they were hiding, I was sure they wouldn't want someone to scream out what was going on on the other side of the door.

The man looked at the note. The door to the peephole slammed shut without another word from him.

I stared at the peeling paint. *Seriously? Did I just get rejected?*

Suddenly, the door swung open, revealing a small foyer. On the other side was a woman wearing a brown monk-like robe that totally washed out her skin. She gave a small smile, her pale face gentle as dew. "Welcome, seeker." She bowed at the waist and motioned me inside.

"Oh, okay." Stepping in, I was barely out of the way before the door slammed shut with a dense thud, enclosing me in a small, bare room.

The peephole guy stood next to the door, a perma-scowl on his face. He wore a matching brown robe, the hood pulled low over his brow, but the most eye-catching thing about him was that he was a human. The woman was an E, but this man was unmistakably a human. In Eden.

Visiting hours had ended over six hours ago. It was illegal for a human to be in Eden after 5:00 p.m., and each entry was strictly recorded. If a human didn't leave on time, there was literally a manhunt to expel said human. But this guy, though grumpy, was obviously not worried about being found. So how did he get in here?

The Hunter motioned to the side with her arm. "Follow me, and all your questions will be answered." She turned and walked to a narrow hallway in the back right corner of the small room.

I doubt it, I thought, trailing after her. My hands were itching for my kindjal more than ever, but I had a feeling it wouldn't go over well if I took it out.

The hall was short, barely four feet long, and barren. There were no pictures on the tan walls, with only a simple mushroom light on the ceiling. The hall veered left and ended at the top of a staircase.

She stopped and motioned down it with her hand.

The long stairway was perfectly lit, revealing white walls and dark wooden stairs. Despite the creepy guide and the faint, earthy smell lingering in the air, the staircase came across as perfectly safe.

The woman waved her hands like she was performing a magic trick, twisting her fingers and swishing her wide sleeves. With one final flick of her hand, a plain white masquerade mask appeared in her palm. She offered it to me. "Dr. E is waiting for you. Follow the stairs and be enlightened." She smiled, her gentle eyes like brown glass.

"Thank you," I whispered, taking the mask from her. I fitted it to my face and stepped down to the first stair.

CHAPTER 33

An average staircase in a house had roughly thirteen stairs. This one had at least twenty. It was brightly lit and clean the whole way down, but I couldn't help but be on edge. I remembered one of my last conversations with Healer Jonovan, how he'd let it slip that this cult was dangerous and to stay away. I'd promised him I would, yet here I was.

The stairs bottomed out to another hallway with white walls, a ceiling with mushroom lights every five feet, and a dirt floor—which explained the earthy smell I'd picked up before descending. The hall was at least the length of a football field, and there wasn't another soul in sight, but there was noise coming from the stairway at the other end. It sounded like a lot of people.

As I walked closer to the noise, I played over what the woman said before I left her. She mentioned someone named Dr. E. Ironically, that wasn't the first time I'd heard that name. The first time was from Green five days ago, only he'd called him a quack. I heard it again just yesterday from Yellow. Dr. E was the client the rainbow brigade was getting the cyan-agaric for. Did they have a tie to the cult? I hoped not.

I was curious about the cult, true. But honestly, it was because if this cult had some knowledge of the parasite planet, I hoped there'd be someone here who could help me save Earth; that I'd make an ally. I wouldn't have to convince them about the threat against Earth or the danger of the crystals; they'd already know. And maybe the Hunter's Association would take my reports more seriously if I had someone else backing up what I said.

Even as I thought through my plan, I remembered what Healer Jonovan had told me about the drugs dealt here. *They secretly lure people to their meetings and fill their heads with nonsense while releasing a vaporized drug into the air.*

And it could be instantly deadly for humans.

If it was that dangerous, it needed to be stopped.

I came to the bottom of the stairs and looked up to the opening above my head. As brightly lit as it was down here was how dim it was up there. Many voices echoed from the open doorway, too many to count. The words overlapped and drowned each other out, some yelling, some talking quietly, some excited, some nervous.

I couldn't stay down there forever, so I climbed up. The narrow space opened up to a large room—a gymnasium, maybe? It was hard to tell. Even with my enhanced eyesight, the large cloth sheets which hung on the walls blocked any distinguishing features. All that was left was a huge room with hundreds of people standing and a large stage set up at the front of it all. There were no visible windows—probably covered with the dark material—just dimmed hanging lights from the high ceiling. It was enough for the average human to see the person next to them but not be able to make out someone five feet away.

Not that it mattered. Everyone was wearing white masquerade masks, just like me. They seemed to glow in the dark, and I felt like I was standing in a crowd of ghosts. Some people stood together, strangers becoming acquainted, and others were groups of people who obviously knew each other. There were some people like me, stragglers who stood alone, some fidgeting nervously, some looking around with interest.

What surprised me was the wide range of apparel in the crowd. There were Hunters with good gear, Hunters with cheap gear, humans with expensive clothes, and humans with discounted clothes. I was actually surprised at how many humans there were. They made up almost half of the crowd.

Then I saw something which sent a chill down my spine.

Ten feet away from me were two young men standing together and talking quietly. One of them was wearing a varsity jacket from Aliya's school. It had this year's graduating date on it and everything. These boys were Aliya's high school peers. I turned my head and noticed another group of kids, obviously not old enough to graduate.

How far-reaching was this cult?

Suddenly, fog started to billow from the side curtains around the stage. It spread over the stage and spilled down on the floor, twisting around people's feet. More fog came from the top of the curtain and spilled down like a waterfall.

The crowd instantly hushed.

I frowned and covered my nose as the chemical smell of the artificial fog caused my eyes to sting. It sure as hell wasn't the refreshing breath my mist had, that's for sure.

Blue laser lights burst from the top of the stage, five from each corner, and low mystical music started to play in surround sound from speakers hidden behind the hanging sheets. The lights shot into the fog then started to twist and turn, creating distorted images in the white substance. The earth and stars were depicted. Suddenly, two lightning strikes came from both sides of the curtains. They hit each other and exploded into a blindingly bright flash behind the waterfall of fog. When the light faded away, the laser lights depicted a dragon fighting Hunters, the colors changing from blue to red to green.

I gasped with the crowd, watching the story play out. I'd never seen anything like this. I didn't have the time or money to go to shows and concerts with my friends, too busy trying to keep my family in order. I definitely didn't think I'd see something like this here, though.

The Hunters in the light show teamed up and attacked the dragon. Swing by colorful swing and flash by colorful flash of magic, the Hunters slew the dragon.

The crowd around me cheered, completely entranced by the light display. If I wasn't so on edge about finding an ally *and* worrying about human teens present, I might have cheered, too.

"That's what it's supposed to be like, huh?" a man's mellow voice echoed around the gym.

Another flash of lightning bolts collided with each other. When the light faded, a man was standing on the stage. He was tall and slim, and his white priest robe with vertical blue accents only emphasized his lengthy build. His face was covered by a full mask, making it impossible to tell if the features indented on the white surface were his own or made up. The mask went up his forehead and cut off in sharp square lines, bleached hair spilling around it and down his narrow neck to brush at his shoulders.

He walked forward on the stage, fog wafting around his white boots. "The monster gets defeated by Hunters and everyone cheers, right?" He motioned with his white-gloved hands. "Isn't it?" he asked, prompting the crowd.

A couple people in the front gave weak sounds of agreement.

"But that's not what's really happening, is it?" he concluded, his soothing voice rich with disappointment.

The crowd murmured with confusion as they looked at each other. That *is* what happened inside the Gate every day.

The man on the stage lifted his hand. The laser turned on again, showing the dragon and Hunters light show. But another element had been added. Underneath the fight were smaller figures: Hunters holding weapons and people without weapons—humans. Every time the dragon and bigger Hunters acted, the smaller people were stepped on, blasted with the attacks. Died. Until at the end, it was simply the larger, stronger Hunters standing. The dragon and smaller people were snuffed out.

"This is how it really is," the man concluded. "The unspoken rule: the strong survive and the weak are simply their stepping stones for success."

A hush fell over the crowd. Not a single person tried to argue.

The fog stopped billowing over the stage as the man walked forward till he was at the edge of the platform. "I am Epson. And I speak the truth. The truths you have come to find. The truths that the government, both human and Hunter alike, want to keep hidden."

Okay, so far, this was not what I expected. But maybe now, maybe this was the moment this leader guy would validate what I knew about the parasite planet.

The crowd drifted closer to the stage, staring up in interest. I slipped around milling people, also edging my way forward. There were some who didn't move, their posture indicating they were still on edge, but I wanted to get a better look at Epson—and the handful of Hunters behind the curtains. Two had to be the mages who crashed their lightning together. Who else was behind there?

"For two decades, our planet has been wracked with danger. We hide inside our cities, not braving to go out of the Walls that imprison us just as much as they protect us. Do you remember what it was like before the Gates came?" Epson looked around the crowd.

For a second, his eyes landed on me. I frowned and stared back, refusing to look away. His gaze moved on.

"I do. I remember going camping with my family in the forests, not caring about what dangers were out there because we were at the top of the food chain. I remember being able to go to every part of the city. There were no walls, no restricted access in and out, like with Eden and Garden City. I remember a government that cared for its people. They gave food to the hungry, provided housing for the homeless, healthcare to those who couldn't afford it." He paused and looked around. "I understand that this sounds like a myth to some of you, since you aren't old enough to remember. But others can attest for me."

Younger people glanced around, looking for validation to this man's memories. There were murmurs of agreement from the older people in the crowd—the veterans who'd lived through the collapse of society and were there every grueling step to get back to the life we had today.

I had to admit, the world Epson talked about sounded like a dream—everyone had food, housing, you could go anywhere. None of that came without a heavy price nowadays. Even with food and housing handled, the movements of the people were still very restricted. It was safe to say that the government knew what part of the city every individual was at any given point of the day.

It was even more so with Hunters and their Guides. The pearls embedded in our temples didn't just provide help; they also served as a potential tracking device outside of the Gate. Granted, the person had to do something really big before the government allowed law officials to track a person's pearl, but the possibility was always there.

Epson looked around. "Back then, we were the *land of the free.* We could do anything we wanted, be anything we wanted, live anywhere we wanted. Tell me, is that possible today?" When the people responded more than ever before, he shook his head. "No. Of course not. Every person in this country is told what to be from the time they learn to walk. I am no exception. I wanted to be a surgeon when I was a boy. The Gates opened, and I awakened as a melee Hunter when I was a teen. There were no other choices left. I only had one choice—to fight. It didn't matter if I liked it or not; that's what I was told to do. Going to medical school and *saving lives,* which I had been studying for my whole life, wasn't possible because I didn't have healing magic and wasn't a normal human anymore." Sadness dripped from his compelling voice. "That same thing goes on today."

I stood there, surrounded by people, hearing Epson tell his story and hearing other people agreeing with him. Some shared their own experiences with their companions; a couple girls not far away even sniffled.

I couldn't help but admire the guy. A surgeon, huh? He sure had a steady hand for when it came to handling this crowd with finesse, something I could never do. First, he amazed them with the light show to perk their interest, then he shocked them as he hammered a stake into their sore spot labeling them all as cannon fodder for the strong; next, he won their hearts with a sob story—one they had all experienced. The man on the stage did a fantastic job making himself seem just like everyone else.

Would his tales evolve into the truth behind Earth's greatest threat? Would this Dr. E be my ally?

A System message popped open before me. [**Noxious contaminant detected. Please beware.**]

—

CHAPTER 34

Noxious contaminant? My eyes widened, and I looked around. Jonovan said that Epson used a vaporized drug, so it must have been in the fog that spilled from the ceiling and sides of the stage, accumulating on the floor to knee height.

A slight headache throbbed at my forehead.

Up on the stage, Epson, surrounded by the gas and lit like a pillar in the dark room, kept talking in his soothing yet riveting voice. "Let me tell you a secret." The people around me hung on his every word, as if they needed to hear it to survive. "The government wants us to stay this way. Oppressed. Under their control. Ignorant of what's really going on."

It was like his surround-sound voice was drilling into my head. Even if I didn't want to hear, I couldn't keep it from penetrating my skull and polluting my thoughts.

One of the young guys from Aliya's school pressed his hand to his forehead and wobbled.

His friend reached over and grabbed his shoulder. "You okay, man?"

"H-Head," the kid groaned before dropping to the ground.

He wasn't the only one affected by the vaporized drug. One after another, people's eyes went out of focus as they wobbled in place. Some sat down, others just grabbed onto the person next to them to stay up. The people affected the most were the humans, but I noticed the lower the Hunter's rank was, the more they were influenced.

The light show came back on, drawing a picture of Earth in the air. The crowd looked up at it with dazed expressions.

I scowled as the headache pulsed stronger, glancing up at the light show and at Epson behind it. My vision blurred as the image of Earth intensified, consuming me as if it was growing larger. I flinched and shook my head, trying to clear my vision.

"Ten months ago, I accidentally discovered a secret the government is trying to keep hidden from us at all costs. The secret behind the Gates," Epson announced.

I gasped and looked up, squinting to bring him into focus. *This*, this is what I wanted to know about. This was why I came even though I knew it was dangerous. More dangerous than I thought it would be.

Frustrated, I created a barrier around me, pushing back the artificial fog with my own fresh mist. It was a long shot, but I wanted something to ease up the influence of the drug.

It didn't work. I could feel the particles of the drug-laced fog slowly seep into my mist, contaminating it like a drop of food dye in water.

[Cultivate the fog.]

The System notification shocked me. *Cultivate it? Are you kidding me?* It'd just warned me it was full of poisonous contaminants. Still, I put my hands together in the right position. I didn't sit down because I was worried someone might fall on me, but hopefully, it wouldn't make too much of a difference. I didn't close my eyes as I pushed my senses out and latched onto the artificial fog, grabbing it and slowly forcing it into my body.

It felt awful, like trying to chug water that was too carbonated as it popped and fizzed painfully all the way down your throat, but I continued to absorb the artificial fog. Amazingly, my head started to clear up a bit, enough that my vision stopped swirling.

"You see," Epson said slowly. "The portals in the Gate aren't just one-way passages meant to spit out monsters and make our lives hell." He motioned with his hands to the light show. The picture changed to a loose depiction of Gate Vale before zooming in at a dizzying pace to a portal on the south side of the Vale. "What the government doesn't want you to know is that through the Gate"—the light show lit up again, like traveling through a warp tunnel—"on the other side of a portal, is a paradise."

The picture opened up, showing a gorgeous land with bright green plants, blue water, and rich soil. There were mountains, lakes, oceans, and deserts, as beautiful as Earth was before the Gates appeared, before monsters and weapons of mass destruction damaged so much of this planet.

The people around me gasped in delight.

My eyes widened. *No, that isn't right . . .*

"A paradise full of luscious green plants that aren't trying to kill you. Deep blue fresh water that's safe to drink or swim in without fear of being poisoned or attacked. Gentle weather where the air is sweet and the sunlight is warm on your skin." Epson's words bore into my brain. "There are no monsters there. It's a perfect place to finally reproduce the DNA extracted from our natural animals before they went extinct a decade ago. In as few as a couple years, thousands of our precious wildlife could be reborn and live free. No more getting eaten by monsters. A new Earth. That's what's on the other side of the portals."

"New Earth," the crowd whispered like a broken choir. They stared at the picture with fascinated, blurry eyes.

No, I thought. *That's wrong. There isn't a utopia on the other side of a portal. There's nothing but death. A parasitic planet that will destroy us.* But I was too disabled with cultivating to voice my thoughts aloud.

"A new Earth," Epson said, his voice heavy with accusation, "that people like us will never see." He paused dramatically, waiting for the shocked gasps to die out before going on. "For years, the government has been secretly going into this very portal and building a city there. They have been using our resources—using the energy crystals that we have spilled blood and tears to collect, energy crystals that are supposed to be used to keep us alive—to fund the construction of their new Utopia. Because to them, we are *nothing.* Worker ants, meant to be walked on. Weaklings to be trampled over. And when they're done with their new city on their new Earth, they will leave us behind."

Small cries of outrage echoed around me, but all I was noticing was that more people had collapsed on the ground. Most were bent over, breathing in the artificial fog heavily, while others were completely unconscious—like the school kid with his friend now fretting over him.

I took a breath and sat down, assuming the full cultivating position and increasing the rate in which I absorbed the fog. Maybe I could absorb the drug out of the air and help the people around me. Was this idea what was behind the System's suggestion to cultivate? The fog pooled up to my chin, the heavy artificial smell burning my nose.

"Yes, the strong Hunters will leave. Who wouldn't want to? This planet is dying," Epson said, finally telling a truth after a load of bullshit. "Before the Gates opened, there were seven billion people on Earth; now, there are less than three billion. Over sixty percent of Earth's human population has died, and of those few billion left, thirty percent of them are in a coma. The government claims that they're creating a cure for Dreamers, but it's a lie. They're taking all that money and putting it into making their lives easier on the new Earth."

He opened his arms, and the strobe lights changed again, creating a swirling effect that my already aching head could barely handle. Half of the crowd that remained standing fell to their knees, holding their mouths or heads with obvious disorientation.

"And in that diminishing population, less and less are Awakening as Hunters. The ones who do are getting weaker and weaker. Fifteen years ago, the average Hunter was a C. Nowadays, that average is a D. In fact, there are more Ds and Es than the rest of the numbers combined, yet we are sandwiched together and unappreciated. Even though there are fewer numbers in the higher ranks, the bulk of the Hunter's Association money is allotted to the stronger ones, all with the claim that they need the money to get good enough gear to handle the stronger monsters they fight."

Epson hissed out a breath. "What about us? The greater population of people? What about the ones who don't have enough money to buy good enough gear to handle what we're dealing with? What about the E Hunter who died today because he couldn't afford a sword that didn't break after one hit? What about the Hunters who go hungry because they can't kill a monster with their inferior gear, surviving on rice and vegetables? What about those people?"

His thundering voice propelled the crowd to call out in anger, even those who were on the ground.

I frowned, peering at Epson between the few bodies still standing between us. He didn't seem to care at all that the people he was preaching to were collapsing. In fact, he spoke more passionately the more people fell down. Disappointment and anger built in me. Someone like this was too dangerous to be around people.

"Every year," Epson went on, "more and more people become Dreamers. The numbers have gone up so much that hospitals don't have the appropriate amount of staff to take care of Dreamers. If you fall into a coma now, they will only house you for four years before they kick your inert—yet very much alive—body into the street. Or inject you with drugs and kill you right in your bed."

My eyes widened, shocked despite myself. Was that true? I could call foul on his description of new Earth, but everything else he'd said about Earth was true. Was this information about Dreamers correct? Then again, I only had six more months before my mom's plug was pulled.

A hunched man beside me lifted his head and howled, "My wife! Give me back my wife!" He wasn't the only one who reacted to these words.

I gasped. Did that mean it was true?

"But I mean, why should the government spend so much money on a group of people who will never wake up?" Epson's smooth voice smothered the rest of the cries. "Why not use that money to make the new Earth better? It's only a matter of time before it's ready and the Hunters leave." He paused, looking around at the few remaining people. "Yes, the Hunters will leave. But only the strong ones. The Ss, the As, maybe even a lucky few Bs who are rich enough. The rest of us will be left on our destroyed Earth."

"Good riddance!" a woman yelled from the front of the crowd.

"Get out of here and let us live without your oppression!" another man yelled.

Epson chuckled. "If they leave, who is going to stop the monsters from coming out of the Gate?" His words were met with silence. After all, the answer was clear. If all the high-ranked Hunters disappeared, Earth would be overrun with monsters in days.

"The Hunter's Association created this world," Epson continued. "They are the ones who scorched our precious land with nuclear weapons, making twenty percent of Earth uninhabitable. They forced society into a mold, separating Hunters from humans. Splitting up families, couples, friends. They are the ones who made our very survival completely dependent on the government and Hunters. And now that Earth is ruined, they're going to pack up and leave. Dump the problems that they made on us, the weak, as usual."

No, I thought. The Hunters and the government didn't create this mess. The parasite was the one that opened the Gates and spilled the monsters over the world. And the reason why Hunters and humans were separated was for the survival of humanity. Sure, there were some things wrong, like the level of control the Association had over Hunters and the blatant discrimination that was going on.

But, like what Epson said, the planet was dying. It was slowly being consumed. In fact, from what I'd learned from Kesstel, the reason why Earth hadn't collapsed so far was because of the strict society that was created to deal with the Hunters and monsters. After all, the parasitic planet's energy that made a Hunter into a Hunter was poisonous to the average human. If Hunters and humans lived together, more humans would fall into a coma than what we had now. Earth probably would have collapsed already.

With all the little truths laced through so many lies, I could see why Jonovan had warned me to stay away. And I could see that I'd find no ally here to help me fight the parasitic planet.

Ding! A System notification popped up. [**Task: (Collect three Cyan-Agaric) Completed! +125 EXP**]

CHAPTER 35

I gaped at the System message, so shocked that I stopped cultivating. Seriously? How was that possible? I wasn't anywhere near the Gate right now. How could I have collected a cyan-agaric?

Wait, I was cultivating the artificial fog, just like the System wanted me to. So the noxious contaminant that was poisoning everyone was derived from a cyan-agaric? Well, that made sense, since I already knew that the rainbow brigade was trying to find one for their client "Dr. E"—in other words, Epson.

But my surprises weren't over yet.

Ding! [**Gained Ability: Poison Fog.**]

Ding! [**Gained: Resistance to certain poisons.**]

"Cool," I mouthed, letting Epson's words fade into the background as I focused for a minute on the notifications. I quickly opened my Abilities menu in the Guide and looked at it. A wave of shock and satisfaction washed over me.

There was now a new ability listed: [**Poison Fog: Add Bleed and Poison to Mist. Some monsters might experience disorientation as well. Cost: 25 MP.**]

The man next to me collapsed in my direction, drawing my attention. I reached out and caught his bulky body just before he landed on my head, grunting as I shifted him around and more or less dropped him on the ground next to me. At least he didn't take the damage a dead faint would have done to his head.

That was when I noticed that everyone in the crowd was on the ground. Some higher-ranked Hunters were still conscious, but they were high as a kite, giggling and staring up at the ceiling as if it was a movie screen instead of a bunch of support beams. Most of the people were out cold.

The artificial fog stopped flowing from around the stage, but there was still a large pool of it that bubbled and flowed over the unconscious people. The laser show turned off, leaving the room dim and smokey.

Four people entered the stage from the wings and stood next to Epson. They wore dull bull-brown priest robes, just like the woman who'd led me to the stairs, but their faces were covered in white, full masks. The craftsmanship on the newcomers' masks wasn't as high quality as Epson's, but still impressive.

The five people, three men and two women, looked down from above.

Then Epson tilted his head to the side. "Get going." The lyrical, compelling tone on his voice was gone, leaving only a cold command.

My eyes narrowed as my opinion of this whole thing dropped another notch.

One of the girls not far from me moaned and shifted. I glanced at her, then did a double take. She was curled on her side, a cell phone lying in her lax grip.

I cast Stealth and hurried over to her. I didn't know much about phones, since I'd never owned one, but luckily, this was an old model with cracks webbing across the screen. It was the same one that Marcie, my high school bestie, had.

Swiping the screen, I opened the camera without needing a password. But my Stealth didn't work on the device probably because it wasn't mine, resulting in a floating phone. Not optimal, but workable. Switching it over to video, I hit record then aimed it at the people on the stage, and started to creep closer.

The four people in the brown robes jumped down to the slumping crowd. They split into pairs, the men going left and the women going right, and started to walk around the people on the ground.

A thin man dropped to his knees beside a human and felt around the downed man's body. A second later, he stood up. "Found one." He waved a wallet in the air.

The masked man, who was slightly smaller in size, came over and took out a tablet. "Give it here." He flipped open the wallet and started to swipe every card on the tablet's reader.

My eyes widened as my opinion of them hit rock bottom.

So they weren't just antigovernmentalists, they were thieves, too. Carefully, I crept closer and zoomed in the video. I didn't know how good of a picture it was taking with all the residual fog floating between us, but hopefully, it would be good enough.

The women were doing the same thing, searching the unconscious people on the ground for wallets and cards. Their search was limited to humans because Hunters kept their money attached to their Guides and their cards in their Items Bags. But out of the nearly three hundred people here, almost half were human. There were still a lot of cards to pick from.

The taller man stood up with another wallet. Unlike the first one, this one was made out of fine leather. He flipped it open and fingered the cards inside. "I don't know why we can only take fifteen dollars at a time," he whined. "This fatty can handle it if we take more." He nudged the unconscious man's belly with his toe.

"Because any more than that is too noticeable, dumbass," his partner snapped back. "We've been over this already." He put the last card back into the wallet and stuck it back into the pocket of the person he took it from.

"Yeah, but just five more bucks a person. A measly five, and think of how much more we'd make," the tall man persisted.

Epson, standing over them, made a dismissive sound. "Think of how much we'd make if you actually got that mark like you said you would. Easy money, my ass. All you did was bring the police down on us with that stupid gunshot."

The slight man jumped to his feet and glared up at Epson. "If you think putting a hit out on someone is so easy, why don't you do it? You gave the okay, too. Go on, I think it's time for you to get wet in that damn rainforest. You don't know how hard it is trying to kill that little E bitch."

My mouth opened in a silent gasp as something about their words clicked in my mind. *Mark. Gunshot. Rainforest. Little E bitch.* These people . . . were the ones hunting me. At least two of them were.

The shorter woman from the other pair stood up. "Let's just focus on the task at hand. They won't stay unconscious forever."

Epson huffed. "Right, hurry it up." He turned and started to walk off the stage.

I stood up. "Do you believe the words you said?" I called out. My voice carried through the quiet gym.

All five of them froze.

Epson whipped around on the stage, his white robe fluttering with his movements. "Who said that?" Then he must have noticed the phone floating in the air. "Who are you?"

I ended the video before putting the device into my Items Bag, then I put my street clothes in there, too, revealing the under-armor suit I wore underneath. They couldn't see anything because Stealth was still on, so I took out my leather chest plate and quickly strapped it on. "Do you believe the words you were spewing all over the crowd? Do you think a new Earth is real? Or are you just sharing conspiracy theories from a rambling antigovernmentalist?"

"Where are you?" Epson looked around, trying to figure out where my voice was coming from. Luckily, there was enough of an echo in the building that it semihid my location. Which was unfortunate for him, since I bet one reason he chose this place was for the dramatic echo.

The four Hunters on the ground started to stalk closer to me, every inch of their bodies alert and ready.

I took out my thigh cuisses and strapped them on with well-practiced hands. "It doesn't matter who I am, but I want to know what makes you think anything you said was true?"

The taller of the men, a C Hunter, moved within ten feet of me. I was dying to do something about him, but I wanted to finish my conversation with Epson. Slipping around the man, I walked closer to the stage while the rest of them moved toward the back of the gym.

With a cock of his head, Epson opened his arms and slipped back into the persona he had while the show was going on. "What do you mean? Everything I said *was* true. You can look up the facts yourself."

I shook my head, even though he couldn't see it. "No, the only facts that were true were the ones you said about Earth's population. Everything else was a lie. There's no paradise on the other side of a portal." I quickly strapped on my greaves.

The people behind me gasped as they realized I'd slipped right through them and they had no idea. Spinning around, they started to walk back toward me.

Epson scoffed and folded his arms. "How do you know?"

I stared up at him as I put on my boots.

Funny. He spoke about how unfair life was. How the weak were beaten down and stomped on by the strong. But this man, Epson, was a C Hunter. Unless he did something illegal, he should have had a cushy life. Either way, he sure as hell wasn't oppressed like he said he was.

"Have you ever been to the other side of a portal?" I asked. "Because I have. Let me tell you, it's no heaven. In fact, I'd take Hell over it." I slipped to the right, away from the woman getting too close to me. I looked up at him. "What do you know about the parasitic planet?"

The woman made an annoyed sound, obviously frustrated that she didn't catch me.

Epson laughed. "Parasitic planet? What the hell is that?"

"It's what's on the other side of portals. You're right—Earth is dying." I jumped up on the stage with him. Since it wasn't my mist, the artificial fog rippled when I landed noiselessly beside him.

The white-robed man startled and turned. A long, serrated dagger appeared in his hand as he swung in my direction, but I reached out and caught his wrist, stopping the tip of his dagger inches from my cheek. Flinging his hand to the side, I reached for his mask. It annoyed me that I couldn't see his face. A contradiction, I knew, since I was invisible and still wore a mask, but hey . . .

My fingertips wrapped around the edge of his mask. With a hard yank—coupled with the momentum of his tipping body—the mask ripped right off his face.

I didn't know what I was expecting, but it wasn't a pretty-boy face. Thin, coquettishly tilted brown eyes, a narrow nose, and full lips. I bet he was twice my age, but he didn't really look it. If it wasn't for the lines around his eyes and mouth that were only noticeable at a close distance, I would have pegged him at thirty. His long, bleached hair only added to the youthful look.

He gasped and staggered back, and taking advantage of it, I swiped his feet out from under him. He yelped and landed on his backside, faint coils of fog washing over his head.

Inside the mask was a filter, obviously to protect him against the poison he unleashed on his audience. All so he could make a couple bucks from people who could barely survive as it was.

I scowled at him and flexed my hand. The mask in my grip cracked, the thick white paper-mache breaking like it was porcelain. I threw the mask to the floor, shattering it, and the small air filter slid out of sight.

"Earth is dying," I reiterated. "And you're making it harder to save it."

CHAPTER 36

Three magic attacks—two lightning strikes and a fire blast—shot at me from below the stage. Since my invisibility proved difficult for them to detect where I was, none of the attacks were aimed at the same place. Magic and fire spread through the air three feet above where Epson lay on the stage.

I dodged a bolt of lightning that arced around me, but a stray electric tentacle struck my arms and left a burn mark. My arm went numb for a second before it started to tingle as the nerves began to wake up. Luckily, the lightning was from an E mage. It hurt, but it wasn't fatal. A moment later, a C-ranked fire blast hit the right side of the stage and exploded in a hot boom that evaporated all the fake fog within three feet of it.

In the middle of the stage, Epson threw his hands over his head and gasped like a pansy as magic struck around him. I guess he was fine when it was orchestrated as part of his show, but in the middle of a real battle, he lost his cool. Well, he did say he wasn't made for being a Hunter. But after twenty years, you'd think he'd grow a pair. Then again, maybe that's why he stole from unconscious victims.

The artificial fog left on the stage swirled around my feet as I skipped out of the way of the magic, bending and twisting as needed to stay safe. Stealth made me invisible for now, but to anyone paying attention, the movement of the fog was a dead giveaway to my position.

I landed on my toes and ducked under another arc of lightning.

Before I could recover, a fire blast shot toward me. Throwing up my arm, I formed a mist barrier half a second before it hit, the attacker's magic and my barrier connecting with a deafening *boom*. The force threw me back into the dark curtain that spread across the back of the stage, which ripped off its support beam and tangled around me as I continued to fly backward. The material slipped over my body and fell away seconds before I slammed against something solid and flat.

The impact forced the air from my lungs and sent my head reeling and spinning. The wall I slumped against vibrated slightly, and a second later, a large metal cylinder landed on my shoulder. The lid popped off, and something wet, cold, and sticky spilled down my hot body. I gasped painfully for air as a strong smell of paint covered the stink of the artificial fog.

My eyes cracked open, coming into focus.

God, that one blast had shot me back over thirty feet to the space behind the stage and taken out thirty percent of my HP—and that was after my barrier took the edge off the actual attack. I glanced down at my body and the royal blue paint that spread from my shoulder to hips. The paint revealed my torso and completely negated the reason why I had Stealth activated in the first place. *Well, I might as well not waste the MP to maintain it, then.*

I canceled Stealth, taking comfort that my identity remained concealed behind the mask I still wore.

The four Hunters leapt onto the stage.

The two women went to Epson, who was struggling to his feet. From the way he tottered as he stood up, the effects of the airborne drugs were getting to him now that he didn't have a mask on. They held him up on each side, leaning over to check his condition.

The two male Hunters shot at me. Jumping to my feet, I dodged to the side as the tallest one attacked me with dual daggers. The serrated edge of the blades struck the metal wall behind me, sparking as metal hit metal, and a gash was left when the stainless steel yielded to the Hunter weapon. I twisted out of the way and kicked out, my heel hitting his masked forehead.

He grunted and staggered back as his mask cracked and warped. The top half fell apart and revealed a face I recognized. I would never forget a nose like that. It was Beak Nose, one of the hitmen hunting me.

My eyes narrowed. So then the mage who just hit me with fire must be Beak Nose's companion from the rainforest, Mage Buddy. I knew they were the men who were hunting me, but for the moment—thanks to the mask—they had no idea exactly who their target was.

Before I could attack Beak Nose, a whip of fire arced toward me. I dodged out of the way as the fire struck the ground, searing the concrete black. Flipping around, I lunged at Mage Buddy, kindjals out. He staggered back as I closed in on him, obviously not expecting me to go on the offensive so fast.

I stabbed at him. He dodged to the side and flicked his fire whip at me again, but I moved to the right and swung out with my left kindjal. The blade hit the line of fire and sliced through like hot butter, making the flame that had been cut off evaporate in the air. I moved to attack him again but paused and jumped backward at the last second.

A bolt of lightning struck the place where I had just been standing. The taller of the women was guiding Epson off the stage, but the other one stood with a hand out, lightning still crackling between her fingers, obviously ready to join in the fight. She was an E, completely over her head, but I respected that she wasn't backing down. However, that didn't mean I was about to let her stand there and zap me every time I took my eyes off her.

I closed in on her in a second. She gasped, her reaction time a million times slower than mine. Before she could move, I kicked out and caught her across the chest. She flew back, landing on the floor below. She didn't move, but her chest was still rising and falling. I didn't have a big beef with her; she was mostly just in the way, so I didn't exactly want to kill her. If possible, I wanted to turn her into the police alive.

A tingle of awareness shot down my back. I spun around, blocking Beak Nose's sneak attack with my kindjal. Our blades collided, and sparks flew.

"Are you the police?" he gritted out, trying to overpower me.

My arms started to give way under his pressure; after all, he was stronger than me. My boots were sliding slowly across the polished floor of the stage even though my rigid posture hadn't changed. My eyes narrowed. *Man*, he really needed to brush his teeth better. "No. Just a pissed off girl who's gone through too much shit because of you." I slashed up with my left hand.

He bent back to get out of the way and responded with his own attack. We exchanged blows in rapid succession, both trying to take a chunk out of each other and coming up a hair too short. It was a little odd to me, since all of my battle experience was against monsters and not Hunters with familiar weapons, but Beak Nose seemed like he was in his element. His moves were practiced and methodical, attacking me with two daggers. After ten or so exchanges, I finally started to pick up on his rhythm and worked to throw it off. He hissed as I left a long cut from his left shoulder to his elbow, leaving a long gap in his brown robe that slowly turned red with blood.

A long whip of fire cracked in my direction, forcing me to back up before I could pressure Beak Nose more.

Beak Nose grabbed his bleeding arm and scowled at me. "Who are you?"

I jumped out of the way of another snap of fire. Almost casually, I reached up and pulled off my mask before I tossed it out and used it to block the next whip attack. The fire hit the white masquerade, and it cracked in half before falling to the ground, blackened and smoking. Instead of answering with words, I simply glared at the men. If they didn't recognize me, they were truly failures as hitmen.

They gasped in unison, obviously shocked. "But you're an E," Mage Buddy denied. "How can you . . . " he trailed off.

I smirked. "Your information is out of date."

The two men gave annoyed growls at almost the same time, giving a messed-up sense of surround sound. They attacked in sync—the mage flicking his fire whip and Beak Nose lunging for a kill. Between them, there was very little room to dodge. Instead, I went on the offense.

My Poison Fog thickly filled up the air, blinding them. They were so startled that the trajectory of their attacks shifted. Beak Nose missed completely, and I cut the fire whip again. They still had their masks, meaning they had air filters on, so I didn't know how damaging the poison was to them, but I was pissed off enough to find out.

The fighting escalated quickly with both men against me. They were higher level and a team, but I was faster than them by a hair, and Poison Fog gave me enough of an advantage to dodge their most powerful attacks. I continued to go at them, leaving cuts here and there. I couldn't seem to get any good, solid hits in, but I noticed they were dripping blood more than a normal cut should. They must have been inflicted with Bleed.

I, of course, wasn't able to dodge everything they threw at me, not by a long shot. My own HP was nickeled and dimed down until my HP was in the orange. What I had going for me was that I didn't have a status effect.

"Just die already!" Mage Buddy hissed, throwing out a huge fire blast, completely ignoring the fact that his partner was right next to me.

I dodged to the side and activated Critical Hit as I threw my right kindjal at Mage Buddy. Simultaneously, I solidified a wall of mist in front of me. The mage's fire blast hit Beak Nose and exploded. He didn't even make a sound as he was blown through the air until he smashed against the back wall with a horrible crunch. The outer rim of the explosion hit my shield, shattering it, and I was knocked off my feet, rolling a couple feet before I stopped.

My whole body hurt from the long battle, the dried paint irritated my skin and stuck my clothes to my body, and I was too hot from the fire, but still, I struggled to my feet. Breathing hard and ready for another attack, I looked around but couldn't see the two men.

The curtains and framing on the stage had been destroyed in our fight, and scorch marks dotted the stage and backstage area like a toddler on Red Bull with a black paint brush. Some marks looked like they were still hot, but they hadn't lit on fire just yet.

Unconscious people remained slumped against the floor around the open space below. Since I purposefully guided the fight away from the crowd, it didn't look like anyone was hurt, and the fog was starting to clear up. Hopefully, they'd start to wake up soon.

The kindjal I threw at Mage Buddy returned. I held both swords at the ready as I walked to the back of the stage where Beak Nose had been blown to, then turned my head and paused. There was no reason to go any farther.

He was crumpled against the back wall like a broken doll, bent nearly in half, his head down in his lap. The wounds on his body had been seared shut, so there wasn't a lot of blood around him. Smoke rose from his back and limp arms. Without a doubt, he was dead.

I stared at him, frowning. I considered myself a good person. Too good, in most cases. I wanted to be an example for my sister to look up to. But I couldn't bring myself to feel bad at all that Beak Nose was dead. In fact, I think it was for the best. As a hitman and thieving cultist, he was a danger to the public.

A moan followed by a gurgling sound came from below the front of the stage.

I turned around and hurried in that direction. I thought I'd kept the fight away from the people. Did someone get hurt after all?

I stopped at the edge and looked down.

Mage Buddy lay spread-eagle on the floor below, just a couple feet away from the unconscious female cultist. A line of blood leaked down his cheek from under his mask, and the left side of his chest was covered in blood, the red liquid puddled around him.

So my thrown kindjal had hit him after all. The force must have knocked him off the stage, and Bleed was still plaguing him.

His chest shuddered as he gasped again.

I jumped down to his side and stared at the dying man. "Who hired you to kill me?" In my mind, that person should be Blake Hans, but after the mix-up with Bethany, I wanted to hear a name.

His mask had slipped to the side, but I could still see his eyes flutter open from the eye slots. "Wou . . . ldn't . . . you . . . like to . . . "

"I don't think you're in a position to be cocky." I reached down and pulled off his mask. "Who wants to kill me?"

His head tilted to the side from my rough handling, the blood leaking from his lips smearing across his pale cheek. His lips stretched in a distorted sneer. "You . . . should . . . die."

The life left his eyes.

CHAPTER 37

I stared down at the corpse, frowning. I might have had a hand in the death of Beak Nose, but I didn't actually claim that kill. In the end, the one who did the killing attack was Mage Buddy. But I was one hundred percent responsible for this mage's death.

I should be upset that I killed a human. It was something I swore I'd never do. But I felt nothing. Technically, I should have captured him alive and turned him over to the police, let the officials take control and get as much information as they could. But it didn't happen like that. In the end, it was me or him—and I wasn't going to lie down and die.

As the pool of blood around Mage Buddy grew bigger, the strongest emotion I felt was disappointment that I couldn't get any more information from him. I never got the name of who hired him to kill me. Or found out what they were doing in the cult. No matter how long I stared at him, he wasn't going to open his eyes and tell me.

I turned and looked at the female cultist still unconscious on the ground. Man, I must have hit her hard for her to be out this long. Well, it was nothing a healer couldn't fix. Hopefully she was a talker. Walking over to her, I pulled out the rope from my Items Bag. I wasn't a pro at tying people up, but after wrapping her in ten feet of nylon rope with multiple twists and knots, in theory, she wasn't going to go anywhere until the authorities got here.

I just didn't plan on being here when that happened.

I turned and walked toward the stairway that led back to Eden. Technically, since I was in Garden City, I could easily spend the night with my family, but then I'd have to explain to the front gate officer in the morning how I got out of Eden without approval when I tried to get back in.

Just before I took the first step down the stairs, I paused, my foot hanging in the air. Slowly, I turned around and walked to the middle of the gym where the drugged fog still pooled the most. I took out a water bottle and poured the contents out onto the ground. There were still a few drops left inside, so I waved my hand over the opening. The drops evaporated into mist, and I guided the mist out of the bottle.

I mentally reached out to all the remaining mist that I could and condensed it into a thick cloud. I scowled, feeling the particles of something impure inside—the drug. It was different from my Poison Fog. This foreign stuff felt coarse and clunky, like backwash floaters, obviously not natural in the water vapor. Still, I guided the drugged fog into the empty water bottle and packed it in there as much as I could. It wouldn't all fit in the bottle so, after twisting the cap tightly and storing it in my Items Bag, I guided the rest behind the stage area where it couldn't affect anyone—at least not anyone alive.

I hurried down the stairs, through the long hallway, and back up to the small building on the other side. The man and female Hunter who were here when I first entered were gone. For all I knew, the Hunter was one of the lightning mages. I wasn't exactly paying attention to the stairway after I exited it earlier, but I wasn't worried. It was better that they were gone right now.

I pulled out the cell phone that I took earlier and fiddled with it until I accessed the emergency setting before I took a deep breath. *Think panicked thoughts. I'm a pathetic, scared, useless girl.* I repeated the thought over and over in my head, trying to drill the idea down. Then I dialed 991—the Hunter's three-digit emergency number.

"991, what's your emergency?" a woman said over the microphone.

I took a couple breaths, trying to make my voice airy and panicked. "I need help. I don't know what's going on. They're just . . . falling over, everywhere." Was that good enough? I'd never been good at acting.

"What's your name and where are you?" the woman asked.

I completely ignored her request for my name. "I don't know exactly where I am. I don't think I'm in Eden anymore. My friend brought me to a building." Quickly, I spit out the address. "Then we walked down some stairs and came out in this building in Garden City." That will freak the authorities out real fast. I took a break to hyperventilate a little more before rushing in, completely cutting the woman off. "Then this guy in white started talking about weird stuff and there was this fog. Then everyone started to pass out. I don't know what's wrong; there's hundreds of them. I feel so dizzy and sick. Please hurry."

"Okay, miss, what was—"

I gasped like I was looking at a monster and moved the phone away from my face. "Wait! Who are you? Don't touch me!" I screamed and rubbed the speaker on the only part of my pants that wasn't covered in paint or battle grime. Without waiting, I hit End Call and shut the phone off.

"That should freak them out good enough," I whispered, putting the phone back in my Items Bag, then I cast Stealth. It wasn't completely effective because of the paint, but hopefully, the night's darkness was enough to hide me.

I exited the building, taking care to lock the door behind me. It would be nicer to leave it unlocked for the authorities, but I wanted to keep it as authentic as possible.

I could already feel the presence of dozens of high-leveled Hunters closing in on the area. Without waiting, I activated Feather Step and sprinted away as fast as I could.

"Did you hear about the cult bust last night?" a middle-aged Hunter gossiped to her friend as they walked in full arms toward the Gate. The morning sun winked off a large red pendant around her neck. "Those crazies actually burrowed a tunnel into Garden City." She *tsk*ed with disdain. "It makes all the regulations we do to keep humans safe pointless, don't you think?"

I found my head turning toward the woman as I focused on her conversation. I was openly eavesdropping, but because of my Stealth, they couldn't see me.

Her friend covered her mouth with her gloved hand. "Is that true? What are they thinking?" They passed the raised planter boxes around Gate Square and walked into the open area, their boots clicking on the concrete.

"No good, that's for sure. Those people will say anything to cause panic if you ask me." The first woman nodded righteously.

Her friend bobbed her head in agreement. "Yes. So they finally caught them?"

The first woman shook her head. "Only a couple of them. But the ringleader is still out there . . . " Their voices trailed off as they moved out of my hearing range.

They weren't the only ones talking about the cult raid last night. I'd heard quite a few things the people were saying—some of it true, some of it not. But there was one thing that remained consistent: Epson was still at large. And they were still trying to figure out what was in the drug. Which is why I was here.

From my spot under a tree, I looked up at Eden's hospital. The glass surrounding the building reflected the picture of Gate Square and the buildings around it. The green foliage was bright in the late summer heat, but I wasn't here to gawk over architecture.

Walking up the few steps to the entry, I stopped just outside the sliding glass doors and waited a beat before the doors slid open as a Hunter exited the building. I took the chance to duck into the hospital, then silently and carefully, I slipped down the hall leading to where the doctors' offices were.

Several people, mostly nurses in scrubs, passed me in the hall, but I didn't run into a problem. Only one of them turned as if they could somewhat sense me, but in the end, they walked away looking confused. After a couple twists and turns, I stopped outside a thick wooden door, the brass nameplate to the right reading Healer Jonovan Setter.

I bent over and pointed to the ground right by his door. A small brown cardboard box appeared there, the top taped together with a printed label which read, To Jonovan. That was going to cause some panic when he saw it. Hell, they might even call in the bomb squad. They were doomed to be disappointed, though.

Inside was the cell phone I took last night and the bottle full of drugged fog. By now, the fog had liquified, but the drug agents were still in there. There was also a printed note which read:

Look at the video taken last night at 11:24 p.m. It might give some insight on the cultists. The leader calls himself Epson or Dr. E. He's a C-ranked melee Hunter but isn't well trained. Then I went on to describe him as detailed as I could before I moved to the next subject. *The bottle contains some of the drug in the fog that was used on the crowd. The main part of it is derived from the cyan-agaric that's found in the Josu Rainforest.*

I turned and left.

That was everything I knew about the cultists, and a lot of good information. If they couldn't locate Epson from that, it was on their heads. I was sure they had a way to open up the cellphone and look through the photos and videos. I mean, they could in the movies, so they should be able to in real life . . . right? Push comes to shove, they hunt down the girl the phone belonged to and make her open the phone. I'm sure they had a list of people involved in last night, so they just needed to ask around.

As for the drug, I knew they had the technology to break it down. Even if it was watered down by the fog, they should be able to get the general gist of its makeup. And hopefully come up with a recovery method for the people who were still affected by it.

As I walked out, I took a deep breath of the fresh morning air. No matter what happened now, it was all on the authorities' heads. I just wanted to wash my hands of the whole thing. I didn't have any more time to spend on a bunch of thieving wackos. I still needed to find an antidote for Dreamers, figure out how to find my way to a parasitic planet to destroy it before it ate Earth, and find Kesstel. But to do all that, I needed to get stronger. A lot stronger.

My eyes narrowed in determination, and I walked toward the Gate.

A week later, everyone and their dog was talking about how the leader of the cultist group was finally caught. And he wasn't just a crazy antigovernmentalist—he was also stealing from the people who went to listen to him. It was a horrible thing for him to do, but it also served those saps right for going in the first place.

Another bit of news which quickly gained momentum was how the cyan-agaric in Josu Rainforest was now a controlled substance. It would be part of the morning cleanup crew's job now. After the crew who killed the worst of the monsters left, they would search the rainforest for the mushroom, and they were either supposed to destroy the cyan-agaric or carefully collect it for further Association research.

None of that had much impact on me. They never did put me together with the person who crashed the cultist meeting or handed over the information.

As for myself, I was too busy grinding levels to care, but even though my levels were increasing every day, it just felt like something was . . . missing. I couldn't resist going to the Josu Rainforest every morning. And every morning, I left disappointed.

Alone, without Kesstel.

—

CHAPTER 38

The Josu Rainforest floor spread out sixty feet below me, a mix of dark soil and pale green moss that climbed the trunks of the massive trees. An ever-present light drizzle flattened my pale brown hair to my head. My wet black-and-gray leather armor gleamed in the faint greenish light glowing from the leafy canopy above.

A drip collected on the point of my nose, making it itch. Wiping the water off, I pinched my nose to keep from sneezing. Silence right now was key. With one more deep breath, I stepped off the branch and dropped to the forest floor.

Landing silently on the soft ground, I stepped back, pressing my body tightly against the smooth tree bark behind me. My kindjal, a short blade made of clear crystal and steel blended together, appeared in my right hand. Each water droplet that caught and lingered on the blade soon evaporated into mist, dissipating into the air when I didn't collect it.

My senses spread out, making me aware of everything within forty feet from me. Thirty feet away, I could feel three large monsters, velociorheas, walking through the forest. They were bobbing almost leisurely around the tall trees, soundlessly moving over the moist ground. Getting closer to me.

In the blink of an eye, an exact replica of my sword appeared in my other hand. Like a ghost, I leaned back against the tree and waited.

A velociorhea approached the other side of the tree. Several loud sniffs followed, then I heard the ground squish as it was compressed—a footstep. Then another. Four feet from me. Two feet from me.

On my right, the huge claws, bigger than my fingers, of the three-toed foot sank into the moss as it stepped next to my feet. A large, elongated head appeared. The huge, pointed teeth were bright against the multicol-ored skin of the bird dinosaur's bald head. The circular yellow eye pointed straight at me.

I swung my kindjal before it could alert the others, my sword sink-ing into its chest where the long, thin neck met the gray-brown feathered body. The monster's mouth opened, but no noise escaped. Jerking my kindjal, I ripped it out of the side of the velociorhea, nearly severing off its wing in the process. It collapsed to the ground, writhing in pain.

The other two instantly reacted. They whipped around the tree, trying to pincer me in the middle, but I jumped up and kicked one head while I stepped on the other, landing five feet from them and turning just as they got back to my side. They attacked, snapping and scratching at me, and I parried, but one attack was soon followed by another. More and more, they pressed me, forcing me back.

Teeth gritted, I cast Poison Fog, covering the whole area within forty feet of me.

The velociorheas shrieked in alarm and turned to run away.

"Not this time," I whispered, thrusting out my hand.

Ten feet away, a solid mist wall appeared in their way. They hit it and bounced back, obviously confused.

This fog wouldn't only benefit me, but it would ensure that no other velociorheas got in my way. I'd found that these monsters were sensitive to Poison Fog, as in, they could detect it every time, and they would always run away. Now that I finally had them in my trap, I wasn't going to let them go.

As soon as they realized they weren't getting out easily, the velociorheas turned on me, more aggressive than ever. They worked in perfect unison, a unique trait to the species, to take me down. It was hard work to keep a step ahead of them, and I still lost HP in the process, but they were losing it faster, susceptible to Poison.

"Ha!" I slashed out with my left kindjal and left a gaping wound on the side of the breast of the velociorhea. Then I spun and stabbed into the hole with my right kindjal. There was a slight resistance as my blade hit the energy crystal inside before it shattered, and the monster exploded into tiny lights that quickly disappeared, leaving two glowing item drop orbs behind.

[+ 346 EXP]

A heavy force slammed into my back, knocking me to my knees. The other velociorhea pressed down on me with one foot, its long claws digging into my leather armor and painfully piercing my skin. Then it snapped down at the back of my head.

Twisting my body, I leaned my head to the side. The toothy mouth slammed shut right next to my ear, the sound sending shivers down my spine, as I jerked my kindjal around and stabbed it right into the monster's head. The velociorhea screeched, painfully loud, and lurched off me. I jumped to my feet and turned around, swords at the ready.

The bird monster shook its head, flinging black blood out of the hole where the right eye used to be.

I lunged forward, closing in on the left, the monster following me with its good eye. Five feet from it, I created a solid block of mist on its right and, with a flick of my wrist, sent it smashing into the blind side of the velociorhea. It screeched as it was taken by surprise and thrown to the ground, and I jumped to stab both blades into its chest. The energy crystal shattered, and the monster disappeared, leaving a couple drop items behind. When it disappeared, all its blood on me and the surrounding area vanished as well.

[+346 EXP]

Breathing heavily, I scooped up the drop orbs. They disappeared as soon as I touched them, depositing their contents in my Items Bag, then I turned and walked back to the tree where I originally started.

The first velociorhea was still there, spilling black blood all over the pale green moss, but alive. The slit in its yellow eye constricted when it saw me, and it struggled to get up, but the most it could do was flop to the side.

I walked up and stabbed down. The velociorhea vanished, along with the black blood and any other traces it had left.

[+365 EXP]

[You have Leveled Up!]

[Gained Ability: Mist Blade.]

[Daily Task: (Destroy ten Energy Crystals) Completed. + 215 EXP]

Every time I leveled up, every one of my stats increased by one, and I was given three bonus points to assign wherever I wanted. It was kinda nice being able to choose what changes I wanted to make in my own body, considering how little control I had over the System that was making me stronger. It decided the minimum of how many monsters I could kill a day, how long I cultivated for, and also sent me on random quests for items that I had no idea why I was getting.

There were a lot of things I didn't understand about the System, but one thing was for sure: it *was* making me stronger. And that was all I needed. As long as I was strong enough to protect my family, I didn't need to know anything else.

Satisfied for now, I opened up my System menu and assigned my extra stat points.

Jynn Devhro

Rank B		**Level** 50	
		EXP to Next Level 6885	

HP 1174/2842		**Stat Points** 0	
MP 732/1253			

Strength 90 (+20)	**Agility** 83
Magic 80	**Perception** 83
Constitution 83 (+20)	**Intelligence** 76

Skills	**Abilities**
Throw	Mist (Improved) (50 ft)
Critical Hit	Feather Step
Quick Hit	Regen (Limited)
Mirror	Stealth (Limited)
High Jump	Poison Fog
	Mist Blade

My eyes widened when I noticed my rank. I was finally a B. After all this work, I was halfway to where I wanted to be. I should be whooping and jumping around, but I couldn't muster up the excitement. I still had so far to go.

It had been two months since Kesstel disappeared inside a collapsed portal, and my life had fallen into a routine: wake up, kill as many monsters as I could before the sun went down, cash in the drop items, go back to E Hostel, sleep. Get up in the morning and do it again.

Still, no matter what I did, it wasn't enough. It was frustrating to know that a giant dimensional monster on the other side of a portal was in the process of destroying Earth, and yet I couldn't do anything about it. I wasn't strong enough to go into a portal myself. Hell, I couldn't even survive in some areas of Gate Vale by myself.

All I could do was focus on helping the research for Dreamers. Out of the sixteen areas that Gate Vale was divided into, I'd killed one of every monster in seven of them. The System had notified me of four monsters which could help with creating a cure for the Dreamer's disease, but those four items were already known to the medical world and already being worked on.

In the end, I wasn't any closer to finding the missing ingredient than I was two months ago—when Kesstel said there was no cure. The disease was caused by the magic of the parasitic planet attacking Earth. And since the Gates, the monsters, and even the superhuman abilities that the Hunters had were created by the parasitic planet, it wouldn't create a means to cure the disease. The parasite wanted the people to die so that the planet would finally die.

At least, that's what Kesstel said, but I couldn't believe that. I needed to believe there was a cure. I might collapse if there wasn't. Only, there just wasn't enough time. I only had four more months before my mom had to leave the hospital. Without the medical support, a Dreamer would die.

I waved a hand, and a solid piece of mist appeared over me like an umbrella. A piece of paper with a list of every area and known monster listed on it appeared in my hand, and I took a pencil out, drawing a line through velociorhea, thus completing the Josu Rainforest list. This location was good for leveling up and cultivating, but it was time to find another place. The missing piece to the cure wasn't here.

A teal screen flashed before my eyes, telling me I needed to go. I put the list away and started to run through the forest, not bothering to go up to the treetops. I wasn't at risk to run into monsters with my Poison Fog activated in Josu Rainforest. If I were in another location, that would be a different matter, but here I simply ran full out over the soft, wet ground.

Two hours later, I stood in front of my family's apartment door. My knuckle made a soft sound as I rapped on it.

There was a clatter of movement from inside the apartment, then the door swung open.

Aliya stood on the other side, a wide smile on her face and a fluffy pink cat-ear headband popping out of her light brown hair. "Happy birthday!" she squealed, throwing herself at me.

I caught her and grinned as I held her warm body close. So, so much better than the cold chill and death inside the Gate. "Thanks," I murmured, her hair in my face. Ah, had she grown another inch since I last saw her? I swear she wasn't this tall. Wasn't this old.

Aunt Mina and Uncle Carl sat at the battered square table on the other side of the small living/kitchen area. They smiled at me, love in their tired faces. There wasn't much in this tiny two-bedroom apartment—all the furniture was old and worn, the electronics were out of date, and even the decor was lacking—but this small unit held all my precious memories and the people who created them with me.

"Come in, come in." Aunt Mina stood up and walked over.

Without waiting, Aliya dragged me inside and shut the door. I took a second to hug my aunt and uncle before I was pushed into a chair with a loose leg.

My sister hurried over to the kitchen counter and returned, holding something behind her back. "Tada!" she sang, pulling a sparkly gold-crown headband from behind her back. "It's your special day, so you get the crown." She slid it onto my head, the fanged snapper bracelet I made her tinkling soothingly from her wrist.

I cringed and laughed at the same time. Seriously, bling wasn't my thing. But anything Aliya gave me was perfect. I just hoped she grew out of her glitter phase soon.

Still, I took a flip phone out of my Items Bag and opened up its camera. Smiling, I grabbed my sister and pulled her in for a selfie to show off our headbands, then I turned around and took a picture with all four of us together. It had been so long since we were all in the same room, I wanted to capture it.

"Have you had lunch yet?" Aunt Mina asked.

I nodded. It was almost two in the afternoon—I hoped they hadn't put off eating for me.

"Then it's already time for dessert," Uncle Carl said. He went to the counter and picked up a large plate covered by a metal mixing bowl. He carefully walked the short distance back to the table and set it down, then he took the mixing bowl off, revealing a sword-shaped birthday cake.

Since we never had money for a lot of presents growing up, Aunt Mina always made sure to make us a special birthday cake. She'd spend hours, sculpting cake and frosting, trying to make whatever wild request Aliya or I asked for. She wasn't a cake master by any means—like the time Aliya's unicorn looked more like a dying dog—but she always put her best into it, and some of the pieces were actually fantastic.

This sword looked more like a fat dagger, but I liked how she'd used sugar candy as gems on the hilt and blended two colors of gray to represent the pattern weld on the blade.

I grinned wide. "It's wonderful. Thank you!"

I reached out and hugged her. I could feel the pounds she'd lost in the last couple months from stress at her job. Her eyes—the same hazel as my dad's, Aliya's, and mine—were tired, with bags under them from not sleeping. And there were more gray hairs than last time I saw her, I swear. Even so, she was grinning as happily as ever.

"Ah, I can't believe you're already nineteen. I remember when you were *this* big." Aunt Mina held her hands in front of her, indicating a tiny bundle. "You were such a fussy sleeper, your mom would come and crash at my place while I watched you in the afternoon just so she could get enough sleep to function." She laughed, alight with memories. "Now, you're such a strong young woman. Your mom and dad would be so proud."

A happy blush burned my cheeks. I hoped they would be proud of me. I was trying; really, I was.

Aliya and Aunt Mina worked together to put a one and a nine candle on the cake, then Uncle Carl lit the candles. As the people I loved sang, my chest tightened painfully, and a big smile split my face.

"Make a wish and blow out the candles!" Aliya urged.

I blew them out.

Aunt Mina got some plates while Uncle Carl dug out a tub of ice cream from the back of the freezer.

My sister bumped her shoulder against mine. "What did you wish for? I won't tell anyone."

I laughed and shook my head. "If I tell, it won't come true."

"Aw, that's just a myth," she complained.

I bumped her shoulder back. "So is wishing on candles."

But I'd do it again and again, if it kept my loved ones safe. After all, it was a wish I was willing to pay any price for.

CHAPTER 39

And that takes game," Aliya announced, slapping down a red eleven Rook card.

My game partner, Aunt Mina, moaned and set her green ten down. "I swear, I've done nothing but feed you points all game." She huffed. "I really thought we were going to set you."

Uncle Carl happily dropped his black five on the table over the two other cards. "Good job." He laughed and patted my sister on the shoulder.

"Good job, Aliya," I said, dropping my card on the table. "It was a close round."

Aliya looked down and gasped. "Wait!" She pointed at my red twelve. "Where did you get that?"

I laughed at her shocked expression and swept the cards over to Aunt Mina to join the small pile of Rook cards in front of her. We didn't take many hands this round, but every hand we took was full of points.

I planted my elbow on the table and rested my chin in my hand. "You didn't count your cards right. If you had led red one more round, you would have forced my last trump card out. I bet you would have taken the last couple points if you had."

She moaned in defeat and rested her head in her hands.

"Thirty, forty-five," Aunt Mina counted the points of the cards in front of her out loud. Since we had the smaller pile, it was better to count what we had versus Aliya's and Uncle Carl's large one. "Fifty-five." Aunt Mina put down the last card. "That's a set!" she announced, holding up a high five.

I clapped her hand. "By five points!"

"Darn it!" Aliya collapsed on the table like an emotional teen and let out a mock wail.

Uncle Carl tsked in disappointment. "Aw, I thought we had that," he grumbled, but his lips curled in a smile anyway. He pulled the score paper closer and wrote the tally, then quickly added or subtracted the numbers. "That makes game," he said in his slow voice. "Jynn and Mina win with 525. Me and Aliya have 325."

Aliya huffed and looked at me. "I went easy on you because it's your birthday."

I laughed.

Aunt Mina looked at the clock. "But it's getting late. Why don't we open up presents now?"

I followed her gaze and frowned at the big hand getting closer to the five. It was funny how, since becoming an adult, my curfew time was stricter than it was when I was a kid. Back then, if I didn't get back in time, I was guilt-tripped to death, but that was it. Now, the Association actually slapped a fine on Hunters, the penalty getting bigger and bigger with each offense.

"I'll get them!" Aliya jumped up and hurried down the hall. A couple minutes later, she came back with two small boxes wrapped in red paper. She set them on the table then plopped back into her chair.

My family sang happy birthday to me one more time, then Aunt Mina handed me a long, thin rectangle. I opened it and pulled out the maroon shirt inside.

"It's pretty, thank you," I said, running my hand over the soft material. It was fancier than all the other plain tees in my closet at the hostel, but not overkill enough to make me awkward.

Aliya beamed. "I thought it would look great on you. When you get a boyfriend, you really should bring him home, you know. I need to make sure he's good enough, right?"

I choked. "Yeah, right. As if that's ever going to happen. Out of the very long list of things I need to do, romance it absolutely on the bottom, let me tell you." I put the shirt away in my Items Bag. "Why don't you get a boyfriend, and I'll check him out to make sure he's good enough, huh? Choose carefully, 'cuz I might beat him up if he's not."

Aliya jumped like I'd touched her with a live wire. "What?" she yelped.

My eyes narrowed. "Is there—"

"No!" she protested too passionately and waved her hands in front of her red face.

"Both of you girls are thirty years too early to talk about boys," Uncle Carl announced over our antics, but he gave Aliya a second glance, lips pursed with suspicion.

Aunt Mina seconded the notion, her eyes peeking at my little sister before she passed me the next package, a small square box.

Inside was a dime-size circular white magic crystal on a long silver chain.

"Wow," I whispered, touching the stone, noticing the glint of light it gave off. There wasn't a doubt that it had a small magic buff on it. When I was growing up, I always wanted something like this. Something elegant and simple enough that I could wear all the time without worrying about it sticking out too much. I just didn't think I'd get it now.

"We thought it would look good with the shirt," Aliya added, beaming. "And it kind of matches Mom's bracelet that you have. So, you know, you could wear them together."

I smiled at her as I put on the necklace right there. It lay over the rough blue fabric of my plain T-shirt. I couldn't resist rubbing my hand over the clear stone, its smooth surface cool on my skin. It might match with my mother's bracelet—they were both made out of silver—but they would never be worn together. Not because I hated the idea but because my mother's bracelet was so precious, I couldn't bring myself to put it on.

But this—I could wear this and proudly show the world what my family scraped up to get for me. After all, I knew how much they would have spent for a simple necklace like this. And with the budget they lived on, it was a sacrifice.

"Thank you," I said sincerely, my hand over the necklace. I got up and hugged each one of them, then I sat back down in my seat. "I have a present for you too." Tapping on the middle of the table, a pile of papers appeared, the top-most showing a large picture of a handsome building, followed by a house layout map.

"What's this?" Aunt Mina picked up the papers and gasped. "Jynn?"

Uncle Carl and Aliya leaned over her shoulder as they flipped through the pages.

"It's for a condo about a mile from here," I explained. "It's still a two-bedroom unit, but it's three hundred square feet bigger, with designated kitchen and living room spaces, and Aliya would have her own bathroom." Before they could say more, I rushed on. "It's not the fanciest place, I know, but it's only fifteen years old and in good shape. And the area it's in is safer than here."

"We can't afford something like this," Uncle Carl said slowly, self-loathing low in his tone. He glanced at Aunt Mina as she slowly put the papers down. With him out of a job and Aunt Mina only working part time, there was no way they could afford to buy a home.

Aliya bit her lips and didn't comment. She was in school full time and barely had time to do small odd jobs for the older widows around the apartment complex, just like I did before I became a Hunter.

"I have been earning a lot more lately," I said. "With what I've saved up, I can make the down payment. In the end, the mortgage would be less than what we're paying for this place right now, even with all the utilities. It would be a better, safer place for less money a month. I heard that the neighborhood next to it is going to go under construction next year. The plans are to really update that area. It would boost the appraisal value of that condo without us lifting a finger." I tapped on the stack of papers.

Aunt Mina still shook her head, frowning. "A down payment is a lot of money, Jynn. You should use that money for yourself. Buy a place in Eden."

I shrugged. "I think it would be better to use it like this first. And I can always make more money."

Now that I was stronger, drop items I got from monsters were worth more. With how I was grinding levels right now, I was making bank. In six more months, Aliya would graduate and get tested as a Hunter, which was plenty of time for me to save up another down payment for a place in Eden—an apartment or a condo. Granted, real estate in Eden was forty percent more expensive than in Garden City, but I could make it work with two mortgages. Somehow.

Assuming Earth hadn't collapsed by then.

But first, I needed to make sure my family was okay, then I could think about myself.

Uncle Carl rested his arms on the table and picked up the papers, looking at them carefully. "I think it's a good idea," he said slowly.

"Carl," Aunt Mina scolded.

I was glad he agreed, but I was a little surprised. He hated that they had to rely on me to afford to live. It drove his self-esteem down the drain and was a major part of the nearly fatal depression and anxiety that had plagued him for the last year.

He shifted through the papers, his face serious. "I was waiting to tell you after I got my first paycheck, but I got a job in Bill's Market. It's actually only a mile and a half from here." He tapped on the paper. "I could walk and save on bus fare."

Aliya and Aunt Mina gasped, just as surprised as me.

"Wait, when did you get a job?" Aliya asked, cautious excitement on her face.

Uncle Carl set down the papers, his lips twisted in embarrassment. "A week and a half ago. It's nothing big, just a part-time day shift stocking stuff and organizing the back. But Mr. Atwell promised that if I keep up the good work, he'd promote me to full-time at my two-month eval."

"That's fantastic," I piped up, throwing in all the encouragement I could. Still, there was a bit of concern. "How . . . do you feel there?" It wasn't like he hadn't gotten jobs in the past; it was just that he couldn't handle the environment. He always felt like running away. Was it going to be the same this time?

He smiled almost shyly. "It's good. It's a slow place, and if I feel too pressured, I can slip into the back to breathe."

Tears pooled in Aunt Mina's eyes. She got up and hugged him. "That's wonderful, honey. Really."

Uncle Carl gave a breathy laugh and patted her arms around his neck. "It will be." He kissed the side of her head. "But what I was thinking was, when I get a full-time position, I'll be able to cover almost eighty percent of the mortgage. With both of us working, we should be able to cover all the costs." He looked into my eyes. "So you won't have to worry about us anymore. We'll be fine."

I grinned. As much as I loved my necklace, my uncle's news was the best present I got today. Not because of me but because he was so optimistic about his future. Unfortunately, I couldn't stay much longer.

I stood up and gave another round of hugs, then went to the door.

I tactfully paused and looked at my aunt and uncle. "Can I talk to you guys?"

They nodded and followed me to the door. Aliya's face scrunched up in annoyance that she was left out, but she stayed at the table.

I led them out and shut the door. A second later, I felt Aliya's presence creep to the other side. I smiled and shook my head before leading my aunt and uncle to the top of the dingy stairwell, away from her prying ears. I didn't want her to hear about this yet.

The parking lot spread out under me, a small collection of cars in various conditions on the cracked pavement hiding under the shade of the trees. It was getting colder, but my enhanced body didn't feel the fall chill as the sun started to set below the skyline. However, Aunt Mina and Uncle Carl didn't have coats on, so I'd keep this short.

"I talked to the hospital and applied for an extension for Mom," I said bluntly. "If it's approved, it will only be for another six months—so ten months from now in total. But that time wouldn't be at the discounted Hunter's Benefit rate."

They looked at each other, grief on their faces.

"It would be at the same cost as the hospitals on the East Coast. The only difference is we wouldn't have to pay for moving costs," I added. "As it is, it sounds like the doctors don't think—" I paused, my throat suddenly threatening to tighten up. I swallowed and forced the knot down without changing my expression. "They don't think she'll last the year."

"You won't be able to go with her if she's moved to a different hospital," Uncle Carl pointed out.

I shook my head. I had a five-year obligation to stay in Eden. A higher-ranked Hunter, after that probation period, could apply to be a Guard to the cities without a Gate. But someone with my rank would never be hired outside of Eden. "Neither will Aliya if she tests as Hunter after she graduates. She could choose to go to the Quebec Gate or stay in Eden, but both are very far from where Mom would be."

Aunt Mina pulled me into her arms and hugged me tight. "You do what you think is best," she said, her voice cracking. Even though she was my mom's sister, they always let me have the final say on Mom's medical situations.

I nodded. Today was such a roller coaster, from low to high and back down to gut-wrenching low. But I couldn't keep holding onto this alone. "I don't want Aliya to know yet. Maybe a cure can be made in time. Either way, I don't want her to get distracted and her grades to suffer. It's her senior year—she needs all the happy memories she can get."

God knew, happy memories were few and far between in Eden. And if there was a god and Aliya somehow didn't become a Hunter, she needed good grades to get into a good higher learning program. Even if she hated me later for holding out on her, I could handle that. As long as she had a bright future.

Because I was going to do everything I could to make sure she had a future.

CHAPTER 40

In the last two months, the thing that had changed the most in my life was . . .

A knock echoed on the door of my dressing room. "Come on, are you done yet? It's just a couple of clothes, not a European dress," Bethany Wilks asked on the other side.

. . . *her.*

I'd spent an entire month thinking that she hated me enough to send hitmen after me, only for it to turn out that I was wrong on several accounts. She ended up being dead serious about wanting to be my friend and attached herself to me like an appendage. When she first proposed the idea, I thought she'd be like all the other high-ranking Hunters—constantly trying to knock me down to my place and treat me like a grunt. Surprisingly, she wasn't. In fact, all she wanted to do was hang out.

Oh, and talk. *A lot.*

It wasn't so bad. I'd come to realize that she was as shallow as a teaspoon but as vast as a lake. She knew about a lot of random things. Like, just a couple weeks ago when I mentioned researching Garden City real estate in passing, and the next day she handed over a thick stack of papers on the best properties in a variety of income ranges. Seriously, who needed the internet when there was Bethany? She even knew stuff that wasn't available to the public—like the future construction plans around the condo I'd bought, which was going to make the property values boom. And now, thanks to her constant chattering, I did too—whether I wanted to or not.

"Jynn," Bethany called again.

I shifted and glanced at myself in the mirror. The "couple of clothes" involved a pair of . . . pants? Shorts? Short-pants? I didn't know what they were called, but they were dark gray and skintight. The right side was a long pant which went all the way down to my black calf boots, and the left side was a short which left two inches of skin visible before a dark gray thigh-high started and covered the rest of my leg. A black leather strap in the front and back attached the short to the thigh-high. It was cute but weird. She had paired it with a white cut-off tank and a short black-and-iridescent-blue jacket left open.

I finally opened the hot-pink door and stepped out. This store wasn't anything like the discount clothing stores I'd shopped at my whole life. It was glitzy and glamorous, decorated in black and white, with splashes of bright colors which popped and drew the eye to the expensive displays and even more expensive clothes.

"Look, Bethany, it's cute and all, but that doesn't mean I'm going to spend two hundred dollars on four articles of clothing." I couldn't resist rubbing my hand over my bare stomach. As a Hunter, it just felt so wrong to leave such a weakness open. I know this wasn't armor, and I'd never wear this to a battle, but I couldn't resist the need to protect myself from everyone.

Bethany looked me up and down, appraising me like a new car. The wrap-around short dress that she was currently modeling shimmered between white and blue as she moved around me. "Of course not," she announced happily as she tipped her head to the side, making her gorgeous, wavy blonde hair spill over her shoulder. "I am." She hummed under her breath, completely ignoring my pained look, and pointed to the white pendant hanging from my neck. "A blue necklace would look better, but that has sentimental value, right?" She sighed as if in reluctant acceptance. "Oh, well. I'll just have to find an outfit to match that too. The tab's on me, of course."

"Bethany," I moaned. She was always trying to give me stuff. It drove me crazy.

"What?" She crossed her arms and pouted. "Look, I just want to take you with me to some of the parties I go to, okay? I want to hang out more, let you experience more than the streets and the Gate. But I'm not going to let you get mocked for wearing discounted clothes, alright? Even these are barely in the acceptable range."

I sighed silently. "I really appreciate that." I knew her well enough now to know that she honestly meant well. "But I just don't think that any of those places are for me."

She huffed and planted her hands on her curvy hips. "Look, you have backing now. *Me*. And if you want to get out of the hole in the ground that society put you in, you need to use it."

I scowled. "But that's not why I'm friends with you." Technically, the reason we were friends was because she wouldn't let me go. Although I did enjoy hanging out with her and didn't regret it. I just wished she'd get over this "give Jynn the whole store" thing.

"But I don't know how to be friends with someone who doesn't want anything from me," Bethany half yelled. Distress buckled the eyebrows over her baby blues. "You wouldn't take the smartphone I tried to buy you, and you settled for that little thing—"

"It does everything I need it to," I cut in. It could call, text, and access the internet. What else did I need?

"So why not this?" Bethany demanded. "I'm the one who wants to take you to a party, so I should pay for the clothes."

"Because I don't know how to be friends with someone who's always giving me stuff," I replied softly in the wake of her tantrum. Granted, Kesstel had a habit of always giving me food, but that was completely different. That was a cupcake or a snack-size bag of nuts, not a thousand-dollar phone.

For a second, Bethany looked like she was going to cry. Her hands tightened at her sides, and she looked away, scowling with tears in her eyes.

I frowned, feeling bad that it sounded like I was rejecting her. At least the only audience in the store was a shop clerk who was trying to make herself disappear behind the racks of clothing and two bodyguards who were always invisible. It made it easier to explain myself, because I didn't want her to misunderstand.

"We couldn't be more different," I said slowly. "You're from the top of society in every way. I'm on the bottom. Even our personalities couldn't be more opposite. This kind of friendship is new for the both of us. A lot of people would think we shouldn't hang out at all."

She frowned but didn't refute me. After all, it was true.

"So let's work to figure out a friendship that's only our own, okay?" I continued softly. "Not based on past relationships we've had with other people. Not a transactional one, but a real friendship for the sake of being friends. Is that something we could do?"

She threw her arms around me. "Okay."

I awkwardly patted her on the back and let her cling. The number of people I let touch me had forcefully increased by one since I met her, and I was still getting used to it. After a while, I stepped back. "I'm going to change now." Then I paused. "But I really like that dress on you."

She beamed. "I do too."

Suddenly, an alarm rang from every light post outside the clothing shop.

I froze as I recognized the sound. A Gate Surge was coming. Why? The phenomenon when all the monsters inside Gate Vale rushed the Gate at the same time was rare. In fact, there'd only been a couple times in the last five years, and one of those was just this last summer. Why was there another one so soon? The last one had been caused by a portal in Gate Vale collapsing, which had triggered a Surge in every Gate on Earth.

What was causing this one?

Another thought struck me. *Please, please tell me this isn't a worldwide one. Earth can't handle too much more of this.* Every Gate Surge spilled more magic and energy crystals into Earth, hurting the planet more and more. In fact, Earth was still recovering from the last one.

I looked at Bethany, her face just as shocked as mine.

Hurrying back into the stall, I changed into my armor as fast as I could. I felt a little bad about carelessly throwing the outfit to the side, but I was in a hurry. When I came out, Bethany was waiting in her street clothes.

Several of Bethany's bodyguards stood around her, finally visible, scanning the shop for threats. They all wore matching black, first-rate armor. One guard with brown hair waxed back away from his face stepped forward, his angular features tight. "Miss Wilks, we need to move to a secure location." He motioned toward the door, where the store clerk stood in full armor and waited to lock up the store.

She nodded as if it was expected.

By law, all Hunters had to take part in Gate Surges. Monsters were instinctively drawn to kill everything that breathed and were also immune to Earth-made weapons. Even the weakest monster would walk away from a nuke. The only weapons that could kill them were weapons made with monster byproducts wielded by Hunters, which is why Eden was built around the Gate. If a monster got out of Eden, the humans in Garden City could not stop it.

But Bethany Wilks, the daughter of a High Councilman and the face of Hunters, was so pampered that, apparently, she didn't have to help with Gate Surges. Never mind that she was an A-ranked mage. She grabbed my arm. "Jynn is coming with us." She glared at the guard as if daring him to argue with her.

I blinked at her in surprise, then my mouth pulled up in a lopsided smile. Gently, I took her hands off my arm and stepped to the side. "I'm fine, but thank you."

She turned her scowl at me. "Gate Surges are dangerous! You're just an E; you could die!"

I grinned and patted her shoulder, trying to comfort her. "I'm not going to die anytime soon. There's too much stuff I have to do first. And too much I have to protect." I slipped around the guards before she could protest any more. "I'll see you later." I waved and ran out of the store.

"Jynn!" her wail cut off when the door slammed behind me.

As soon as I was out of her view, I lengthened my stride and sprinted at full speed toward the two-hundred-foot-tall black arch looming over Eden. The autumn sun was high overhead as I entered Gate Square. There were already Hunters set up in formation, and more were spilling in from all directions, adding to the army. It was set up so that the strongest Hunters were in the front to deal with the strongest monsters while they let the weaker ones through to the weaker Hunters in the back.

Technically, I should be on the rim with the rest of the Es, but I wormed my way up to the gray area between B and C. Since I could take on stronger monsters, I should pull my full weight. Most of the Hunters were in groups and guilds, grouped together in formations to be their most efficient, so it was really uncommon for a random Hunter to be standing alone, the complete opposite of the E and D Hunters, where groups and guilds were less likely—the turnover rate was just too high.

The group of Hunters looked at me like I had a death wish, but I ignored them. My whole attention was on the Gate towering overhead.

It wasn't like the last time I saw a Gate Surge or Portal Burst. The rim of the Gate was wrapping and shifting around, but the black 2D arch looked stable. It wasn't bubbling and twisting like a drop of water in hot oil, nor were there battered Hunters stumbling out of the Gate, desperate to escape the hell army of monsters attempting to escape from the other side. Still, the alarms were ringing, meaning the Gate was unstable, and that could only mean a Gate Surge. What was going on in there?

Suddenly, the Gate's movements stilled. The calm before the storm.

"Get ready!" a man yelled from the front of the Hunter army. It took me a second to place the voice as Blood Sword.

My heart skipped a beat, a mix of anxiety and fear. I was experienced and strong enough to not be mindlessly scared anymore, but there was always a bit of tension when facing the unknown. My kindjal appeared in my hand, and I took a breath, steadying my breathing and killing the butterflies in my chest.

From my place in the middle of the crowd, I could see the Gate ripple, but I couldn't see the monsters. Or hear any.

A gasp rippled through the crowd. That was it. No other noises.

The people around me looked at each other. "What's going on?" a woman whispered to her friend.

The friend shook her head.

A dense pressure swept over the crowd, starting from the Gate and spreading out like a tidal wave. One after another, every single Hunter was forced to their knees with the pressure, no matter what their rank was.

The feeling hit me, and I stumbled back, but I wasn't brought to my knees like the people around me. I bent over, gasping for air as my eyes widened.

I know this aura.

My whole body was shaking, and my knees wanted to give out, but I lifted my heavy head to look over the downed crowd. Hundreds of bodies were between me and the Gate, filling the ground like a messed-up puzzle, but that didn't matter.

The only important thing was the man who'd just walked out of the Gate.

He was covered from head to toe in black blood. His armor was missing, and his clothes were in shreds. His pants were passable, but his shirt was in pieces, hanging on his broad shoulders by threads and revealing his pale skin underneath. It didn't seem to matter how he was dressed— his head was high, chin up, and eyes narrowed like a lord surveying his people. And finding them wanting.

"Kesstel," I mouthed the word, but the pressure was so intense that I couldn't make the sounds come out.

I peered at him, trying to see if there was any red mixed in with the black blood. From here, I couldn't see any injuries, but that might not mean anything. I was dying to grab his shoulders and shake him. Yell in his face, "*Where did you go?*" Make his chest hurt just as much as mine did just by seeing him in that dilapidated state. I'd been waiting, searching, missing him for two months.

Now he was *back.*

I stumbled forward, slowly limping toward him through air as thick as cement.

The S gods were also being affected by Kesstel's aura. The only S-ranked Healer had fallen against the man at her side, gasping for air. Two others grabbed their heads, as if they had the same headache that threatened to split my skull open. The other Ss looked uncomfortable, but they weren't downed like the rest of the Hunters.

Blood Sword stepped closer to Kesstel, his face tight. "Noble." His shaky voice was barely audible from my distance. It was only because the rest of the square was so quiet that I could even hear him. "Put away your aura."

Kesstel turned his head and looked at Blood Sword. His face was apathetic as usual, a blank slate of cold granite. Then a slight frown pulled down on the corners of his lips. That was the only warning he gave before his hand shot out, so fast I couldn't even see it moving.

A second later, Blood Sword was on his knees with Kesstel's fingers around his throat.

CHAPTER 41

The other S Hunters yelled in shock and jumped forward.

"Noble! Stop!" one man shouted, grabbing Kesstel's arm. He pulled at Kesstel, but his S-ranked melee strength wasn't enough to budge Kesstel's arm an inch.

Another man grabbed Kesstel's fingers and tried to pry them off. "Let go!"

Blood Sword knelt on the ground, gurgling, his face turning blueish red as the chain mail under Kesstel's fingers warped and broke, a sliver of blood mixing with the steel. The S healer put her hands on Blood Sword and started to heal him with bright golden magic while the rest of the people tried to separate the two.

It was like ants on a titan. No matter how much they pulled, nothing worked.

Another frown pulled at Kesstel's lips. Blue magic pooled around his body, swirling chaotically and threatening to explode. The magic ate at the arms of the Hunters grappling Kesstel, slicing through armor and skin with ease. They flinched at the pain, but they still didn't stop.

My mouth parted in horror. He could flatten the whole city if this went on. Hell, Blood Sword alone could flatten the city. If Kesstel could withstand the other Ss so easily, how much power did he really have? It might not be just Eden and Garden City that disappeared off the map.

"Stop," I mouthed, trying to get my voice to work. The more time passed, the more pressure Kesstel emitted, and the harder it was to make noise come out of my tight throat.

Kesstel had always been apathetic, but never destructive. Never murderous. Never like this. I didn't even know what *this* was.

The Hunters on the ground around me groaned in pain, clutching their heads. They withered and gasped in constant pain as Kesstel's aura grew stronger.

My breath was fast and shallow as I limped toward the commotion. "Stop," I whispered. "Kesstel, stop."

His blue magic grew like a flame, rising ten feet in the air and casting a blue sheen on everything around him.

"Stop! Noble, stop!" an S yelled.

A man in black full armor stepped back and pulled out a longsword. With a deadly move, he stabbed at Kesstel, who grabbed the blade with his bare hand before it pierced his side. Just like that, the man's sword was completely stopped. He puffed and shook as he tried to finish the attack, but the blade didn't move; then, with an almost casual flick of Kesstel's wrist, the S Hunter was thrown in the air, landing twenty feet away in the downed crowd. The people he landed on groaned in pain, but they couldn't move enough to dodge out of the way.

"Don't," I mouthed. *Don't hurt Kesstel. He's doing wrong right now, but don't hurt him!* There was something wrong with him. I didn't know what, but he wasn't himself. "Kesstel," I whispered.

His magic grew five feet taller and started to pulse like the timer on a bomb.

Three Ss abandoned the struggle to get Kesstel off Blood Sword and jumped back. The man in armor gripped a claymore while the woman at his side held a sword and shield. The other person, a mage, brandished a staff with three brightly glowing white magic stones on top. Lightning magic crackled around the magic stones as power pooled around the mage. At the same time, the two melee Hunters relaxed into an attack position, like lions ready to charge.

"This is your last warning," the woman holding the shield and sword announced. "Release him and put your magic away."

Kesstel's mouth pulled up in a sneer.

Wait! No! I drew in a large amount of air, so much that my chest hurt. "Kesstel!" I yelled for all I was worth. My small voice was like a fly's buzz compared to all the noise the Ss were making. "Kesstel, stop!"

Kesstel froze. Slowly, his head turned until he could see me through the people surrounding him. Our eyes locked. The magic around him vanished in an instant.

The Ss paused, completely confused. They gave cautious glances around, trying to see what he was staring at while keeping Kesstel in sight.

"Kesstel," I said as loud as I could. "Please stop."

He stepped back, away from the group of people holding him. Blood Sword collapsed to the ground, gasping for air, and the rest of them were forced to let go of Kesstel. The healer and a couple others dropped to Blood Sword's side to check if he was alright, while the armed Hunters watched Kesstel vigilantly then glanced at me in confusion.

Kesstel stared at me, his eyes like blue glass. I'd seen corpses with more emotion in their eyes. Slowly, he started to walk toward me. The people on the ground scurried out of his way, creating a path; they couldn't get up because of his Hunter aura, so all they could do was avoid getting stepped on.

As Kesstel and his overpowering aura got closer and closer, I bent over, propping my hands on my knees to make sure I didn't fall. I'd go to meet him, but my legs were shaking so badly I didn't dare move anymore.

He stopped in front of me and looked down with an apathetic expression. I didn't know what he was thinking—if he was thinking anything at all. All he was doing was standing there. In a silent town square. Under the eyes of everyone in Eden. As he stared at me.

I swallowed a couple times before my tight throat was moist enough to work properly. "What happened . . . to you?"

His expression didn't change as he reached out to me.

The closer his hand came, the more my very bones ached under his aura. I couldn't help but flinch back.

His hand paused. His aura vanished, pulled back inside him.

A great sigh of relief hushed over the square as everyone was finally able to breathe.

My tense body went soft at the sudden release of the painful pressure, as if a thousand-pound weight had been removed from my shoulders. My knees wobbled, and I stumbled back to try to stay up.

The next second, a strong force wrapped around my body. I blinked, shocked at the feel of sticky flesh under my cheek, and I looked up into Kesstel's glassy blue eyes. His arms were wrapped around me, pinning my own arms at my sides and caging me against his black blood–covered body. My eyes widened. I mean, we were friends, but I didn't think we were at the hugging stage.

Before I could open my mouth and ask, the world blurred around me. Kesstel hoisted me up in his arms and moved so fast that I was dizzy, since I hadn't had time to recover yet. I knew he was running, but he was going too fast for me to see properly. The world was a dizzying whirl of colors, and I was too disoriented to keep track of our location.

All at once, he stopped, placed my feet back on the ground, and before I could fall over from the sudden movement, trapped me in a hug again.

I was completely shocked, and at a total loss. What was going on in this man's head?

When my vision stopped spinning, I finally noticed we were in the backyard of a modern-looking two-story house. The yard was a modest size, with a small patch of grass, a small well-kept flower garden with a cool rocky water feature, and a hot tub on the patio. A seven-foot privacy wall blocked the view from the surrounding houses, but what was most noticeable was the fact that it was a detached house with a yard. In Eden, neighborhoods like this only existed in A District and were absurdly expensive.

I tipped my head back and looked up at Kesstel. He was still staring down at me with that blank expression.

Trying to wiggle my arms free so I could wipe the black blood off his cheek, he responded by tightening his arms around me. Not hurting me, but enough to let me know he wasn't going to let go. In the end, I gave up struggling and just stood there while he held on. I didn't know what was going on, but if this made him feel better, I could stand here for him.

After a minute, I opened my mouth. "Kesstel, can you understand me?"

At first, I didn't think he was going to respond, but then he slowly nodded.

"Are you hurt?" I asked.

He paused then shook his head. The muscles on his face relaxed, not quite to an expression, but he didn't come across as a tense bomb ready to explode anymore. His arms loosened a little around me.

He wasn't hurt now, but I could tell from his clothes that he'd been hurt a lot in the two months we were separated. Clothes didn't get torn like this just from walking around.

My chest tightened painfully just thinking about it.

I wiggled again. This time, he let my right arm slip loose, then immediately tightened his arms to keep the rest of me still. A handkerchief appeared in my hand, and I slowly wiped the blood off his face and off his pale blond hair. He just stood there, letting me.

"You're covered in blood," I whispered. "What happened to you? Where did you go?" I paused. "Hang on, we should get this off you first." I looked around, craning my neck as far as I could to look around his large body. "Where are we?"

I really hoped we weren't in some stranger's backyard. That was a conversation I really didn't want to have. Not only would it be embarrassing, but Kesstel's hostile attitude still had me worried. What if he attacked them? I didn't even have a snowflake's shot in hell of stopping him if he did. Maybe.

Why did he respond to my words earlier?

Kesstel turned, finally giving me a good view of the house behind him. It was shaped like a box and painted white with blue trim. There were French doors on the right side of the back, a long window, then a glass door on the left. Kesstel kept his arm around my shoulders as he walked to the French doors, putting his thumb on a print scanner next to the door. The lock clicked, and Kesstel opened the door.

"So this is your place," I muttered. That made things a little easier. Maybe.

Without waiting for me, he marched me inside and shut the door.

CHAPTER 42

—

We came into an L-shaped living space. A square dining table made of dark wood was set up in front of the French doors we'd just entered through, and to the left was a large off-white modern kitchen, complete with marble countertops and top-of-the-line appliances. Ahead was a big living room with a navy-blue sectional couch, dark wood furniture, and a TV nearly as long as I was tall. Everything—the features, the furniture, the delicate decorations on the shelves, and the pale wood flooring—screamed of money and wealth.

Given who he was, it didn't shock me he had such a nice house. What did surprise me was how empty it felt. It was like a model house that no one had ever lived in; just for show. Maybe I shouldn't be surprised. After all, I already knew he considered Earth just another pit stop on his journey to find the path to the parasitic planet—the place where he wanted to die, hopefully taking the parasitic planet with him.

I glanced up at Kesstel, still covered in black blood and holding me like a lifeline. He turned his apathetic eyes in my direction and silently stared back. I sighed, my chest aching all the more.

"Let's get you washed up," I said softly. This place was so nice and clean, it felt wrong to talk too loudly. It felt just as wrong to walk across the clean wooden floors with our dirty shoes, as evidenced when I tried to take a step but couldn't bring myself to put my foot down. Finally, I placed my boots in my Items Bag.

Kesstel watched my actions before staring down at my white socks on the wood.

I frowned up at him. What was he right now? A robot? "You should take off your shoes too," I suggested. My boots were dirty from walking in the city. Who knew what was on his boots? At the very least, there was a lot of blood, but what had he stepped in that had already sloughed off?

His boots disappeared, leaving black socks.

I'd bet a million bucks they were white before he disappeared. Thankfully, I didn't have to say anything before they disappeared into his Items Bag too. But that left his very dirty feet.

I bit my lips to keep from scrunching my face in disgust. It had been a long while since he'd taken a shower, that was for sure. "Is your room upstairs?" Given how nice his house was, there had to be a master suite in here.

He nodded.

"Come on," I ordered, steering him around the furniture to the stairs on the right of the front door. It was odd. I was treating him like a drunk, telling him what to do and stuff, but he obviously wasn't drunk. He was like a fleshy robot, only responding and acting when I told him what to do.

His large room was decorated in navy blues, pale grays, and deep black. Just like downstairs, it was model-room perfection and not a place anyone had ever lived in.

I pushed him into the bathroom.

At first, I thought he would drag me inside with him, but I put on the brakes and wouldn't willingly cross the threshold. "No, Kesstel. Let me go."

He stared at me for a whole minute before he slowly released his hold.

I stepped back and pointed toward the shower. "Clean up and get dressed. I'll meet you downstairs." Then I shut the door on his blank face.

I hurried out of his room, eyes locked on the light gray carpet in front of my toes. As empty as it felt, it didn't change the fact that this was my first time in a man's bedroom. It wasn't until I stepped into the hall and closed the door behind me that I relaxed.

With a sigh, I looked down at my body. After all his handling, I was just as covered in monster blood as him.

When I was fighting monsters, as soon as I destroyed their energy crystals, all of their remains disappeared. Even the blood that got on me. It kept me relatively clean throughout the day. But I didn't have access to the energy crystals tied to the blood on me now. I just hoped that the armor's nightly regeneration and cleaning also worked on third-party messes. As someone who'd cleaned armor more times than I could count, I couldn't say I enjoyed it.

I walked down the hallway, opening doors as I went. I found another bedroom, a home office, a linen closet, and another bathroom. After snagging a fluffy, navy-blue towel from the linen closet, I went into the bathroom and locked the door. Luckily, I now had the habit of carrying around a travel kit with me which included minute-size washing supplies.

Fifteen minutes later, I walked down the stairs to the living room with damp hair and wearing my street clothes. I hadn't taken that long. There were some girls—*cough*, Aliya, *cough*—who could easily take an hour-long shower and still cry that they weren't done before the hot water ran out.

Even so, Kesstel was already seated on the couch. He was like a statue, perfectly still and expressionless. He was perfectly clean, wearing black sweats and a white tee with a small towel draped over his shoulders. It wasn't until I was closer that I realized his hair was still wet and plastered to his forehead.

"Honestly, you," I whispered, walking up to him. Without asking, I took the towel and started to scrub the water out of his hair. Man, guys had it easy. In a minute, his hair was pretty much dry. I'd spent easily three times the amount of effort, and my hair was still wetter than his.

Kesstel waited until I set the towel on the coffee table before he reached out and grabbed me again. He stayed seated as he pulled me to stand between his knees.

My eyes widened when he wrapped his arms around my waist and buried his face into my stomach. "Kesstel, what's gotten into you? What are you doing?" I mean, he hadn't let go of me since he saw me. I wasn't uncomfortable, outside of how my heart hitched every time he hugged me. In fact, it felt quite nice, and he smelled fantastic right now, but hanging onto me like this wasn't something he'd normally do.

"Purifying . . . " he whispered slowly. His usually smooth voice was low and rough, as if he hadn't used it in a long time. For that matter, this was the first time he'd actually said anything since he came out of the Gate.

"Purifying?" I echoed. I couldn't resist resting my arms on his shoulders, consequently hugging him back. It wasn't on purpose! I just didn't know what to do with my arms, and this was the most comfortable position.

"I collected too much tainted energy," he said haltingly, as if he had to think about each word before he could make it come out. With each word he said, his speech slowly evened out.

Energy . . . purifying . . .

Suddenly, I remembered one of the last conversations we had before he disappeared in the Josu Portal Burst two months ago. The one where he explained how every time I destroyed an energy crystal, my kindjal absorbed the energy then returned a portion to me, but what I was given was clean and purified.

My eyes widened, and my hands tightened on his shoulders. "Are you okay?" I'd seen someone absorb an energy crystal, and seen several Hunters have energy crystals implanted into their bodies. All of them had turned into monsters.

I grabbed his head and tilted it back. Frowning, I stared into his passive face, trying to find if there was anything out of the ordinary. "Do you feel weird anywhere?"

"I don't feel yet. Give me another minute," he said softly, burying his head back into my stomach.

"No, this is serious!" I wiggled around but couldn't get out of his grip or lift his face back up to me. "Everyone who absorbs the energy of a crystal turns into a monster. What if you turn into one too?"

He let out a dry laugh, the bitter sound eerie in my ears. "Too late."

I froze, a chill running down my spine. "W-What?"

"I've been a monster for a very long time," he whispered softly. "So long, I forgot what it felt like to be human until I met you."

I was frozen, feeling like a bucket of freezing water had just doused me. I slowly pressed against his shoulders, steady and firm. This time, he slowly leaned back until I could see his face without letting me go. "Are you talking about your apathy?"

He shrugged a shoulder, for the first time moving in a way that I associated with his normal behavior. "That's a part of it. Or, more like a byproduct of it. I thought it was permanent. Until I met you, and you slowly purified the energy in me. Then I could finally feel emotion again."

My eyes narrowed, and I focused on him. For the first time, really focused on him, just like when I'm facing a monster and I want to find its weak point. There, on the lower left of his rib cage, was a faint white glow.

The same glow an energy crystal gave inside a monster.

My eyes widened, and my knees nearly gave out. My head felt a little dizzy as all the blood left my face. If it wasn't for Kesstel holding me, I might have fallen back.

"Just being with you had that effect," Kesstel kept talking as if I hadn't gone white as a sheet. "If I had known holding you accelerated the effect, I might have hugged you sooner. Then again, it might be related to your strength. You are a lot stronger than when I last saw you. Congratulations."

"You . . . you have an energy crystal in you," I whispered in horror as I reached out to touch where the glow was.

My mind short-circuited.

No, that was impossible. He couldn't have one. Only monsters had energy crystals, and I could see with my own eyes that he wasn't a monster.

My fingers pressed against his side. The warmth of his skin passed through his shirt, and his chest muscles moved with each of his steady breaths. I could see the glow, but I couldn't bring myself to believe it was there. I wanted to actually see the energy crystal in him. Then again, it was inside him. The only way to know for sure would be to cut it out.

Kesstel took my fingers away from the spot and held my hand gently in his. "It's always been there. You just weren't strong enough to see it until now."

I stared into his glassy blue eyes. "Why do you have an energy crystal in you?"

The corner of his lips hooked up in a smirk. "I'm the Boss of my world. Of course I'd have an energy crystal in me."

CHAPTER 43

—

H-how is that possible?" I whispered, staring at him with wide eyes. "You look perfectly human."

My hands shook as I urgently ruffled through his soft hair. I didn't find any horns or any other monster characteristics hiding in his bleach-blond locks. There were no scales hiding behind his normal ears or on his neck. The clothes he wore when he came out of the Gate were shredded. Although he was a mess, his chest had been perfectly visible. There wasn't anything there. Granted, I'd never looked below his belt, nor did I have the guts to.

In the end, I stopped moving and just stared at him, trying to wrap my mind around the mental bomb he'd just exploded. I shook my head, instinctively rejecting the idea. "That's not possible."

Meanwhile, Kesstel had just sat there on the couch, letting me touch him without objecting. When I finally stopped, the corner of his mouth kicked up again. "Do you think a normal being could hop from world to world?"

No. Honestly, I didn't think that was possible. But I admit, there was a part of me that had purposefully put blinders on when it came to Kesstel. It took me so long to trust and rely on him—on anyone—I didn't want to accept that there might be something which could damage my faith in him.

He kept his hands resting lightly on my waist as he spoke. It was like he was giving me some space but didn't want me to get too far away. I guess he was still purifying?

"Scared?" he asked, his lips quirked up in a mocking smile. Who was he mocking? Me or himself? I couldn't help but think it was the latter. "But

I won't let you run. I thought I was just lonely at first. Now I'm thinking it was instinct that drove me to get you to accept me." He looked up into my eyes. "I won't hurt you. Out of everything and everyone in the world, you are the only person I will never hurt. For the sake of my sanity, I can't afford to."

A part of me was nervous. The same part that always ran away when he tried to get close. The part which instinctively knew he was too dangerous to be around. Ironically, that little part had been right. As a stray Boss who had made it out of the Gate, Kesstel could wipe me out of existence if I made him mad. In fact, after the scene earlier today, I doubted there was anyone who could stop him. At least not in America.

Another part of me, the part that had agonized over his disappearance and drove me to search Josu Rainforest for him every day, was more scared *for* him. Not of him. It ached, seeing the out-of-character mania he had just displayed in Gate Square.

The two parts warred inside me, clashing and scratching to get control. One trying to make me run; the other wanting me to soothe Kesstel's wrinkled brow. In the end, I simply stood still between his hands, swallowed, and shook my head. "I just don't understand."

"Every time a world is devoured," Kesstel said, "all the remaining inhabitants are injected with an energy crystal, the animals and the intelligent species who control the planet alike. Those crystals turn every surviving living thing into monsters, which are then released onto the next world the parasitic planet attaches to. I've already explained this, correct?"

He didn't fully wait for me to finish nodding before he went on. "This same thing happened on Kathar, my planet. I must have been the strongest living person left, because while everyone around me was turning into ape-like monsters—covered in long hair with elongated arms and flat faces—I was fine. I could feel myself getting stronger and my mind going blank, but I didn't physically change." His fingers stiffened on my waist but didn't squeeze me. "My memory was vague from that moment on. I remember the remnant of Kathar attaching to a Gate Vale on the next world. I remember at one point the intelligent species came into my world's portal. And watching my ape-like little brother being cut down by one of them."

My eyes widened, and my heart squeezed painfully for Kesstel. I didn't say anything. I couldn't. It was like he needed to say these words. Had he ever been able to say them to anyone else?

Kesstel's glassy eyes started to glow neon blue as he was wrapped up in the memory. "I don't remember what happened after. Just anger. I think grief? That was the last time I felt emotions. My body was moving like a puppet, attacking those intelligent species who invaded my world. I didn't have control at all. I don't think I wanted control. My memory blackened at that point. That world collapsed, then another. And I had a heavy hand in it."

Gently, I reached out and brushed his hair, soothing him as best I could.

Slowly, the light died in his eyes until they returned to a normal color. He glanced up at me, coming back to the moment. He sighed and rested his forehead against my stomach again. "I regained my consciousness some time around that point. I couldn't feel emotions, but my mind was awake enough to know what was going on. To know that all my people were dead, and I was the only one left. All the monsters that remained in Kathar's remnant land were external ones that appeared there when the parasitic monster devoured the last world and moved to the next. I figured if they could come into my world, then I could leave.

"It wasn't until the next world that I gained enough control of the barrier to break out of my portal. When I left it, since I was the Boss, my remnant world collapsed and disappeared. As it should. Everyone was already dead; it was time to let Kathar and the memories of it fade away." There was a sad note hiding at the back of his flat voice.

I wrapped my arms around his shoulders. He might be a Boss, but he was still hurting from losing his world. I couldn't even imagine continuing to go on after that. I'd give up and die from the sheer heartbreak.

He turned his head to the side and hugged me back.

For a second, we just stayed like that.

"What happened next?" I asked. This couldn't be all of his story.

He breathed a dry laugh. "I came out into a world which was much more technologically advanced than Earth. The problem they faced was that they were so reliant on their technology, when it all stopped working after the parasitic planet attached to their world, they couldn't recover. I warned them so they could use their technology to destroy the parasite. They didn't believe a word I said. They were only interested in the fact that I was an alien with black blood. They thought I would be more beneficial to them sliced up into pieces so they could experiment on me. I had to destroy one of their few remaining cities before they finally left me alone. That planet was devoured not long after, and I appeared on a random remnant world, since my original one was gone."

An alien with black blood. No wonder he'd had such a reaction when I suggested he use his blood to prove the story of the parasite. Maybe the outcome might have been different, but it was just as possible that it would have repeated.

"Wait, black blood," I whispered, looking down at his blond head . . . which had been covered in black blood when he came out of the Gate. "How . . . how much of the blood on you earlier was . . . " My voice died out as my face contorted into a horrified expression. There had been blood all over his body. And it hadn't been a light, single layer.

No, it had been caked onto his body. Repeatedly.

"Mine?" Kesstel finished for me, not nearly as upset. His lips dipped down in a thoughtful frown. "Maybe a little less than half? I wasn't really paying attention; since I heal so fast, blood loss wasn't an issue. It's not like the worlds I went to had showers. If I wanted to be clean, I had to jump in a lake or wait for the rain, but that wasn't really an option."

"Wait, what happened after the Portal Burst collapsed?" I asked for the umpteenth time. "Where did you go?"

Kesstel finally let me go and leaned back on the couch. I couldn't help but notice that even though he wasn't holding me anymore, his left knee shifted until it was resting against my right one so he was still touching me. He looked up at me. "As soon as I walked in, I knew that portal wasn't connected to the parasitic planet. I just didn't expect it to fall apart so quickly after I killed the Boss. Usually, when the Boss is killed by someone, that person becomes the new Boss. But this time, the fragment of that world collapsed before I could take control, and I was in the void—lost between worlds." His lips pressed tight.

I gaped at him. "The void between worlds?"

He nodded. "If you fill up a bowl full of marbles then pour water into it, the water between the marbles is like the void between the fragments of the worlds the parasite has collected. It was troublesome, but I was able to break into the closest neighboring world fragment, then I had to skip around before I found one that was connected to Eden's Gate Vale."

His nonchalant way of explaining something so complicated nearly blew my mind. "How many worlds did you go through?"

He shrugged. "Four."

Four worlds? Four portals? All alone?

I sighed, pressing the heel of my hand to my forehead. God, he really was a Boss, wasn't he? "I can't believe you did all that in just two months."

I stepped to the side and dropped down on the couch next to him. The plush, navy couch instantly formed around my body.

Okay, I needed a couch like this. I didn't know where I'd fit it in my tiny room, but I wanted one. As long as I didn't have to pay for it.

There was a comfortable space between our bodies, but Kesstel still shifted until his knee was pressed against mine again. "Oh, is that how long it's been here? I'm glad it wasn't too long. I would have been angry if I came back and you were an old woman."

I tilted my head to the side. "Old woman?" Since I knew the reason why he wanted to touch me, I didn't shift away. In fact, I kinda liked the warmth I felt through my jeans.

He shrugged one shoulder. "Time works differently in each world. It took much longer than two months for me to get back through the four worlds."

I blinked at him as a thought came to my mind. "How old are you?"

On Earth, the stronger the Hunter was, the slower they aged, which is why Bethany looked less than twenty even though she was twenty-six, and Jonovan looked to be only in his early thirties even though he was almost fifty. E Hunters weren't as affected by this phenomenon, but still, Henry looked about sixty even though he was closer to seventy years old.

But how did it work for a Boss from another world?

Kesstel looked amused. "You mean, how much of a monster am I?" He leaned his head back. "I was twenty-two when my world was invaded and I became a Hunter. I stopped aging at that moment. As for how many years it's been since then, I can't tell you because of all the time differences—and I don't know how much time passed before I woke up. After I regained consciousness, I spent a year and a half in the first world according to their calendar, two years in the world after, and four years in the next. I've been on Earth for seven years so far." He slanted me a look. "When you decide how old I am, let me know."

I snorted. "It's like playing roulette with your age, just waiting to see what number the ball falls on."

"I'll have to take your word for that," he muttered.

I blinked at him. "Huh?"

"I don't know what a roulette is," he commented. "Other than it's a 'little wheel.' But I have a feeling that's not what you're talking about."

"It's a gambling game," I explained, completely confused by his words. "And yeah, it's played on a wheel. And, um, a ball that lands on numbers." I knew what it was, but I had to admit, I'd never played it before. I wasn't old enough to legally gamble, and there weren't a lot of options around Garden City or Eden. "Where did you get a 'little wheel' from?"

He shrugged. "Roulette means *little wheel*. At least that's what it translated to when you said it." When I continued to stare at him in confusion, he elaborated. "I have the ability to understand all languages. It has something to do with this." He rested a hand over where the energy crystal was in his chest. "But I don't exactly know how. I'm not even speaking English right now, but that's the language you're hearing because it's the language you know."

I gaped at him. "That's . . . amazing. So you can understand all languages?"

"Yes. I rarely have problems hiding it unless there are multiple languages being spoken in the same conversation." Kesstel reached out and gently pushed my half-dry hair behind my ear. "But it's just the speaking part. It doesn't work the same with text. I learned to read English after I came here. It was . . . uncomfortable until I could."

"I bet," I muttered, just thinking about all the paperwork required for starting a new job, like he did as soon as he came out of the Gate. It also basically meant he had to sign it all blindly because he couldn't read what the contract said. And I knew Kesstel well enough to know he would never admit that he was disadvantaged in front of people he thought might be a threat.

But there was something else which caught my attention. If Kesstel had that language ability, and he'd gotten it from the energy crystal, it meant the parasite had it.

A chill went down my spine when I remembered how the red orc had a language and could respond to what I said. Was that why? That meant all monsters with the intelligence to speak could understand everything the Hunters around them said.

"Kesstel," I said slowly, thinking about the possibilities. "Can the parasitic planet hear what the monsters are hearing?" I looked down at the faint glow coming from his chest. "Can it . . . hear everything we're saying right now?" My stomach twisted painfully. What was the use of all this planning if the target we were after knew every move we made?

He frowned, understanding what I meant. "All monsters are connected to the parasite. That's how it can control their movements, such as urging Gate Surges and driving them to target living things on the planet the parasite is attached to. So yes, it has the ability to hear what the monsters hear."

My stomach went from painful to downright nauseous.

Kesstel shifted his knee, pressing it closer into mine. "However, when I broke free from my remnant world, I broke free from that connection. Which is why I can move freely without its influence, and why I believe that it reacted so strongly when I collapsed the portal. And why it tried to keep me from exiting the Gate today." He stared down at his hands, eyes narrowing maliciously. A faint glow appeared in the depths of his icy blue eyes, even more obvious in the dim room. "It's angry that its own weapon attacked it."

Any relief I might have felt that the parasite couldn't eavesdrop on us was completely washed away by the dangerous glow in Kesstel's eyes. It'd only been an hour since he last went berserk. It wouldn't do anyone any good if he did it again. I only hesitated a second before I reached out and rested my hand on his arm.

He blinked, as if shaken from his thoughts. He glanced at my hand, the hard lines on his face softening a bit, and his eyes returning to normal. "Never mind, we're getting sidetracked," Kesstel said. "Since you are so intent on finding the parasite with me, I just wanted to tell you something I found out when I was lost between the remnant worlds."

I instantly straightened up and stared at him.

"None of the portals attached to Eden's Gate Vale lead to the parasitic planet."

CHAPTER 44

It's impossible to get to the parasitic planet through Eden's Gate?" I whispered. After all the ups and downs I'd had in the last day, this felt like a crushing blow. A defeated sigh escaped me as I leaned back against the couch. "Really?"

Kesstel nodded. "When I was in the void between worlds, I could somewhat see where the worlds aligned and where the portals led. There was no way out of the portals attached to Eden's Gate. In fact, I didn't see a current portal that was even attached to the parasite. It was hard to tell because of the sheer size of everything." Kesstel scowled. "I think there might be a connection with a Gate on the other side of Earth. Somewhere very far north with a lot of snow and no people. But I don't know what it's called."

I blinked at him. Other side of the planet, north, with a lot of snow. "Siberia," I said slowly. "That sounds like the Siberian Gate. It's a no-man's-land. The monsters are so strong, and the weather is so bad there, every Hunter who's gone has died. Very quickly." Despair was heavy in my voice.

Kesstel smirked. "You really think it's going to be a problem for me?"

I shook my head. "No, I think you might be the only one who wouldn't have a problem. But that's not what I'm worried about."

It had to be *there*. Just traveling from the closest settlement to the Siberian Gate would take a long, long time, and that was with the proper equipment. I didn't know how to drive, and I didn't know how skilled Kesstel was at it, but I really didn't want to run hundreds of miles in the snow.

That was if we could even get out of Eden.

I stood up and paced around the room, thinking. "The hardest part might be getting out of the country—well, for you. I don't think I'll be able to get out of Eden." I looked at Kesstel, who didn't seem alarmed. "Hunters are stationed at their Gates for five years. I still have more than three left before I can apply to leave. But the biggest problem is, S Hunters aren't allowed into other countries. It's like sending a warhead in." When he didn't react to the explanation, I went on, in case *warhead* was a word he didn't know. "It's like declaring war on another country. The only way you'd get through customs is if you're signing an agreement to be that country's citizen."

He didn't look impressed. "Do you really think any of that matters to me? I'd like to see them try to lock me up."

"It matters to me," I shot back. "Even if we have a way to get to the Siberian Gate—flights to the other side of the world and vehicles to make it up to the Gate—if I just up and leave without permission, that would be breaking the law. If they can't find me, my family would take the fall. My aunt and uncle would be locked up. If my sister proved to be a Hunter, she'd have to deal with the extra daily fines because of me." My hands jumped up and grabbed my head as panic set in. "If she wasn't strong enough to handle the fine, she'd be locked up, too. My mother . . . would be removed from the hospital."

I'd be thrusting them into hell. Over something which might or might not actually be there. My fingers tangled in my hair and fisted. My mind registered the pain, and I focused on it to calm my nerves. I didn't know that I could do it. Leave without permission like that. Even if I was successful in destroying the parasitic planet—given I even *had* a chance—there was no guarantee my family would survive long enough for me to come back. Especially if the times between the worlds were different.

"Hey." Kesstel's hand grabbed my wrist while his other one reached out and untangled my fingers from my hair. "Don't hurt yourself," he ordered.

I let him move my hands as he wanted, but I shot a glare at him. "Says the man who was covered in his own blood an hour ago."

"That's beside the point," he came back. "I couldn't feel the pain, so I didn't even know I was hurt." He shook my wrist, making my lax hand flop in the air. "This is different."

It was funny. The way I viewed him had changed drastically in the last hour. He wasn't just a freakishly strong Hunter from another world anymore. He was a Boss. It made him so much more. More dangerous. More powerful. More of a threat to me and everything I loved. I would have thought it would change how we interacted, but here we were, acting like this.

A grateful little flame grew in my chest as a small smile curled my lips.

Kesstel let go of me and sat back down. "If freely leaving agitates you so much, I'll find another way to let you leave without repercussions." He snorted and tilted his head like the lord he was. "As if a bunch of humans are really going to tell me no?"

I rolled my eyes at him. Then I paused.

I appreciated how motivated he was at trying to find the path to the parasitic planet. It made it a million times easier for me, since I wasn't strong enough to do anything about it, nor did I know where to even start.

After months of being stuck, I finally had a direction to go.

However, while for me it was a mission to save my family and my home, for him, it was a suicide mission. The way he talked about it, he didn't plan on coming back to Earth even if we were successful. And if these last two months had been a preview of how my life would be after he was gone, I didn't know—

My thoughts were cut off when I noticed a dozen very strong auras closing in around Kesstel's house, a pair on each side, three in the back, and the rest moving in on the front door.

The relaxed expression wiped clean from Kesstel's face, replaced with an apathetic frown. "I suppose they're here to see if I killed you after I ran off with my prey." He pushed off the couch and walked to the door. "Took them longer than I thought."

I followed a couple steps behind him. From their auras, they had to be Eden's S Hunters plus two more A-ranked ones. They weren't going to attack him, were they?

A soft knock rapped on the front door.

Kesstel opened it.

Blood Sword stood on the other side with the S healer and another S Hunter. From the looks of it, all the damage Kesstel had done earlier had been healed, but there was a wary gleam in everyone's eyes. They all held weapons, half drawn and ready for action in a split second.

"Good afternoon, Noble," Blood Sword spoke slowly, watching Kesstel like he was ready to explode at any time. "It seems like you've calmed down?"

Kesstel nodded to the side. "Is there a reason you're surrounding my house?"

Blood Sword's thin lips pressed together. "Just a precaution. After all, we are charged with defending the lives in this city. Against anything."

The huge sword in his hand vanished, and he took a slow breath. After a second, his face relaxed to a more friendly appearance.

His eyes widened with surprise when he caught sight of me.

A man cleared his throat from behind the small group of Hunters, and Blood Sword and his people stepped to the side, presenting two middle-aged men. Both were dressed in armor, but they held themselves more like businessmen than Hunters. The reason was as obvious as their identities. The man in the front with a short, square haircut and gray hair around his ears was President Paul Anderson, the leader of the Hunter's Council. The man with blond-and-gray hair just a half step behind him was just as influential, the treasurer of the Hunter's Council, John Wilks—Bethany's father.

Kesstel didn't so much as blink an eye. I, however, went stiff as a board.

This was not what I thought was going to happen.

President Anderson walked up to the door. "I was hoping we could talk. That was quite a commotion in the square today." There was a smile on his face and a comfortable tone in his voice, but a sharp glint in his eyes. It was like he knew he had to be careful around Kesstel but didn't want to be steamrolled by him.

Kesstel glanced back at me. "I already have a guest." His look clearly said it was up to me to let them in.

I bit my lips, not sure what to do. Honestly, I didn't want them to come in. I was comfortable with Bethany and her title because I'd been around her long enough, but that didn't apply to big shots who just randomly appeared. At the same time, this was the head of the Hunter's Association and Bethany's father. It would be rude to send them away for no obvious reason. Since it seemed like Kesstel was waiting for me to respond, I slowly nodded.

He turned back to them. "Come in." Waving his hand, he stepped to the side so they could enter.

President Anderson looked a little perplexed at Kesstel's actions, but he stepped inside, pausing as soon as he saw me. "Good afternoon." His gaze flicked up over my head, obviously checking my rank, before he finally looked at my face. A wrinkle formed on his forehead as he glanced between Kesstel and me. I could practically see his mind ticking, wondering why an S was taking an E's opinion into consideration before letting the president of the Hunter's Association in. Still, President Anderson must have concluded that he didn't want to poke a hornet's nest because he flashed a business smile and held out a hand. "Paul Anderson. And you are—?"

"Shy." Kesstel stepped slightly in front of me, blatantly blocking off the president's greeting. Just like when the Stone Mace's president had shown interest in me. "And more of an introvert than I am."

President Anderson froze. Whether he thought Kesstel was being rude or was shocked at the situation, he got over it in a flash, merely nodding at me and walking to the kitchen table.

Mr. Wilks followed behind. He gave me a small smile and nod in greeting, obviously knowing who I was. A testament to how well he knew what was happening around his daughter, I was sure. Still, he didn't mention my connection to Bethany and sat at the table with President Anderson.

As soon as President Anderson's attention was off me, I finally relaxed enough to breathe, and slowly, I slipped further behind Kesstel. Thousands of people had seen Kesstel's reaction to me earlier in Gate Square, and now I was being seen in his home. In a cutthroat city like Eden, I could be considered a tool to influence Kesstel if someone wanted to make a move. Being friends with an S did give privileges, like the top contract President Wardyn Price from the Stone Mace guild was still trying to push on me, but it was also a dangerous thing if I couldn't protect myself.

Paul Anderson had fought his way into leadership during the initial opening of the Gates and subsequent collapse of society. That might have been twenty years ago, but if someone wanted to stay on top, they couldn't be soft. President Anderson might look reasonable, but that could change. Fast.

Blood Sword followed them in. He paused when he saw me half hidden behind Kesstel. "You're that girl from Josu Rainforest. I heard you sat there all day. Why?"

My eyes widened as a bolt of lightning shot down my back. He remembered *that* from the day Kesstel disappeared?

Kesstel glanced at me. His face was as blank as ever, but I knew him enough to see the little light in his eyes. "Josu Rainforest, huh? How long did you wait?"

For way too long, I thought and scowled. My cheeks were burning as I glanced to the side. Damn Blood Sword and his big mouth. Even though I'd been worried about Kesstel, he didn't need to know just how much. It was embarrassing.

The rest of the team ambled in and crowded around, all trying to get a good look at me.

It was more than I could bear.

I turned to Kesstel to tell him goodbye so I could run out, but I paused.

Slowly, I looked toward President Anderson. Months ago, when I first found out about the energy crystals, I made an appointment to see him. That date was still a few weeks away, but now he was right here in front of me.

I glanced at the Hunters around me. Well, they should know too. Honestly, the more people who knew, the better. They hadn't believed Kesstel when he told them seven years ago, and no one had taken kindly to the posts I left on the Hunter forums every month before I got blocked again for causing such a ruckus. Still, even if I made anyone mad, no one was going to hurt me with Kesstel here.

I took a breath and walked toward the Councilmen. As soon as I stepped in their direction, everyone in the room looked my way, eyes wary. I was an E, but that didn't mean I couldn't have a bomb in my Items Bag.

Kesstel's blue eyes narrowed threateningly as he took in their reactions. I could practically feel his tense muscles quivering as I passed him.

I tossed a shallow smile at him then focused ahead. "President Anderson, there's something I wanted to talk to you about."

CHAPTER 45

———

Surprise briefly colored President Anderson's face. I mean, Kesstel had just introduced me to the Councilman as *shy*, so the direct way I faced the man must have thrown him off. His mature features smoothed out. "Yes?"

Walking up past the S-ranked Hunters who were acting as the president's bodyguards, I stopped in front of the table. "My name is Jynn," I stated, trying to get my mind in order. I'd thought I still had a few weeks to come up with an eloquent way to argue my point. Maybe I should have thought first before I went to pitch my idea on the fly. "I actually have an appointment with you in a few weeks, but I was hoping I could talk to you about it right now, since you are here anyway. It's important to everyone in Eden, and a few weeks could make a difference."

The president frowned. "Oh?" He flicked a glance at Kesstel before looking back at me.

Mr. Wilks laced his fingers together and focused on me, his handsomely aged face kind but stern at the same time.

I took a breath. "I want to let you know the dangers of energy crystals." I kept my face serious and strong so they didn't laugh off my words like others had every other time I'd talked about it.

The men at the table looked surprised, their brows rising high on their foreheads.

"I know that energy crystals are used to power nearly everything," I went on. "But no one seems to know that they can turn Hunters into monsters."

The Hunter in light armor just behind me snorted before he cleared his throat. I could feel him shifting around. That one sound broke the tense atmosphere in the room, and I knew in an instant that they weren't going to take my words seriously.

"It's true," I stressed, using my hands to emphasize my point. "I've seen it with my own eyes and had to deal with the aftermath."

The men looked at me politely, but even Bethany's father thought I was telling a joke.

"If a person cultivates the energy inside a crystal, that energy turns them into a monster," I kept going. "I can even prove it to you. Since there's no turning back, if you let me teach someone on death row how to cultivate the energy, I can show you how it can turn a person into a monster."

Mr. Wilks tapped his fingers slowly on the table. "That, Miss Devhro, is actually illegal. We can't just give you a person to experiment on."

I shook my head. "That's not what I meant." Okay, it kind of was. "The point is, it's not an experiment if I know it's true, is it? However, once a person turns into a monster, they can't turn back, so I can't very well ask a good, innocent person to do it." I paused in frustration. I could tell I wasn't getting through to them. "Kesstel can attest for me." I motioned to him.

The S Hunters drew in a breath, and everyone looked in his direction.

He was watching the scene with a blank expression, but when his eyes landed on me, there was a slight tinge of pity in them. "What she says is true. Just as I told you seven years ago."

I turned back to see President Anderson scowl. "We did many experiments on the energy crystals back then," he said slowly, his voice low and even. "Everything you suggested, Mr. Noblé. All that was proven was that we did a lot of work for nothing."

My eyes widened. They weren't even going to take his word seriously? Maybe I should take another angle. "It's not just that, but the energy crystals—"

President Anderson cut me off. "As pleasant as it is to talk to you, there is an actual reason for me and my Councilman to have come here today." His words were generous but carried a definite closing tone.

I couldn't give up just yet. "But they're pois—"

"Miss Devhro," Mr. Wilks jumped in this time. His friendly face had changed to a cautious alarm. Did he think I wasn't good enough to hang out with his daughter anymore? "It was nice meeting you."

I looked back and forth between them. They were being polite to me, probably because they were in Kesstel's house and his heavy aura was starting to leak out in the room, but they obviously didn't want to listen to any more of what I had to say.

My hands gripped at my side. "I'm serious! I'm just trying to keep people safe!"

The president laced his fingers together and regarded me solemnly. "I appreciate your efforts, as misplaced as they are." Before I could come back, he spoke again. "Young lady, you *are* young. I have experienced more than you ever will. From the beginning till now, I have seen it all. Your worries are groundless."

My eyes widened as a blast of anger burst in me. My aura bubbled up, threatening to explode out of the steel-tight cage I kept it in, but then everyone in this room would know the strength of my aura didn't match my rank. I gritted my teeth and kept it locked down.

What right did he have to disregard me so easily? Yes, he was more than twice my age. He was there when the Gates first appeared, watched humanity nearly fall apart then claw its way back up to what we have today, being a large part of that reform. But even before the Gates appeared, Paul Anderson was a big shot, a millionaire from old money who was an expert at making more.

He'd never experienced life on the bottom rung, slaving day after day, knowing that even if I put in every ounce of my energy into providing for my family, I was always going to fall short. And be short-lived. He'd never felt the despair of being toyed with by monsters, degraded from an intelligent being to nothing but a moment of cruel entertainment.

"Yes," I said slowly. "You are older than me. And no matter where I am in my life, you always will be. But just because you have experienced more of life than I have, it doesn't mean I haven't had experiences of my own. It's entirely possible I have knowledge that you don't." I lifted my chin and glared at him. "Maybe because of my *youth*, I can be a little more open-minded and not so blinded by what I might know. I'm able to see things from a different angle and see what's really there. And not some rose-colored dream."

Instantly, their expressions changed from polite disinterest to disapproval. President Anderson's aura flickered out to put me back in my place, but before it reached me, Kesstel's aura flicked out like a whip and slapped it away. Everyone froze as the atmosphere instantly turned tense.

Kesstel's finger tapped on my shoulder from behind.

I glanced back at him, turning my full displeasure in his direction even though he wasn't the one at fault. Why couldn't they believe me? Were their lives really so comfortable that they couldn't accept that the energy crystals were dangerous?

He nodded his head to the side in an *I told you so* way, but he didn't seem happy about it. "I'll find you later, okay?"

"Yeah," I muttered to Kesstel and turned to the door. Pausing half a step past him, I quickly pulled a pen and piece of scrap paper out of my Items Bag and wrote my phone number. I handed it to him then walked out the door with my head held high.

The city was peaceful but still in a state of confusion. After all, everyone in Eden had mobilized for a Gate Surge, only for nothing to happen. Well, nothing outside of an S Hunter nearly leveling the city. More Hunters than normal roamed the streets, discussing what it all meant and what might have happened to one of their S gods.

I walked through the ritzy streets of A District with my hands in my pockets and a scowl on my face. No one stopped to talk to me, and if I was lucky, no one would realize I was the girl from Gate Square everyone was talking about. The one who had soothed a raging S god with just a look. Like I was some gorgeous, awe-inspiring angel. So embarrassing.

My phone rang from my hip satchel, a generic, bubbly ditty.

Taking it out, I flipped the cell open. "Hello?"

"Jynn, are you okay?" a young woman asked urgently.

It took me a second to place her voice. Just to make sure, I pulled the phone away and glanced at the caller ID. I was still new enough with the gadget that I kept forgetting it even had that feature. "Ah, hi, Emma. Yeah, I'm okay."

"Are you sure?" she rushed on. "I saw the whole thing. I've never seen a Hunter lose control like that and just snap. When he went to you, I thought he was going to kill you." Her voice hitched. "I was so scared."

I sighed and looked up at a fluffy cloud drifting across the blue sky. "You don't have to worry; I'm fine. Just antsy."

"Antsy?" Emma mimicked.

My gaze shifted from the blue sky to the black arch towering over the city. "Yeah." My encounter with President Anderson still boiled my blood, even though I'd already left Kesstel's house in the dust. I shouldn't have gotten so worked up like that, but dammit, I was tired of being pushed aside and laughed at for trying to save everyone's lives.

"Oh, what are you doing? Where did Mr. Noblé take you?"

"We took a short stop at his home. Right now, I'm going to head into the Gate for a bit to unwind," I added, spouting the first thing that came to mind. I hated the Gate, but it did serve as a good stress reliever. My feet turned and carried me closer to Gate Square at a faster speed.

There was a pause on the other side of the phone. Then Emma piped up, "I'll go with you!"

"Huh?"

"I've always wanted to go into the Gate with you, just us. You know, girl time. So can I come too?" Her words were energetic at first, then slowly became hesitant. In the end, she sounded like a pitiful kitten meowing for a treat.

It was a tone that Big Sister me had a hard time rejecting. " . . . Okay."

"Great! I'll meet you there." She cut off the call quickly, as if she was worried that I would change my mind.

My lips pulled up in a half smile as I put the phone into my Items Bag. Phones were so finicky. If I left it in my hip satchel, it would break when I went through the Gate. But if I kept it in my Items Bag all the time, no calls would come through because the space distortion in Items Bags interrupted the signal. Since I spent so much time in the Gate every day, I was forever forgetting to get my phone out.

I took a pit stop in a public bathroom to change back into my armor. It was still covered in black blood, but since it was mostly black too, it wasn't that much of a problem—as long as I ignored the smell.

Emma was waiting for me at the Gate, just like she said, once I arrived. Her pinkish-red armor was a stark contrast to the black arch behind her, making her stick out like a sore thumb. Her cute face lit up when she saw me, and her long brown hair bounced in her ponytail as she hurried over to me. "You're finally here." She grinned. Just the sight of her released some of the tension humming in my body.

Nodding in greeting, I accepted her hug without complaining. I'd really been getting used to touching people lately, hadn't I? Well, with a handful of people.

I looked at the Gate and the few Hunters milling around it. "Are they actually letting people in?"

Technically, a Gate Surge had been announced just a couple hours ago. Usually when that happened, the subsequent massive battle took up a lot of time, then there was the sorting of carcasses and cleaning up, which meant that access to the Gate was closed for a whole day. But it wasn't just Earth's side of things which needed time to straighten out—the portal from Earth to Gate Vale was usually unstable, too. Simply put, Hunters couldn't go through the Gate even if they wanted to.

But today was different. The destabilizing of the Gate, which Hunters used to notify of a Gate Surge, had instead been caused by the parasite trying to prevent Kesstel from leaving the Gate. Leaving its influence. I didn't have time to get more details about it before Kesstel changed the subject, so I didn't know how that difference affected the connection between Earth and Gate Vale.

Emma motioned to the Gate. "Authorities announced it was safe to enter about thirty minutes ago. I've seen a couple dozen Hunters go in while waiting for you; from the sounds of it, mostly just people who haven't gotten their quota for the day." She looked back at me. "Shall we?"

There should be a law against sounding giddy about going into the Gate, but I followed her anyway. Gate Vale looked the same as always: a magical valley which hid its horrors under luscious greenery and dazzling views.

A small group of Hunters stood on the edge of the clearing surrounding the Gate, talking animatedly.

One Hunter in battered, mismatched armor looked to his teammate. "I didn't find any. Did you?"

The mage, wearing a patched black robe, shook his head. "No, I didn't find a single monster in Glenn Holt."

Another mage with purple robes stood with them. She ran her hand through her short hair and tsked. "There weren't any monsters in Josu Rainforest, either. Not even the velociorheas. It's like they all vanished."

CHAPTER 46

Emma glanced at me in confusion then walked up to the group of Hunters while I trailed behind her. "Excuse me?" she called out. "Sorry to butt in, but did you say all the monsters are gone?"

They turned toward her.

The man in the front, the D rank with battered armor, spoke up first. "Gone. They're all gone," he lamented. "Everyone who went to hunt came back empty-handed. And I haven't gotten my quota for the day." He moaned, thumping a hand on his helmet.

My eyes widened and Emma gasped.

How was that possible? Gate Vale had been filled with monsters since the day the Gates opened. In fact, the problem was there were *too many*, and like a boiling pot, the Gate would explode, and those monsters would attack Earth. That was the reason Hunters went into the Gate, especially since more appeared every night. But it was the middle of the day now. How was it possible that all of them were gone?

I tapped a finger on my lip. Did this have to do with Kesstel?

Emma thanked the men then turned to me. "Do you still want to look around, anyway? It might be fun to go somewhere we normally can't because of the stronger monsters. You know, the A-ranked places?" Her eyes suddenly brightened. "Oh! Like Rainbow Garden! I've always wanted to go there; the pictures are gorgeous! I'm sure it's prettier in real life."

It was tempting. Very tempting. The Rainbow Garden was known as the most beautiful location in all of Gate Vale. It was a natural garden full of thousands of exotic flowers of every shape and size, and magic sparkles hung in the air as if blessing the colorful petals. All the monsters there were plants . . . and all A rank.

But I had to sigh and shake my head for one obvious reason. "The only place I have a token to is the Josu Rainforest. Rainbow Garden and Josu Rainforest are on opposite sides of the Vale. And I don't want to go to the rainforest; I've been all over that place lately." Like, literally.

Emma paused as she caught on to the major problem. "Oh, I don't have a token for the Rainbow Garden either." She hummed in thought, obviously wracking her brain to solve the problem.

We couldn't just run over to the Garden either. Gate Vale was set up so the weaker locations were on the inside, and the farther from the Gate, the stronger the area was. Rainbow Garden was on the very edge of the Vale, right against the mountain range which circled the valley. It would take half a day, at least, to hoof it there. Since the day was already half over now, we'd get to the garden just in time for night to fall. Then we'd be stuck in the location farthest from the Gate when all the portals in Gate Vale vomited out hundreds of thousands of monsters.

As someone who had seen nighttime in Gate Vale, I was never ever going to let Emma risk that danger.

We could buy a token for it, but that would take time and several hundred dollars. Way too much effort for a quick, girl-time trip.

"What to do," Emma said slowly. Then her eyes lit up again. "But what about the area next to the Josu Rainforest? The *something* desert wasteland?"

"The Alous Wasteland?" I supplied. I'd been in the Josu Rainforest enough to be very familiar with the surrounding areas too.

"Yes! I got a token for the rainforest a bit ago." She nearly jumped up and down. "We can teleport to the Josu Rainforest then walk to the Alous Wasteland. It'll only take like five minutes or fewer."

I nodded. "Or less."

I couldn't say that walking around in a hot desert really appealed to me, but if it made her happy, okay. It was a B-ranked area, and I was confident enough that I had the strength to keep her safe if it wasn't as deserted as that group of Hunters claimed. Then again, Emma was only four levels lower than me. If we tag teamed, we could take down stronger monsters.

Emma happily led me to the transportation circle location. There weren't many people waiting in line for the purple glowing circles, just a handful in each of the ten waiting lines. The reason why was obvious when we got closer to the front.

The Association worker looked at us. A hard life had weathered the woman's face and left deep lines around her eyes and thin mouth. She glanced at the tokens in our hands. "In case you haven't heard yet, there are no monsters in Gate Vale right now. The phenomenon is still being investigated. However, the dangers of the regions are still present. Be careful."

"Are the monster plants still there in the Josu Rainforest?" I asked, curious.

The older Hunter shook her head. "No. Everything monster related has vanished. For now. We expect them to come back at night."

I nodded my head. "Thank you."

Emma thanked the woman and hopped into the transportation circle. As soon as she touched the glowing purple light, her body became a blur of movement as it shot up and through the magical arch which connected to the Josu Rainforest in the southern half of Gate Vale.

I glanced at the Hunter manning the magic circle. "What are some of the theories around the no monster thing?"

She pursed her lips. "Well, when the Gate Surge was announced, an S Hunter was in Gate Vale. They think he was the one who took care of them."

So it *did* have to do with Kesstel. Since all the other S Hunters were accounted for, waiting with the Hunter army at the Gate during the alarm, Kesstel was the only S Hunter she could be referring to. But that was a lot of monsters to take on by himself.

"What about the Hunters who were already in here when it happened?" I asked, curious.

She shook her head, her eyes burning with gossip. "I was here when it happened. When I tried to evacuate with everyone else, a monstrous pressure settled over everything within a mile from the Gate. No one could move. I thought we were dead for sure. Then all at once, the pressure was gone, and Gate Vale was empty of all monsters. Witnesses say that instead of running toward the Gate like in a Gate Surge, the monsters—all monsters, no matter the rank—ran *away* from the Gate. By the time we got out, the mess in the square was already done."

I nodded my thanks. The pressure she'd felt was undoubtedly Kesstel. And the reason why the monsters fled was because they could feel an angry Boss's aura, just like when he controlled the goblins before he disappeared in the Josu Portal Burst. The question that remained was, where did all the monsters go?

Still thinking about it, I stepped into the transportation circle. Instantly, my body became weightless, then I was hurtling through the sky at airplane speeds. The first couple of times I'd traveled this way, the pressure was nauseating, and the speed made me dizzy. Now I was used to it, and my body was strong enough that I didn't feel like I was being squished like a bug.

I flew over Gate Vale and quickly arched down toward the misty, tall green trees of Josu Rainforest. I twisted around until I was feet first as I approached the ground.

Emma was ten feet away from the landing circle, its pale purple glow illuminating her face. Her hands were outstretched, and her face was determined as she watched me come down, obviously ready to catch me. Such a silly girl.

I landed on the ground and braced myself as the inertia sent me skidding across the damp ground in a well-practiced braced pose. I skidded to a stop feet from her and reached out to high-five her hand.

She blinked repeatedly, looking from her hand to me, then back at her hand. Then she laughed. "I should have known you didn't need my help."

"But the sentiment was appreciated." I smiled and stood up.

Emma glanced around at the rainy forest. Outside of the *drip, drip, drip* of the water hitting the leaves and pale tree trunks, the dim forest was still and silent. "I've never actually walked around the ground of the Josu Rainforest. It's just too dangerous, you know? We tried once because Billy wanted a '*challenge*.'" She lifted her hands and bent her fingers in quotation marks. "But we gave up after a little while. With those bird monsters and the tree roots, we all decided it wasn't worth it."

I nodded slowly. I totally knew what they meant. "You're not missing out. Without the challenge, there's really nothing to see here. It's not beautiful like the Feng Jungle, and it doesn't have hidden sights like Glenn Holt. Just the same thing over and over again." I reached out and watched the drizzle wet my glove. In fact, if it wasn't for Kesstel, just waiting for him to return, I wouldn't have spent so much time here.

I glanced across the small clearing, remembering the battle that happened here. Just on the other side was where the Portal Burst had been. The one that almost stole Kesstel from me.

I frowned as I played over the last moments of him leaving in my mind.

A thought came to me, and my eyes popped wide open.

I yelled and slapped my hand over my forehead.

Emma reacted instantly. Her beautiful recurve bow was out and drawn before I could even blink, her naive eyes narrowed with deadly intensity as she scanned the trees, searching for something to shoot. But there was nothing around except for us. Confused, she lowered her bow and glanced at me. "Are you okay?"

I was too busy agonizing to pay her too much attention. "That son of a—" My words cut off because I couldn't bring myself to curse at Kesstel's mother.

What was the last thing he said to me before he disappeared? That he'd personally made sure the Warriors of Mist were extinct. Then he left me hanging for two months! No explanation whatsoever!

I'd been so happy that he was back and worried about how he was acting to even think of asking him about the Warrior of Mist subject. Then the Council showed up and . . .

"Agh!" I covered my face.

"Um, Jynn?" Emma put her bow away with a wave of her hand and reached out to my shoulder. "What's wrong?"

I sighed and dropped my hands. "I just let myself get distracted, that's all. I forgot to do something important before we left." Yes, I'd let myself get distracted for the moment, but no way in hell was he going to get away with it much longer. Kesstel was going to explain why he was going to kill me and why he hunted down all the other Warriors of Mist. No loopholes, no vague answers.

I huffed a breath. "Are they sure there aren't any monsters around?" I'd originally wanted to blow off some steam in the Gate. Emma had preoccupied me from that anger, but now, the tense emotion was bubbling up in my chest again.

"I don't feel any around here." Emma glanced around the rainforest before turning to the region's barrier. "Should we try over the Alous Wasteland? If nothing else, the new sights might distract you."

I bobbed my head in agreement and started heading over with Emma.

We walked out of the rainforest with Emma chattering happily, obviously trying to cheer me up. She talked about what was going on with her group. How the mage, Kip, and the new guy, Russel, were going out, and how he was blissfully wrapped around her finger. Nick was the same as ever, a silent mountain and a steady partner to the more subdued Billy. The healer, Morgan, had bought a puppy who was an angel . . . as long as Morgan was in the room. Billy had threatened to kill it more than once.

"And what about you and Mason?" I cut in. "How are things progressing?"

Emma's face turned pink. "Um, we've, ah, gone on a couple dates." They must have been good ones, from the way her eyes were sparkling.

I stopped on the top of a dune and looked around. We were only ten feet into the area, and I could already feel the hot sun high in the sky pounding down. Even with my enhanced body, sweat was starting to drip down my back. I shifted, trying to put some distance between my skin and the sticky leather armor. The heat made the dried blood that much more pungent.

The Alous Wasteland spread out ahead of us, a mix of sandstone pillars and plateaus between small mountains of sand. There was hardly any vegetation, and what little there was was thin, pointy, and about the same salmon color as the sand and stones. Honestly, the whole place consisted of practically two colors. The sand on the ground and the bright blue of the cloudless sky above.

It was cool looking, I guess, but I felt an ever-greater sense of unwillingness to walk through it. It just looked hot and hard to travel through. There was nothing pretty to look at, *at all*, but at least there weren't any sand sharks under our feet right now.

Or perhaps it would be better if there were so I'd have something to concentrate on instead of how hot it was.

Emma pointed to the right. "Is that some green? Do you think there's an oasis over there?"

I focused on where she was pointing. "It's definitely green. Let's check it out." I lifted a foot to start down the dune.

A huge System message popped up right in front of my face. [**HELP ME! HURRY! SAVE ME!**]

I staggered and lost my footing. Gravity mercilessly grabbed onto me and dragged me to slide down the dune while Emma yelped and hurried down, kicking sand everywhere as she rushed after me. I landed on the bottom, choking on the sand that filled the air and covered me from head to toe.

Where are you? I asked the System in my head.

[**Find the portal with the red orcs. Hurry! I don't have much longer.**]

Jynn Devhro

Rank B   **Level** 50

EXP to Next Level 6685

HP 1174/2842   **Stat Points** 0

MP 732/1253

Strength 90 (+20)   **Agility** 83

Magic 80   **Perception** 83

Constitution 83 (+20)   **Intelligence** 76

Skills   **Abilities**

Throw   Mist (Improved) (50 ft)

Critical Hit   Feather Step

Quick Hit   Regen (Limited)

Mirror   Stealth (Limited)

High Jump   Poison Fog

Mist Blade

CHAPTER 47

Are you sure you're okay? You've been off all day," Emma asked for the millionth time in the last five hours. A pink burn from the scorching sun we'd just left colored her cheeks and forehead. It was so similar to the color of her armor, she was like a rosy-pink doll with brunette hair.

I nodded and waved my hand. "Yes. I'm fine."

Okay, that was a lie. I was reeling inside and didn't have any way to let out the energy. First, I was burning from the Warrior of Mist thing with Kesstel, then that message from the System.

I didn't know how to find the portal with the red orcs. It'd been a random Portal Burst in Glenn Holt months ago. By the time I woke up in the hospital days later, it was already gone. If it was a permanent portal on the edge of Gate Vale, I could go there now and save the System, but how would I find a portal that didn't stay in one place?

If the System disappeared, what would happen to me? Would I lose everything and revert to the weakest Hunter in history?

A chill went down my back, and my stomach twisted nauseously. *God, no. Please no.* My life was finally in order. My family was stable for the first time in years and optimistic about moving into a better place. I wasn't a hair away from dying every time I went in the Gate. I had enough to eat, and I could finally sleep in peace. I didn't want that to fall apart.

Emma grabbed my arm. "You just went as white as a sheet. Are you really okay?"

I blinked down at her. It took me a second to answer her. "Yes. I'm okay." I would be. And so would the System. I couldn't afford for either of us not to be.

Luckily, I could get answers to both of the problems plaguing me from the same person.

Emma and I exited the Gate. The orange sun was low in the sky, causing the buildings to cast long, dark shadows across the square. Streetlamps lit the square, and small groups of Hunters lingered around the space, talking about the lack of monsters in the Vale.

Emma grinned at me. "Thanks for letting me come and play. It's probably the only time I'll ever get to go into that desert. It was a fun, new experience. And that oasis was amazing, so tropical and green, just like in the movies. I can't believe something like that actually exists in real life."

I smiled back. "Same."

She sighed. "The only downer is that we couldn't take pictures. It kinda makes having a phone frustrating, you know? You can have it all the time, keep it tucked safely in your Items Bag, but as soon as you take it out in the Vale—*puff*!" She gestured an explosion with her hands.

"Having it but not being able to use it. Is that what you mean?"

She nodded, her phone appearing in her hand. Instantly, it dinged a dozen times. Emma glanced at the screen. "Oh, whoops. I told Mason I was going to be back an hour ago. He's a worrywart." But she beamed with pleasure anyway.

I laughed. "I actually need to go, too." I had a man to hunt down.

She gave me a goodbye hug and hurried off toward the Guild District.

The smile slipped from my face as she disappeared from view. Taking out my own phone, I jumped when it dinged. And kept dinging. Walking slowly toward A District, I flipped it open. The first was a message from my real estate agent letting me know that the offer I'd put in on the condo in Garden City had been accepted. Now she was just waiting on the inspector, and then it would be time to sign the papers.

I nodded and made a mental note to call my family to tell them the good news later.

The next message was a little harder to think about what to do with. It was from Bethany.

Jynn! What the hell happened today? I mean, there were pictures and recordings of Kesstel walking out of the Gate like a zombie. Then he kidnapped you? Are you okay?

The next message was from her too.

Jynn, answer me! Are you okay? And what did you say to my dad? He's always thought it was great that I was showing charity to weaker Hunters by hanging out with you. (Jerk.) He thought you were a good

influence on me and my image. (Double jerk.) But now he's telling me to find another person to fill in that role? The hell? What's going on?!

What followed were another half dozen texts and calls from her.

Well, at least she's feeling energetic, I thought, texting back.

I'm fine, but I can't talk right now. I'll call you later.

Even if I called at one in the morning, it wouldn't be a problem.

The last message from an unknown number had two simple words:

It's Kesstel.

I scowled just seeing his name. I didn't normally hold on to anger long. Usually, I let it simmer down to a cool rage, which was easier to think through and gave enough of a push when I needed it. Hot emotions led to mistakes. Mistakes led to a short life. But I was feeling irrational right now.

Where are you? I texted him back.

I was halfway across A District's shopping street when my phone dinged. Instead of telling me, Kesstel simply shared his location—a park about a mile away, on the west side of A District's residential area. Not too far from his house. I set out at a jog, following the instructions my phone gave.

A couple minutes later, the park came into view. It was more of a garden than a park, with winding paths between lots and lots of flowers. Well, flowering plants. The chill in the prefall air was wilting the flowers, so only the resilient ones still had blossoms. In the back, illuminated by several strings of lights, was a pretty gazebo over a table set. Trees grew in just the right places, their branches stretching out to give privacy in several different locations. It was an amazing park, even with the dying flowers. Hopefully, I'd get to see it in full bloom someday.

I entered the park and headed toward Kesstel's presence next to the gazebo.

He was staring off into the distance, his eyes blank and obviously lost in thought. The low light highlighted half his face, while the other half was left in shadows. Just like everything else about him: half illuminated in light with a long, dark, unknown history hiding behind that glowing perfection.

When I came closer, he looked up, and a welcoming light entered his eyes. "Evening."

I walked up to him. Without a word, I reached out, my hand gripping his navy shirt while my foot shot out and hooked his knee. It buckled, and I shoved him down to the ground. In the same movement, I planted a knee on his chest and scowled down at him.

He looked up at me, his brow wrinkled in confusion and amusement. He could have easily stopped me, but he didn't. Instead, he just lay there and asked, "Is this where I deny any involvement or where I plead for mercy?"

"Oh, you bet you were involved," I snarled. "And this time, you aren't going to get out of explaining it to me."

He put his hands up in surrender. "I just got back. I honestly can't think of a single thing that I could have done to make you this mad in the last seven or eight hours."

"You and the Warriors of Mist," I snarled. "You can't just drop a bomb like that and then disappear."

I felt a barrier settle over us, and all the world went silent. I was familiar enough with his barriers that I didn't have to ask to know no one could hear our conversation now. "Oh, that," Kesstel said in a heavy voice.

"Yes, *that*. I've been looking for information about the Warriors of Mist for months, ever since I became one, and you've been holding out on me this whole time." My hand tightened on his shirt as a new wave of boiling anger surged in. "Not only that, but I also find out that the guy I finally learned to trust has been thinking of killing me this whole time?" There was a faint ripping sound as the material under my fingers gave way. I was too mad to care right now about how much I was going to have to pay to replace his shirt.

Kesstel glanced down at my hand. "How about you let go so we can sit down and have a proper conversation?"

It felt kind of nice to subdue this overpowered Boss, but I was trying to be a good example for my sister—even if she wasn't here at the moment. That included being a civilized person.

I huffed a breath and got up. Five clear holes were torn into Kesstel's obviously ruined designer shirt.

He rolled to his feet in a smooth, predator-like move, then glanced down at the holes. "I normally don't change this much in a day." Without pausing, he pulled his shirt off over his head.

My eyes widened, and I instinctively looked away. It wasn't the first time I'd seen his chest today, but his moves were so sudden, the sight shocked me.

Out of the corner of my eye, I could see a black shirt appear in his hand, and he pulled it on before brushing off his light-colored pants.

"Shall we?" He motioned to the gazebo. Without waiting, he walked to the table and tapped on it. A familiar pink pastry box appeared, spreading the smell of sweets and sugar into the air.

My lips twitched. "Bribing me with sweets still?"

I couldn't resist staring at the box. I knew it was full of heaven. It was also a taste I hadn't had in months, since I couldn't seem to bring myself to even enter that pastry shop without him.

"It worked last time." Kesstel shrugged. "Besides, it took a lot of time to get you to a healthy weight. I don't appreciate you losing it all again while I was gone." He pulled a chair out and motioned for me to sit.

I gaped at him. "A healthy weight? What?"

When I didn't sit down, he moved to the next chair and sat down, leaving my chair open for me. "Yes. You were underweight when we met, and I didn't like it. It baffled me that I could even feel that emotion at the time; enough to draw my attention. When I first gave you food, it was to let you relax enough to stop running from me. When I decided to take care of you, it became a habit so you'd finally be healthy." He paused. "If you hadn't noticed, not everything I gave you was just sugar. There was protein and whatnot included. It's a little ridiculous the percentage of snacks I have in my Items Bag right now."

My jaw dropped. *Really? That's what all the food is about?* I mean, I really enjoyed the snacks, even if they were an odd thing to bond over. I shook my head. "I'm so confused. Don't you hate the Warriors of Mist? Why else would you kill them off? What did they ever do to you?"

He pointedly glanced at my chair before he opened the box. The faint smell of chocolate came out in all its glory. He reached inside and took out a small chocolate bundt cake topped with raspberries and chocolate shavings. He set it in front of my chair, then he locked his pale blue eyes on mine. "They annihilated nearly every living thing on my planet, which led to Kathar's collapse."

CHAPTER 48

I slowly walked over and sat down in the chair Kesstel had left for me. The intoxicating smell of the chocolate bundt cake seductively wafted around me, and it looked so heavenly, but I didn't touch it. Instead, I watched Kesstel, waiting for him to explain.

Kesstel pursed his lips and tapped on the wooden table as if thinking about how to word his thoughts. The pale light from the string of bulbs hanging on the gazebo cast a sort of glow on his bleach-blond hair.

"On my world," Kesstel started, "we didn't know what those monsters were originally called. I only found out their name after Kathar fell. We called them Blood Mists."

His heavy words landed like a sledgehammer, and my eyes widened.

"They weren't quite human and not quite ghosts, but something in between. Magic could affect them, but plain physical attacks went right through them. They looked like someone had taken them and stretched them out, each standing over seven feet tall, their features distorted and elongated, glowing white eyes and ghostly clothes flowing around them. Each step sent out a wave of fog. As soon as the fog started to roll out of the trees, smothering everything in its wake, everyone knew it was time to run. Anyone who didn't leave would die, turning that everlasting fog red and soaking the ground. Those monsters didn't even eat; they just slaughtered everything that moved." He paused and pressed his hand against the table, blindly staring down at his long fingers.

His eyes narrowed and started to faintly glow blue. "I personally watched six Blood Mists take out an entire legion of magic warriors. My father was leading the people. Those ghosts faded into the fog which flooded over the army, thick as ink. Then the screaming started. My mother and brother held me down, crying and pleading, to keep me from rushing down there. When the fog moved away, there was nothing but a bloody soup of bodies where brave men and women had been. We never found all of my father's body." Kesstel's fingers pressed on the wooden surface, turning his fingertips pale. The wood began to crack and splinter under the pressure.

My heart bled for him. I'd seen a lot as a Hunter and had been desensitized to human death, but I would never be able to handle watching my father die in front of me. I reached out and gently tapped a finger on the back of Kesstel's hand. The table wouldn't hurt him, but still, he shouldn't destroy public property. And it wouldn't do anyone any good if he slipped back into a mindless rage again; himself most of all.

"I'm sorry," I whispered. "That must have been hard."

Kesstel blinked and looked up at me, the glow fading from his eyes. He turned his hand over and gently pinched my finger with his. The glassy look in his eyes vanished, replaced with an almost smile. "It was. Every time one of my family died, it was hard." He played with my finger in silence for a minute, but he obviously wasn't done talking. "After my world was devoured and I regained consciousness, I discovered those monsters were originally called Warriors of Mist. Their world was the one that fell right before mine, and the Blood Mists were what was left of the population after they were injected with energy crystals. After that, I set out to kill every one of them."

I shook my head. "How did you know where they were?"

Kesstel frowned. "When I first threw off the parasitic planet's control, I was still connected enough to know about the monsters under its control. It's like a queen ant, a single brain that does all the thinking for every monster in its massive army. The parasitic planet has a consciousness, you understand? It wouldn't be able to do all this without one, and it's quite smart. The parasite remembered enough about the Warriors of Mist that I was able to piece together this much information about them before I completely broke out of its control. And when I came out of my portal, they were in the world the parasitic planet was preying on. So I hunted the ghosts down and killed every single one of them. The current intelligent species praised me for helping them, but I was doing it for me. I couldn't feel any emotion in the act, but I knew they had to die."

"I see," I said softly. Honestly, I had been hoping he would have more information about them than that. Or maybe just different information. Like more about where they were from. "Since you killed all the Blood Mist monsters that killed your people, why did you want to kill me?"

His lips pressed together. "If you got sick after eating something for the first time, would you want to eat it again? If the first time you saw a rose was when your sister died holding one, would you ever want to see one again? Visual cues are just as effective to induce trauma as smell is."

So every time he looked at me, he thought of his dead family? *Oh my god.* My heart squeezed tight, so painful it was hard to breathe. When I tried to pull back, he tightened his fingers around mine, holding it captive. It wasn't painful, just strong enough that his opinion was obvious. In the end, I stopped pulling away. "I'm sor—"

He cut me off. "That was then. My first instinct was to kill you, but I was also curious because the first two times I saw you, you weren't a Warrior of Mist. My curiosity and logic won over the predator instinct. So you lived." He shrugged. "Simple as that. I didn't want to tell you because I thought you'd be scared of me."

"You were right," I muttered under my breath.

"But since we're companions, I decided to tell you everything," he concluded.

I was quiet for a minute. I wasn't being fair with him. He'd told me so much about himself. As for me, other than my simple day-to-day things and about my family, I hadn't told him anything about the System or the Warrior of Mist thing.

"I don't know how the Warriors of Mist were in their world, but I have a feeling I'm nothing like them," I started slowly. "I—" My voice was suddenly cut off. I couldn't move my lips, couldn't make any sound.

[Warning. Warning. Information not authorized for sharing.] the System flashed in front of my eyes.

I sighed. I'd thought at this point I'd be able to tell him, but that was wishful thinking. Outside of what he already knew, I couldn't add more. "I'm sorry," I concluded.

Kesstel watched my actions, his eyes serious. He had noticed when I stopped as if someone had pushed a pause button. His eyes narrowed. "Something or someone is preventing you from talking about it?"

I didn't say anything. I couldn't, anyway.

He nodded slowly, taking my silence as a confirmation. "I see."

I bit my lips and stared down at our fingers. "I actually need your help," I said slowly.

He focused on me. In all the time we'd spent together, this was the first time I'd ever asked for help. All the other times, it was him acting on his own, guessing what I needed. And he was usually right. But this was different.

I pursed my lips. How much was I allowed to say? "For reasons," I started slowly, "I need to find the remnant of the world the Warriors of Mist came from. It still exists, but not for much longer. I think." So I could talk about that much. It was a start.

Kesstel shook his head. "I don't know what it looks like. I only know what happened to the people after that world collapsed."

I tapped my finger on his fingertips, bouncing from one to the other while I thought. "I've been there, once." I had to assume that the remnant world on the other side of the Portal Burst in Glenn Holt was it. It was the only other world I'd been to, and where I'd made my contract with the System. "It's a Mediterranean-type place, inhabited by red orcs."

Actually, now that I thought about it, if all the people from that world had become ghost-like Blood Mists, where had the red orcs come from?

Kesstel leaned back a little as if thinking, but he kept his hand in the same place for me to keep playing. "I don't recall seeing a world with red orcs attached to Eden," he spoke slowly.

"You mean, when you were checking out the portals around Gate Vale?" I asked hopefully. "Is it possible the portals changed while you were gone?"

He shook his head. "No, I meant while I was coming back here today. In the void between the worlds, most of the remnant worlds look like glass balls with pieces of land or ocean inside. I could see what the world looked like as I passed by, and I got a good look at all the worlds attached to Eden, since I wanted to find one that was connected to both Eden and the parasitic planet. But I do admit, I wasn't able to see all of them, given the scope of things. I must have overlooked it, since I wasn't searching for a world like that."

I leaned back against my chair. The warm touch of his skin disappeared from my fingers, but instead of reaching back for it, I closed my hand to keep from following the sudden strong instinct. I looked up at the string of lights above, thinking. "I need to find that portal. It's . . . vital," I whispered. "Where do I even start?"

Kesstel was silent for a minute. "I could go back into the void and look, but I don't know how long I'd be gone because of the time differences. Earth could be gone by the time I'm back," he said. "I'm very reluctant to go that route."

I nodded. "Yeah."

"How important is it that you find this portal? Does it have to be before we try to attack the parasitic planet?"

I blinked in surprise and looked at Kesstel. "I don't actually know." What would happen to all the remnant worlds caught in the parasitic planet's void after it was dead? Would they simply vanish? If so, the Warriors of Mist's world would disappear . . . along with the System. What would happen to me after that? Was it possible to save it before that happened? Was that what it meant by *save me*?

"First," I said, "I need to find that portal before we attack the parasitic planet. If we don't, I don't know that . . . I'll be strong enough to help you." If something happened to the System, I'd be back to what I was the first time I met Kesstel. Weak and useless.

Hell, maybe I'd end up like that after the parasitic planet disappeared anyway, if we managed to destroy it. Since the magic which created Hunters was tied to it, maybe everyone would revert back to being human. As long as the monsters died at the same time, that actually wouldn't be a horrible thing. It just meant humanity would be what it was twenty years ago, except they'd have to learn how to live without energy crystals. I could handle a life like that, as long as I was on the same level of playing field, which I should be.

"So finding that remnant world is very important," Kesstel concluded. "It's not going to be easy, but we'll come up with something." He frowned and looked in the direction of the Gate blotting out the stars from the darkening sky. "Apparently, I have a lot of paperwork to do. Keep your phone on you."

I leaned closer to him. "Why?"

He shook his head. "Since you want to use the legal method to leave Eden, as time costly as it is, it's going to require a lot of paperwork. I don't know what the forms might require. Keep your phone on you so I can fill them out as needed."

"Hang on." I grabbed his hand. "You're talking about filling out paperwork for both me and you? You're going to do my paperwork too?"

He nodded and looked at me like it was obvious. "I grew up handling mountains of paperwork and handling people the right way to get what I want. How hard would it be to do one more form?"

"Oh," I muttered. Honestly, a part of me was happy that I didn't have to worry about that stuff. Just dealing with the paperwork involved for the condo I was buying was terrifying enough—and that was with the nice agent explaining everything to me every step of the way.

"Let's get approved to leave Eden legally," Kesstel said. His thumb rubbed across the back of my hand, but he was looking over my shoulder into the dark garden, lost in thought. Did he even know his thumb was moving? "Once that's done, we can move on to the next step and figure out how to find that portal."

I nodded. "Yes. Let's start with that."

CHAPTER 49

ome on! Come on!" Aliya squealed with excitement. She grabbed my shoulders and shook me so hard I could barely insert the key into the door.

With a twist of my wrist, the lock clicked, and Aliya flung the door open. I stepped to the side so she could rush inside the front room of the condo we now owned. She spread her arms wide and did a circle on the off-white carpet.

"Oh my god!" she squealed. "It's so big! We can actually fit a couch and a coffee table in here. And a TV stand. Maybe even a rocking chair." She danced in place, then stopped and drew in a deep breath. "And the air! It doesn't have an old, musty odor."

"I hope not." I stepped onto the small tile patch in front of the door and kicked off my shoes so I didn't leave tracks on the newly cleaned carpet.

Aliya winced and hurriedly pulled her shoes off, wobbling dangerously in the process. I stepped over and steadied her before she really did fall.

She yelped and looked over at me, holding one shoe in her hand with her sock halfway off. She blinked from me to the door and back. "How did you get over here so fast?"

I laughed and patted her head like a little puppy. I really didn't think I'd moved that fast. "Hunter, remember? Never mind. Let's take a look around. You haven't seen it yet, right?"

Her face lit up. "Yes!" She ripped her other shoe off and tossed them next to mine on the tile. Turning around, she pointed to where the honey wood laminate started. "This is where the dining table goes, right?" She trotted in that direction. "It's so big. We could totally buy a bigger table than that wobbly thing we have now."

I nodded and trailed behind her. I was already planning on dumping another couple thousand dollars to buy things they'd need for the house as soon as they moved in, like a living room and dining set. But Aliya didn't need to know that right now. She'd tell my aunt and uncle, and they'd ixnay the idea. "Over here"—I pointed to a door on the left wall—"is a coat closet. It's pretty big, has good storage. Oh, actually, this unit comes with a small storage shed down by the parking lot."

"An actual storage shed included," Aliya muttered like it was the most novel idea ever.

To the left of the dining room was a G-shaped kitchen. The honey oak cabinets were about the same color as the flooring, and the appliances showed definite wear, but it was big enough to fit two people comfortably, and it was clean.

I bumped Aliya with my elbow and grinned. "Uncle Carl has a lot more room to hide his candy stash now."

She laughed. "As if that's ever worked." She bustled about the kitchen, opening every cabinet and drawer, experimenting until she found the right way without slamming it too loudly. I leaned on the small bar and watched her, absentmindedly thinking that one of the first things I needed to buy were barstools.

When she was satisfied, Aliya grabbed my arm and dragged me down the short hall between the kitchen and the coat closet. She opened the first door on the right. "This is the master, right?"

I nodded. "Right, their own bathroom is right there." I pointed to a door in the corner of the room. "The bathroom at the end of the hall is yours. Well, yours and guests, so keep it clean."

Aliya leaned into the master bathroom, just big enough to fit a shower, toilet, and vanity. It was like the kitchen—not much to look at and a little dated, but clean and functional. She came back out, shaking her head. "I can't believe I get my own bathroom. It's like a dream come true." She sighed then perked up. "Let's go check it out."

I watched her rush out the room and shook my head. I didn't even have my own bathroom; I was still sharing it with all the other women in E Hostel. But I only had to deal with the cold showers for another six months. By that time, I should have enough to put a down payment on a condo in C District for when Aliya graduates. The quality might be a little worse than this, but it would have everything we need: a safe place for Aliya to live. Maybe it wasn't fair for me to take advantage of the free housing at E Hostel when I wasn't an E anymore, but I didn't feel bad for milking the Hunter's Association's system until I could give my sister a comfortable life. Not with how much I went through just because I didn't fit in their mold of what a Hunter should be.

Aliya chattered nonstop about everything she was going to do with her bathroom. When she ran out of words, she rushed into her room and started another wave of excited explanations.

I leaned against the doorjamb and watched her with a smile. After the last couple extrahard days in the Gate, this was the perfect thing to relax me.

She paused midsentence and turned to me. The exhilaration in her eyes dimmed a little. "I wish we could have gotten this place before you went to Eden. It would have been awesome living here with you." She shifted. "I feel a little bad about being so excited about taking advantage of all the hard work you've done."

I walked over to her and hugged her. "I work hard for you. That's the only reason I do it. It's the reason why I'm breathing and living today. To see the smiles on our family's faces." I leaned back. "Besides, you won't be here for that much longer. You're going to graduate and join me in Eden, right? Then you can help me pay for this place."

Energy surged in Aliya's eyes again. "Right!" She raised her left fist into the air, making the red fanged snapper bracelet on her wrist shimmer and rattle soothingly.

I laughed and wrapped an arm around her shoulders. "Come on. You'll get to spend all the time in the world in this house in a couple weeks. For now, let's go down and work on your balance and footwork."

"What?" Aliya gaped at me as we walked to the front door.

I leaned my head over and bonked her head with mine. "You couldn't even balance while taking off your shoe a minute ago. Don't tell me you expect to pass the Hunters course in school like that?" I let her go and put on my shoes.

She pursed her lips in a scowl. "Jeez, you sound like my teacher. She said the same thing. Is balance really all that important?"

"I'm going to pretend I didn't hear that. Balance and footwork are *vital*. Nearly every technique requires both. I mean, how are you going to kill a monster if you trip over your own feet and fall flat on your face?"

She stood up and tapped her toe on the tile twice to settle her shoe. "You know, I like the 'bash them to death' strategy. Or maybe I'll just be a mage and zap them black from a distance." She thrust out her hand and moved it around like she was pretending to shoot magic. "No footwork involved," she reasoned happily.

"Or you'll just rely on your sister and become a useless bum who can't do jack," I muttered.

"Ah, that's cold!" Aliya opened the door and stepped out.

I followed her, shutting the door tight before locking it. "Then work on it," I said.

A lazy Hunter was a dead Hunter . . . Blake Hans excluded. And technically Bethany, but I'd since learned that what she didn't do in the Gate, she made up for in the media front. Aliya wouldn't have the same backing as they did, so she had to be strong enough to live. Even without me.

If Kesstel was right, then there wasn't much time left before Earth collapsed. It could be tomorrow or a year from now. By that time, he and I could have found the portal which led to the parasitic planet, and hopefully, the monsters wouldn't be a threat anymore. But then Earth would be back to where it was twenty years ago, learning how to rebuild their society again while finding a new power source, since I was hoping they'd all vanish when the parasite died.

Or maybe Kesstel and I would find the portal but never come back, and the monsters would be just as strong until the world failed. Either way, anything could happen in the future, and I wanted Aliya to be able to handle whatever came her way.

"I love this view." Aliya sighed and leaned against the railing. Three floors down was a parking lot, but on the other side was a large park, all grass and flower beds. Granted, the beds had been cleared for the winter already, but it was a lot better than having another dingy complex staring at your face on the other side of the lot.

"Let's go down there." I pointed to the park.

She nodded and followed me down.

There weren't a lot of people there, so we easily found a secluded place under a tall, aged tree.

Aliya clapped and grinned at me with excitement. "Okay, teach. What am I learning today?"

"Yoga." I smirked.

Her expression fell. "What?" She groaned. "I hate yoga."

"But it does exactly what it's supposed to. Teaches balance and control over your body," I lectured like I didn't hate it too. "Start with just a few poses and once you get them, I can teach you something else that will help."

"A more advanced yoga posture?" Aliya guessed, completely nonplussed.

"Nope." I shook my head, a smug smile on my face. "Not yoga." There were quite a few moves the System put in my Guide when I got it that I could teach her. The difference was, I'd had a year of living as a Hunter under my belt, so I had the fundamentals down already. Aliya did not. "It's cool, but I can't teach it to you until you master the poses I'm going to teach you first."

Aliya huffed but reached down to take off her shoes. "If it's not cool, I'm gonna guilt-trip you for the rest of your life," she promised.

I opened my mouth with a comeback ready, but paused. All of my senses, from the top of my head to my toes, screamed in warning. The next second, the ground started to shake as ripple after ripple writhed under our feet.

Aliya screamed, reaching for me. I hugged her protectively and looked around. Branches creaked and broke as the park's trees swayed back and forth, smacking into each other. Casting a thin vapor of mist, I created a barrier over us; bark and twigs hit it and slid down to the ground.

More screams came from the buildings around us. The taller and older the building, the more it shifted with the earthquake. A five-floor apartment complex right next to us shook for only a couple seconds before a loud cracking rang out, and a split opened up on the building's north wall. Terrified screams echoed louder than ever, but the building didn't collapse.

The tree to the left of us groaned loudly and fell in our direction. I stepped back a couple feet, dragging Aliya with me, and it hit the ground with a thundering crack, splintered wood exploding like darts in every direction. They hit the barrier around us with solid *pop, pop, pop* sounds then dropped to the ground.

Aliya gripped my shirt and peeked over my shoulder, shivering in fear. "What's happening?" she yelled in my ear over the loud bangs of moving earth and destruction.

I shook my head. "I don't know."

But the feeling of alarm I got right before the quake hit didn't come from the Gate in Eden. No, it'd come from somewhere southwest, outside of Garden City.

CHAPTER 50

Slowly, the ground stopped rolling. Natural disaster sirens rang from tilted street posts, car alarms beeped, and people screamed in fear, wails for help echoing in the air adding a sense of despair.

All the noise faded to the background as I listened to something more than the superficial sounds around us. I was feeling for that alarming sensation I'd had right before the earthquake, but whatever it was was gone.

I let out the breath I didn't notice I was holding and released Aliya.

As soon as I stepped back, the ground rumbled again, but it was at a fraction of the intensity, enough to shimmy the ground under our feet but not enough to freak me out. There was no feeling attached to it, and the earthquake was coming from the opposite direction.

"An echo?" Aliya asked, grabbing my arm to stay stable.

I frowned. "I . . . don't think this earthquake is attached to the other. Maybe it was caused by the first, but I don't think they're from the same place."

Slowly, the rumbling stopped.

"Why do you say that?" Aliya looked at our feet and hummed in confusion. "Weird, the debris fell in a perfect circle around us."

I took a deep breath and answered her in my head. *Because the first earthquake was caused by magic.* I didn't say the words out loud because I didn't want to scare her.

My phone started ringing from my hip satchel. Pulling it out, I flipped it open. "Hello?"

"Where are you?" Kesstel asked. There was no "Are you okay?" As if he knew this wouldn't hurt me.

Aliya reached out to poke at the circle of shattered wood around us, but her finger was stopped by the semi-invisible barrier. "Huh?" She pushed against it. "What is this?"

I canceled the mist and watched as my sister yelped and nearly fell into the wood pile. "In Garden City," I said into the phone.

"Come back to Eden," Kesstel replied immediately.

I hummed under my breath and looked at the chaos around me. Quickly, I examined everything and started to plot out my next moves in my head. "I don't think I will just yet. There isn't a Gate Surge right now, is there?" I asked him even though I could already feel the answer.

Kesstel paused before he reluctantly said, "No."

I jumped over one of the downed trees and walked toward the complex with the huge crack on its side. "I think I'm going to hang around here for a bit to see if there's anything I can help with."

Aliya scrambled over the tree and caught up with me, looking from me to the apartment complex.

"It's useless," Kesstel warned, his voice low in my ear. "You'll only get blamed for not doing enough if someone dies. You shouldn't bog yourself down with unnecessary blame."

My lips curled in a bitter smile. I was sure he was talking from experience. "I know that might happen, but I'm going to help anyway." The phone started to beep, indicating an incoming call. I glanced at the name before saying to Kesstel, "I have another call coming in that I have to answer. I'll call you when I get back to Eden."

Aliya grabbed my arm. "Who are you talking to?" she whispered. Then she looked at the leaning building. "How can we help?"

There was silence on the other side, then Kesstel slowly replied, "Okay."

The call ended with a click.

I snorted. He's never been a big goodbye person, but that was almost cold. Was he mad I went against his wishes? I didn't have time to think about it long before Aunt Mina's voice came over the phone.

"Jynn! Are you okay?!" Her voice was thick with hysteria. "Do you have Aliya with you? Oh my god! Is she okay?"

Screams for help echoed from the complex, getting louder with each step I took. "Yes, we're okay." I looked at my sister. "I'm actually going to have her tell you about it; I gotta go." I handed Aliya the phone. "Talk to Aunt Mina," I instructed her. "Calm her down and don't move from here, got it? I don't want you inside that building." I pointed to the complex in front of me.

She took the noisy phone and nodded at me, confused. Then she realized I was leaving her out. "Wait. I can help too!"

"Stay there and help Aunt Mina calm down," I repeated before running closer to the building.

Disheveled people were running out of the stairwells, coughing from dust lingering in the air and yelling with panic. Mothers clung to their crying kids, and men carried other people out. They rushed across the street and into the park, forming a noisy crowd with the rest of the people.

I stopped in front of the building and spread my arms. A thick mist covered the apartment complex, seeping into every nook and cranny accessible to air, and a 3D picture of the entire building appeared in my mind. There was an influx of terrified screams because of the sudden mist, but I ignored that as I started to scan for injured people who couldn't escape themselves, starting on the bottom and working my way up.

My search stopped just seconds in. On the first floor was an older woman on the ground under a pile of books and broken porcelain dolls which had obviously fallen from the shelving on the wall. Next to her was a crying little girl. Something inside that apartment was contaminating my mist. I didn't know what chemical was mixed in the air, but it wasn't oxygen or hydrogen.

I frowned and sprinted to the apartment, stopping just outside the window. There was a large crack in it, but it was still intact. Materializing my kindjal, I lightly hit the window with the crystal-steel blade, and the glass shattered into pieces, raining down at my feet. Instantly, I smelled a gassy odor emanating from the apartment.

Oh shit, I thought, jumping through the window into the messy home. The girl and the older woman were in the back room, on the floor by an off-centered bed.

The black-haired child was shaking the woman. "Grandma! Wake up!" Her high, hysterical plea was painful to my ears. A large bruise was already forming on the side of her face, but it was nothing compared to the damage done to the woman.

I dropped down next to them and paused. With a sigh, I touched the side of the woman's neck just to be sure. There wasn't a pulse, and her body was going cold.

The girl jumped and let out a piercing scream. "Who are you?"

"I'm here to help," I said. "We have to go. There's a gas leak."

I needed to look at the rest of the building before a fire sparked. I was certain there was a sparker somewhere in the building that had malfunctioned. Energy crystals weren't electric, so house fires were less common compared to a couple decades ago, but that didn't mean they didn't happen. And I didn't know when the police or firemen would get here. The closest one was at least a mile away, if I remembered correctly; it could take over ten hours before they arrived, and that's if they worked fast, helping everyone between us and them.

I grabbed the girl and spun around.

She screeched and reached over my shoulder, struggling and sobbing. "Grandma!"

I didn't pause as I ran through the home and jumped out of the window. She was still screaming and wiggling as I darted around the people exiting the building. I stopped next to Aliya and handed her the crying child. "Take her. Her grandma's dead, and someone needs to watch her until the authorities get there."

The girl froze at my words and crumpled into Aliya's arms, sobbing uncontrollably. "Save Grandma," she pleaded in a broken voice. "Save . . . Grand . . . ma."

My phone slipped out of Aliya's hands as she fumbled with the girl until she was holding her better. My sister's eyes were wide with shock as she looked between the girl and the building, then she nodded, her face settling. "Okay," she promised me and started to pat the girl's back soothingly.

I picked up my phone and slipped it into my hip satchel. "I don't know how many people I'm going to bring back," I warned her. "You might need to get some help, depending on how many are injured. There's a gas leak, so tell everyone to back up. I don't know if this building is going to blow up or not." I turned around to go back.

Aliya gasped and caught my arm. She shifted the crying girl in her arms as she stared at me. "Don't go! What if it blows up with you in there?"

My lips curled up in an almost bitter smile. "I have to say, I've been through worse. I'll be fine." Hell, I'd already been in a burning building, and that was before I was level fifty. "I'm counting on you," I told her before running back to the crumbling apartment complex.

According to the 3D picture from my mist, there were four people on the second floor, lying on the ground. I wouldn't know if they were alive or not until I checked every single one.

My eyes narrowed in determination, and I put more speed in my step.

I walked slowly through Eden's front gates a minute to 5:00 p.m. The quake happened at 11:00 a.m., and I'd been running constantly in and out of buildings since then, collecting injured and disabled people into a growing pile in the middle of that park. Luckily, there were two other Hunters in the immediate area who'd been able to assist me, and Aliya was able to rile some people into helping her tend the injured and the five orphaned kids we'd found. All the first aid items I had in my Items Bag, as well as the ones in the other Hunters' bags, were used up.

After hours of running and lifting, even at the level I was, I was tired. I stopped by a bench at the end of the main street and sat down.

Eden wasn't nearly as damaged as Garden City, as buildings in Eden were made to handle destruction. They were also newer, all built with reinforced steel structures that could bend and settle back into place. Most of the damage I could see were things like cracked brick walls and broken windows. There were a couple fallen trees and tilted street posts, but it was all superficial.

Garden City had already existed before the Gates appeared, so when the city was taken back, it was cleaned up and the buildings were modified to be powered with energy crystals, but most of the structures were original or half original to the way they used to be. The apartment building my family was currently living in was well over fifty years old.

When Eden was built, they knew it was going to be under heavy attack, given the monsters and monster-like people living in it, so extra care was taken with each building. It was like a fortress, built to withstand anything. Well, at least in the majority of the city. The living structures in E District fell under that category, but things like storage units, sheds and other smaller buildings in that part of the city were cheaply made. I wasn't too excited to see what that part of the city looked like right now.

I leaned back against the bench and sighed.

Hunters ambled down the street in front of me, looking just as dirty, flustered, and tired as I felt, all coming from Garden City. Most were on their phones, talking to family and whatnot.

My own phone was out of battery, or else I would probably be on mine too. Surprisingly, my family's apartment was fine; rattled and a mess, but structurally sound, so they were back home for the night. As for the condo, I was going to have to wait for the building to be checked out before I knew, but it seemed okay. Hopefully, I was right.

My aunt and uncle were beside themselves with worry when I brought Aliya home. As soon as they were convinced we were okay, despite all the dirt and—other people's—blood on our bodies, they were proud we had stayed to help. Both of them had been at work when the quake happened, so they had walked home since transit wasn't working, arriving home only a couple hours before Aliya and I did.

As for my mother, the phones at the hospital were so busy, we couldn't get through. But the hospital did put out a statement that all Dreamer patients were safe and to please give the hospital space so they could care for the injured people faster.

A large group was marching down the street toward Garden City, opposite of the direction most tired feet were moving. I turned my head and watched as the tired Hunters stepped out of the way for the large group of fresh people to pass through. There were over three hundred Hunters, melee and mage alike, mostly in street clothes or in a semiarmored state.

I noticed a couple familiar faces in the crowd, like the rainbow brigade, whom I hadn't seen since the Josu Rainforest's Portal Burst. Since they didn't get arrested with the cult, I could only assume they'd only been contracted to find the cyan-agaric and didn't know that their employer was using it to poison people. The rainbow brigade looked healthy—albeit worried—as they marched with the rest of the Hunters.

I also noticed Emma walking with her group and called out.

She heard me and waved, working her way over to me as her group followed behind. "Hi, what are you doing here?" she asked.

Billy, just to the side of her, muttered, "You look like hell."

I rolled my eyes at his comment. He should have seen me before I washed my hands and face at my aunt's house. Instead of commenting, I motioned to all the people. "What's going on?"

"The Council is letting Hunters assist Garden City," she explained. "These are the people who have registered and been allowed to go out and help."

I nodded slowly then glanced at Morgan, the healer. "I'm a little surprised. Healing magic doesn't work on humans."

"There's more than just injured people out there; there's a lot of damage that needs to be cleared and whatnot," Mason explained. "Besides, Healing might not work, but first aid does. We're supposed to record any materials that we use so the government can reimburse us."

I nodded slowly. "It's a mess out there. Be careful of gas explosions and falling buildings." The first apartment building I cleared never did blow up, but quite a few people suffered from gas poisoning. While none of the structures I'd worked on collapsed, I knew of at least a dozen that had between the condo and my family's apartment.

Emma gasped. "Were you just out there?"

"Yes. I was in Garden City when it happened. I just got back."

Someone from the army called out to Mason and urged him to hurry. The army of Hunters had reached the front gate and were funneling out into Garden City.

Mason tapped on Emma's shoulder. "We need to go." He nodded a farewell to me while Emma waved bye, and they rejoined the rest of the Hunters in the back of the army.

A moment later, I felt a familiar, powerful presence behind me. I turned my head as Kesstel sat down on the bench beside me, holding out a small bag of chocolate-covered pretzels.

"You're so weird," I said, but my lips hooked up in a small smile as I took the bag from him. I'd been so busy today that I hadn't eaten much. Most of the food in my Items Bag had gone to Aliya or the victims that I helped. "Thanks."

"You don't need to thank me for this." He pulled out a bag of peanuts and munched on them as I ate my own snack.

I took a second to savor the salty sweetness in my mouth before I spoke. "This earthquake wasn't natural."

"No," he agreed. "The first quake was not. The second was a reaction to the first and could be considered natural, though, I suppose."

I blinked up at him. Why wasn't I surprised that he knew what happened? Then again, he'd grown up training to be the secret eyes and ears behind the crown in his world. I guess some habits died hard, even if this wasn't his natural world.

"What happened?" I asked.

He paused and munched a couple more peanuts. "It probably had something to do with me," he admitted softly.

My eyes widened. "What?"

He glanced at me. "A portal appeared in the Las Vegas waste, which caused the first earthquake. Earth is so unstable that the act of the portal ripping open caused what was left of the Florida peninsula to sink into the Atlantic Ocean. That was the second earthquake you felt."

CHAPTER 51

—

I gaped at Kesstel. "The . . . Florida peninsula . . . *sank?*"

It technically wasn't that big of a deal. There hadn't been people living in that area for two decades, ever since the Gates first appeared and one opened on the southeast corner of Alabama, where monsters quickly overpowered the humans stranded on that part of land.

In the government's panic to get rid of the Gate, and since all known humans were already dead, they dropped an H-Bomb on the Alabama Gate. The burn scar contaminated the southern half of the East Coast. Animals, any possible remaining humans, vegetation—it was all destroyed. The land in that area, which already had a high level of water saturation, mostly sank, leaving a weird land bridge to the Florida peninsula.

The monsters and Gate were just fine, completely immune to the bomb which devastated Southeastern America. Suddenly, the area was so toxic that humans couldn't touch it, but the monsters were still there. The ground under the Gate eventually sank, submerging the whole Gate in the Mexican Gulf. Monsters still come out of it today, giving the few remaining communities around the Southern Burn Scar daily trouble.

But to hear that the rest of a landmass that big sank into the ocean . . . it boggled my mind.

"Like, it's all the way gone?" I asked. "How is it your fault?" How did he sink hundreds of miles of land into the ocean from here, in the Midwest?

"I had to rip my way into Eden's Gate Vale to come back. Earth is already unstable, and I agitated the parasite with my actions. I'm ninety-five percent sure the portal opening up is a direct response to my actions." He pulled out his phone and tapped on the screen a couple times then handed it to me. "As for the peninsula, the government is keeping it under wraps for now because they don't want people to panic."

My eyes were wide as I started to swipe through picture after picture of a bird's-eye view of what should be land. Only now it was nothing but a raging wave with huge random rocks that were still slowly sinking into the water. The photos ended with a three-minute-long video of the muddy soil bubbling and water slowly spreading over the brown ground. There was a deep, thundering sound that the recording couldn't fully process before the ground shattered like glass and, starting from the outside and working its way in, started sinking into the water in large chunks. Then the camera zoomed back, revealing the whole huge section of land disappearing.

I gaped at the video, barely able to believe what I was seeing.

"At the time, a helicopter was over the area, trying to scope out the amount of monsters present. They were able to record the peninsula collapsing as it happened," Kesstel said.

"How did this happen?" I asked quietly, looking up into his face. "You said a portal opened up in the Las Vegas waste? Don't you mean a Gate?"

He shook his head. "No. It's a portal, not a Gate. Since there's no one living there, they don't know exactly how big it is, or even its exact location. It's hidden somewhere in the rubble. The government was able to track the direction of the earthquake and used a plane to fly over with a detector to figure out it was a portal. Now that area is covered with monsters."

"How do you know this?" I handed him back the phone.

He turned off the screen and slid it into the back pocket of his designer jeans. "From the Hunter's Association. I've been in a meeting with them most of today."

I guess it made sense that they would notify the strongest Hunters of the situation. Especially because we were the closest Hunter city to Las Vegas. There were other Hunters living in settlements across America, but Eden was the largest hub.

Thinking, I spread out the empty snack bag over my thigh until it was flat. Then I started to fold it smaller and smaller. "There aren't any people in that location anymore. There are some in the North Mexican No-Man's-Land, but I don't know how many," I thought out loud. "That was one of the locations that rebelled and created their own pseudocountry when the Gates appeared. Really, there's no unity, just a bunch of Hunters scrambling for resources in the desert heat, remember?"

He nodded slowly. "Yes. I know. That was also talked about this afternoon." He took the wad of plastic from me and put it in his Items Bag.

His actions made me smile. "What is the government going to do with the portal? I assume you know, since you were in the meeting?"

Kesstel nodded. "Even though I didn't want to go, they insisted on me attending." He shifted until he could rest his ankle on his knee and leaned back on the bench. "Since I came back a couple days ago, they got the impression that I knew more about the portals than they did. Most of the afternoon was spent with them pestering me for information on the portals, then arguing if I was right or not." His eyes narrowed and flashed blue light as he scowled. "Annoying."

An angry aura pulsed out of Kesstel. Goose bumps lifted all over my body, but I was used to it enough that I wasn't bothered. A Hunter walking by was smacked with it midstep, however; he reacted like a spooked cat and leapt five feet away. His weapon was out before he fully landed, and he looked at Kesstel, eyes wide in fright.

Kesstel didn't even fully glance at the guy.

I almost felt bad for him. Being struck with Kesstel's aura—a *Boss's* aura—while walking down a peaceful street would freak anyone out. I waved my hand and drew the man's attention, pressing my lips into a smile. "Sorry."

The man shot Kesstel a worried and confused look before he hurried away.

Kesstel's attention locked onto my wrist and the fanged snapper bracelet that was making a soothing *sh-sh* sound with my movement. He reached out and touched the red scales on the bracelet, his finger slowly moving them around on my wrist, his skin sometimes brushing mine. Each time it did, I felt a warm thrill down my arm. His expression relaxed, and the heavy atmosphere evaporated.

I stayed still and let him play. "What did the Council decide?"

"They want to close the portal," he said, softly clicking the scales against each other. "In two days, a large team of the best American Hunters are going to be sent to Las Vegas to clear out the monsters and locate the portal. They didn't believe me when I explained what was really going on, but they did accept the fact that there's a Boss inside. When the Boss is killed, the portal will close."

"Are you going?" After all, it was a fact that Kesstel was easily the strongest Hunter in America, and most likely the world.

He hummed under his breath in a noncommittal sound. "They want me to. If I go, I should be able to keep the portal open long enough for all the Hunters to get out before it shuts. That way no one gets lost in the void between world fragments. Of course, they don't know that, but it could be done."

I frowned. "You aren't going to get lost again, are you?"

The side of his mouth cocked up, and he glanced at me. "Worried?"

I mimicked the tone of his hum and didn't say anything definitive. But honestly, yes. I was. I didn't want him to disappear again. Even with grinding levels and Bethany and Emma, I was . . . lonely, missing Kesstel. Even when I was angry with him for leaving me hanging like that.

"I'm currently planning on joining the party." Kesstel shrugged his shoulders. "I think it's a good place to search."

I also thought the same thing. There was an opportunity here. We knew there wasn't a portal which led to the parasitic planet in Eden's Gate, but this was a new portal. A new tunnel.

Even if this wasn't the path to the parasitic planet, it might be the way to the System.

I looked up and opened my mouth. We spoke at the same time.

"Can I go?"

"Come with me."

I paused and smiled. "Ah, it sounds like we had the same thought."

He nodded. "This could be the portal we need. After all, it's so unusual." He paused. "Either way, I still want you to go with me." He dropped his foot to the ground then leaned forward and rested his elbows on his knees. "This world is so unstable. It could collapse at any second. I want you to stay with me so if that happens, we won't be separated."

I swallowed hard, suddenly nervous. If that was the case, I didn't really want to leave my family, either. But I couldn't save them if I stayed here in Eden. If I wanted any chance of preventing Earth from collapsing at all, I had to leave.

"Are there any strings we can pull to get an E-ranked Hunter on that team?" I asked.

This rank was starting to get annoying. I mean, I'd always hated it because of the discrimination I suffered from it, but now, it was preventing me from doing things I could do now that I wasn't weak. Unfortunately, if I got retested and lost the E rank, I'd have to start paying rent, and

I doubted I'd be able to afford a down payment for a good place to live in by the time Aliya graduated. I wanted to hold off until then.

Kesstel glanced at me and smirked. "I already did. It was part of the deal I struck with them for me to go. If they wanted me there, I had to bring you too. You are officially my emotional therapy—"

"If you say dog, I'll make you bleed," I threatened.

"—person," Kesstel finished without missing a beat. Whether or not that was what he was going to say, he smoothly sailed through a crisis.

My eyes narrowed as I looked at him, trying to see through his perfect face. He didn't seem the kind of person to play a prank like that. Still . . . "That's the oddest thing I've ever heard." I paused and added, "In the last couple months." Seriously, I really did hear a lot of odd things. If you thought about it, this whole experience since I got the System was odd.

He breathed a short chuckle, as if remembering something. "They thought it was odd, too, until they remembered a couple days ago when I came out of the Gate. Then they agreed really fast. They want all your paperwork in tonight, and it will be approved in the morning. As of tomorrow, you won't be tied to Eden. You could go wherever you want, even Siberia. After you get a passport."

I shook my head. That was probably the fastest leave approval the Hunter's Association had ever given. I guess it did make sense that he'd want to keep me close, since I helped purify the energy in his body. I wouldn't want to lose control and be an emotionless robot, either. Glancing up at Kesstel, I asked what I'd been wondering for a while. "So, why were you going crazy when you came out of the Gate?"

He frowned and tilted his head to the side. "I don't exactly remember. By the time I made it back to Eden, my memory was starting to slip, and my vision was hazy. I didn't even fully remember why I needed to go to Eden at the time. I just knew I needed to find someone. I was under the parasitic planet's control enough that the order to kill was in the back of my mind, but I was trying to repress it. When Blood Sword stopped me and he wasn't the one I wanted to find, that order kicked in. The more they resisted, the stronger and louder that command was in my mind." He paused and turned his face to lock me in his bright blue gaze. "Until I heard your voice. It was like a clear bell in a hazy mess of noise."

My face suddenly became uncomfortably hot. I pursed my lips and looked away. "Oh." I didn't know what else to say. After a second of desperately reaching for something to talk about, I asked, "So if you go into the portal to close it and lose control, you think I can stop you again?"

He nodded. "I'm counting on it."

"Deal." I gave him a half smile. "But 'emotional support person' is a really weird title."

He shrugged and mirrored my half smile. "We could just be partners. That doesn't sound so bad."

I paused. "True. It doesn't." If there was anyone I wanted to be partners with, anyone whom I knew I could trust my life and back to, it was Kesstel. I held out my hand. "Partners?"

He grinned and gently but firmly took my hand. "Partners."

ABOUT THE AUTHOR

M. L. Reid is a walking contradiction. She loves art as much as science, so her collection of random knowledge is as eclectic as all the fungi in the world. She's a Kingdom Hearts and Final Fantasy fanatic and spends too much time reading Asian webnovels. Although a peacemaker, her favorite scenes to write are fight scenes. After her kids get older, she's totally going to start a sword collection.

Podium

DISCOVER
STORIES UNBOUND

PodiumAudio.com